Sweet Dreams are made of Teeth

Richard Roberts
BESTSELLING AUTHOR OF
Please Don't Tell My Parents I'm a Supervillain

A Division of **Whampa, LLC**
P.O. Box 2160
Reston, VA 20195
Tel/Fax: 800-998-2509
http://curiosityquills.com

© 2011 **Richard Roberts**
http://frankensteinbeck.blogspot.com

All rights reserved, including the right to reproduce this book or portions thereof in any form whatsoever. For information about Subsidiary Rights, Bulk Purchases, Live Events, or any other questions - please contact Curiosity Quills Press at info@curiosityquills.com, or visit http://curiosityquills.com

Cover design by Lisa Shevchenko

ISBN: 978-1-62007-080-2 (ebook)
ISBN: 978-1-62007-081-9 (paperback)
ISBN: 978-1-62007-082-6 (hardcover)

Table of Contents

Chapter One: *First Step Into The Dark* 4
Chapter Two: *Destruct Testing* 33
Chapter Three: *Prove It* 71
Chapter Four: *Just Friends* 113
Chapter Five: *Letting Go* 172
Chapter Six: *Exeunt Omnes* 214
Epilogue 259
About the Author 261
A Taste of *Please Don't Tell My Parents I'm a Supervillain* 262
More Books from **Curiosity Quills Press** 283

Chapter One

First Step Into The Dark

My name is Fang, and I'm a nightmare. I like to think I'm pretty good at it, but as you can tell from the name, I'm not exactly subtle. Those are the really great nightmares. Jeffery can drag a dream straight into the Dark just by showing his teeth and what he's eating. I don't know why he wants me as his best friend, but he keeps telling me I don't know how good I could be.

We were about to find out.

We lurked at the edge, the borderline between the Dark and the Light. Tonight it looked like a wide stretch of road edged by grass on either side. On our side, of course, it was brown and dead, and on the other side there were budding flowers. The border wasn't always so obviously symbolic, but I was happy because it meant the barrier was wide tonight. It would be easy to get across. I waited, crouched low like a dog, which was a pretty good description of me. Jeffery just sat there on a ragged tree stump, lazy and calm and thoughtful. For a nightmare, he could look so much like a human boy you'd think he was the dreamer. That was part of it. We had a plan.

Dreams drift like soap bubbles, and the dreamers rarely have any say in where they go. I wasn't going to wait for one to wander over the line into the Dark tonight. I was going hunting.

I saw one that would fit perfectly, gathered myself, and raced across the highway into somewhere too bright, somewhere that felt wrong, where I wasn't welcome. If I didn't have a clear goal in sight I'd have gotten turned around and ended up heading right back into the Dark where I started, but there it was, a soapy window into a little house where everything was perfect and pretty and orderly. I could spot the dreamer clearly. She was the only thing truly active, a short-haired woman in a modest flowery dress pushing a vacuum cleaner. A soothing little dream about a simple life I suspected didn't exist. Perfect for what I intended to do.

First, I had to circle around and leap through into the dream from the back. I landed in a kitchen, but since the dreamer wasn't in it, the room was mostly just a bunch of sterile and shiny surfaces. She'd know somehow that I was here, but she wouldn't know she knew. It gave me time to hide. She had a dog, an absurd little poodle, harmless and pretty to match the rest of the dream. I grabbed it in my teeth, pulled it open with my claws, swallowed my pride and dove into its skin.

Even knowing the payoff, this was more than a little humiliating, especially with Jeffery watching. I trotted out into the living room where the dreamer performed her meaningless domestic chores, and as I came into her view I actually turned pink. It was that kind of dream. So I wagged my stumpy little tail, yipped a couple of times, and trotted off again into what might be a bedroom.

The plan was working. She was watching me, with that vague stare I see a lot from dreamers. She knew something was wrong, and the dream would be floating closer to the edge, to the Dark. I couldn't just let this slide if I wanted to do it right. There was a crib, my real target all along. I trotted up to it in my stupidly harmless pink body and lifted myself up onto my hind legs to peer into it.

I gave her just a moment. Timing was important, to let the dread start to flicker without letting her quite realize it. What I saw in the cradle meant this was going to work very, very well. The dreamer must have really had a baby, because this one was so well defined, every hair and curve of pudge and faint stain on its pajamas perfect.

I let out a growl, loud and abrupt, hunger and pleasure, and the poodle started to tear off of me as I lunged my teeth down and bit into the dream baby. I shook and shook, and behind me the dreamer screamed. I felt the lurch, saw the lights dim around us, blackening the edges of the dream. This dream had plunged hard into the Dark, and now there was blood spraying everywhere as I ground my teeth into the thing in the crib.

And all of a sudden, the dream broke. I had terrified the dreamer into waking up in only a few seconds. I was surprised at how far from the border we were, too, and as the dream dissolved around me black fog swirled, visceral traces of the woman's fear. They began to tighten around me, clinging, and I shook them off. If you did something like this, there was always that temptation to become what you'd been pretending to be. That wasn't me.

Which is why, as Jeffery wandered over, grinning with a mouthful of little bitty teeth sharper than mine, I felt both exhilarated and triumphant, but not satisfied.

"That was beautiful!" he crowed, slapping me on the flank. He reveled in this kind of thing, and why not? He was a top nightmare, an artist of bad dreams. "No, more than that. It was delicious. You're always telling me you're too simple to be one of the great monsters. I told you, that's your strength. You can do anything with it, and in the back of their heads they're all afraid of the teeth in the dark."

That didn't make me feel any less conflicted, honestly. I could feel the thrill of that dream. I wasn't sure I'd ever done such a powerful job, scared a victim so hard, so fast. It was something you could make a reputation with, and part of me felt good. The problem was the other part.

"It wasn't me, Jeff," I told him exasperatedly.

"You performed it," he argued back, as smug as if he were arguing that it was his victory after all, "It was nothing you don't know how to do. You picked your target, you adapted everything, you had the timing and the voice. That wasn't me out there, it was completely you."

"No, it wasn't," I retorted firmly, "Maybe you're right, maybe I could have thought of all of that myself. But I never would, and do you know why? It's not me, Jeff. That was beautiful, all right? It was. But it was the kind of thing you do, not the kind of thing I do, and I don't feel like me when I do it."

"It can be," he insisted, "That's the point. You could be that monster, every night."

"I don't want to be," I groused back. "That wasn't a chase. I'm the teeth snapping one step behind you, and you know it. This kind of thing doesn't make me feel good."

He left it for a moment. We had this kind of argument a lot, although not usually this vehemently. He felt like he'd proved his point and so did I, and he didn't see it. He didn't want to push, either. He wanted me to be as good as he was, and I wanted it too, but I wasn't going to become him to do it.

The whole thing made me feel wrong. Just wrong, like the dream was still clinging to me, telling me to be something that pounces on weaknesses instead of the thrill and violence of the chase. "It didn't work, okay, Jeffery? I'm sorry. I'm just not the nightmare you think I am. And after that dream, I'm starting to forget who I am. So if you'll excuse me, I've got to visit my Muse."

"You mean your girlfriend?" he asked, flashing those teeth. He liked to save them, but I was his friend and he was teasing me. The argument was on hold until another day.

"I wish," I snapped back, thankful I couldn't blush. Okay, she was my girlfriend. She was also my Muse, and I needed inspiration to see who I was again. I turned my back on Jeffery and went loping off into the Dark.

I always had to wander a little to find my Muse. I knew where she was because she never left, but where that place was could be a bit of a question. All the professional Muses, the nightmares and other things who were devoted to making themselves into art, into something that would inspire the rest of us, they stayed near the Gate. I think Jeffery had one. I'd seen her, if 'her' can be used to describe something that was just a mass of geometry. My girl was just herself, and that was why I needed her right now.

This time, I found her home near the border, so close that it was just this house all alone, looking over its lawn at the highway and across to brood on brighter days that would never come here. That's the kind of feel I got. It wasn't quite the stereotypical haunted house, but it was big and tall and abandoned, with bay windows and a turret and a big porch and a cellar door. It was obviously abandoned, the paint drab and peeling and many of the windows broken and boarded up, but it wasn't falling apart and there weren't bats or spider webs or anything obvious. Just derelict. I loved the loneliness of it.

Inside, it had the same abandoned house feel, with only a little furniture, some of which was knocked down, and a lot of dust. As I walked down a hallway that was longer than the house itself, I passed a statue bulging from the wall, a greyish shape of a human man with arms thrown up in fear. The statue didn't move, but sometimes an eye would open on the wall and stare at me as I passed, an eye that could be any size and any color.

That set me on alert. The house was more active than usual, and I doubted it was because of me. It was because… of the dreamer appeared, walking down the hall in front of me. There was that feel, my hackles slightly raised like I was being watched. We were in a dream now. I couldn't have asked for a better opportunity, because I was about to see my nightmare girl in action.

There was hardly any for a while. The dreamer was blurry and I thought it was male, but some people don't really know what they look like. He wandered slowly down the hall, reaching up to touch a chandelier and watch it sway, edging away from another statue jutting from a wall, this one a child. There were eyes staring at him, but always behind him.

The hall just didn't end, so he turned a corner and wandered through a library where all the books were blank and most of them had fallen off their shelves. That just led into another hall, and now he walked a little faster. This one wouldn't end either, so he ducked into a nursery playroom blackened by old fire. He edged around a teddy bear that was half ashes and wrestled with a stuck door for a moment before forcing himself impatiently into a pantry. The food was all ancient rot, fungus and cobwebs too old to even smell. After that a little hallway with no wallpaper, just bare wooden walls. He was no longer trying to follow it, ducking from room to room instead as he tried to find the way out. I followed, keeping to the edges of rooms, lurking in the darkness. Maybe he knew I was there, or maybe felt the eyes watching him. He looked sharply behind him a couple of times, but I would hide and the eyes would close and there'd be nothing to see.

Finally, a door let him into a large parlor. Here was the most furnished room so far, although there were dust covers on most of the chairs and couches, and the huge windows looked out on nothing at all. Four of those statues stuck out of the walls, but the dreamer was staring at my girlfriend.

She was, I had to admit, beautiful. She looked so human, pale and nearly bone-thin with long hair that was dark but not black. Her dress was lace and moth-eaten holes, black and wine and stained with dust, and she sobbed quietly with tears leaking past the gloved hands covering her face.

The dreamer stared. All she did was cry without acknowledging either of us, curled forward in a rickety wooden chair much too big for her. Eventually her hands fell from her face, shaking as one reached out to take a brush off a side table and start pulling it awkwardly through her hair. Her face was perfect, her features delicate but wasted. A hint of grey made her skin look unhealthy and she had no eyes, just black and empty sockets from which tears steadily ran. She still sobbed even as she wrestled with her hair, until the brush fell from her hand onto the floor.

The sound of it broke the dreamer. He ran past me, back the way he came, down that wooden hallway. It just wouldn't end, and he ducked into the laundry only to stagger back out of a demolished kitchen. The eyes watched him from in front and behind, no longer hiding, and I sort of lost control. He was running. He was lost in my Muse, and I had to be a part of it. I growled, the ragged sound of a dog about to attack, and I started to run after him.

Room to room to room, he ran. Every room was darker than the last. He didn't have to climb any stairs to pass through a slimy, dirt-floored cellar or an attic layered with dust and things broken and forgotten. I was always a room behind him, slamming a door open as he ducked through the next one. He burst into a bathroom with no other exit and a trapdoor opened up beneath him, dumping him down a long chute into the coal cellar again. Just as he ran up the stairs and threw open a door, I came crashing through a grimy window, landing on all fours in the cellar behind him. He ducked through into the next room with a deliciously satisfying urgency.

We were back in the sitting room again, and my girlfriend was still there, crying softly. Nothing had changed at all. Maybe he realized he only had one way to get out, because the walls around me smeared and twisted, the house jerked a couple of times, and the dream broke as he woke himself up.

Which left me alone with my Muse. She didn't react to me, of course. She hadn't reacted to the dreamer. I had no reason to believe she knew either of us was here, because she never spoke, never did anything but sit there and cry.

That was what made her beautiful, and I prowled over to her chair, stood up, and drew a fingertip over her hair. She didn't have to work or plan to be a nightmare, she just had to be. Sometimes I wondered if she was even a person at all, or just a concept. I liked to think there was someone inside there and she wasn't just a prop for the house.

"I'm back," I told her. "I hope you didn't mind my taking part, but I love watching what you do to a dream."

All I got were quiet noises of sadness. I drew my thumb over a tear and raised it to my tongue to taste the salt. She couldn't just be a piece of furniture. She was too exact, always the same, and she had a feel and sounds and taste. I was sure the house was part of her. It couldn't be the other way around.

"What's your name?" I asked her for the fiftieth time. I took her wrists and gently pulled them away from her face, but it just made her lean her head back and close those empty eyes, whimpering slightly as the tears continued to come.

She just didn't know I was here. She'd never known I was here, but this time it sucked the satisfaction out of seeing her. I didn't want her to change. I just wanted to touch her, somehow, just the slightest bit. I leaned in close, my face an inch from hers. Nothing. I wrapped my arms tightly around her, and in a moment of desperation I bit down on her neck.

I bit hard, letting my teeth sink in, and my claws dragged down her back. I didn't have time to do anything worse or to feel good or bad about it. I tasted her blood instead and it was awful, so bitter and nasty it made me jerk away convulsively. When I looked back there weren't any marks, just slight stains of blood. I'd ripped her dress, but the fabric raveled back up before my eyes. Now I felt worse. I'd forced my love on a girl who wasn't even aware of me, and she hadn't noticed.

I had to give up. Maybe I'd be able to face her again later. I fell back onto all fours, heading for the door, but there was another dreamer in front of me.

This one was a little girl in a white nightgown, with short brown hair and big blue eyes, and she just watched me. I was pretty big and black and hairy at the moment. I loomed over her, but she just stared solemnly and nothing changed around me. There was no sense of being in a dream.

Of course, she might not be a dreamer. Hardly anyone in the dark looked so harmless and human though, and you did get dreamers who just wandered into the Dark without bringing a dream with them.

"You shouldn't give up," she told me. That was even more odd. Dreamers rarely speak. Most of them can't really get words right while asleep. "I know there's more to her. You just have to get through the sadness."

I stopped and sat down on the floor. My Muse wouldn't talk to me, and apparently this little girl would. It felt a bit weird, because I didn't get lonely much or seek out other people, really. Some part of me was the lone wolf, and that's not a metaphor. "I don't even know she's really sad," I told her frankly, "It could be an act, crocodile tears, a recording. Sometimes I think there's nobody in there at all."

The little girl walked into the room, and as she passed she ran her hand over the top of my head, petting me like I was an actual dog. "No, I think it's the other way," she argued, although she did it calmly and delicately. "I think she's like me, not like you. I think she's a person who got lost."

It does happen. They say Lucy is like that, a human who woke up in the Dark and realized that it's the dreamer who can kill the nightmare, not the other way around. "She doesn't act human. Even when they're dreaming, they have, you know—they have depth."

"That's why I think she's a person," the little girl replied. "It's the things around her." She walked up to one of the statue things stuck in the walls, the man, and touched it carefully. "Have you really looked at these? They're all the same. The same man, woman, and two little boys. Everywhere in the house. Look at their faces. I think they're memories."

She was right. They were scenery, but they were always there somewhere, and when they were in this room they always faced my girlfriend. Every fold of cloth and wrinkle in the faces showed. I glanced back at the beautiful, crying figure in the chair and tried to think of it like the little girl was suggesting. That was her face. The house was the person underneath.

The little girl patted my flank, treating me like a dog again, and I tried not to wag my tail.

"You're in love, aren't you?" she asked, and she was smiling now.

Everybody had to rub it in. "Yeah, I guess. She's just so perfect, okay? But whether she's a human or a nightmare or any kind of person at all, I can't get her to feel the same way about me."

The little girl giggled, and I certainly didn't hear that much from dreamers. "Maybe you're going about it the wrong way?" she pointed out, "Human girls don't much like being bitten. I always wanted a boy to bring me flowers."

Flowers? That was the craziest thing I'd ever heard, but only something unexpected was going to work here. At least this girl had made me feel like I really could get through to my Muse somehow.

As I pushed myself back up and turned to the door something nagged at me. "What's your name, anyway?" I asked her.

"I'm Anna. I'll probably see you again some time." She told me.

"I'm Fang," I told her in return. She started giggling again at my name, and I suddenly felt kind of embarrassed. Seriously, had I ever had a conversation this personal with anyone? So I ducked the issue and bolted out the door. Where in the Dark was I going to find flowers for a girl?

There was one obvious place. You could get most anything at the Gate, or at least in the city around it. If no nightmare could bend the Dark enough to make flowers out of it, a demon would have stolen them from the waking world, or they'd have been constructed, string by thought by atom by line of paint, by one of the things from outside. Little girls who show up when you least expect it and give you relationship advice aren't the weirdest things in the Dark by any measure.

I wasn't going to take that option. I didn't like the crowds, didn't like dealing with strangers, and wasn't a scary enough nightmare that I could expect good service. I'd have put up with all of those things if it meant getting my nightmare girl's attention, but flowers made by someone else weren't going to do it. Winning her heart with someone else's creativity? I was too proud to do that even if I thought it would work.

You see a certain amount of flowers in dreams, at least if you're brave enough to go get them from the Light, and Anna was right. There's flowers around a lot when dreamers are cooing over each other. As soon as I remembered that, what I needed to do was obvious.

I went back and found that the border had become a fence, high and cross-slatted, and our side was just rocks and sand while the other side sprawled lushly green and drenched in sunlight. Not what I wanted to see, and the occasional little daisy or whatever in the grass didn't comfort me. There were only a few, and they were plain and hardly there. I needed the kind of beauty only a human imagination could make and the kind they stopped making when their dreams drifted this close to the Dark.

Gritting my teeth, I went for it. I jumped the fence, hit the real divide the fence only symbolized, and went rolling into the grass in the Light. The sun baked me, burned me. Tonight the Light wasn't accepting any intrusion. Things like me weren't allowed and it was trying to force me out, or boil me away if I wouldn't go. I had to think about my Muse, and how she made me feel. Not just the way I wanted her to notice me, but the way she reminded me of who I was. I was teeth, the thing that chases, a wolf and a hound and a tiger and things that don't have names. If it sounds like I was dizzy, I was. The Light had never hated me as much as I felt that night, and I had to hold onto myself, make myself steady so it couldn't burn me down.

Instead, I went charging into the Light. Like the Dark, it had... places. Bits of landscape, drifting in the endless glow. Sometimes I ran across grassland, or along a beach, or everything became blank and white. I didn't have the attention to spare to think about them. I was keeping my back to the fence, running in deep, with the glare blinding me and leaving paw prints that were smudges of ash.

I needed a good dream, a beautiful dream. I hardly realized when I found it. I was running through some kind of park, and slowly I realized it wasn't random. It had a purpose, and I could see a rainbow sheen around the its edges. A dream had closed around me and I'd been too dizzy to notice. The trees were covered in tiny blossoms I couldn't quite use, the bushes were verdant with leaves, and a young woman, a dreamer, stood on a little bridge in a nightgown. Out of nowhere a horse trotted up with a young man on it. His face was very clear, so he must be someone the dreamer knew, and as he reached down to her flowers sprouted everywhere.

I got the vague sense that this dream was repulsively stupid, but I was still burning hot and the Light was grinding at me. Anyway, I'd gotten what I wanted. Huge, luridly colored flowers of every shape, multiple blossoms to a stem, sprang from the grass on all sides. I yanked a few up in my teeth, and instead of disturbing the dream, it was me that twisted. Something tried to lurch out of me, to go trotting up to the lovers with this bouquet. That meant I was way, way too far into the Light, and I couldn't stand up to it much longer. I knew who I was, though. Fangs, long and sharp and white, gripped those flowers. I growled, growing as big and black as I could, and turned and ran for the edge. Now it was the dream that shuddered. The boy grabbed the girl's bodice harshly... and the whole thing broke up. We were too far into the Light for me to drag that dream back with me, and I didn't want to. As it burst I was leaping out of the skin of it, holding my prize in my teeth.

I ran. It didn't matter in which direction because I would be pushed toward the border. I could feel that sun, pure and golden, beating down on me. I had chosen the wrong night to cross into the Light, but that just meant it pushed me out faster, and when I saw the fence I leaped, holding tight onto the flowers as I crashed through the division between Light and Dark, spinning and falling, and came to rest in sweet, cool shadows.

The flowers were still in my teeth. Ripped raw from a strong dream, they remained bright and lovely and uncorrupted. I felt shaky for a moment, but soon I was racing off into the Dark. My Muse's lonely, rotting house wasn't far. I trotted in through a front door hanging open off the hinge. She had lured in no dreamers tonight, and the hallways were dark. I passed only one statue, the grown woman, and caught no eyes spying on me. Nothing moved at all until I reached the sitting room, and then it was only her, hands over her face, weeping softly as she had been since we first met. She was one thing barely alive in an empty and lifeless building on an empty and lifeless estate, and my heart was pounding at how lovely she was.

Probably I'd spent too long in the Light, but I always felt a little like that when I saw her. I actually felt nervous as I crept up to her and laid the flowers in her lap. They were by far the brightest thing in the house, the only thing that seemed alive except for her.

But nothing happened. She sobbed softly into her hands, on and on. Tears fell, became spots on her dress that slowly disappeared, replaced by new spots from new tears. Every once in a while she would fumble with a button on her dress or the laces at her wrists and her black, empty eye sockets would be revealed, but they never turned toward me or my gift. So I sat there. I sat there until the color leeched out of the blooms and they became grey and faded away into dust as fragments of dreams that didn't belong.

It had always been a silly idea. I had listened to a dreamer, and it had turned out the way I should have expected. Maybe Anna was right and this girl I wished was my girlfriend, who I claimed was my Muse, had been human once. A mouthful of flowers was not going to get her attention though, not if she'd ignored me for this long.

I padded gloomily out of the building. My Muse had failed me. She didn't care, and didn't want to inspire me. I felt empty, so my path immediately turned toward the Gate and my guiltiest pleasure.

The city around the Gate is a confusing place. Like everywhere in the Dark, places aren't really fixed. A building or a forest or a beach might always exist, but they moved around each other without warning. The shops and tenements and clubs and offices and all of that surrounding the Gate moved too, but they stayed near the Gate itself. The streets might rearrange themselves, but there was always a knot of buildings tethered around the Gate by the desire of the owners to be easily found.

I avoided the place when I could. I was a nobody and no one would want to serve me, and there was nothing I wanted anyway. Every nightmare in the city knew who Jeffery was, and he could sit down in any bar and everyone, even ghosts and the damned, fallen angels and alien things would want to talk to him. Fortunately, I wasn't all that social to begin with. There was really nothing for me here.

Well, there was one thing for me here, a weakness I gave in to when I had no pride or strength to resist anymore. I found her salon the same way I find everything, by knowing where I want to go and walking until I can see or hear or smell it. In this case it was a glowing red sign over a nearly hidden doorway. On the sign was the blade of a safety razor—which everyone knows isn't safe at all.

I padded down the steps and into the parlor, and the emptiness inside me became a leaden weight. Not surprisingly, she had customers. I was hardly the only person who wanted her, and 'person' didn't just mean nightmares. There was a silhouette moving in one of the walls, stretching its surface sometimes as it leaned out.

Something that seemed to be all legs that ended in needles might have been a nightmare, or a thing from outside the Dark. Neither of them mattered. By the door into the back rooms, smoking a cigarette and leaning on a cane, was a man dressed all in fine black with deep red skin and eyes that glowed like coals. A demon. A smart demon, one of the ones with style, maybe even one of the ones that claimed they were really angels.

I dragged myself around, tail hanging, and tried to keep my head from hanging too as I wandered back out onto the street. There was no way she would choose to take me as a customer tonight, and the others were probably fooling themselves too. She would see the demon first and they'd be busy for a long, long time. I couldn't compete with something like that.

I didn't know Jeffery was there until he grabbed me by my shoulders and exclaimed, "Fang, you dog! So this is what it takes to lure you into town?"

If I'd known he was there I'd have tried to sneak away. Now I wasn't sure if I cared how humiliating it was to have him look up at the sign and comment, "Masochism, huh? You're one of her clients? What does your girlfriend have to say about that? Don't give me that look. I'm honestly relieved. I thought mooning over a ghost was the only thing you ever did besides chase dreamers. You like to tell me I'm going to get Lucy on my trail, but I've been more worried you'd fade away."

The idea of doing that, of just becoming a set of fangs with no thoughts or feelings, chasing dreamers mindlessly through the dark—it was entirely too soothing and attractive. I didn't want to be the kind of nightmare Jeffery was, my Muse was never going to know I was there, and I was too much a nobody, another unimaginative nightmare from the edge of the Dark, to enjoy the one pleasure I had left. "I'm not one of her clients, Jeff," I told him flatly, "Yes, you caught me here, but she won't see me. You know the kind of guys who come to her. I don't rate."

"You rate if I say you rate," he corrected me, and grabbed me by the collar and dragged me back inside.

His intention was obvious. Jeffery has a reputation. He commands respect. He can get anything in this town, and usually be served first. There aren't a lot of people or things that are higher on the food chain than him around here, but a demon is one of them. I was about to point that out, but when he saw the man with the red skin he didn't even hesitate. Jeffery dragged me right up and dropped me in front of the curtain.

"Excuse me," he told the demon, and his tone wasn't polite at all, "My friend here has the first appointment."

The demon might have been even more stunned than I was. Not that he showed it, but he took a long puff on his cigarette before answering flatly, "No."

Now they were eying each other and not saying anything. There wasn't anything left to say. Either one of them would back down, or—was Jeffery seriously picking a fight with a demon? He could choke a dream with terror until the dreamer couldn't get free and that had made him strong, and he was fiendishly smart. The problem was that 'fiendishly smart' were words invented to describe the black-suited figure watching him now. I had no idea who'd win, but they were too proud to surrender and the loser would be hurt, maybe beyond healing.

Instead, a weak, high-pitched voice interrupted. "Fang?"

I knew the voice, or at least I knew the way she talks. Jeffery called her Masochism because everybody does, but she's the Demiurge of Self-Loathing. She probably had a name, but no one knew what it was or what she'd been before she obtained the title. I knew she was starting to fade, to become a concept rather than a person, but she hung on because it hurt more. Demiurges are important. They have power, and they can't be killed, but she spent her nights in this little salon, giving herself to one customer at a time as we came out of the Dark.

I didn't try to see her very often, and usually I turned away because of how popular she was. I was shocked that she even remembered my name.

So was everyone else, although Jeffery looked distinctly smug as Self-Loathing stepped out past the curtain and addressed the demon, "I'm sorry, but you'll have to wait. This is a very special, personal customer, and he goes first."

He was probably furious, but it didn't show and there was nothing he could do. She picked who she would see and when, like every Muse and decorator and fortune teller and vendor in the Dark. But she was popular, and I could see why. Right now she looked a lot like Anna, like a little human girl. She was thinner, fragile and shaking and bruised. All I could be sure she was wearing was a white sheet wrapped around her. One arm was holding it closed, but the other was hidden and I knew she didn't want us to see what had happened to it.

I followed her beckoning hand through the curtain into a dim little hallway, and whispered to her, "Did you call me because Jeffery wanted you to?"

"Is that why he was here? He's never come to me before," she answered. Our voices were low. Who knew how good a demon's hearing was?

"Then… you picked me over him and a demon? Why?"

She smiled, and I could feel the bandage on one of her fingers as her hand stroked down my neck. But instead she asked me, "When you talk to your friends about me, what do you call me?"

I didn't talk to my friend about her, but I understood the question if not what it meant. "Self-Loathing," I answered disbelievingly, "You picked me because I don't call you Masochism?"

"I'll always pick you, Fang," she told me, "I pick you because you care, but you hurt me anyway." She laid a finger to my lips and added, "Give me a moment to slip into something more comfortable, and you can come in."

So she stepped through another curtain into one of her special rooms, and I gave her a moment. It was hard. So close to a session with her, I was getting a thrill, but I was also getting nervous. How could I perform better than Jeffery or a demon? What could I do but disappoint her?

There was a noise, something faint and high-pitched, and my feet sort of walked me into the room. I couldn't describe the room. I didn't see it. All I saw, sitting in a wicker basket on a ragged old pillow, was a kitten maybe a day old, laboring to open pale blue eyes for the first time and look up at me. Feebly she mewed, and I lost control.

I chase. It's what I do, who I am. But if you chase, some part of you wants to catch. I grabbed that tiny, flimsy body in my teeth, and I stopped even trying to restrain myself. I shook and I chewed and I remember at one point hitting her against the wall a few times, and that's more than I should have said about that already.

Which left me, a long time later, lying on the torn pillow among the scattered bits of the broken basket with my head lying on something that had once been a kitten. The room was a mess and there was a lot of her smeared all over it, but those bits were still moving. A Demiurge can't be killed, not in any way I know of, but they can feel pain. Most of her face was left at least, and as I lay there panting she lifted it, and I felt her tiny, raspy tongue dragging up the side of my muzzle. In the far corner I could see most of her tail, twitching contentedly.

I guess I'd given her what she wanted the same way she'd given me what I wanted. I wasn't really sure what either of those things were. I was exhausted, panting, but every part of me felt good again. I felt like I was worth noticing. But if I was worth noticing, my Muse was worth trying for. I would stuff her house with every flower in the Light and the Dark if that was what it took to let her know how I felt. It didn't matter if she thought they were romantic or not. She'd know that I was willing to do anything to get through to her.

There was a faint bubbling noise and a tiny head pressed against my jaw, and I realized Self-Loathing was trying to purr.

I found a field in the Light, a place that didn't depend on dreamers to remain. I knew I wouldn't be able to find it again, so I raced back and forth across it to each patch of flowers, yanking them out with my hands and then stuffing them into my teeth so I could dash off looking for the next one. It was perfect, every flower sweet and subtle, petals soft and with delicate aromas. Dreamers forget smells most of the time. Only the Light scouring me raw eventually forced me to take what I had and bolt for home.

This was a mild night in the Light, which is why when I got back to the border and wriggled my way through a crack in the crumbling wall I had a huge pile of flowers waiting for me. I'd been able to go back and forth pretty freely, and I was determined to do this right. Still, the flowers on the bottom were starting to lose their color and I'd been baked until my fur was starting to get crispy and fall out in places. It was time to make another delivery.

This would be the biggest yet. I grabbed as many stems as I could in my jaws and got fistfuls of more, since it's not like I can't walk on my back legs if I want to. There was a heavy pile left, but I couldn't carry it all at once. I'd be back for it. Off I ran, heading for an estate of dead trees and brown grass, and I'd been there so often tonight it was easy to find. I felt good, very good as I trotted up the stairs onto the porch. Eyes in the hallway watched me, but there was only one hall. I felt like the house was leading me right to her, and I when I reached the sitting room the girl in the chair seemed more delicate and lovely than ever.

There were a lot of flowers. The prettiest, the most vibrant and colorful that stood out like a flame in this grey room, I piled up in her lap. Then I arranged a few over the little tables on either side of her, among sewing supplies and heaped atop her brush and her empty bottle of perfume. There were a lot of roses. Dreamers seemed to go nuts for roses. They were falling apart, but I just tore off the petals and scattered them in a circle around her feet, then sat back to watch my Muse.

Yes, I'd been hoping something would happen. Something other than the quiet, endless whimpering and sniffing, so that maybe by covering up her brush she would have to accidentally pick up a flower. Instead she just seemed to have forgotten about the brush entirely, and her face remained hidden in her hands and the room was still.

It was painfully disappointing, but she hadn't responded to the last load of flowers and I had more waiting. I would keep trying. Something would get through. I watched as a spider, just a little dark, leggy shape, dropped down from the ceiling on a thread until it landed in her brown-black hair. There was a gloss to that hair, every strand unique, and a few here and there were a colorless grey that just made the others richer. I would keep trying. My Muse was beautiful beyond belief and she didn't have to try at all to be like that.

Still, my heart felt heavier as I ran back to the border to get more flowers. I'd collected a lot tonight. I'd see if I could cover every inch of her room in them, and if that would get her attention. Then when it didn't I'd try some more. It might only be through sheer persistence, but I was going to get through to her, wake her up somehow.

I was disappointed when I reached the pile I'd left, because a lot of them had gone grey and crumbled already. I'd taken them from dreams that weren't vivid enough, most likely. I couldn't focus on that, because I wasn't alone. A woman stood over my flowers holding up one of the richest, a pink star threaded with purple, and running a fingertip over its arching, pointed petals. Not just a woman, an angel. A fallen angel.

The look was so obviously perfect and deliberate I wondered if she was faking it. Her hair was red like blood and she had a halo that was nothing but rust, a dull and unlit hoop, and she didn't have grand, white wings but rather the mutilated remnants of them on her back. Her clothing wasn't clothing. It was just white cloth that swirled and floated around her, hiding everything without deigning to pretend to be what humans wear.

Her posture was still and graceful, and she had a peacefully sad look on her face as she admired the flower I'd picked. It convinced me she wasn't a nightmare. Anyway, you'd be a fool to try and imitate a fallen angel long. The demons tended to fight among each other for trying it, so she had to be either powerful or dumb.

"A nightmare picking flowers?" she asked me as I trotted forward, "You went in very deep for some of these. I'm impressed." The flower she held had a bouquet, and as she lifted it up and smelled it I could tell she appreciated that.

It was just smart to be polite to a demon, but what should I say? "Yeah. They're for a girl," I told her. Might as well come out and say it, I guess.

"If I were her, I'd be flattered," she told me warmly, "I never thought of nightmares doing something this sweet, but I guess we all can fall in love, can't we?" She stroked the petals of the flower she'd chosen again, and now she was gazing across the border. It had become a railroad track with nothing obvious on either side, just a twilight nothing here and a pale, hopeful dawn over there. "I didn't know nightmares could spend so much time over there."

Her voice was drifting, but dark eyes stared fixedly at the paler nothing across the tracks. "It gets to you," I conceded, "I probably have to stop for the night once I deliver these. Can't you go get flowers yourself? You look like you want to, really bad." I stopped myself. Demons were prickly. I corrected as best I could, "You're not really trying to hide it."

She smirked, but she also hesitated before she pulled her gaze away from the Light to look down at me. "I'm not allowed over there. Well, I could go back any time I wanted, but I'd have to renounce everything that makes me who I am." I understood that perfectly, and why there was so much emotion in her voice when she said it.

I didn't really have time to figure out what to say, though. She was pointing back across the border and telling me, "You know we have a Gate here in the Dark, and you've heard stories about what's on the other side. Well, there's a Gate over there too, which you'll never get to see and I'll never see again. I like to come here and remember it sometimes."

In a few nights I'd gone from avoiding everyone but Jeffery to having personal conversations with people I would have sworn would never want to talk to something like me at all. The whole idea made me feel uncomfortable at first, but then I just gave up.

"It's an act, right?" I asked her frankly. "You're putting on a show. I don't talk to a lot of demons, but you don't look or act like this."

Rather than be offended she reached out a wing, heedless of the occasional drop of blood it left on the flowers, and brushed the pile into an arc. "Is this an act?" she countered with an impish smile, "Are these really your feelings?"

"Sort of?" I hedged. She'd made her point.

She held out her hand, smiling, and introduced, "I'm Lily."

I laid my paw in it. I can shake. "Fang."

With both ended up snickering. Half the demonesses in the Dark are named something like Lilith, and half the nightmares are Fang or Claw or something. Names so generic they had to be real.

She had never put down the flower, and now she was touching it again. I had to listen to a demon actually try to sound gentle as she asked, "The girl these are for—she's another nightmare, I take it? Are these really what she wants?"

She'd gone straight to the question I'd been trying to avoid. Of course. "I don't know what she wants," I had to admit, "But probably not. Someone suggested flowers and the best I can do is give her so many it has to get her attention."

"I know I'd be impressed by the effort," she admitted, "But I'd trade a house full of regular flowers for just one, if it was picked because it was perfect for me. Think about that."

I thought about it. It was an idea. My strategy certainly wasn't working.

It also would have been easier without an actual angel hanging around behind the border watching, but Lily seemed to be interested and how do you tell someone like her she makes you nervous? Thanks to Jeffery's never-ending attempts to teach me to be more subtle I thought I knew what to do. It wasn't hard to find the right dream. All this hunting for dreams with flowers in them had made me sensitive, and the hard part was waiting for one to drift close to the border. I wanted one on the edge.

When I broke into the one I'd picked I saw flowers, but only a few. The dream was a sort of a forest, or a garden, or something in-between. I couldn't even tell if the dreamer was male or female. They were just a vague shape drifting peacefully through a lush arbor.

This wasn't about the chase. It was about setting a mood. I hid myself inside a tree until the dreamer floated past. As it did I shoved my head out through the trunk, letting the skin of the tree cling to me as I snapped and growled, claws showing through a branch and thrashing at the dreamer. By the time I ripped through and leaped out onto the grass the whole dream had changed. We were in the Dark now, and everything had turned grey and shadowy, and the dreamer had sharpened into a young man in bulky pajamas. He wasn't drifting anymore but running, dashing through bushes and between trees to escape me in the little forest.

But most dreams just aren't that big. Seconds later I leapt out of the dark at him from another direction, and when I let him pull out of sight I just waited for him to loop around and did it again. Now he was stuck in the Dark and everything was changing shape, but I couldn't let this be a dream about a big, black dog. The next time he passed by it was a pile of moss that fell out of the web-haunted branches in front of him and I was inside it, just snapping teeth and a body forming out of the grey strands. When he escaped that I found a little patch of sunflowers in a clearing. They had almost faded into the shadows, but I hid myself in one and as the dreamer was about to run right through them I lunged.

I didn't break out. Like the tree, I stretched the skin of the flower over me, giving it a muzzle that reached, snapping with violent bloodlust to either side because I was getting into it now. The rest of the sunflowers stopped fading and grew their own teeth, and as I forced an arm out and started dragging myself toward him with my claws they were mutating too. Behind him thorns sprouted from the trunk of a tree and its branches curled around to yank him in, and as I burst free of the sunflower the dreamer woke up.

Around me the dream spasmed, but it didn't pop. I was actually proud as I looked around. Every vine twitched threateningly, every leaf had an oozing sheen, bushes thrashed and bit with a hundred mouths. The dream had taken on a sense of identity. It knew what it was. A new nightmare was waking up.

I had come here with a purpose, though. A clump of flowers with heavy purple-and-black blooms edged with teeth and shifting, slitted eyes between the petals—that was perfect. I grabbed a bunch of stems in my jaws and tore them free, and with a squeal of pain the dream broke up.

They were gorgeous and the dream had been so close to consciousness, so specific, they weren't going to fade any time soon. They might never fade at all. That didn't mean I wasted any time. I bolted through the vague mists that are so much of the Dark as fast as four legs could go, only partly because Lily was whistling appreciatively behind me.

My Muse's house had lodged in some kind of withered field, so dead grass stretched all around it as far as I could see, and above its peaked roof hung a crescent moon. It was a good place for her to have wandered, and I hoped she'd stay there because I thought it looked very pretty. At least, I thought that as I barged in through her front door and raced into the sitting room. I might have been hurrying too much. I had to make turns through several rooms, ducking back into the same hallway a second time until I found the right door. The house was trying to keep me out.

But there she was. The flowers from before were gone already, but they'd been so out of place here it was no wonder they hadn't survived. These flowers were better, and I padded up to her as calmly as I could and laid them in her lap. Their vivid markings, along with the wine colored lace on my girlfriend's dress, were the only real colors in the room. The eye in each flower still moved, peering up at her, at me, at everything, hostile and staring and not quite intelligent.

But still nothing happened. I sighed as the quiet sobbing continued. The flowers at least would last a long time. I hoped they'd be there in her lap forever.

Something touched my shoulder. Lily had caught up to me, or that weird little girl Anna had dropped by again. I looked around, both proud and embarrassed, but what I saw was a thin chain stretching out of the floor, hooking itself into my spiked collar.

I felt a sudden tension. A light thrill of fear that didn't come from anything, that was impressed from outside. Shadows in the corners of the room went pitch-black, and the four statues were looking at me.

A dream had formed around the house, but this time there was no dreamer. This was my dream and she was my nightmare. More pale lines snaked out and took hold of my legs, and they were starting to pull me back toward a blank stretch of wall. The four statues, a man and a woman and two little boys, were watching me with expectant faces. Four people encased in something white and stuck in the wall.

I was in trouble.

I almost wasn't willing to hurt her enough to try and get away, but as I ripped at the chains trying to drag me into place I tried to reassure myself that it would take a lot more than this to do her any lasting harm. I, on the other hand, was about to be eaten. That thought drenched me in panic. Panic is never very far away in a nightmare and I ran, slamming the door to the sitting room open and bolting out into the hall. Eyes were everywhere, all of them watching me, and one of the statues had moved out here. A white hand groped at me as I fled past it into the atrium, heading for the front door.

Of course, it wasn't the atrium. It was, nonsensically, the cellar. That was the kind of nightmare she was, a dream of being trapped. A pile of stacked boxes tried to fall on me as I ran in. She wanted to pin me, hold me still so she could absorb me. I ran faster.

A half-collapsed library where books tried to grab my feet. An attic where the dust clung like tar. A pantry, unnaturally long, racing past unidentifiable foodstuffs that stirred on their shelves as I passed. A kitchen with a heart painted on the tile walls in crude swathes of blood. I had wanted to see that for a long time, but now it just scared me more. Knives fell off of hooks and I danced between them to keep myself from being nailed to the floor, then burst into the fire-blackened children's room. Both of the little boys were in the walls and one was groping for me—but the other was pointing at the window.

A window onto the dead field surrounding the house. Outside I could see some figures. The one not in white, with the yellow hair, that had to be Jeffery. He was heading for the front door. He was going to try and free me.

Either he'd kill her or she'd kill him, and I wasn't looking forward to either. "Stay there!" I yelled through the broken pane, "I have an idea!"

And I did. I backed up a few steps and ran, leaped for the window, eyes fixed on the view outside and daring my Muse to try and pull a switch where I could see and weaken the dream.

Instead the roof fell in on my head. I went rolling as bricks and beams of wood and dirt and rusty pipes fell out of the ceiling, blocking the windows. As I ducked out of the room it collapsed completely.

This was a hall, and there was a window in it. As I ran for the glass the opposite wall fell forward to smother it, and I turned and dashed into a studio instead. Cloth-covered easels were too symbolic. A modeling couch was already sending links threading through the floor toward me. It was an attempt to get the nightmare back on track, except that studios had to be well-lit and I was turning toward the huge windows already. There was no way she could block those believably. Oh, except for the house's tower falling over onto them.

The crash was loud and violent and glass shards sprayed across my back, some of them digging in painfully as I fled into the next little hall. It had a window at one end and the roof was already sagging, beams falling in down there, so I turned and bolted the other way.

Into the sitting room. The sitting room with the bay windows. The extra second of knowing they were there was what I'd needed. In the corner of my eye, was that a glimpse of a pale girl with empty eye sockets holding up a fanged purple flower to her nose? I couldn't look. Like the heart, more likely it was wishful thinking, something that as the dreamer I'd made myself. That grim thought came as I was already leaping for the windows and the ceiling tumbled down, but she was too late. I crashed through the glass, hit the lawn outside and rolled to the feet of my friends as I felt the dream finally let go.

I lay there panting, letting the artificial fear of the dream fade away. Not to mention the all too real fear of being devoured, becoming another statue on my Muse's wall. But the house was a pile of rubble behind me now. Anna crouched behind me with that serene dreamer's expression that suggested she wasn't quite there, picking bits of glass and nails out of my hide.

Jeffery rubbed me between the ears. "I heard you twisted a good dream into some kind of nightmare garden, then killed it just as it was waking up," he told me, his voice drawling with pride, "And then you got out of a nightmare by yourself. That was amazing, Fang. I'd say I didn't know you had it in you, but I've been trying to tell you that you do since we met."

If Jeffery was condescending, it was the condescension of a friend. A friend who'd been willing to try and fight his way into a dream he'd known he might not have been able to get out of.

"That was love, Fang," Lily added, leaning over me familiarly and brushing dust off one of my ears. "Pretty pink roses and milk chocolate aren't for the likes of us. Obsession, puppy. That's what we want. She didn't ever want to let you leave her again."

I felt relieved. More than relieved, but I couldn't describe it any better. The girl I loved had torn herself apart rather than let me get away from her. However much I'd projected onto that dream myself, she'd noticed me. There was no question at all, she'd finally noticed me.

As I pushed myself shakily back to my feet Jeffery told me, "Soak up the accomplishment while you can. I'm going to be telling everyone what I saw tonight, I know. But Fang, my chum, when you've got your wind back come and see me in town. I need your help, because you've given me an idea that's going to show everyone what I'm capable of. I don't mean to leave you in the dust buddy, but you'll have a lot of company there when I'm done."

And that was also Jeffery. He never let up for a moment. Still, I grinned up at him. "Okay, okay. I get it, I spend too much time hunting alone." There was nothing for it. I was going to have to be more social. A jolt of worry wiped away that resolution for an instant, but I looked back over my shoulder and the house was back. Forlorn, lonely, and unaltered. That hadn't been enough to kill her.

As I stared I heard Jeffery start to say something, but Lily interrupted him. "If you have to talk about your scary plans, you can tell me over a drink. Can we leave the young lovers alone?"

So she dragged him off into the gathering mists and left me in silence. It was just me and the house. Oh, and the little girl in white with the gentle, almost blank expression and her hands resting on my back.

"'Young lovers'. Nothing has changed at all," I told Anna mournfully.

"Hasn't it?" she asked. Her eyes hadn't changed, but her voice was knowing and alive. "I think you should go inside."

Which might be dangerous, but my Muse was probably as weak as I was. I left Anna on the lawn and climbed the stairs to the front door. Everything was quiet, but the house was as I remembered it.

No eyes watched me and there were no statues in the hall, although as I peeked into side rooms I saw the woman glued to the inside of the door of an open refrigerator. She might have been asleep, but my Muse didn't seem to be damaged. I'd gotten through to her, but only for a moment.

It only took a couple of twists to get into the sitting room and there, like always, she sat in her big wooden chair with hands in fingerless gloves covering eyes she didn't have. Four statues watched her with expressions whose horror I felt a little sympathy for now, but they ignored me. The only thing I didn't remember being exactly like this was the vase.

The vase was new. There'd never been one before, sitting on her little table beside her brush. The flowers it held were long-dead roses, mostly bare stems, with only a couple of dried and blackened petals clinging to the ends so that I could tell what they'd been. And there had been a vase and roses like it in the hallway, hadn't there? And I thought I'd seen one in all the other rooms I'd peeked in.

My Muse remembered me.

Did that mean she really was my girlfriend now?

Chapter Two

DESTRUCT TESTING

I tried not to get my hackles up as I slunk into town. It wasn't dangerous, there were just too many people. I could wander the leafless arbors and sunken caves and featureless mists of the Dark and hardly ever see anyone but dreamers in their dreams, so having someone brush shoulders with me on the street wasn't a thrill. Ah, who am I kidding? What I didn't like were the stares. I would look away from the blindingly colored storefront I was passing and there'd be a thing, like a toad made out of a toddler, sitting on a cardboard box and watching me. Whatever it was thinking, it wasn't admiration. On the next street corner there'd be something like a goat with extra arms like sickles on its back. The glow in its eyes would say 'demon' as it glanced at me and dismissed me as beneath it. Up above, on a metal frame balcony, a porcelain goddess would watch me for a while, then unbuckle her face to check her makeup.

The whole thing made me uncomfortable, so I kept my nose to

the ground as much as possible and followed Jeffery's scent, that special cruelty that was calculated rather than passionate and made him easy for me to find. I followed it into a building of dingy brick and boarded up windows and failed to be surprised when the inside was a bar. There were too many people here also, but at least their looks all said 'nightmare' to me and the big room was smoky and dimly lit. Nobody much cared about me.

Jeffery was sitting on a stool at the counter, and next to him was Lily. She was putting on the fallen angel act hard, glowing faintly but pearlescent and the white sashes she wore slithered over her constantly. The way she cradled a frosted glass and sucked off of her spoon got stares. Everyone likes style.

Then she reminded us it wasn't an act by crooking her finger and beckoning me, and I knew, we all knew, that I didn't mean to come romping up to her with my tongue lolling out like an eager lap dog. These kinds of games are another reason I didn't like coming into town. It was just hard to resent the affectionate way she scratched me above my spiked collar or the delight in her voice as she told me, "Is this your first time here too, puppy? Jeffery tells me this is where the nightmares hang out and compare scars." There was snickering from across the room. Of course everyone was listening to her, especially the nightmare who was himself little more than a notched and twisted cadaver of furrowed flesh.

"You're like some underworld debutante," Jeffery told her, and only he would have the guts to say that to something like her. And probably only he could get a laugh out of her for it.

"I kind of like it," I admitted and sat down on the floor next to her.

"I hope so," Jeffery told me, showing off his little bitty needle teeth, "It's you she's trying to impress, not them. She was as cool as ice until you walked in the door."

Lily laughed again, and whatever the truth was I definitely wanted to change the subject. "You had some kind of plan, Jeff?" I asked him awkwardly, "Something you needed me for?"

"I do, and stage one is getting you to relax and socialize for a few minutes," he answered. When I gave him a stubborn look he amended, "You don't have to go chat up a bunch of strangers, but at least have a drink with us before we run off. Bar Number Three serves the best you can dream up. He's some kind of genius."

"He's right, puppy," Lily told me, licking her spoon again theatrically, "This is the most convincing chocolate malt I think I've ever had in the Dark. Just trust me? Have something, and then we can go."

A nudge of her foot pushed me up to the counter, and I decided not to argue. I'd told myself I was going to come out of my shell a little. Heaving myself up onto my hind legs and resting my hands on the surface was rewarding already, because waiting bar was a shiny black mannequin with unnecessary sharp edges at every joint. Strings held the barman up, making it an oversized marionette, and those strings connected to a pair of wooden crosses and those crosses were held by huge hands jutting out of the ceiling. The puppet itself had no eyes, but grey domes with multicolored lenses would bulge out of the wall behind it occasionally and twist around to stare at me.

I didn't know what dreamer had come up with this nightmare, but I liked something this creative on sight. The scratchy, synthetic voice came out of a metal grill where the puppet's mouth should be as it asked, "And that would make you Jeffery's friend Fang? We're delighted he's finally lured you out of the Dark. Call us Bar Number Three, after you tell us what you want us to make for you."

"...I have no idea," I confessed. I rarely ate or drank anything. Blood or water, sometimes, as part of a dream. I struggled to remember some of the things I'd seen dreamers enjoy, but labels you can read are a rarity in dreams.

To my relief, nobody laughed. Bar Number Three didn't have any expressions, but Lily looked entirely sympathetic and Jeffery nodded like he was taking my ignorance seriously. "I swear, he never comes into town, Bar," Jeffery told him, or maybe them, but there was hardly any teasing in his voice. "We need to make him feel comfortable. Do your trick for him, would you?"

Giant hands twisted and the head of the puppet was dragged around to regard Jeffery. "There's such a thing as too much hospitality, Jeffery!" it protested, its voice screechy and staticky, "What if we got a special visitor? I'll be too tired to do it again for the rest of the night."

"More special than me and the lady here?" he countered, "Besides, you heard about the arbor nightmare. That was Fang. He needs some congratulations."

The eye dome things bulged out of the wall and ceiling and the bar top itself now, and all of them focused on me. "That was you? Birthed it and killed it in the same bite? We saw the dream painters do a picture of it tonight. For that lovely dream, we will find the taste you dream of."

"I don't dream. That's the—ow!" I'd started to back off, but before I could physically back away something jabbed into my head. Peering up resentfully I saw an arm with a needle on the end withdrawing into the ceiling. If he'd meant that to hurt me it might have been ugly.

For a moment, Bar Number Three went still. Then the mismatched eyes started withdrawing into the walls until only three were left staring at me. The puppet body pulled a mug out from under the bar and set it in front of me, then poured something black out of an equally black bottle into it. "Try that," the artificial voice urged me, and it sounded slow and slurred. "Jeffery was right. You're full of surprises."

Now Jeff, Lily, and the Bar itself were watching me expectantly, and probably a couple of people from the crowd. It made my skin want to crawl right up my back, but I wasn't going to give in to nerves. Lowering my muzzle to the top of the mug, I gave the stuff inside a lick and then tried very hard not to fling myself to the floor and go into convulsions.

It was awful. It was nasty. It was vile. It was bitter and warm and had a vaguely salty and metallic aftertaste. I was reaching my tongue out for another lick before I'd figured out why. As the muscles of my neck knotted, trying to yank me away, I recognized the taste as the blood of my Muse, my love, my girlfriend, the eyeless girl in her abandoned house. It wasn't quite as intense, didn't have her chill, wasn't quite as thick, but as foul as it was the moment the taste had faded off my tongue I wanted another lick. After three or four the mug was empty. That was fine. By then my knees shook and I could smell my girl all around me. That flavor was pure sentiment with an edge of long-rotted milk. Ugh. It had been horrible, and I'd loved it.

"Would you like another?" asked Bar Number Three cautiously. Lily and Jeffery were still watching me, although they were smiling as well. Lily's was slight and affectionate, I suppose. Jeffery's had pride and approval written all over it.

"Not... any time soon," I panted, trying to stay upright as the weakness slowly passed.

"Now that we know what you like, we can make it at any time, Mister Fang," the mannequin insisted.

"Not... any time soon," I repeated. It was teasing me, but I let it. That had been amazing.

Flowers with teeth, the smell of tears and a dress full of holes... Jeffery was standing beside me. To change the subject I asked the most inconsequential question I could grab. "Why aren't you drinking anything, Jeff?"

He flashed his grin, but this wasn't for fun. He ran his tongue over his teeth, and I could smell the blood, human blood from a dreamer. "I can't. There's a taste I can't afford to lose tonight." And now I knew what the second stage of his plan was, and why I was here.

"A recurring nightmare. You want me to help you pull a recurring nightmare? You hate those," I accused him, "You say they're unimaginative."

He crouched down by me, bringing his face to my level so he could keep his voice low, just loud enough for me and Lily to hear him. "No, this is an experiment. I've been looking for just the right dreamer, and I think I found him. But I need you to track him down again, Fang, so I can test this. I don't have your nose." He hesitated, and for once he really looked honestly concerned. "If you've got your strength back."

I tested my legs, and they were only slightly wobbly and getting better by the second. "It wasn't me who met this dreamer, Jeffery. You know what we'll have to do to follow him. I hate doing this," I griped.

That wasn't a refusal, and he knew it wasn't. Which is why I clenched my jaws as his teeth sank into my shoulders, tearing open my back so that he could slither in.

Jeffery was exactly the only person who might possibly ask for this who I'd let do it. I could taste the dreamer's blood now. Not just blood, but the lingering traces of the dream itself. I could follow that. He let me work my own legs and I raced off after that fading dream as fast as I could without stumbling. I hoped Jeffery's experiment was worth this itchy feeling of having to share a body with someone. He certainly thought so. I could feel his attentiveness to the trail, ready to leap out of my body and follow it himself if he could.

Even with a friend, sharing the same skin for the whole hunt wasn't easy. An empty shell in a dream is one thing, and with a light touch—that I don't have—you can slip inside a dreamer and make them do things, but there just isn't room for two people in one body. Not in mine, that's for sure.

The trail led toward the border. I'd known it would. Dreams that have already fallen into the Dark aren't satisfying for Jeffery. I hardly noticed the edge. We were crossing a blank, flat grey plane when I started to realize that behind me everything was black and in the distance ahead everything was white. That hit me almost exactly the same time as Lily spoke.

"You boys will have to go ahead without me," she called from behind us, "I'll watch for you from this side. I want to see what the fuss is about."

We both turned my head back to look at her. I hadn't been aware she was following, as fixated as I was on trying to find a dreamer Jeffery had bitten only once. I knew she was prone to being dramatic about her appearance, but the beautiful white wings she'd had in Bar Number Three were now bent wrecks and a trail of feathers caked with black and red followed her through the night. The moving sash she seemed to favor was now knotted and binding, her rusty halo glowed orange, and she just wasn't elegant anymore. It was Jeffery who noticed her hiding her left hand behind her. He didn't think this was an act. She couldn't cross the border.

"Don't worry, we'll be back," I slurred as he spoke through my jaws, "The farther in I have to go, the farther I'll pull him into the Dark when I'm done." Then we staggered as I took over our legs and leapt forward into the rapidly lightening grey.

There were a lot of dreams around tonight, but Jeffery wasn't interested and I had to keep my full attention on the trail. I knew we'd found the dreamer a split second after Jeffery did, because he threw himself out of my skin and left me panting and wriggling. The Light wasn't getting into me as I closed up. I knew that. It just felt like it.

Jeffery wasn't paying attention. When I looked up he'd already dived into the dream. It was like this big pink heart-shaped bubble, because the Light could be just as symbolic as the Dark. Someone was dreaming about love. Human dreams tended to get physical when they did that, but I pressed my face to the membrane to peek inside and the dream was all very much in the pretty and nice stage.

Too pretty and nice, come to think of it. I couldn't figure out quite what was going on. The dreamer was a man, and he was walking with a woman hand-in-hand and they were whispering the gibberish to each other that most dreamers think is language. That was normal enough. But while nothing was exactly vague, I couldn't tell if any of the other people they passed were male or female. Nobody had any figure except for his dream girl, and she was exaggeratedly curvy. And they'd pass buildings so well-scrubbed they had almost no color. Everything was neat and perfect, every line exact. When they'd wander off a street into a grove the stream was blue, the trees were brown, every blade of grass was even. I couldn't even see Jeffery. He was good at hiding.

Pretty quick, things started moving on. The dreamer and his girl sat down on a pink and white blanket that was mathematically exact and perfectly clean, and there were giggles and a heated tone in their babbling. They kissed, and then she kissed his neck, and then she kissed a little lower down, and then she opened her mouth and I had just enough time to see Jeffery's needle teeth before she bit him.

The dream convulsed, shrinking violently as shadow seeped over its surface, and it shoved me aside as it raced for the border. I did what I do, of course. I chased it, barking and growling and snapping my teeth, watching the surface turn black and the whole thing twist and roll. This was pretty tame by his standards, but Jeffery loved his nasty little surprises to yank a dream from the Light into the Dark.

White blankness dimmed into grey blankness until the dream, still heart-shaped, was spinning into a night that doesn't end. I caught up to it and pressed my face to the surface again, wiping it with my paws a few times to get it clear enough to see through.

Nothing had really changed. The dreamer and his girl were sitting on that blanket in some kind of park, but most of that had faded into darkness and it looked like soon the dream would be nothing but the two of them. There was no question Jeffery was inside the girl. She kept biting off little strips of flesh, chewing and swallowing them one by one, again and again. Most of his shoulder and throat were gone already. The dreamer gasped, fought for breath, and every time she bit the dream jerked, so he was really feeling the pain. His girl still held him tenderly, and her expression was sultry and affectionate as she bit and bit and bit. That was a Jeffery touch.

Finally the dream broke and the dreamer disappeared. The cloud of horror it left behind was sickly sweet and so thick I couldn't really see Jeffery until he walked out of it, and a lot of it was clinging to him, seeping in. He had no reason to shake it off. That had been exactly the nightmare he is.

I wasn't alone. Lily had been on the other side of the bubble, and Jeffery walked out between us—and as the cloud thinned I saw Anna sitting behind her as well.

"I don't have a lot of these myself, boys," Lily commented curiously, "but didn't that one last longer than it should have? Much longer?"

"He wanted it," commented Anna, sprawled out on the ground lazily.

"No, he hated it, he was terrified," I disagreed, "The dream was shaking. It just wouldn't let go."

"You're all right," Jeffery husked. He looked drunk. He was weaving a little and licking trails of blood mixed with the clinging fog of the dream off his clothes. "He's just what I was looking for. This is going to work!" He shot me a blurry glance and added, "Thanks, Fang. I've got the taste of him now. I have to keep following. I have to be in every dream."

The three of us watched as he raced off into the Dark, following a trail only he could see or taste or smell. I didn't know quite what to think. It had been a vicious, scary little dream, but they all are when Jeffery gets into them. Before I figured out what to make of it Lily asked suddenly, "Is he gone?"

"Uh—" was exactly how witty I had time to be before she stepped into the lingering cloud of the broken dream. Ribbons of it clung to her and she licked them off herself with an expression that wasn't at all angelic.

"This stuff is delicious," Lily told me throatily as she devoured it, "Your little girl is right. Fear and pain don't do much for me, but there's something else in this. I'm surprised we haven't been stampeded. Anyone from my side of the Gate could smell this dream halfway across the Dark."

Lily's smile was much too much like Jeffery's when she turned it on me, and her eyes glowed like heated coals. Anna just giggled, and after a moment I laughed too. Lily was too good at her game. She'd really made me forget for a minute that she was a fallen angel, not the pure and innocent kind. Not that I'd ever met one.

I didn't have time to say anything about it. Anna's normally peaceful face frowned and she told me, "Puppy? You should stand behind me."

"Is everyone going to call me 'puppy' from now on?" I demanded, ears and tail hanging low.

But while Lily laughed affectionately Anna just repeated, "Really, you should stand behind me. Right now. It's not safe."

I padded over behind her, although it seemed like a silly demand, exactly the kind I'd expect from a dreamer. Whatever kept her here in the Dark, maybe it was letting go again. I thought that if a dream bubble formed around her I'd try and nudge it into the Light before she woke up. Not that I was sure how to do that.

I was flat wrong. Dead wrong, almost. Lily spotted it before me. She stepped out of the fading black smoke from the recently popped dream and stared off into the distance. Then I heard sniffing, and a little girl came creeping up to us out of the shadows.

I thought for a moment she was a nightmare. She was a parody of a little girl, almost. Around Anna's age, whatever that was—I was no expert in how humans grew. She had on a pink and white dress I'd seen only in the goofiest of dreams, all unnecessary ribbons and frills. Her hair was coppery red, long and tied back in another ribbon. But she walked crouched forward, following a scent, and each hand held an obviously oversized knife. It took me a moment to realize she was a wandering dreamer like Anna, and then another moment to put it all together.

Oh, Hell. Oh, Hell, Hell, Hell. Lucy.

"Hey, you! You're not a nightmare!" she declared, pointing a finger at Anna. She stomped right up to her, the girl with the knives and the grin looming over the girl with the peaceful expression who sat splayed out on the surface of the Dark. "What are you doing here?"

It wasn't really an aggressive question, just a brazen one. I hardly noticed. Lucy was right on the opposite side of Anna from me. Something clung to the edge of the knife she held out as she pointed. Just a smudge, a trace of shadow. She'd used them tonight already.

"I can't seem to wake up," Anna admitted. She was still smiling and easygoing. Of course, she had nothing to fear. If she died it would all be a dream.

"That's sweet!" Lucy declared. She stuck the knife in her hair, somehow without cutting her hair or herself, and offered her hand to Anna. "I'm Lucy. I thought I was the only one who'd worked it out!"

"I'm Annalisa," Anna replied, giving Lucy's hand a gentle shake and then leaning back again. I wondered if I should huddle down behind her. I was too big; I reared up over the little girl. If I were curled up on my belly I'd still be too big to hide behind her. I wasn't hidden; Lucy was just ignoring me. It was a nightmare game. She was playing with me, letting me scare myself. It was working all too well.

Lily just looked the slightest bit cautious and awkward, but mostly interested. "You're not alone," she interjected, "I've seen any number of dream walkers over the years. Magicians, humans about to die or taking the wrong drugs, and a few lucid dreamers who start wondering what's outside their dream."

"I was like that," Anna agreed pleasantly, "I kept dreaming, over and over, and I never woke up. I finally got bored and thought I'd go look around. I stayed on the bright side for a little while, but it's prettier over here and the people are more interesting."

"Oh, it's way more fun on the Dark side," Lucy drawled, pulling her knife back out of her hair. Did she glance at me, just for an instant? Then she straightened up and sniffed. "Sometimes the nightmares have too much fun. One of them's started some fun right here. Something special. You know what they say? The nail that stands up gets hammered." The knives in her hands were suddenly a mallet, a huge metal thing bigger than she was, and she slammed it into the ground. Splinters sprayed around. We were sitting on a wooden floor in some kind of loft, although it seemed to go on forever in all directions. Lucy was a dreamer and she could make the Dark be whatever she wanted.

"I think they're kind of sweet," Anna replied lazily, "They can't really hurt us, and bad dreams are just who they are. I like mice, but I don't blame owls for hunting them."

For some reason this just made Lucy laugh. "I like you soooo much!" she drawled, "It's like talking to a funhouse mirror. Can we hang out? Everything may look the same in this place, but I bet we could find each other again easy. I thought playing with demons was pretty fun for a while, but they're all 'I'm so evil, ooh!' and it gets tiring. They're so full of themselves."

Lily just nodded at that, smiling whimsically. "We really are. Most of us are really into the power games, too."

Lucy rolled her eyes exaggeratedly. "Oh, yeah, I ended up killing, like, half the ones that wanted to hang with me before I got sick of them."

"I'm not surprised," Lily confirmed, and she looked amused rather than upset by it. Anna shook her head, like she was the adult and they were two little kids being difficult.

Then Lucy straightened up abruptly, and as she shot a hard look at Anna I went rigid. It felt like my bones were made of ice. But the copper-haired girl didn't sound angry, just a little accusatory as she told the pale one, "You really just distracted me, didn't you? That was deliberate! You kept me here until I lost the trail!"

I didn't know what would happen next. I certainly wasn't expecting Lucy to drop her hammer and throw her arms around Anna's neck, hugging her tight and laughing, "That was great! But don't think it worked. I'm going to find him and I'm going to cut him." And with that she bolted away, running flat out, arms behind her and knives clenched again in her fists. The hammer had disappeared and the wooden floor faded first into blank shadows, then melded into nighttime grass, probably something Anna wanted.

As soon as I couldn't see Lucy or hear her giggling anymore I started breathing again, panting desperately while my body shook. I'd met Lucy and lived.

Lily glided over and stroked her fingers down the back of my head and neck, musing, "So that's the girl the nightmares are all afraid of? It's okay, puppy. She didn't seem to notice you."

"She saw me," I wheezed, "I'm just not worth her time. Talking to you two was more fun than killing a nobody like me. She likes to hunt down the big nightmares, anybody who steps out of line. And she's the one who decides what that means."

I shuddered as it hit me. "She's after Jeffery. This thing he's doing, she knows about it. It's got her attention. I've got to stop him!"

And I left Lily and Anna behind, running as fast as four shaking legs would carry me. I knew Jeffery and I could find him. Hopefully Anna had bought him enough time.

I found him in a strange place. The border is always changing, and always at least a little odd, but this was new. The border itself was a stream tonight, choked with slime and rocks on our side, with a gentle slope and strawberry bushes on the other. I could have cleared it in a single jump and that promised a sharp, painful transition from Dark to Light, but I didn't have to find out.

Jeffery's trail led downstream instead, and downstream was something I wasn't used to. A dream had lodged in the middle of the stream, and it hadn't just diverted the stream or caused the water to spill around it. The whole symbolism of the border was breaking down, replaced by a whirlpool, spirals of it glittering with sunshine or dark and reflecting the stars. Jeffery was in the dream. The whole thing smelled like him. How hard had he been pushing this? How many dreams had he invaded, following this one human? The endless night of the Dark didn't match with the regular stopwatch rhythm of the waking world, but we did have time and Jeffery hadn't had much of it.

There was only one way to find out how he'd done this. I went charging through the shallow, confused waters and dove into the dream.

I almost thought this was still a good dream, floating in the Light. It was much like the last one, with the same people and colors and objects that were deliberately generic rather than accidentally vague. Now there was one street, but wasn't very dense with buildings. The layout made sense rather than being random, and there were a couple of signs on shops that would've been readable if I cared, so it might be a place in the human world. The dreamer was there, and again he was walking with that woman. They mumbled gibberish to each other, but they seemed happy enough just taking in the sights. They seemed completely unaware of what was going on around them.

The dream wasn't crowded by any means, but there were people and a few animals, always one or two everywhere I looked. They were all eating. Something androgynously human sat on a bench having a snack of an arm. Sitting at a plastic table in front of a tiny café two more people shared a human head between them, cutting it up delicately with a knife and fork. Everyone and everything living was doing that, except me.

That fact was pointed out to me as a small child with a bag of ears walked past and whispered to me in Jeffery's voice, "Don't mess this up, Fang. He's at a very delicate stage. Join in, eat something!"

This being a dream there was now a dead body in front of me, so I started ripping off chunks while the little child picked up the bits I dropped to eat them one by one. The body was much more detailed than any of the living people. It had a face and the meat—the meat tasted real. It had flavor, it was rich and faintly salty and there was texture. It resisted and tore as I pulled at it. It was delicious.

Nothing else seemed to be happening. I didn't get time to find out if anything would. I was near the edge of the dream and I could see out of the skin to the vortex outside, so I was looking right at it when the goldfish swam by.

It was big and orange and yellow and red and it was a fish, although it looked kind of like one made from strips of paper. It was a goldfish. At least, until it swam up to the edge a little above me and the fish became a swirl of paper around a girl who peered inside as I stared out at her.

Jeffery saw her too. A squirrel holding a badly chewed finger in its teeth skittered down a tree and whispered to me, "Fang, get rid of her! If she gets inside this whole process will be ruined and I'll have to find a new dreamer."

Which made my thoughts jump. "Forget her, Jeffery. Whatever this is, Lucy knows about it! I met her, Jeffery, she's coming for you!" I whined at him desperately.

"Do you think this is the first time?" he snapped, "That fish is the problem right now. Get rid of her and I'll start dodging Lucy after this stage is over. Please, Fang!"

My own thoughts snarled. The first time? Of course this wasn't the first time. Jeffery was probably at the top of Lucy's hit list already. Just because I'd never gotten her attention didn't mean it wasn't a danger he was used to. And my thoughts derailed again. The need in his voice. He was my friend, and he'd rather be in danger than let this fail.

I was worried I'd pop the dream by breaking out of it, but something was holding onto it like a vice now and I had to struggle and force my way through the edge. It sealed up instantly behind me. Outside, the waters were still spinning, lit and shadowed, and the fish glided through the air around the dream bubble. One pale, feminine arm emerged from the body and fingertips trailed lines of color over the dream's surface. Enough of that and the dreamer would notice, or she'd find a way in.

I had no idea what to do, so I did what I always do. I growled and snarled and leapt at her. She yelped and fled, so I chased her.

She swam straight into the Light, but she was fleeing so I followed her. I just stopped thinking about it. Ahead of me was a streamer-trailing, shining fish who wriggled as she sped along, ducking behind dreams, weaving through a carnival that loomed up out of the glowing nothing, or sometimes abandoning me and soaring upwards. I followed behind, fangs slavering, bouncing heavily off of anything solid and snapping when I got close or barking in frustration if she pulled ahead. When she went up into the sky I ran up a slope that hadn't really been there before. The Light was as fractured and responsive as the Dark, it seemed, or maybe more so. The gentle warmth bit at me like ants, but I ignored that. For a chase I could ignore that heat forever.

At least, I could ignore it until I noticed the sound. The goldfish, huge and supple and trailing streamers of color as bright as its scales, was laughing. She led me into a springtime glen where every tree had little pink flowers and the sky was blue and the sun bright, and we twisted and dodged between the tree trunks while everywhere she passed the flowers spun out of the grass and flew around us like fairies. Finally she swam right up into one of those trees and laid herself out on a branch.

I can't fly. To do it I'd have to become a different nightmare. I can have hands, so I stood up and started pulling myself awkwardly up the trunk. Big or small, wolf or dog or man beast, no version of me is good at climbing, but what else was I going to do? Stop chasing her?

She giggled, and streamers and scales in every color a goldfish can be rained down around me, leaving behind a young woman. Well, sort of a young woman. She was simple, mostly white, and no matter what direction you looked at her from she looked like she was flat. She wasn't wearing any clothes, but even if I'd cared there wasn't much to see. She was like a painting, an impression of a girl rather than a human.

"I'm Coy. Do you have a name?" she asked me as I tried to get enough of a grip with my hind claws to push myself up a little further.

Which was a useless effort, because the question made me lose my grip and fall sprawling on my tail. "Fang. I'm Fang. You can talk?" Cue babbling like a moron.

"Oh wonderful, you can too!" she laughed. More 'bubbled', I guess. It was a fish's voice, like I was hearing it through water.

I still didn't know what to say. I've never been a good conversationalist. "Aren't you scared? Why do you keep laughing?" I asked her, grabbing whatever came to mind.

"Oh, I was scared at first!" she told me enthusiastically, "But you know, it was like a big game of tag wasn't it? You obviously didn't want to hurt me, just chase me. And then I got a look at you. You're like this big black smudge, a shape rather than an animal. Just teeth and eyes and hulking blackness. You're art, Fang. Didn't you know that? I was dreamed up by an artist, so I love pretty dreams. You'd scare a lot of normal dreamers, but I've known some that would love you."

She giggled again. I stared at her in bafflement, watching the airborne flowers flutter around her and red and orange streams of paper spin about her, too thin to guard the modesty she didn't have. To my growing discomfort it occurred to me that she was beautiful. Her eyes were just these triangles outlined in thick black brushstrokes, and her red lips were always smiling.

"I've got to go," I announced, leaping to my feet, "I have to get back to the Dark. We're too deep in the Light. It's doing things to me."

I started turning away, but I froze when she called out, "Wait, Fang!" When I didn't start moving again immediately she told me, "You're a nightmare, aren't you? You have to tell the nightmare who was in that dream to stop. I know it wasn't you who did it."

I looked back up at her, and then looked away. She was so white, and for all that she looked like a cutout edged in rough brush strokes, she moved with the sinuous girlish grace that Lily had. If I didn't get back to the Dark soon I wasn't sure what would happen to me. "You're sort of like a nightmare, but for the Light, right? I'm not going to tell Jeffery to stop making bad dreams. He's good at it. I think he's found some way to show that he's the best at it."

I'd turned my head away, so I didn't see her change. She was a goldfish again as she swam around me, wriggling and floating and circling. She wasn't laughing anymore. She sounded completely serious as she explained, "I'm a fantasy. It's not really the same. I don't just make a dream better, I try and make a dream something that makes the dreamer better. Humans just shrug off dreams, so it's really hard. That other nightmare, Jeffery, he's found a way to hurt the dreamer. He's scaring him somehow so that it's following the dreamer to the waking world. Is that what nightmares are supposed to do? Because I look at you, and I don't think it is."

It wasn't. There were no rules against it exactly, although there was a big, fat Lucy against it. It just wasn't supposed to be an option. What could you do to a dreamer, to someone who would just wake up and forget? And that dream hadn't been all that scary. Well, it would have scared a lot of dreamers rigid, but that one seemed to be finding it natural.

Why was I caring about any of this? I was too deep in the Light. I could feel it, and every time I glanced at this iridescent fish girl swimming by me it got into me a little deeper.

Still, actually hurting a dreamer?

I wasn't going to think about that. I threw myself forward and started running. I didn't pick a direction, and since I didn't I knew I'd head straight for the border. I had to get back into the Dark and get myself back before I thought about this.

Behind me Coy's pretty, bubbly voice called out to me, but I growled as loud as I could so I couldn't make out the words.

Getting back into the Dark was a relief, like I was alone in my skin again. I needed to center myself.

I found the house high on a hill that curled out like a hook of stone over a barren farm. Above us an oversized moon grinned ominously, and the wind blew cold over my shoulders. Already I was feeling better. I could rely on my love to find the most picturesque places to settle. In the field below, things stirred, pale but half-seen shapes. I thought those might be real ghosts, humans who had found no peace after death but had gotten lost in the Dark and unable to find reward or punishment. Like the drifting dreams, they were now just one more of the Dark's curiosities. When I threaded my way through the maze of rooms and halls inside the house I was not surprised to find my Muse's sitting room looking out over the edge of that cliff. For once her hands weren't covering her face, and instead she rocked slowly in her creaking chair, staring out the windows with empty eye sockets.

But some things never change. Tears ran down her cheeks, and I could hear the rough fluttering of her breathing, and she paid me no attention at all as I crept in.

I was glad that her face was uncovered. I got to pad over to her chair and lay my head in her lap and stare up at that face, every feature exact and delicate like glass. Her eyes were black pits, and her skin was as pale as the paper-white smoothness of a girl who could swim as a goldfish.

I'd chased Coy much, much too far into the Light. So I lay there and listened to my Muse cry and wondered what this blighted farm and its misplaced souls meant that she would rearrange her room to watch them. I watched tears slide down her cheeks one by one and fall onto her ruined dress, and restrained my urge to lick them off her face to try and taste her sadness.

Yes, I was feeling a lot better. Which meant I had to figure out what to do next.

"I don't want to take her advice, my love, but she was right," I murmured quietly to a girl who couldn't hear me, "Jeffery's doing something crazy. Maybe I should trust him. He's smarter than me and I'm not really sure what he's doing, but this bothers me. It feels like he's not content to be a nightmare anymore. Can you be too ambitious? And it's driving him crazy. He doesn't even care about danger at all."

Of course she didn't respond. She just sat and rocked and sniffled occasionally as the tears dripped down, one by one. But above the windows an eye the size of my head had opened, sickly green, and it stared down at me fixedly. Accusingly, even.

I knew she wasn't really looking at me. The eyes just watched, they didn't seem to take anything in or express her feelings at all. But still, I had to confess. "Yes, I met this girl. She's like a Muse for humans, on the other side of the border. I… had to come back here to remember which of you is more beautiful." I hated myself for saying it, but at the same time I felt better. The eye watched, but nothing else changed. Whatever mysterious feelings she had for me, my eyeless Muse didn't change them just because I'd had my head turned for a moment by the topsy-turvy prettiness on the far side of the border, where everything is wrong but beautiful anyway.

I took a deep breath and lifted my head. I was cool and strong and dark again, and I knew who and what I was. I still wasn't sure what I would do, but I couldn't just sit around.

"You're more lovely than anyone could ever be," I whispered into her ear, and I meant it, "But I have to go find Jeffery. I don't know what I'll say to him, but he's destroying himself with this and taking a dreamer with him. I can't just let him chase his own tail until Lucy cuts it off."

As I loped out of the house, I tried to fix every peeling strip of wallpaper and cracked china vase in my memory. I was going to need all the determination I had to argue with Jeffery over anything.

I found him at the border, of course. I headed there even before I started picking up his trail. I knew he'd be following his dreamer around from dream to dream, not giving either of them a chance to rest. I caught up to him there, or at least I almost caught up to him.

He was sliding through the surface of a dream floating in the shallow end of the Dark.

I trotted up after him, ears perked and nose sniffing for any hint of Lucy, any sign of the Dark warping or some other disturbance. I was starting to feel like I'd gotten worked up over nothing. It looked like a mildly bad dream and the chaotic part of Jeffery's plan was over.

I tried to push my way in after him, because a dream just drifting near the border couldn't be that critical, but I couldn't. It wouldn't let me in. So instead I pressed my face against the edge and peered inside.

It turned out the interior really was just dark. The only two things in this dream were the dreamer himself and his girlfriend. At least, it looked kind of like his girlfriend. It wasn't really that curvy anymore and it was getting hard to tell if it was a man or a woman. They were kissing, and she kept biting off little bits of his neck and shoulder, which seemed to justify the way the dream drifted slowly on the Dark side of the border. After a while the girl kissed the dreamer on the mouth, and they seemed to be getting into it, and then blood poured out from between their lips. From the way his jaw was working, the dreamer must have been eating her tongue.

The dream stayed where it was, but the surface was going opaque. The last thing I saw was the dreamer biting into the girl with a feral excitement, but a gap in her cheek showed tiny sharp teeth. Jeffery was possessing the girl, not the dreamer.

I didn't know what to think. The one thing I was sure of was that this was dangerous. This dream wasn't deep enough in the Dark for what was going on inside it and it was closing up around itself, so it couldn't pop or be diverted again. Jeffery wasn't getting out of there until the dreamer let it end. It wasn't just that by then Lucy might be waiting for him. The dreamer could kill him in there. He wasn't even trying to be safe.

"Jeffery, come out of there! Or let me in!" I barked desperately. I bit and clawed at the edge, but of course that didn't do anything. "This has gone too far, way too far! You're losing your mind. You're fading, Jeffery. This, whatever you're doing, you're becoming this thing that eats, not yourself anymore!"

I whined. I raced around. I scratched at the surface, over and over. I wasn't even sure he could hear me, until something scraped words on the inner surface of the dream. "Go away. I can do this."

I gave up. I just slumped down on my haunches and stared for a minute, although I couldn't see anything through the surface anymore except the occasional streak of blood. I must have been losing my own mind to think I could talk Jeffery out of this. Was it even my business to talk him out of it? It was his life to throw away, even if I wished he wouldn't. And he wasn't telling me what kind of nightmare to be. I was the one telling him he couldn't be the kind of nightmare he wanted.

Those were the kinds of things I thought about as I dragged myself back toward the Gate.

I knew where I was going, and I stayed away from it. I'd already been much less faithful to my girlfriend than I was comfortable with tonight. It was hard to think of that face, thin and delicate-looking as glass, and feel that I deserved her. So I just wandered the city, which I'd never really spent enough time in to look at, and when I would get tired of not knowing what kind of service a shop offered or what kind of thing the proprietor was I'd turn and look toward the center and the massive, gargoyle-pocked edifice that was the Gate.

This left me padding across the mismatched flagstones of a public square just as a clumsy metal figure lurched up to the top of the stage overlooking it. The square probably had only been brought here for this announcement, and the crowd had happened to be passing through it the same way. Perhaps the Dark itself wanted something. So I stopped long enough to listen.

"A year has passed," the metal thing announced, lurching as awkwardly in its words as it had in its steps, "The powers that be are proud to announce that the time has come for the annual challenge tournament! If you believe you are something more and better than those around you, hone your skills, and if you're as good as you think you are you'll have the chance to prove it. The most serious challengers will be selected automatically, and a schedule posted for the edification of the public."

It was an amusing distraction to peel away the carnival barker nonsense from that. Years were something that happened in the waking world, but still, it was challenge time again. Whoever or whatever you were you had the right to challenge a Demiurge. If you could prove you were better than they were at being what they were, the title became yours. There were no judges, no organizers, no powers that be that anyone knew of. Challenges might be posted, competitors worthy of taking part might be selected, but these things just happened. The possibility of being killed by a Demiurge who had just defended their title kept the tournament small. I'd avoided the city most of my life, so I'd never really watched a challenge.

Before my thoughts got any further the announcer was speaking again. "Also, anyone who knows anything about a nightmare pursuing some kind of campaign against a single dreamer, there is a reward for information leading to him being found." What? "The nightmare is reported to go by the name of Jeffery, and his appearance is as follows." On the front of the stand Jeffery's picture was rapidly being painted in. It was crude, but the dark clothes, the sandy blonde hair and the sharp teeth made him stand out. I was apparently the first person to realize what the picture drawing itself meant, which meant I was backing toward an exit to the surrounding streets by the time the metal figure finished, "Anyone who knows how to find this nightmare, please report his whereabouts to the young lady holding a blade to—"

His head came off, and as his body fell limply from the stand Lucy stepped up to the edge. She wore a fancy blue and green dress now, and had huge bells in her hair that tinkled with a sound far too sweet and merry to match her gigantic scythe.

"Look at this!" she called down to us with delight while the crowd was still frozen, "It's a street full of victims! Hello, street full of victims! I'd love to chop you all int- YOU! You know where Jeffery is!"

Yes, she was pointing straight at me, but I was almost at one of the exits. I'd have been there already but the crowd had started to move, some of it surging forward, some of it trying to get away. As things thinned I had a few seconds to see more than I wanted to.

Lucy jumped down off the podium into the crowd, and a swing of her scythe cleared her a spot by cutting two nightmares in half. Now the crowd was really panicking, but not all of it. I almost had a flicker of hope. This deep in the city she'd jumped down into a ring of creatures ready to fight.

In the few heartbeats before I found a gap I could slip out through into the streets, I saw how this was going to go. The massive brute made of plates of old bone was probably a demon, and the clawed hand it slammed down on top of Lucy was bigger than she was. Except she wasn't there, she was behind it. She hadn't moved, she was just there, and the tension and panic I felt in the air, the faint gleaming in the skyline, told me how.

Lucy had enclosed the entire city in a dream.

There was nowhere to run. I could only hope there were so many nightmares caught in a dream this big that she couldn't pick me out from the rest. I ran anyway, ducking into the street and churning my four legs as fast as they would go toward the edge of the city. I wasn't watching the square anymore, but a dreamer is the center of a dream and I could still see what was going on. I saw her cleave a huge rent in the demon, hit a spiked gargoyle of a nightmare so hard that she punched a hole through its chest, then grab what I thought was an actual ghost and rip the transparent skin off of it, making whatever was inside dissipate like a burst of glowing mist.

Again I had a flicker of hope as a weird, discordant note rang through the surrounding streets and a split was carved into the flagstones so violently that shards of it sprayed everywhere. At the other end of the crowd was one of the… things, from outside, from somewhere that doesn't touch the waking world at all and has nothing to do with humanity. It was just a bunch of grey, transparent globes that floated vaguely through each other. Lucy's response was to grab a wiry feline nightmare that had been clawing at her, and although he screamed and writhed I saw him turn into a spear that she hurled straight at the outsider. There was a demon in the way, a thing of fire and scales, but rending it apart didn't even slow the spear down. Neither did the thing from outside. The spear passed through it with no effect. It wasn't really there, but one of those globes shivered and sounded another note, and another stretch of rock shattered violently.

Lucy wasn't standing on it anymore. Bells chiming, her red-brown hair flying, she hopped from head to head across the city's protectors until she landed atop the highest floating globe. At least she bounced off of it, touching it only with one fingertip as she launched herself past. When she did the globe went solid. They all did, falling to the surface of the plaza and splitting into shards. Lucy laughed even as a few drops of blood leaked from her ears, and I think that's what did it. She had lost her concentration and the weak dream burst.

I didn't know what was going on behind me anymore, but I hadn't wanted to. I just ran, and although the streets were always random and changing anyway in this town, I zigzagged through them, trying to leave no obvious trail.

I nearly tripped over my own feet when I heard Lucy yelling behind me, "Here, doggy doggy doggy! You want a bone, right? I just left a big pile of them in the street back there. Once you show me how to find your friend, you can have all you want!"

I could hear myself whining as I skidded around and threw myself into an alley, but I couldn't outrun a dreamer. As I ducked past some character wearing black leaning against the wall, I heard her shout again from the alley's mouth, "Don't you be a bad boy like Jeffery, doggy! Come back here!" This was all a big joke to her.

And then she yelped. The sound was so unexpected I jerked my head around to look back over my shoulder and saw her suspended against the brighter light of the street, impaled on a hundred pencil-thin blades that stuck out of the walls and the ground from every direction. I had barely registered the sight when she burst and disappeared.

I managed not to fall over as I ground to a halt. Behind me the blades withdrew into the walls, and then I saw them sliding back into the hand of the figure behind me as he pulled that hand away from the wall. The skin on his face was red and his eyes glowed, and little horns stuck out of his black hair.

"You lured her to me perfectly, boy," the demon informed me as he checked the buttons on his cuffs and started walking away from me into the street, "I'm going to be very popular tonight, so to repay you I will give you some advice. Fighting a dreamer head on is stupid. A sharp shock that they aren't expecting will wake them up."

Panting for breath, I lurched the other way and tried to get a grip on myself. I didn't want to talk to him anymore.

Who I did want to talk to was Jeffery, which was why I shouldn't have been as surprised as I was when I trotted out of the other end of the alley and nearly knocked him over. I'd wanted to warn him. If raw fear had been on the surface of my thoughts, he'd been everywhere underneath. I'd tracked him down without meaning to and nearly led Lucy right to her target. That might even have been her plan.

"Jeffery, what are you doing to that dreamer?!" I barked. "Lucy came into town to get to you, Jeffery. She came into town. She chased me over half of it. You had to have noticed the dream."

That, finally, got through to him. He stared at me for a moment with those blue eyes he used to make dreamers think him harmless. And he sounded grim and serious when he told me, "I didn't want to drag you into that. Any time a nightmare tries to put himself beyond the pack she comes after him. I knew before I started that she'd be chasing me, but I convinced myself she wouldn't be interested in anyone around me. That's all the more reason I need to finish this now, and I need you to come with me."

"I don't want anything to do with this," I growled at him. If he was going to be stubborn, I could be too. "And I might just as well say that I can protect you better by splitting us up so she can only follow one at a time."

"Come with me, Fang," he insisted, "She's not as good at finding people as we are and I'm sure there's only one more dream."

"I told you, I don't want to be involved," I insisted. I couldn't justify it. I couldn't explain why what he was doing was wrong, it just felt that way.

"But I want you to be there to see it," he told me.

I had no immediate reply to that, and even less of one as a stuffed scarecrow that was vaguely female climbed the stairs from the sunken shop next to us up onto the street. I stood aside, grateful for the excuse not to answer until I recognized the nervous, halting way she moved and I looked up and saw the little wooden sign with a black razor on a red background.

"Ready to go, Miss Masochism?" Jeffery asked her lightly.

"I think so," she answered cautiously, looking around, "The city's gotten bigger, hasn't it?"

How long had it been since she'd been outside her little salon, serving people like me night after night? Would I know what the answer meant if I got it?

She was looking at me, or more like peeking at me, big button eyes glancing in my direction and then away. It made Jeffery smile very widely and tell her, "Fang helped me get this started and he's been protecting me along the way. He's a very good friend."

I was still totally blank on what to say about that when she answered him, "Yes, you said he was involved. I want to be, too. It will be nice to get out again and take part in a friend's life instead of waiting for him to come to me."

They were talking past me, but they had to because it's not like I was saying anything. The little catches in her voice, the faint rasp—she had agreed to this, taking part in whatever scheme Jeffery had come up with, because she thought I wanted it. And the way she talked, I got the feeling she was finally fading enough that it scared her. If she expected me to save her, I didn't know how. If she thought this would help her get herself back a little, I wasn't going to so much as hint that she shouldn't.

I was also trying very hard to believe that Jeffery hadn't tied the two of us into this knot deliberately.

"There's really only one dream left?" I asked him exasperatedly as we started walking.

"I think so. I'm almost sure of it," Jeffery affirmed, "There's just one obstacle left and then we'll see fireworks. It's still all a dream to him, some kind of fantasy. His human morals are like a wall and I can't get him to break through them myself. I need an expert."

"I know what makes someone do things they know are wrong and will hate themselves forever for," Self-Loathing sighed, "I'm not sure I can remember the last time I played with a dreamer, but I know what to do. If it's what you two want I'll get him past that wall."

"It's all that's left to do," Jeffery insisted vehemently.

At least, I thought he did. As the distractions of the city faded behind us I had noticed a teasing smell. It made me look up at Self-Loathing ambling slowly beside me. Thinking of her as a scarecrow had been a mistake I'd made before my panic had faded. She was a rag doll, slim and made with a delicate skill that even gave her individual fingers, but the fabric was coarse, maybe burlap, and her seams were coming undone. She was old and battered everywhere and covered in stains. Grease. I could smell the stains, animal grease, and underneath I could smell the dusty wood shavings her body was packed with. She would crunch and tear between my teeth, and taste like meat and fat and resin...

I lowered my ears and hoped as hard as I could that I wasn't blushing. Normally I can't blush, but I couldn't shut out the smell or the faint crunching noise of the shavings as she walked. I found myself noticing the careful way she took each step, like she was terrified something would jump out at her, and I had to turn my head away.

After a while she laid her hand on my shoulder, and it was all I could do to keep my breathing steady and keep walking. I was very grateful when we got to the border.

I almost stumbled over it. It was a street again, this time covered in bricks instead of asphalt or concrete, and across the way it was lined with brightly painted homes and jolly store fronts. I glanced back as we walked across and behind us loomed boarded up windows and decaying wooden warehouses. The crossing was easy, but the Light didn't want us tonight.

I felt it when we passed between the too-pretty buildings and into a sort of country town mixed with a fair. Little buildings were interspersed with children's rides, like a carousel and a tiny roller-coaster. Despite the glaring sunshine, bright lights hung everywhere and they all focused on us. We weren't in very far, but it was intrusive. It nagged at me, but at least that let me think about other things than who was walking right beside me. Come to think of it, I could see steam rising faintly off Jeffery, but Self-Loathing looked no more or less comfortable than she ever had.

That was definitely symbolism of some kind. The dream we were looking for was here, resting between two buildings. I'd had enough of the scent of it by now to be sure it was Jeffery's dreamer and he'd led us straight to it.

For once it really looked like an innocent dream worthy of the Light. I could look inside and see the dreamer walking slowly down endless hallways, everything plain, maybe a little patched and worn but painted white. It was a building, not a home, with windows on the inside and doors you could see through. Every once in a while, a small child in a clean but slightly ragged little outfit would pass by carrying some toy or other. It was more subtle than most, but this was the kind of dream of a simple, peaceful life that made a target for a nightmare. I was sure Jeffery had something less obvious in mind.

When we got to the dream Jeffery instructed me, "I'd like to let you watch this from the inside, but I need you to stay out here. He has to feel me in there, but it's all up to Masochism now. She can't have gotten to be a Demiurge without being good at this. At least, I hope so."

She couldn't answer herself. She hadn't stopped at the edge; she'd just walked right into the dream bubble and apparently disappeared. The last thing I saw was the thread running up the back of her crude dress, already coming undone. One swipe of my claws would have opened it, and the smell of grease still lingered.

"She is," I told Jeffery fervently. I didn't want him to do this, I didn't want to be a part of it, and I didn't want to have dragged Self-Loathing into it. But he wanted it. I reared up on my hind legs and put a hand on his shoulder and told him, "You're wasting time."

I pushed him in, and unlike Self-Loathing he didn't disappear. He just ducked behind a door and hid in a corner and waited. He wouldn't have to do anything. A dreamer can feel a nightmare in their dream, and his presence would bend the way the dreamer thought.

The dreamer kept walking, but as he passed one door a little girl, a really little girl, like the kind who can't read yet, pushed it open and started walking next to him. One of her hands reached up and took his, and he smiled down to her. I couldn't hear what they said. It was probably nonsense anyway. She had a face, detailed and individual. All the children did. Unlike the not-men-not-women in the other dreams, to the dreamer these were real people. And I knew that little girl's walk, and the way she hesitated for a moment before she moved or spoke.

The dream showed no sign of moving, and there was no sign of why it should. If anything, Jeffery lurking in it might have been the only reason it didn't drift further into the Light. She might be finding too many reasons to touch the dreamer or to brush up against him, but the little girl who I knew was Self-Loathing just wandered around this dream building with him, and occasionally he'd hold her up to sip from a water fountain or try and get her to sit and play with a toy only to have her follow him around and hold his hand again.

Eventually she stumbled and he had to catch her. When he sat down in a chair and put her on his lap, I saw why—a lace in her sneakers had snapped. They chatted and smiled at each other as he rethreaded it. When she leaned up against him I noticed the dream start to shudder, and when she lifted one small hand to run a thumb curiously over his lips the whole dream jumped and shadows started spreading over the walls on either side.

I didn't have much time to wonder what was going on. The dreamer rather hurriedly finished tying the girl's shoe, but when he went to put her down she threw her arms around his neck and hugged him. She was talking, she hadn't stopped, but I couldn't hear it. And she pulled back and gave him a sweet little smile and kissed him on the lips.

He bit her. There'd been a moment when everything froze, but by the time I noticed it his teeth were sinking into her lips. This wasn't like the last dream I saw. She didn't like it. She screamed and struggled and bled as he bit her again and again.

I didn't want to watch it. I didn't want to see Self-Loathing let a dreamer do this to her. It was… intimate, more intimate than anything she'd let me do. It made me more uncomfortable than I would have imagined.

Fortunately, I had plenty of distractions. The dream hadn't moved. It wasn't a bad dream, it was a good dream, and it wasn't going to leave the Light. Shadows whiplashed out of it, staining the fairgrounds around me, and I felt the burning sense of being in the Light slowly fade. Looking back at the horizon I saw an approaching grey line. The dream was dragging the border to it?

In the distance a young girl's voice yelled, "I saw that!" Lucy's voice. Lucy was close, and she couldn't fail to find us with the dream spraying tentacles of the Dark to mix with the Light.

I dove through the edge of the dream and got in much more easily than I expected. The dreamer was a little excited, but not tense. I landed in the back room where Jeffery was hiding, out of sight.

"Jeffery, she's here!" I hissed at him, trying to keep my voice as low as possible, "Lucy is here! We have to go right now!"

"Not yet!" he whispered back. His eyes had gone wide, and he was panting. I couldn't say I could blame him. There was this weird feeling in the dream, like when Jeffery was inside my skin and hungry to get to his victim.

"She's going to kill all three of us, Jeffery! If we wait any longer she'll be waiting for us when the dream ends. For all I know she can break in and rip it away from you! We have to run!"

"No, you do!" he told me, and he burst away from the corner and gave me a shove back toward the surface of the dream. The shove was clumsy. He was too wild and unfocused. "If this succeeds it'll be worth it, but it won't be worth you dying with me. You run, and if I get away I'll get away and catch up with you."

I stood up and grabbed him in both hands. I would have sworn he'd be stronger than me, much stronger, but he wasn't. He might just have been weak from what he'd put into this dream. Maybe I was going to say something noble, but instead he lashed out, not at me, but at the wall. He'd grabbed fistfuls of a wall? I'd seen stranger in dreams.

"Just a few more seconds!" he yelled at me, "Can't you feel how close he is?"

Jeffery was right. He and I had both lost control because the dreamer had lost it. It was filling the dream. And he was right also because the time it took me to register this and realize I was still going to try and get us both out was enough to end it.

The wall was sucked out of Jeffery's hands. The dream broke with a violent tremor, but it didn't disappear. Instead it pulled inwards, and we were left in the space between two buildings that were now so fallen down they were almost rubble. The dream was gone, but the dreamer was still there, standing over the remains that must have been Self-Loathing. And before him there was a split. Beyond it I could see a room, kind of dark, but it just looked like a regular bedroom I'd see in a dream except that the detail was amazing. The dreamer walked through the gap, and it closed up and they were both gone.

That was when the border caught up with us. We were, suddenly, in the Dark. That was also when Lucy caught up with us, walking around a corner into the now abandoned gap between two desolate wrecks that had once been architecture.

"You have been a bad, bad boy," she announced, pointing something at Jeffery. I wasn't even sure what she was carrying. It looked like a couple of axes connected by a chain. The weapon was more than a little at odds with the overalls and bright red shirt she was wearing. These were all more scare tricks, and knowing that wasn't making me less scared. Self-Loathing was dead and Jeffery and I were about to be. I might be able to escape if I left him, but he just lay there in my arms, laughing breathlessly and staring at the sky.

Self-Loathing wasn't dead. If I'd let a dreamer do that much damage to me, meaning to hurt me, I'd never have recovered. But the gory wreck was climbing to its feet.

Now she and Jeffery were both helpless and in trouble. I put Jeffery down and bounded forward, planting myself between her and Lucy and growling as loudly and threateningly as I could. "Take Jeffery and get back to the Gate! I'll hold her off or slow her down or something!" I whispered back to Self-Loathing.

And Self-Loathing hit me, hit me so hard across the muzzle that she knocked me into the far wall. My face was splattered with her blood now, and she yelled at me, "Who do you think you are? Do you think you could delay a dreamer even for a second? I did what you wanted. I've destroyed another life for you, maybe several. Take your friend and get out of here."

"I'm not—"

"Go!" she yelled. Her voice hadn't really changed. It was still hoarse and quavering, but raised in anger and contempt that made it all the more shocking.

I skittered over to Jeffery. He was a little more under control, whispering deliriously, "I did it. It works!" He still wasn't going anywhere under his own power, so I grabbed his scruff in my teeth.

"I'll admit that was the coolest thing I've seen in months," Lucy told us from the other side of the lot, "But I think I'm going to kill them first and come back for you. You're not going anywhere, so why should I let you get in my way?"

I hauled Jeffery up off the ground, but I paused to watch Self-Loathing change. She grew, and filled out, and long coppery hair stretched down, and another Lucy stood in the gravel-strewn patch between the buildings. This one wasn't a healthy little girl full of energy and murder. She looked like she'd been starved, and the green and purple mess swelling one eye shut wasn't her only bruise. There were stains on her nightgown, and it wasn't just worn, it had been torn repeatedly and not so much sewn as tied shut.

Shaking, this new Lucy who I almost forgot for a moment had been Self-Loathing slumped down and whined, "You're right. I'm not even interesting. No wonder."

The axes became gloves, at least twice the size of her real fists, with a band of metal over the knuckles. The real Lucy didn't so much run as fly forward, punching the new one and knocking her down. I noticed as she fell that one of the arms just kind of flopped at an odd angle, as if it had already been useless.

"Die! Die! You… will… die! You don't exist!" Lucy screamed, but I wasn't watching. I was running as fast as I could while carrying Jeffery, heading straight into the Dark. Somewhere in that direction was the Gate.

Lucy didn't stop screaming, but I stopped being able to understand it. I did hear when the thumps became the meatier whacking of a blade biting into flesh.

She didn't come after us. After things had been quiet for a little while I realized she wasn't going to. We'd gotten away. Jeffery was still laughing a lot, but he mumbled something about being able to run on his own, so I let him.

Lily met us first, as the city around the Gate loomed up ahead. She actually flew, although the flapping made something crimson show through under the ragged white feathers of her wings. She catapulted into us, wrapping her arms around us both, but it was Jeffery she spoke to.

"Was that you?" she demanded, "Was that what you were working on? He didn't last long. There was bad luck, but you turned him so hard he didn't try to be cautious. They think the kid will live and the woman won't, but it's not who he took with him. They were pure anyway. It's what you did to him, with only bad dreams!"

Jeffery laughed again, but he was upright and strong and in control now, and I could see every one of his sharp little teeth. It hardly mattered that he could stand, because a crowd had spotted us and they pulled him off his feet, hoisting him into the air and asking him a barrage of questions. I heard one ask which Demiurge he was going to challenge.

Lily's hand stroked me between my ears. "You going to be okay if I leave you alone, puppy?" she asked me sweetly.

"I think so. Go celebrate," I told her. I was trying not to sound sardonic and tired. I wasn't sure if I succeeded or not.

"Celebrate?" she countered wistfully, "I don't have time. Our little sandy-haired glutton has opened up a giant can of worms, for himself and everyone else. I have to go play angel politics. If I'm good at it he'll never know I had to, so don't you tell him." And she sighed, sounding almost as tired as I was.

"I don't think he should have done it, Lily," I told her. I had to tell somebody. "That was a demon thing, or—I don't know. He wasn't being a nightmare there."

"I'm impressed. I'm dearly, dearly impressed," she told me, giving me another petting, "I do have reservations of my own, but I don't have time to talk about it. Try and be happy for him, puppy, it's what he wanted. Now I have to fly. I need to get through the Gate before my relatives start coming out."

And she flew, like before, trailing the occasional feather. I padded into the city alone. There seemed to be a party going on, but most of it happened somewhere else, and if I saw too much light and noise I turned away.

Eventually I found myself passing by a set of steps leading down to a sunken doorway, beneath a red and black sign with the picture of a blade. The salon hadn't disappeared, but the door was ajar and everything was dim and quiet inside.

I wandered down the steps and nudged the door open with my nose. Either she was dead or she didn't want to see me again, but I would get one last look at her chintzy waiting room.

I heard a noise. A moan. There was nothing theatrical or passionate about it. I could barely hear it at all. Curiosity tugged at me, and at that moment it was the only emotion I seemed to have left to feel. I wandered back through the bead curtain and listened carefully until another tiny whimper told me which back room to go into.

The set-up was impressive. Candles stood everywhere, but none of them were lit and I could hardly see. Someone had been writing in red and black all over the walls and the floor, and although I didn't recognize them the letters probably meant something to someone. And something had been nailed to the wall.

Rather, someone had been nailed to the wall. I thought it might be female, but it was withered almost beyond recognition and the nails were the huge kind used in construction, driven right into her. Still, she was alive. She breathed, she moaned faintly every once in a while, and I could make out her eyes moving a little, although they didn't seem to fix on anything.

In fact she didn't seem to notice me at all. The voice was familiar, what little I'd heard of it. As a Demiurge, I supposed even Lucy couldn't kill her. But this thing hanging on the wall wasn't really conscious. It was an idea. She had faded. I wondered if by morning even this would be left.

Hoping I could at least stop the decline, I nudged at her leg with my nose. "Self-Loathing? Please wake up. It's Fang. Do you remember me? Can you hear me at all?"

Nothing. It was worse than talking to my Muse. And in frustration I did the same thing to this girl I'd done to the other. I bit her.

This time it worked. She blinked and let out a cry, and the nails made loud ringing noises as they popped out of the wall and she fell on me.

I was alarmed, then relieved, then I started to worry again. "Are you in there? Do you hear me now?" I asked her in a low voice.

Weak arms wrapped around my shoulders and her hoarse voice responded, "I hear you, Fang. I'm so sorry I said those things to you. I had to make you run away. I can't believe you came back for me."

"You were right anyway," I confessed, tired and full of regret, "I'd have been dead before I hit the ground if she did to me what she did to you. I was useless."

"Aren't we all?" she asked wistfully, "It's not so bad to be weak. It's so much worse to be strong, and still do the wrong thing."

I wasn't sure she was really talking to me, now. She was still badly faded.

"Are you going to be okay?" I asked her, since I had no idea what I could do to help.

"I'm better than I should be," was her answer, which was both a relief and worryingly vague. "Just stay with me tonight, okay, Fang? I just want to lie here on top of you, and tomorrow I'll be as good as I was before."

"I—" Was I about to argue with her? "Why me? I'm just a customer. I don't even come to see you very often."

"Well, maybe after we wake up this will mean we're friends," she answered. The basic question of why me hadn't been answered, but I supposed she wanted what she wanted.

I lowered myself gently to the floor so that we could both rest, and she was right that it was helping her. She was no longer a wasted wreck, although I couldn't quite describe the shriveled thing holding onto me as a person. A lot of nightmares look worse, but I'd always known her to have complete control over her shape.

Breathily, she whispered, "I know I'm going to be challenged again this year, Fang. Would you come? I don't think I'm going to be able to win this time. I know it's a lot to ask to make you see that, but I want my friends there."

By the time I figured out that I should at least tell her 'yes' her breathing was so slow I knew she was asleep. I lay my head down and let exhaustion claim me, too.

I knew my girlfriend couldn't hear when I spoke to her, but I still wasn't looking forward to having to explain this.

Chapter Three

PROVE IT

I ran. I was being chased. Black and white trees flashed past in a monochrome forest. Some dreamers were less interested in color than others. This dreamer charged through the underbrush behind me, his gun held close, his body low. He was fast and sleek. The idea that he could keep up with me on two legs was absurd, but this was his dream and we moved almost in lockstep. Every time he lifted his gun, I would twist around a tree out of sight.

Soon the forest gave way. Now we ran through a narrow canyon. I snaked around, letting him get only glimpses of me. Each turn came closer than the one before it. He was gaining. The darkness drew in overhead, and the dream became tense. He nearly had me, and it was all coming down to that breathless moment. That breathless moment when he heard the footsteps behind him.

They were heavy. Paws are soft, but these thudded into the rock floor. He ran on, no longer watching every turn for the fierce black wolf he wanted to bring down. He was trying not to look behind him, trying not to know what was making either that sound or the heavy, rough panting that seemed to come from so high up.

Excitement was excitement. Adrenaline was adrenaline. The sweet thrill of pursuing seeped away to become the cold rush of being pursued. I grinned as I listened to his suddenly rapid breaths running behind me, and I grinned wider as I looked down at the tiny man with his ineffectual gun trapped in a winding rock tunnel. Every moment he refused to look behind him the fear solidified its control and the dream ground its way farther into the Dark.

The dream broke disappointingly soon. The dreamer had been weak, or just not sleeping very deeply, because he wasn't all that scared yet. If he'd held on he'd just have gotten more and more afraid.

Still, I was very satisfied, and I ran in circles, romping in the remains of the dream dissolving around me. It smelled like me. Only belatedly did I even notice the little figure in a plain white nightgown standing nearby and watching.

I trotted out of the mist and grinned down at Anna. "How much of that did you see? I'm really proud of that one. He thought he wasn't scared of teeth in the night, and I ran him in a circle until he was. I'm just glad he likes the chase that much. He really, honestly could have killed me if he'd tried hard enough."

"Why didn't you get out of the dream? I'm sure he'd have imagined something else to chase," she asked while scratching me under the jaw. I really don't get into that the way waking world dogs apparently do, but she was just being friendly.

"It didn't occur to me," I admitted. "If it had, I'm sure I'd have lost my nerve, but it didn't. I had no choice but to find a way to make it work."

"I liked it," she told me mildly, "I'm glad I caught you performing. But why aren't you at your friend's challenge?"

Oops. "Did I miss that?" I asked her cautiously, "I haven't seen a—" Next to me, lying on the ground, was an announcement sheet.

And another. I looked around and the area was littered with them. I was talking to a dreamer. I doubt she'd even thought about it. Around her, things like that just happen.

There was nothing to do but read one. Most of the page was random letters that were hard to focus on, but 'Challenge' and 'Demiurge Of Self-Loathing' were clear. The time and date were probably on the blurriest part. I just knew when I read it that the challenge would start any minute now. I had heard that dream writing is very frustrating for anyone who isn't a nightmare or a dreamer themselves.

I was already trying to think around the issue, wasn't I? "It doesn't matter, Anna," I made myself confess, "She doesn't want me there."

"She said she did," Anna replied unflappably. I didn't ask her how she knew. The calm, spacey eyes said it all.

I didn't want to meet her gaze anymore, even if she never quite seemed to meet mine. "She was being nice. She thinks she likes me, because she likes everybody," I told the pile of announcements.

"Is she your friend?"

"She's a Demiurge, Anna. I'm not someone she'd want to spend time with." I really didn't like spelling it out that plainly.

"Is she your friend?" Anna repeated.

I bowed my head. She was making me argue with myself, and the moment I started, I lost. "I'd better hurry."

As I ran through the Dark toward the Gate, I started thinking of things I could have said. We were talking about the Demiurge of Self-Loathing. If I stayed out of the way, she'd find it less easy to settle for someone who was beneath her.

I stopped thinking about it. She'd asked me to come, and I was coming. I was good at finding my way in the Dark. I could see buildings ahead, and soon the looming gothic edifice of the Gate above them. Tonight it glowed a sinister red. Even I was a good enough nightmare to realize the whole thing was too over the top to scare anybody.

I almost ran right into the challenge ring, and probably would have were it not for the crowd. The ring was big, but they'd just marked the edge with blocky white stones and left it at that. As I wandered around looking for a good, spot the ground shifted underneath me so that the space around the ring sloped up and we could all get a view. Of course, right by the edge, I saw Jeffery leaning over one of the stones with a clear space around him. Nobody wants to get on the bad side of a nightmare who can—actually, I still wasn't clear on what he'd done exactly, but it had reached out of dreams to touch a human in the waking world.

He'd earned his clear spot, and I was just looking for a space where I wouldn't have to stand up on my back legs to see when he waved me over. I hesitated, but I had been Jeffery's friend for ages and shouldn't have expected him to change just because he'd gone from being one of the best nightmares to the uncontested best nightmare.

I wormed my way through the crowd until I broke through into the little space around him, and sat down by his feet with a nice, clear view of the ring. It was just a big, sandy white circle with two people in it. The only other thing to see at all was a big bale of sticks sitting a few feet away from me. They were just low-quality dream stuff, without even any smell.

As for the people in the ring, the one closer by had a smell. He stank. He stank worse than any demon I could recall. I couldn't tell anything more because of the robe that covered him completely, although it certainly wasn't occult or mysterious or even creepy.

On the other side of the ring stood a vague, transparent specter of a woman. I could hardly make anything out until her eyes wandered past me. The moment they locked with mine she became solid and flesh. It was hardly an improvement. She had mid-length brown hair, a faded blue dress about to her knees, and was absolutely the most unremarkable looking person I'd ever seen. Only the way she looked at me, with eyes clouded by unhappiness, told me that this was Self-Loathing. She'd always worn different shapes with no loyalty to any of them, but they'd always been unusual somehow. This was just dull.

I'd never watched a challenge before, so I leaned up to Jeffery and whispered cautiously, "When does it start?"

"When they decide it does," he told me. He sounded very serious. It was serious. In fact, I felt like kicking myself for thinking I could miss this. Whether I was beneath her or not, if she lost this challenge she would no longer be the Demiurge of Self-Loathing. The odds were good she'd just be dead.

A moment later one of them decided. The man took his robe off, and I learned the reason for the smell. He was sick. Horribly so. Big black bumps swelled up here and there on a body already scrawny but immaculately clean. He stood there for a moment, perhaps trying to make a point, but was broken out of it by a fit of wet coughing that doubled him over. Even when the coughing stopped he staggered as he walked. Walk he did, though, over to the bale of sticks to scoop up an armful.

When he came close I recoiled, backpedaling around to the other side of Jeffery. It wasn't the smell, it was the fleas. I didn't know what he was that he was carrying around fleas, but I didn't want them.

Stumbling, lapsing into fits of coughing, he hauled armload after armload of sticks back to the center of the ring. Curiously, I glanced over at Self-Loathing.

"She's not doing anything," I told Jeffery. It was more a question, really.

"She never does," he explained. He laid his hand on top of my head, although to be honest I was nearly his height. "I've seen her challenged several times, and all she does is stand there. She's trying to lose."

Was that some kind of strategy? I looked up at her. She really was just standing there. She would watch the man with his black lumps sometimes, and sometimes she'd look out at the crowd, and a lot of the time she'd look at me, but she just seemed to be watching and waiting. No, I didn't think it was a strategy. She just didn't care.

"I didn't think she was going to make it to the challenge," Jeffery added slowly, in a hush, "Before you showed up she was fading while we watched."

Ah. That was why the hand on my head. He knew I visited her professionally, knew that I knew her, and he was trying to comfort me because she wasn't going to make it. I was surprised to feel myself drawing back from that thought and concentrating on the touch instead.

The diseased man, now naked to the waist, had apparently gathered enough wood. He started climbing clumsily up on top of the pile, coughing and wheezing and muttering to himself as he struggled upwards. Sticks rattled out from under his foot as he slipped, and the edge of the pile scattered. He grumbled something I couldn't make out and struck the pile with his fist in frustration—and the sticks strewn at his feet began to burn.

He'd only barely resumed his climb and the little flame had just reached the edge of the main pile when Self-Loathing walked silently over and put the fire out with her foot. She reached out and touched his chin with one hand. One of his black sores cracked and shed all over her fingers as she turned his face to her.

"You've already lost," she told him. I could barely make out the words, but anyone could hear how tender and concerned her tone was. "Why are you still trying?"

He looked stunned. He coughed again, and I hated to think what that got on her, but it didn't break the spell.

"What is your name?" she asked when it was clear he wouldn't answer.

"Anno Domini Sixteen sixty-five," he answered hoarsely, just staring at her. I think he was starting to shake. The smell twisted my insides.

"Zeitgeist. The London Plague," she concluded, stroking his thin, matted hair with her other hand. "Why are you still alive?"

He didn't answer that, either. He was breathing heavily. I knew she wasn't doing anything to him, because she didn't have to.

She closed her eyes and her face tightened with pain, but she dragged them open again and answered for him. "You don't want to live, but if you die you'll be gone."

Now it was his turn to close his eyes, and she held his cheeks in both hands and pulled him close like she was going to kiss his forehead.

Instead, she ate him. Not in a bloody ripping and chewing way. She just swallowed him whole like a snake, and it happened so fast I barely understood what I'd seen.

She was alone now next to a pile of badly-dreamt sticks. She kicked them listlessly, and while the crowd stared and began to talk amongst themselves, she walked straight over to me and Jeffery and put her hand on my shoulder. In fact she squeezed it, hard, and she seemed much thinner than she had at a distance. I could see bones through her arm, a sick fragility that would have made me hungry if it weren't for what I'd just watched.

Jeffery looked at her and then turned his face away. "I'm not going to congratulate you," he commented vaguely.

"Thank you," she told him with hoarse gratitude. Her hand gripped me tighter, and I thought I felt her trembling. The noise was increasing, though, and people were pushing their way through the crowd toward us. I heard a lot of variations on cries of 'Masochism, my dear…!'

She didn't get a chance to reply. Jeffery stepped forward, and right now his reputation was enough that everyone fell back like he would bite them. "Lady Masochism is not available tonight," he announced with a flat and arrogant dismissal, "If she chooses to discuss the match with you during her professional hours, I can't stop her. Right now I'm going out with my friends, and I've decided she's one of them."

Glancing back at us, he added, "Fang, you may have to carry the lady."

"I'll be fine," she assured him quickly. She was blushing. She was actually blushing? But Jeffery started to move, so I padded along after him and Self-Loathing walked at my side as the crowd parted in front of us. I was a little worried that Jeffery was spending his infamy too fast and asking for trouble. I was more worried about how heavily Self-Loathing leaned on me and about the tightness of her grip on my shoulder, even though her walk looked stable.

The challenge had been short and unexciting, but I still could feel the relief trickling down my spine as the three of us walked down the street together. Self-Loathing might have been feeling the same. The grip on my shoulder didn't waver, but the trembling slowed. She also grew thinner and thinner, showing a boniness that I found entirely distracting and turned more than a few heads as we passed.

I was just about to sneak a peek up at her and really see how she was doing when Jeffery stopped, which meant we all stopped. I ended up looking up in the other direction, to see Lily come slinking out of a building built like a small church but festooned with garish signs like a pawn shop. They were marked with the funny symbols demons used, so I had no idea what went on inside. Whatever it was, it had her dressed up in the kind of clingy dress and long gloves, all in black, I'd seen in the fancier human dreams. She was always graceful, but tonight she descended the stairs like an eel, twisting and curving everywhere. She pulled one of those gloves off slowly, calling out, "Boys! Just in time. How did the challenge go?"

"See for yourself," Jeffery told her, nodding his head back in my direction, "I found it educational."

It was Lily's sly grin that made me realize he was talking about Self-Loathing and me standing together. "Oh, puppy," she drawled in absolute delight as she drifted over, "Don't you already have a girlfriend? Where did you pick up this masterpiece?"

"It's not—" I barked, but I choked it off as Lily reached out and took Self-Loathing's now skeletally sharp chin and lifted it.

"The Demiurge of Self-Loathing. The girl they call Masochism," Lily announced, sounding quietly surprised. In fact, she sounded impressed. "Puppy, do you know who you picked up? I like to think

I'm corrupt. I like to think I invented it. But this..." She trailed off, looking down at me. No, she was looking at my shoulder, at the twig-thin fingers squeezing it so tightly, even tighter than before. Since she didn't try to hide that she had noticed, I saw Self-Loathing blushing hotly and felt more than a little uncomfortable myself. But instead of asking us, Lily turned her questioning glance back at Jeffery.

"Everyone likes Fang," he explained with a shrug, "But until today I assumed they only knew each other professionally. He's been going to her off and on as long as I've known him."

I didn't have time to become outraged at that subtle mischaracterization. The cynical delight in Lily's smile as it turned back to us blanked out everything else. I just stared, mortified, as she let go of Self-Loathing and proceeded to stroke me between the ears instead, crowing, "Oh, puppy, I had no idea. I had you pegged as the last innocent. I of all people should have known those are mythical."

Self-Loathing looked as shell-shocked as I did when Lily turned back to her, took her free hand, and told her liltingly, "It's a pleasure to finally meet you, Masochism, and welcome you to the little family we're putting together. So many of my friends speak highly of—"

"Lily, let them alone. Don't treat Fang that way," Jeffery groused. It wasn't loud or nasty, but the exasperation in his voice did the trick.

Lily held onto Self-Loathing's hand for one more moment, gave her a wistful smile, and then let it go. Her hand went back to my head, but only to ruffle the short fur between my ears before stepping back and giving us a much more gentle and bemusedly thoughtful smile. "You're right, Jeff. Sorry, puppy. I've had to put on my professional face the last several nights, and I sometimes forget there are people with feelings left on this side of the border."

Just as I started to let my breath out, Self-Loathing gave Lily a timid nod and assured her, "Fang came as a surprise to me, too." Well, so much for feeling less embarrassed.

It only got worse as Lily put on a doubtful expression. Jeffery saw it and started to reach out to her, but she lifted up her hand to intercept his and continued, "Puppy… don't you have a girlfriend, though?"

I wasn't sure if it was ice or fire that ran through me as I barked, "It's not like that, Lily!"

Self-Loathing's hand lifted up to my neck, quieting me as she explained, "Fang is just being nice to me, Baroness." Baroness? Oh, right. Demons love titles. Lily probably had one. Or fifty. "We like each other, but Jeffery is right. We've hardly met, really."

Lily was obviously unconvinced, and whether she was right or not she saw more than we were saying on the surface. She didn't bother to hide that stare. Still, she reached back and took Jeffery's hand and suggested to him cautiously, "Jeff, I've been looking for a good time to take you to see… well, there's a place where my family keeps… broken things. You would find it educational, and I believe Fang would not enjoy the experience, and if I tried to bring Masochism they'd try and keep her. Let's do that right now and let these two go off alone. I think I'm interfering with Fang's chance to make a new friend."

I bared my teeth, but Jeffery looked at her and then Self-Loathing and finally me, and there was no teasing in his expression. "Sure," he agreed, squeezing her hand in return before letting go, "I'm getting sick of the crowds anyway. I can't seem to get them angry no matter what I do."

So they walked off, and it's not like I could follow them after that. I just stood there in the middle of the street with Self-Loathing's hand on my head, and I think we both felt mortified from the tips of our ears to our toes.

What was worse, there was something I had to say. Looking up at her, I apologized, "Lily thinks this is a date. She thinks she's setting us up as a couple. I don't know how to explain to her that that's not how you feel about me."

Ascetic lips pulled up in a flattered smile as Self-Loathing met my eyes. "I don't mind. People say a lot of things about me that aren't true. They say even worse things that are true. I've been shutting myself away for too long, and I wanted to get out and relax and spend time as a person, with someone who sees me as a person. Would you be okay with spending the evening with me like that?"

I found myself grinning. "I'd love to. I kind of have exactly the same problem, just not as bad. We should do something. I just wish I had any idea what. I hardly know this place at all."

"Are the dream painters still around?" she asked, looking about with an expression of curiosity.

"I've heard about them," I remarked with just as much curiosity, "Do you want me to find them? I bet I could."

"I'd like that a lot," she agreed. So I put my muzzle to the flagstones, began to sniff around, and led us around the corner and up the next street. Shortly, Self-Loathing asked, "You have a canine sense of smell?"

"Sense of direction, really," I corrected, but my grin was back. I could hear the approval and interest in her voice. "I guess I got lucky that way. I find things really well."

There was quiet, but I had the trail and didn't really have to concentrate on it now. They weren't far away. "Is it okay if I ask about the challenge?" I asked her cautiously.

"I guess," she answered just as nervously, "I don't want to talk about it, but I also do want to talk about it."

I wasn't quite sure what it was I wanted to ask. "I've never seen one before," was the only place I could start.

"They're all different," she told me distantly, "It depends on who we are. As you can imagine, my challenges are usually very sad. They're people in too much pain to come to me in any other way, and if they're not using it as an excuse to kill themselves while everybody watches, I end up eating them to take their guilt away."

"They die either way. That can't be fun to go through every year." It sounded pretty ghastly.

"No. I eat them to spare them that. To spare them everything. This one was a zeitgeist. They live in the human world and don't usually linger when their time is up. But I was a very bad time. The humans were mad and they hurt each other from fear, and when they ran out of fear they hurt each other from despair. I became that, and I fed it back to them. They made me make them do terrible things. I whispered into their ear and they shut each other up to die, in cities and towns and houses. If they were strong enough to help I told them to run away instead, and if they were pious I taught them to give the victim blame instead of compassion." She said it slowly, and with a dreamy melancholy.

"You say 'I'…" I pressed, curious and a little horrified.

"I took that part of him. It was me that did those things now, not him," she continued as harshness crept into her voice. "What was good about him I let go. Where it went, what happened to it, I have no idea. But I took more than the blame. I really am that person, or it's part of me and it's no longer part of him. He's free. It's the only good thing I can do for anyone. I was meant to save everyone else."

"That's not true. You make me—" I stammered, "I mean, it's not just that I enjoy coming to you. You make me feel better, you make me strong and focused and positive again. You must do that for a lot of people. You haven't changed, and you're not like that person you just talked about."

Her hand strayed to my neck again above my collar, and she gave it an affectionate squeeze. She smiled. Not much, but it was an improvement. "You don't see the difference because I already know how to hurt people because I've given up."

"I shouldn't have asked," I apologized. How could anyone just talk about herself like that so matter-of-factly?

"You shouldn't have apologized," she corrected me, her smile widening. It was almost convincing now. Almost. "If you hadn't asked, I would have said it all to myself. Instead I said it to you, and you don't blame me."

"Why would I?" I asked her. I mean, I knew why she thought I would, but taking away from someone a bad thing they'd done hundreds of years ago because everyone around them was crazy… I didn't get to finish the thought. "Oh, hey!"

We'd found the dream painters. They're all animals, and they'd found the side of some big building tonight, a space that wasn't being used. Most of them could fly even if they were something like a weasel, and they painted with their paws and noses and tails all over the wall, making a mural out of colored earths and thick dyes. The colors weren't quite right, but the effect was evocative.

I stared. They were painting some kind of room, several rooms. Someone had dreamed about a comfortable house, furnished in wood and with knickknacks everywhere.

"It's been a long time," Self-Loathing murmured beside me. Her voice was full of wonder, and that was a welcome change. "They look so happy. I bet you've never been to the Light, not really. They work there, too. But they don't care. It's all the same to them."

I didn't answer, I just stared. They were getting close to done. Not surprisingly, as they filled in the dreamer he was drawing back in fear. A lot of fear.

I glanced up at Self-Loathing again, and she'd changed. She was a girl instead of a woman now, but not a child. The kind of girl who'll be a woman very soon. Her outfit was simple and old-fashioned, and everything was red. More than red, a rich and vibrant scarlet, down to the bonnet that tied back her shining copper hair. Instead of skeletal she'd become pink with vibrant health, although I'd certainly call her slender. Her dress had some kind of bodice, and it showed off the shape of her very well, every slight but distinct curve. She looked young, really young, and fresh and hopeful and happy and innocent. As I caught a trace of her clean and human scent I couldn't push away thoughts of how badly I wanted to see that young body move as it ran away from me, too scared to run fast enough. To look into those eyes and see them widen with fear because she had no escape, nowhere to run anymore.

I yanked my eyes back to the painting. I'd been drooling. Actually drooling. I hoped she hadn't noticed. Then I blinked. The painters were just putting in the last finishing touches, and the dream was clear now. Dogs were scattered around the picture, different sizes but all of the harmless pet variety. Except they didn't look harmless. They all had the same mouths full of big, white fangs, the same staring eyes, and there was no mistaking the malignant threat in their poses.

As I recognized those teeth, so did Self-Loathing. In a warm voice as girlish as her new body she declared, "You did this, Fang? Look at him. They haven't attacked yet, and he's out of his mind."

"I didn't!" I insisted, "This is the first time I've seen this dream!"

"They don't just make them up. At least, they didn't used to," she pointed out doubtfully.

"No, but I swear that's not me," I told her, ears tilting back in alarm. Then I figured it out, and instead I merely felt guilty that she'd gotten such a mistaken impression. "Actually, I wasn't in that dream, but I think—I think I've chased that dreamer. It happens sometimes. It stuck with him somehow. Now he's scared of all dogs, even the ones he loves."

"That's really impressive," she told me, and she sounded like she meant it.

"I don't think it was really that good a dream," I denied stiffly. The dream painters were putting up dreams I'd caused? "Really, it wasn't. I'm pretty good, but I had to have gotten lucky on that one. Sometimes dreamers have a weakness they didn't know was there."

"I'm going to ask," she announced, and walked up to the wall and the painters. I quickly turned my head so as not to watch that skirt sway, the bare legs showing below the hem slim enough I could probably get my jaws around them.

I wanted to find out if it was true, and to distract myself from that urge I listened as she talked, but I didn't understand anything she and the painters said to each other. All human languages are the same language in dreams, more or less, so I was surprised.

The discussion grew heated, at least on their side, and she quickly came walking back to me with a pained look on her face. "They won't talk to me," she sighed, "They remember me too well."

"Why not? How were you even able to talk to them?" I asked, baffled. I regretted rubbing it in immediately, but it was too late to take the words back.

"I remember them," she explained, distant again, but she looked back at the painters with something like admiration. "A long time ago humans didn't care about the Gates, and the Light and the Dark were just as good in their eyes. It was all the world of dreams and that was heaven, a place of secrets and perfection. That's how they thought about it. They would come seeking mysteries, and they had guides. Then one day the humans just stopped thinking that way. The dream painters found another way to talk about how important dreams are."

"Is that something you got from a challenger you ate?" I asked. I had forgotten everything else. I was amazed.

Her arms reached out to me, and I was still so astonished and wondering that it hardly affected me as she wrapped them around my neck and shoulders and held herself to me while she talked. "It's hard to tell it all apart," she admitted, "It's all just me now. I think that's from the original me. I knew them back then, and they didn't like me. I was important to the humans." There was a moment's pause as she remembered, and I had to notice her changing the subject slightly. "I think that was the original me. I remember when I challenged the old Demiurge. He was an angel. He really believed he'd made the world and messed it up somehow."

Straightening up again, she actually giggled and started fussing with her skirts. I'd probably gotten fur on them. "Angels are crazy. I'm so glad I didn't eat him. Stay away from angels, Fang," she told me lightly.

Wow. She really was a Demiurge. She was everything they'd gotten the reputation for. I could either stare at her in shock, or stare at her and think about her skirts and the tenderness under them again. I chose a third option, and in a hurry.

"I'm glad we saw this," I suggested, "But we need a change of scenery, don't we? Like, right now? Let me take you to this place Jeffery goes to. I need to visit more often."

So a few minutes later I pushed open the door to the hidden nightmare bar, holding it open for Self-Loathing as she followed me in, and regretted my decision just slightly when the whistling started. At least it stopped very quickly.

As I trotted up to the counter I told her, "This is Bar Number Three. He can dream up drinks. I hope you remember some, because it's not something I stop and ask dreamers about much."

"Ooh," she cooed as she looked over at the mannequin bartender, "You're so complicated and stylish. And a nightmare that gave up making bad dreams, I guess?"

"We were a dismal failure at it," Bar Number Three replied drily, "We came out of the dream of a sketch artist, and our creator was more than a little mad. What we did to a dream could make it quite creepy, but very few dreamers were really scared."

"Yes, it's nightmares like Fang that are the best," she agreed, sliding her fingers teasingly over one of my ears. I just rolled my eyes. She thought I was one of the best? "Simple, but flexible. Dedicated," she explained.

"We quite agree," Bar Number Three drawled, while it extruded more eyes to look at her. If it had had a real mouth, I swear it would have leered as the marionette part leaned forward and added, "We didn't have dedication. We weren't satisfied at all, and instead wanted to use our talents to mingle with others of our kind and perhaps see a pretty girl walk through our door."

That got the faintest little chuckle from her, and a wistful little smile. "I'm with him," she warned Bar Number Three, pointing down at me. She had to lift her hand over my head to do it. I was bigger even than usual tonight, wasn't I?

"It's not like that!" I protested. Would people keep thinking it was? I wasn't even sure exactly what the 'that' was, but this wasn't it.

"It still means she's accompanied," the marionette told me whimsically, "We attempt to be more businesslike. Would you like your usual, Fang?" Before I could stop him, he put a little glass on the bar with a few spoonfuls of glistening black liquid in it.

"Not tonight," I told him archly, trying to suggest with my expression that company, especially this company, wasn't the time for something like that. I think I failed completely.

"Well, what about the young lady?" he moved on, turning blithely to her.

"Actually," she mused, "If he's not going to drink that, I'll try it. I want to find out what Fang likes."

I took too long trying to think of an explanation that would stop her. She immediately scooped up the little glass and lifted it to her lips. At least she only took a tiny sip, but that was enough. Her whole body spasmed. I couldn't blame her for that. It was the worst tasting stuff I could think of. That wasn't its attraction.

When she straightened up, she had a kind of unfocused expression. Thoughtful. Withdrawn. A frown started to pull on her mouth, a certain bleakness tighten around her eyes. As I realized she recognized it, she confirmed my suspicion. "Blood. Rotted blood and guilt, dreamed up by the dead," she speculated, "A girl's."

She turned, carefully, and I noticed the easiness she'd started to wear was gone. The hesitation was back, and it drew me. At the same time I didn't want to see her looking at me like that as she set the glass deliberately on the counter between us. "She must be special, Fang," she told me. It sounded accusing, and she corrected herself immediately, "I know she's special. It's in the taste. I can't imagine what she must look like, but if that's an imitation of her blood she must be a broken soul. She has to be beautiful."

What could I say? I didn't want to say anything. I really didn't want to lie to her. "It's what I tasted when I bit my Muse," I had to say.

Self-Loathing leaned over and kissed the top of my head. It was very soft, and I could tell she meant it, but I could also hear the edge as she told me, "I guess our date is over. Please come and visit me soon."

She walked out without another word, and anything I could think to say or do would have made it worse.

As I wandered glumly through the dark I reflected that that had gone exactly the way I had been afraid it would. Whatever she had wanted, I hadn't been it. It was, if anything, more intimidating to have gotten to know her. I was a growling black shape with teeth, trying to keep up with someone who had been sophisticated enough to become a Demiurge back before anything I understood existed. I had thought I understood that she was lovely and unhappy, and tried to be kind. I hadn't understood anything, and I'd ended up hurting her worse.

There are two things I do when things go wrong and I lose heart. There are two people who just make me feel good about myself. I'd just betrayed one of them, and I still didn't understand how. The other—I hadn't meant to go out with another girl behind her back. I wasn't sure I had. If I had, I was going to lay my head on my Muse's leg and apologize. She would be angry or she would forgive me or, more likely, she would never hear my words at all or know anything happened. It was what I had to do, and it would help me understand. That's what a Muse does, isn't it? They remind you of who you are and who you want to be, inspiring you to become it.

It was snowing when I found her house. I didn't see a lot of weather, but the drifting flakes were pretty and the cold was shocking. Rough stone hills and occasional bare trees gave the snowy fields character, and as I looked out across them I realized that not far away the snow glowed almost rainbow-bright. Tonight this snow disguised the border, and my Muse's house lurked right up against it.

I padded up the creaking stairs onto the porch, and saw pasted across the front door one of those posters, 'Announcing The Defense Of The Most Ancient And Primal Title, Death Itself'. It sounded exciting. I wasn't remotely interested. I pushed the door open with my head and wandered into the hall.

The house was quiet and dim. No eyes watched me from the walls. There were no statues, and the rooms seemed to stay in the same order when I peeked into them and at least kind of sort of fit together. My hackles were already starting to rise as I padded into the sitting room at the back, and they were right—the room was empty. She wasn't here, and neither was her chair or the statues stuck in the walls that always faced her. No eyes opened here, either. Nothing moved at all.

I clamped down on my first fear. If she were dead the house would be gone. The house changed sometimes. She changed sometimes, usually in little ways. Still, I felt more than a little on edge when I hurried back outside and found a child on the porch.

It was tiny. It might be around the same age as Lucy and Anna, or maybe even younger. It was thin, not in a starved way but just so very frail that I couldn't tell if it was a boy or a girl. Its skin was darker than theirs, with hair cut haphazardly above its shoulders, a pretty gleaming black. I didn't recognize what it was wearing, but the fabric was very rough and crude and sewn with cords of leather, the result being more of a wrap than a dress.

Boy or girl, as breakably slender as it was, the child moved with ease and even vitality as it looked up at me from where its legs hung over the edge of the stairs. Open and alert black eyes took everything in, and I knew this was a girl when I recognized her voice. "I knew you'd come here," Self-Loathing told me mournfully.

Those eyes watched me. Their irises were as black as the pupils, and they threw me off. I was still figuring out how to tell her I was sorry when she went on, "I wanted to apologize, Fang." She turned her head away, and added, "But I also need to tell you, it would be best for you if you stayed away from me."

The whole thing fell on me like a weight again, but there was no anger in her voice. We could talk about this, and I would do whatever she wanted. I padded over to the stairs and sat down beside her. My head hung a little. I didn't want to make her feel guilty, but I couldn't pretend I wanted this conversation. "You're right," I agreed, "You need someone who's a lot… more than I am. You deserve that."

Her eyes were back on me again, and consternation fell across her face, her lip pushed out and her dark eyebrows pushed together. "You didn't understand what I just said at all, do you?" she demanded. I was about to apologize, but she talked over me. "I don't want you to leave me, Fang. You need to leave me for you. You don't know what I'm doing to you right now, do you? I can't keep my hands off you. Metaphorically." She giggled, but there wasn't much enthusiasm in it.

I put my hand on her back. I was trying to be comforting, but I admit I was nagged by the thought that I could almost feel her skin through that rough fabric. That only lent weight to what I wanted to say. "If you don't want me to leave, I don't want to leave," I insisted, and although it was mortifying I had to say, "I've always liked visiting you and I want to be your friend. I already have a girlfriend, but—" I hit a wall. I realized I didn't know what I was saying. "Nobody told me where the dividing line is. I don't think many nightmares are interested."

"Some. Not many," she admitted. She peeked back at me and then looked away shyly. She sounded a lot more calm than I did about saying these things as she explained, "I want to be your friend, too. I let myself stop having them for a while, because of what I do to them. You're the one who made me realize I have to try again."

"You're… popular," I insisted, trying to be delicate about it, "I can't be the only person who visited you that cared. I can't even be the only nightmare that cared."

That made her hesitate before answering. "You aren't," she conceded, "But they weren't there when I needed them, and I want you, not them."

I didn't know what to say for a moment, and during that moment I realized that my claws had gone through the cloth she was wearing and were sharp enough to have torn the threads. I could feel bare skin underneath, and I knew all I had to do was drag my claws down and I would see just how wire-thin that electrically alive little body was, and she would be too close to escape my teeth. I started to lean in—

She stood up on the step, and I yanked myself back. My heart was pounding, but at the same time I felt like it would be crushed with shame. This wasn't the time or the place!

She was the one that sounded guilty. Her voice was harsh and raspy with it as she tugged her wrap down and announced, "I can't stop myself forever, but I can stop this. Fang, go to town. Right now. There's something you want to see."

"What?" It was just a word.

"Go to town," she repeated stiffly, "If you don't see this you'll never forgive yourself, and then I'll never forgive myself. I'd like to be able to do that just once, at least."

I looked around desperately. Where was my Muse, if she wasn't here? What should I do about Self-Loathing, who was here? I had to take her at her word, didn't I?

"Okay," I agreed.

"Hurry," she insisted. She wouldn't look at me, but there was a hoarse urgency to the instruction.

So I ran.

I wasn't sure why I had to run or where I was going until I passed a lone signpost at a place where I could just see the Gate glowing in the distance. It wasn't the arrows sticking off of it, which were unreadable, but there was another poster for the challenge match against Death—and over top of that a new poster blaring 'Come See The Opening Act—Surprise Challenge Match For The Demiurge Of Regret!' Regret? Why hadn't there been one of these at my Muse's house?

Like last time, I was hardly a block into the city when I nearly threw myself by accident into the challenge ring. This time it was a pit, and people were simply gathered around it looking over the edge, although all I could see was a sandy floor. Only a few people were watching, but more of every shape and variety drifted in by the moment. There were a lot of burning eyes and horns and hooves. I saw Jeffery at the other end sitting with his legs dangling over the edge, but by the time I did I was packed in on all sides and trying not to be pushed into the pit.

Something moved, and I looked back down. The pit was no longer empty. On the side close to me was a chair, a huge, battered wooden rocking chair. In it sat a girl wearing a black dress with dark red highlights. Her back was to me, but I knew she was crying and her hands were covering up the fact that she had no eyes.

I had barely registered her when something fluttered over the crowd and landed at the far end, surrounded by waving and snapping white cloth and flying on wings that looked so broken they should have fallen off. Lily set down daintily on what seemed like exaggeratedly high heels and walked forward to the middle of the ring, her ruby lips pursed as she studied her opponent.

Lily and my Muse were fighting for the title of Demiurge of Regret. One of them had challenged the other. Forget that. One of them was going to die. Challengers hardly ever lived. What would happen if I intruded on the ring? If it looked like one was going to kill the other, could I even convince them to stop?

"It's considered bad manners to start without me," Lily announced, producing some rather snide chuckles from the audience, "But believe me, I understand." She took a few steps back, for courtesy perhaps—Lily would certainly care about the look of being clearly on her own side—and got down on her knees and closed her eyes and clasped her hands together in front of her face.

My panic was fading, going numb. I just took in what was in front of me. I couldn't see my Muse, but I didn't have to. She hadn't quite come alone. The four ivory statues that haunted her home sprawled, half-buried in the sand, watching her, and beside her chair stood a little table too tall for its twisted and rickety legs. On it was a knife and a chipped glass vial with a dead, dried rose in it. My heart fluttered and the fear rose up in me, then went dull again.

She'd brought the rose, but she was facing away from me. I didn't think that was accidental.

My Muse wasn't doing anything I could see, wasn't even rocking in her chair. Lily didn't seem to be doing anything either, she was just crouched on her knees with her hands clasped. No, her lips were moving.

"What's she doing?" I asked out loud.

To my surprise the black goat-legged thing beside me answered. "She's praying," the demon said with a sneer, "What a poseur."

And that was all she was doing. That, and glowing faintly. With the lights of the city on the other end of the crowd, she was the only well-lit thing in this eternal night. I hadn't really registered that it was dim until I saw she was bright, and getting brighter.

I kept expecting her to do something more. It took me a few moments more to register that she had dropped a couple of feathers from her wings, and they continued to fall. Her halo, a circlet of rusty iron, started to glow like it had been heated and her normally billowing wrap just hung on her.

The thing next to me sneered more, but then he drew back, watching suspiciously. "He's answering," husked a woman wrapped practically head to foot in black leather and bits of metal. She sounded surprised and upset, and her eyes glowed like Lily's halo.

Still, my Muse just sat there, and Lily whispered. It wasn't Lily glowing. I could see now that light shone down on her, pure and white, and as it got brighter it spread out slowly to illuminate a wider and wider ring. The feathers were almost gone from her wings, and what was underneath was shriveled and red-black, but it was when the first crack splintered over her face and a piece fell off that the shock hit me.

After that it just all flowed together. Her wrap turned brown, charring. Deep cracks, like in pottery or stone, split her skin one after another. Pieces fell and underneath was something deep and bloody red. Her halo caught fire and it too cracked, and what sprang out was something I didn't understand, a tracery of symbols and a pentacle in flickering fire over her head. Her shriveled wings jerked and thrust back and became huge crimson things with long, extended fingers and a membrane like a bat—but that membrane was more holes and rips than solid, and the wings were bent like they'd been broken and set wrong many times. And the light kept spreading.

That might have been what caused the panic. The crowd was full of demons, and they broke first, pulling back and then fleeing. There was a lot of yelling and swearing, and there were fragments of skin and hide left behind like Lily had dropped, looking like bits of an insect's shell. I was lucky I was at the edge or I'd have been shoved away.

I looked back down at the pit, and things had gotten worse. Lily's clothes were gone. Her skin was gone too, and it had been a shell over something skeletal. It was almost pretty, a few sharp, bony joints adding character to a gauntly sinuous shape, but the surface was a hodgepodge of plates and scales with barbs everywhere ruining the lines. Her hair had burned off and more of those barbs had been underneath, a forest of them, some of them long and wickedly hooked. Their lines softened as I watched, and then I noticed the faint haze of smoke. A drop fell from her elbow onto the sand and hissed there. She was melting.

Another drop, two. Very, very slowly. I could just make out a faint rasp to her voice, suggesting this was as painful as it looked. What could I do?

More movement. My Muse hadn't stirred, but the statues scattered in front of her did. The two adults, a man and a woman, had turned away from her and toward the light, throwing their arms in front of them and shrinking away. The two boys were different. One was crawling, pulling itself toward that light with one arm while dragging the other boy along. They had gotten nearly a yard when the chains fastened to their ankles went taut. The chains had been sunk into the ground invisibly, but now the tension pulled enough of them up that I could see them threaded to the backs of my Muse's boots, locking them together. There were links running into the sand from her other boot as well.

I heard a faint clink as the chains went tight, her foot twitched as it was pulled forward, and for the first time I could remember my Muse reacted. She flopped to one side, arms flailing, grabbing at the tabletop. The table fell over, and she twisted herself over the arm of her chair, groping at the ground—blindly. She had no eyes, but she felt around after the dropped knife with increasing desperation. The crawling children kept moving, and when her leg stretched out from the pulling she yelled shrilly, "Fang!"

I leapt, and ended up ramming my face into the sand. At least it was still sand. The pit was gone, and my Muse was gone, and the challenge circle was rapidly fading into a blank stretch of surface like I'd see in the most dream-abandoned regions of the Dark. Hardly anyone was left. Jeffery was one of them, and Lily was still kneeling where the circle had been. The melting seemed to have stopped. Aside from being a thing of crimson knots of bone and scales she looked intact.

Jeffery was already walking over to her, and as soon as I'd gotten a grip on what had changed I went charging up myself. "Lily! Are you okay? Is she okay?" I nearly fell over again as my blood went to ice. "Please tell me she's alive and you didn't kill her! Tell me you're—"

"Fang! Sheesh, get a grip!" barked Jeffery. His look wasn't confident or reproving. It was just a shock to get me to calm down.

"That really was your Muse?" Lily asked, her voice strained but otherwise normal as she pushed herself to her feet. "I didn't kill her. She forfeited, panicked. I'm not even sure she knows she challenged me, but that was the closest anyone's come in a dog's age. She was so totally turned in on herself, alone with her sins."

"I want to know if you're okay, too," I insisted stubbornly.

"I didn't want you boys to see me like this, but there's no harm done," she told me mildly. She was upright now, picking shards of white off her knobby red surface with something of the delicate grace I'd expected of her.

"Your friends didn't like the show. Bringing the Light this close to the Gate? They were scared spitless," Jeffery laughed.

Lily made a little hiss of disgust and added contemptuously, "What a bunch of hypocritical cowards. I didn't want you to see this, but they needed to. They keep telling themselves they won, and I wanted to remind them of just how much we lost." She waved a hand armed with blood-colored claws bigger and sharper than mine and added, "That's why they ran. Right now they're out there making excuses and telling themselves and each other lies about how cool and powerful and independent we all are and this is what we wanted, really."

She sneered, and on that face with red teeth sharp and curved inwards it wasn't a pretty expression. It only faded when Jeffery reached out and drew a thumb up one of the larger hooks on her shoulder, telling her, "I think I like this look more, personally."

"You're a nightmare," she snapped back, but her tone was playfully sullen, "You would think I was more attractive if my head kept coming apart in halves."

"Yeah, I would," Jeffery smirked back at her, "But this is a look. You have style, even like this."

"Not the one I wanted," she sniped back. Crouching down, she began playing her hand over the top of my head as she explained, "I knew you'd find out, but I was hoping I could keep puppy here from finding out I hold Regret. It makes me sound pathetic."

I just shook my head. Lily was the Demiurge of Regret. I couldn't even figure out how I felt about that. If my girlfriend was okay, I began to wonder if she was back in her house and if I could get away to go check.

"We should back up, boys," Lily told us, interrupting my thoughts. She tugged on my collar, prodding me into motion as she pointed out, "The circle's going to set itself up for the main challenge in a moment, and it'll be a big one. I think the contestants are starting to arrive.

There's always more than one idiot who thinks he's tougher than the Reaper. Like… oh, no. Please, Father, tell me that's not an angel."

My head craned around automatically. People were creeping back into the field cautiously, and a lot of them were watching the shining white figure who was striding in without any show of caution at all.

Lily's crimson body was as fast as it looked, and she almost disappeared as she bolted toward that glowing person. She moved more like me than like she did normally, in long leaps, and when she wasn't on all fours she ran hunched far forward while her mangled wings angled and flapped to help her along. I took after her, of course. When someone runs, I chase—I hadn't thought about it at all, but I'd have followed her even if I had.

It became a chaotic obstacle race almost immediately. As she'd predicted, the challenge circle was rearranging, and stone bleachers thrust themselves up out of the ground unpredictably right under our feet. I was thrown into the air by the first one, but I landed smoothly and ended up jumping from ledge to ledge as we circled around the rim.

I managed to keep up with Lily. Enough to see her reach the angel. He looked like an angel. Human, slim, wearing a white shirt over a body that wasn't vague like a badly made dream, but rather smoothly lacking in imperfections like edges of muscle and shades of color. His halo was a golden tracery as complicated as the burning one over Lily's head, and he wore a sword slung between his sculpted wings.

That sword came out as Lily dropped off the nearest bleacher. The way they were made of stone circling a large, shallowly sunken pit, made the place look like a coliseum. Like the angel, the sword was plain. The blade was just shiny metal, sharp and small enough to surprise me. The only swords I was used to were the kind people dream about, and anything shorter than his arm looked out of place to me.

The point in her face made Lily's crouching run end abruptly, and she stood up, back in one of her usual gracefully curved standing poses. "Don't be any stupider, Malachaiel," she snapped at him, and she really did sound exasperated and unhappy. "You know me and you know I'm not going to hurt you."

"I don't know any demons," he answered, stiff and formal and calm. He stood like Lily, poised but not tense anywhere. Elegance was something they didn't even have to think about.

Lily still looked elegant even when she made a growling noise and bared her back-curved teeth. What she did next looked like pulling a mask out of the air and dusting it with makeup, then laying it over her face, all in the space of a couple of seconds. When she finished it just was her face, the lovely, sensually precise human one I was used to. "Don't try and tell me you don't recognize me, Malachaiel," she insisted, "We kissed on the moon when it was waiting to be lifted into the sky for the first time."

The face hadn't made a glimmer of difference, but his mouth tightened at her words and his voice sounded even more flatly unemotional as he told her, "I repented that sin and was forgiven. You went on to kiss half the angels in Heaven before you were exiled, 'Lily'." Only that last word was sharp.

Lily wasn't going to be distracted by it. "Can you tell me without lying that you hate me, or that you need that sword to be safe from me?" she challenged him. Her voice was calming, but cold rather than emotionless. And after a moment where the two stared into each other's eyes, he put the blade away again.

He didn't say any more, and I had a moment to register that Jeffery had caught up. We were the only people standing close to the angel, although we were being watched by a number of the more gaudily dangerous looking denizens of the Dark. As soon as it became clear he wasn't talking, Lily pressed on. "What are you doing here, Malachaiel? You're not stupid. I know you're not. The younger angels think they can come challenge Samael, but you're as old as I am. Why?"

"It's time, Lily," he replied evenly. There was heat in her expression, but his was serene. It didn't convince me at all. "The title of Death is too important to be left in the possession of the Dark any longer, and it is my task to bring it back where it belongs. I am doing the will of our Father."

"Did he tell you that's what he wanted?" she jabbed back immediately.

Even I could tell that ruffled him, because there was a noticeable delay before he answered her. "If you had any place to challenge me on what he wants, you wouldn't look like that now."

She took a deep breath, and her claws flexed. Instead of responding angrily she changed the subject. "Don't throw your life away for this, Malachaiel. You couldn't beat Samael before he became the Angel of Death, and he's become something unstoppable now."

"I haven't been idle, Lily," Malachaiel replied. His voice wasn't entirely even anymore. "I'm stronger than you ever knew me, and I have the will he lacks. Some justice must be brought to Death. It must serve the greater good."

Lily's hands flew up to cover her face at this, and maybe only I saw her tremble as she turned her head away from him. "You really are stupid. It's just a title, Malki. He's going to crush you like a bug for a title. If it was important enough to die for, the Four should have come themselves to be cut down by him rather than this endless parade of well-meaning idiots."

"I serve our Father and I serve him unto death, and that is the difference between us," the angel told her brusquely. The only sign that he was upset when he said it was that he turned his back on her and walked out into the ring.

That seemed to be taken as a signal. Five other things stepped into the wide, shallow pit. The ring was large enough that the other side was dim, and it got darker by the moment. Something darker still lurked inside it. A figure in a ragged black robe, holding a dull black scythe, crouched on a low stone chair. He looked exactly like everyone said he did.

The bleachers were getting rapidly packed, but Lily just walked us up to the front and threw a couple of spectators out of their seats bodily. With Jeffery staring at them the corroded copper cats slunk away rather than argue. As we sat down, Malachaiel evidently decided it was time to begin, because he stepped forward ahead of the others and drew his sword. Holding it up in salute to Death, he then turned and told the other challengers, "This is a contest between angels. Forfeit now, and I will let you leave peacefully."

I would have taken that offer, but I knew what was going to happen. They sprang for him, all at the same time. The thing with the blade arms went first, its head swept off of its body in one slice, and the angel was already turning to jam the tip of his sword into the thing that was so many piercings and implants there was nothing but metal. A twist, and it came apart in fragments. A step back crushed the neck of the smoke snake creeping up on him from behind, and in stepping back he forced the larger thing with claws to shoulder aside the smaller one. An instant later, his sword jabbed through it, out the other side and up and into the little one trying to climb over to fight.

Jeffery clapped, although that was the only sound in the stadium. "He's good," he told Lily mildly. He had been. He'd moved with sinuous ease, always heading into the next strike. It had taken seconds.

"Not good enough," she husked, "You or Fang could have taken those goons. Most people arrogant enough to think they can win against Samael are too dumb to know what losers they are."

I leaned over awkwardly and bumped my nose against her shoulder. "Your challenge looked rough, Lily. I don't think you're in any shape to watch this."

"I have to," she told me tiredly, "He was sent by people who don't care about him to die in front of people who don't care about him. He's an idiot who can't think for himself, but I owe this to him from a long time ago."

Malachaiel was turning back to Death now, and he raised his sword, and it changed. With a noise like a thick carpet being struck, white fire flowed over the blade, lighting up most of the arena. He pointed it at the robed caricature in the chair and announced,

"Fallen, I am making you the same offer. All I want is the title. Surrender it, and I will have no reason to kill you for it."

"Idiot," whispered Lily furiously. Death didn't respond. He just reached one hand into his other sleeve and one by one pulled out five hourglasses and tossed them to the ground. In all of them the sand had run completely into one end.

"You can't scare me with symbols, Fallen," Malachaiel declared solemnly. Death didn't answer. He reached into his sleeve again and pulled out another hourglass. This one was bigger and prettier, gold and crystal, and he tossed it onto the floor of the arena. It was hard to see from here, but it was still obvious that the sand was almost completely run out.

Lily lurched to her feet, wings spread, and yelled, "Please, Samael! You don't have to do this!"

Death ignored her. He got to his feet, took a few steps toward the angel, and raised his scythe. Malachaiel also ignored her. He charged.

"Don't kill him, Samael, please!" Lily begged, while everyone else was silent. "He can't hurt you! Just let him lose and go back and tell the others how stupid their plan was in the first place."

Even while she shouted, Malachaiel moved. It was hard to even call it a charge, he was so fast and smooth. Death hardly had a chance to move before the flaming sword hit him, cutting in deep, charring and spitting. It was elegant, it was dance. Malachaiel struck, up and down and at angles, until the last blow took Death's head off, robe and all. An empty skull fell out of the severed hood onto the ground.

That was when the sand ran out of the hourglass. I couldn't see it. Probably no one could. But Malachaiel went rigid, his sword stopped burning, and he fell over without any further fanfare and was still. Seconds later gently glowing mist flowed from his fading body. And Death walked over, picked up his skull, and placed it back on his neck. He didn't pause to gloat or make a speech. Blackness in the shape of a pair of wings stretched out of his back, then folded around him. He disappeared.

"Idiots," Lily sighed, falling back onto her bench even as everyone around us started to mill around and talk. "I'm the biggest idiot," she added glumly, "thinking that I could change either of their minds. Samael hardly got the title before he stopped being someone you could talk to. He thinks he really is death itself, not someone who represents it."

"Has anybody challenged a Demiurge and won this year?" I asked. I felt bad changing the subject, but I'd have felt worse making her talk about it.

"Nobody," Jeffery answered me, "It's like that most years. If you can get the title at all, you're good enough to defend it for a long, long time. Most of the time a challenger only wins because the Demiurge is fading."

"Even that isn't enough," Lily added sourly, "You saw what Samael is like. It only made him stronger."

"You could do it, Jeffery," I observed solemnly. This was a grim conversation, but some things were clear to me. "You'd just have to pick one. You could go for Fear. You're smart enough to outperform anyone."

"Fear?" he asked me with a grimace, "And face the twins? They're terrified as well as terrifying. They'd have me coming and going. I can make people afraid, but it's a skill."

"You're better at it than anyone else," I pointed out.

"That doesn't mean I'm suited to being a Demiurge. It's something you are."

"He's right," came a tiny, squeaky voice, and something silvery and small, a feminine figure with multiple bug wings, settled on my nose. I knew Self-Loathing even before I registered the cautious, halting tone that gives her away. Guiltily, I suspected I knew her because there was something so quick and supple about that tiny body and its faint glow. I wanted to chase it around a room, jumping and snapping. I had to run my thoughts back to hear her say, "It's a part of you. I just gave up using a name. I am what I am."

"I took the title to irritate my family," Lily commented vaguely, "I was going to regret either way. I wanted to rub their faces in it, because they've lost as much as I have and they don't appreciate it."

"I don't plan on challenging anyone," Jeffery informed us. There was a certain heat and focus in his stare as he looked up at the sky and went on, "I have other ambitions. I haven't made my mark yet, but I'm going to."

"That's you all over. Demiurge isn't good enough," Lily sniped sardonically, but she was smiling again. "It was good enough for the rest of us."

I looked at her when she said that. I was sitting next to the Demiurge of Regret, a real fallen angel. I could feel the tiny body of the Demiurge of Self-Loathing sitting on the end of my muzzle, and as I looked at her she gave me a shy and curious glance over her shoulder. On the other side of Lily was Jeffery, who had cowed every nightmare in the Dark and was only getting started. Only one person was out of place here.

"I need to go check on my Muse," I told Lily abruptly, "I know you didn't hurt her, but she's never left her house before. I don't know what to think." I heard Self-Loathing's sharp, hurt breath when I said it, but that only made me want to leave more.

"I'm touched that you held off long enough to stay with me through that stupid little tragedy," she answered, subdued but warm, "You're really something special. You run off now."

I nodded, and as Self-Loathing flitted up off my nose I turned and padded away, then trotted as I reached the end of the row, then when I was sure I was out of sight I ran. I didn't like lying to them. I had no intention of forcing myself on my Muse now. She wasn't a Demiurge, but she fit right in with them. I just wanted to go far, far away and try and understand why everyone I knew was better at what they were than me.

Instead, I hunted dreams. I ran out to the border, and even though it was a wall tonight I beat my way through it, and some man pretending to discuss business on an airplane discovered there was a looming black thing with teeth at the back of it, and as he ran the aisle got longer and longer and there was no place to go because if he reached the end he'd be trapped.

Then an old woman found that a lump of meat in her freezer was still alive, and angry. She could barely hobble, but she stumbled from room to room as it dragged itself on one leg after her, oozing gore and savaging everything it came near with its jaws.

I went back again and again, until the wall was rubble from all the dreams knocking holes in it as they were driven into the Dark. Every time any recognizable part of the Dark came near I'd move, find a new spot that was out in the middle of the new nowhere. It let me cut my thoughts into pieces, go through them little by little between dreamers. I had been Jeffery's sidekick, one of his projects, and he really did care about me. That was why he'd lured me into town, and I'd let him. And now Self-Loathing wanted to be close to me, and when her shell was broken by fear my Muse thought first of me. What could I offer them? I didn't know what they wanted, and if they relied on me for it they wouldn't get it. It had been a little insulting to be Lily's puppy, but she'd been affectionate about it. Now she was trying to respect me, and I hadn't earned it. And Jeffery had simply moved past and forgotten to let me go.

Then came a new thought, that none of this was reasonable and I was wrong, but I couldn't figure out what right was. I was going to stay out here until I made sense of it all, rather than go back and mess things up, but the thoughts stopped there. I just couldn't seem to go any farther. So I threw myself into dreams harder, waiting for revelation.

Finally one broke, and I lurked in the dregs of it, tasting the confusion and fear clinging to me until the mists thinned and I saw Anna sitting on a tombstone, watching me curiously.

"Where'd this graveyard come from?" I asked bewilderedly. I really had been trying to stay far away from anything that could be called a place.

"I made it," she told me, her tone light and speculative as she looked around, "I was trying for a spooky playground, and I was really hoping for a swing set, but that dream you just dragged in stained everything it touched. It was pretty strong. It looked weird, too."

"It was," I admitted, "All it takes is the teeth and jaws. Every door and window had them, they chased her through every mailbox and trashcan. I was trying it out."

Anna slid off the gravestone, walked up to me and poked one of my legs. No; she was feeling it with her fingertip. "It takes more than that. It takes a person. You haven't got fur anymore. And did you know you're whispering?"

I took a couple of deep breaths and shook my upper body, trying to clear my head. I tried to think about anything other than what I should do about my friends—which I had no thoughts about at all—or how to scare dreamers, which I'd been drifting into doing by instinct. "You sound different too," I realized.

"I think I'm waking up," she told me, just a little wry sharpness in her voice. Her eyes were certainly focused as she looked up at me, and when they left my face to look around the graveyard they didn't drift. She was just looking around.

"We'll miss you," I husked, trying to get my voice back under control, "I'm sure you'll be happier in the waking world."

"No, I mean the other way," she corrected me. As she talked, she spun around on one foot, surveying not just the graveyard but the surrounding Dark. Her white dress billowed as she moved. She didn't drift like a dreamer anymore. "I'm waking up here. You know, I was just wandering and I saw these things, like wasps, that didn't belong. And they were building a machine to cut a tunnel through the Dark, from wherever they came from into the waking world. Just looking at it I knew it wouldn't work, but I thought—why tell them? It wasn't a waste of time, because the way they worked on it and the idea, that made them special and interesting and worthwhile. When you don't have to be scared anymore you have time to see that everything is special and interesting and worthwhile. And then I realized just how much I'd been thinking."

"I think some of us are more special and interesting and worthwhile than others," I told her. I had intended to be playful, but I was still foggy from all those dreams and the words came out wrong.

"I don't know," she replied, frowning at me, "What makes you worthwhile?" She stepped in closer as she said it and reached up and started petting me. Except she wasn't petting me, exactly. She was just stroking me, and everywhere her hand passed I remembered to grow fur again, and then to have muscles underneath the surface for her to feel.

I sighed, and lay down with my head on my forelegs to make it easier for her. It was comforting, and I wasn't sure if I was doing this or she was. As a dreamer she could probably remake me from scratch if she wanted. I was just a nightmare. "You tell me," I returned glumly.

"I can't," she told me, and her voice was dry and whimsical, but also concerned. She was right about waking up. Her voice lilted with emotion. She was alert. She was here in a way she hadn't been before. I felt her weight sitting on my hindquarters as she explained, "You have to figure it out yourself, don't you? What do you think makes anyone worthwhile?"

"Being yourself, but being good at it." I knew the answer to that.

"Well, how will you know if you are?"

I was silent, thinking about that for a minute, and then another minute, until I knew what I was going to do. I gently shook Anna off as I rose to my feet, and she patted my flank affectionately. "I think you are who you want to be already, you know," she remarked.

"I'm going to find out," I informed her solemnly, and I ran.

I had to run. If I'd waited another moment my legs would have fallen out from under me in fear. I knew just exactly what I should do, what I had to do, and what I was going to do. That didn't mean

I wasn't so scared every joint was stiff and my tail stuck out straight as I headed toward the Gate.

I tried not to think about it, or think about anything, and just ran. It must have worked, because I saw the Gate ahead and the clutter and chaos that was the city around it. Now I realized that I knew what I was going to do, but I had no idea how to do it. There weren't any rules, judges, enforcers, or bureaucracy. Only the blind forces of the Dark.

So in desperation I yelled, "I challenge The Hunt for the right to be a Demiurge!"

I ended up skidding, then falling all over my own feet into the big round plaza where challenges were held, but since I was the first one here at least no one saw it. I glanced at the street behind me and saw a poster that hadn't been there before tacked up on a store's window. I looked around, and people were beginning to wander into the circle to see what was going on. The ring itself was marked out with a rickety wooden fence, so I hopped over it and started pacing around until the horn went off.

It was really loud, and ended on an up note. Dogs jumped over the fence on the far side, but like me they were more shapes than actual animals, and they milled around until I couldn't tell them apart, and out of the mass rose a man. He wasn't so much a silhouette as just drowned in shadows so that he could hardly be seen. He had horns—no, antlers had been crudely tied to his head, and the rest of his clothes were clumsily arranged hides. There were a few dogs left too, slinking around his feet.

"Withdraw your challenge, mutt," he declared, his head lifted and voice booming. He was talking to the crowd, not to me. "You cannot win this. I am The Hunt."

"So am I," I retorted. My voice shook, but my fear was draining away. I meant what I was saying.

"I won't give up my position. Once, The Hunt was everything to the humans. It was in all of their stories, they drew it on their walls and carved statues to it. They worshiped me, nightmare, made sacrifices so that I would inspire them and they would have more to sacrifice tomorrow. No one challenges me these days, but I haven't given up even though the humans have forgotten that The Hunt is in their bones."

"Then I'll make them remember in their dreams," I growled.

It was a stupid thing to say, but I could see him grin. "You are worthy to challenge me, then. I accept. I will show you what you are trying to be."

He couldn't refuse, but I knew what he meant. Even under the shadow I could see those coal-dark eyes boring into mine. This was something we were both dedicated to.

"The Dark has given us our arena," he informed me. Then he collapsed into the dogs, and there were a lot of them splitting up and running around the sides of the house.

The house nearly filled the ring, with only a little bit of dead lawn between it and the fence. It was big, ornate, with a little tower and windows of all sizes bulging here and there irregularly. It was old, and dusty, and some of the boards were crumbling and what little paint hadn't peeled was bleached to grey. It was my Muse's house.

I crept in through the front door and I knew she wasn't home. There were no eyes, no statues, and no vases with dead flowers in them. I would have worried about her, but I knew that if something had happened to her, something would have happened to the house. Instead, this was… a gift? Or just the choice of the inexplicable laws that ran the Dark?

Every room was familiar. The hallway was too long, and the nursery was burned, and every hallway was a different length, but it was all the same. Except I couldn't find the parlor. I was wandering through the painting studio upstairs when dogs crept from behind every draped piece of posing furniture. There were too many of them, growling and slinking closer and closing the gap around behind me.

So I ran, bolting through that gap, and the dogs ran after me barking and snarling. They weren't as big as me, but there were a lot of them. I was faster running straight, but I'd pull away by inches and then lose a foot every time I had to turn a corner, and there were a lot of corners.

So I turned and turned again and turned again, and I charged out of a doorway while they were still in the hall, growling as loud as I could as I plunged into the pack. I grabbed a dog in my teeth, shook him once and threw him, and the others scattered. Two were in front of me and I chased them, hearing yelps of fear all around me. I was the one chasing now, and I knew how to do this. Head low, not snapping—rather, jaws parted, letting them hear how close my breathing echoed behind them.

It was working. I could smell their fear. They ran and I chased, until they ran back into a study furnished in broken bookcases and a charred desk and carpet, and there were dogs growling on either side of me. So I kept running, heading right out the door on the opposite side as they fell in barking insanely. I led them a couple of rooms, lulling them, then twisted through doorways and broke into the middle of them again. They yowled, flying in every direction, but I chased the closest dog only through a single room to find a cellar packed with dogs waiting for me with teeth bared. I turned and ran.

I ran from room to room, none of which were ever in the same order, all too aware of the biting teeth close behind me. If they caught me they could tear me apart and he would have won. If I surrendered he'd probably kill me anyway so I couldn't challenge him again, but he'd know I was no threat, so maybe not. I had lost this already.

No, I absolutely was not going to surrender. I was not going to lose.

I watched every room I ran past. I swerved into the kitchen and vaulted over the counter in the middle. The dogs were too small. They had to run around, or waste a second or two climbing over. It gained me a little distance. I saw the narrow stairs down to the basement, and leapt down as dogs tumbled behind me, struggling with each other because there were so many. That gained me a little distance, too. So

I turned sharply, my eyes darting at every doorway, charging through those doors until I was back in the study and once again pouncing on the middle of the pack, snarling and biting. They were braver now, but I flung three of them into the walls and the pack broke.

This time I didn't chase. I ran into a room at random, turned, and as the dogs poured into a truly decrepit laundry I plunged into the middle of them, sweeping dogs into the basins and wringers and weird churning devices. They weren't scared enough, so I grabbed one and with the tingling memory of a kitten in my jaws I shook it hard and slammed it into the floor twice, while the other dogs ran in circles and then scattered, yipping in fear as they abandoned their broken fellow.

I had to keep them off balance, keep them afraid. I had to chase them until it was clear they weren't going to recover and I won. As the first few tore into a basement to try and gather themselves I came racing down the stairs, snarling at them. When they ducked into a bathroom with only one door and collected there a few at a time, I ran into the next room and threw myself out a bedroom window and crashed in through the window over the bathroom sink. There was no escape from this house. It would herd us together, and I was taking advantage of that. I went charging after them, biting at the closest tail until they all separated. Then I ducked through the study again, lunging at a dog who happened to be passing through. I turned and chased another into the kitchen. I was watching every door, looking for the best places to ambush, and I didn't see the dog in the cupboard until it dropped out and grabbed me by the neck.

The collar is just for show, and one dog is more painful than a threat, but it shocked me. I shook him and threw him off, but now they were plunging out of every cabinet and bread box, from the stove and dropping out of a crack in the ceiling. They'd turned the tables on this chase again. Another grabbed my leg, but I kicked him away and looked for a way to run.

There wasn't one. They were all around me. I bared my teeth, ready to fight my way through if I had to, but I could feel some tension pass like a dream popping. The challenge was over, and I had lost.

I still refused to give up and die. Outside of the challenge there was nothing I could do to hurt The Hunt, but that just meant I didn't have to show any restraint at all. I threw myself violently through the dogs in front of me, biting and throwing without any care for tearing flesh. I broke into the hall and ran out the front door. On the lawn, with my back to the fence, I turned and prepared for them to emerge from the house.

They did, but they weren't running. They trotted easily, and every dog nodded at me as they curved around the house, hopped off the porch and scattering in different directions, squeezing through the fence or jumping it and disappearing into the crowd. The crowd that was much bigger than I'd expected.

"Fang!" Jeffery's voice. He had jumped the fence right next to me, his hands reaching out to the bites I'd taken, checking to see how hurt I was.

"I lost," I told him distantly. Lily hadn't been able to push through the crowd. Instead she landed, a perfect white fallen angel again, drifting out of the air on mutilated wings. I had lost. I hadn't been able to do it. I was laughing.

I almost choked, I was laughing so hard. I staggered and nearly fell over, too. The thrill of it hit me. The chase had been incredible. It was the most perfect and amazing thing I'd ever done. It was me, it was me all over. I wasn't sure if I'd come close to winning, but that didn't seem as important as how it had felt to chase and be chased by the best and push myself to the limit.

"Is he okay?" Lily asked, bending over me.

"He's more than okay," Jeffery assured her. He grinned now, showing off all of those little needle teeth he normally saved for the dreamers. "We could see a lot of it," he was telling me, "That must have been fun. Scare you out of your senses, too?"

"Hell, yes," I gruffed back at him, still laughing. I gave up on standing and threw myself down onto my side.

"Would you like to get your senses back?" a girlish voice with a ragged skip to it murmured from up close. A little hand laid itself on one shoulder, and Self-Loathing leaned over me with a hopeful smile. She was… something out of a little child's dream, all fluffy white fleece and gentle black eyes on a little human body.

That made Lily chuckle wickedly of course, and now Jeffery was just trying to restrain his grin, but as bashful as she sounded Self-Loathing insisted, "I think he deserves a chance to celebrate. You can show him how impressed you are your way, and I'll show him mine." I could feel her breath puffing onto my ear as she whispered, "Whenever you're ready to claim that reward."

"Can I celebrate too?" asked another voice, liquid and girlish, really liquid like bubbles rising up out of water. "That was beautiful. Better than I'd been expecting, even." A fish nearly as large as me swam over the fence, circling around us. Its scales were black and silver, every one gleaming, and tassels drifted from it at every point. Twisting back over the fence, the scales fell away and the tassels floated and spun playfully around the blank white girl. The blank white girl with the triangle eyes and the full black lips, every edge of her painted in brush strokes, who sat demurely on the wooden rail now.

"You look different," I told Coy. If I'd been too overwhelmed to think before, now I really was.

"I had to change my color palette to become a nightmare," she conceded. She leaned to one side and tilted her head even father that way to look down on me, and asked again hesitantly, "Can I come along? I wouldn't be here if I didn't like you already, you know."

"Sure," I told her. I didn't know what to think, but I didn't mind.

"Another girl, Fang?" Lily asked me teasingly, "This one's pretty."

"She is," Self-Loathing agreed. She sounded wistful, but she leaned up against the fence too and took one of Coy's hands in hers, peering at it admiringly. "I haven't met a fantasy in a long time. I can see why an artist's masterpiece would be drawn to Fang."

I thought they were getting it all wrong again, but for some reason it just didn't bother me this time.

Chapter Four

Just Friends

I'd gotten tired of being praised for a challenge I lost. It was great, more than great that everyone seemed to think I'd done well. It was even flattering that strangers thought so, that they would come up and tell me how impressed they were without being asked. It just got old fast. Nobody seemed to understand what they'd seen, but I had been there. It may have seemed close, but I lost. My opponent had been smarter than me, faster than me, and stronger than me. Lily had said something about The Wild Hunt being some old god or spirit or whatever humans believed in a long, long time ago, so that meant he had a lot more experience than I did. Whether I'd lost by miles or inches, I lost because my opponent was better, and I'd never really had a chance. Knowing that, the praise got hollow pretty quickly.

I lost interest even faster because whether or not I'd won wasn't the important part. The important part had been the feeling of it, having to push my body and my mind to chase, to chase like never before, to struggle to be the hunter and not the hunted. It was that feeling of being me, more than I'd ever thought I could be. That was what meant something.

Holding onto that feeling was what I needed, not to be told how impressed everyone else was. That was why I was searching for my Muse. That's what a Muse does. In that starved and eyeless white figure, in its moldy dress and twisted house, I saw everything that was good about myself and what I'd like to become. I'd managed to get away from the crowds before I completely lost that feeling of being happy with myself. She would make it strong again and I would see how I could become better.

I really had it bad, didn't I?

Or was there another reason that image was so strong? I had been following the trail, trotting through dark mists and empty shadows for longer than I'd expected, and the mists were becoming thicker, and the shadows were turning to black. Which direction had I turned after leaving the city?

The answer was all around me. The Gate isn't at the end of the Dark. I'd gone past it, into a place I'd never been before, that hardly anyone goes to. My Muse was this way, though, so I looked around as I went. There wasn't really much to see. Farther out toward the border there are places, bits of landscape drifting past each other like the buildings that cluster around the Gate. Here it was just the Dark itself, so thick that I felt like just eyes and teeth gliding through nighttime waters.

There were still dreams. If no one else came here, dreamers did. I saw one glistening in the distance and veered off to take a look at it. I slid up next to it, gave myself a shake until I remembered I had feet, and rubbed them over the surface to try and look inside. I couldn't. It was just this black and shiny ball, smaller than a normal dream. There was hardly any room for more than the dreamer in there, and the surface was rock hard and wouldn't give.

Teeth flashed, shark-like. They closed over the dream so fast I hardly got the sense of it, whether it shrank or burst as the slender figure left behind swallowed.

The creature was lean, grey on her belly and black on her back, sinuous and flexible with long arms and legs and a mouth full of triangular cutting teeth. Glassy black eyes fixed on nothing, but the rest of it looked entirely deadly except for one thing. Small. It was too small. It wasn't as tall as my shoulder, and hardly weighed anything. That turned this little nightmare from a predator into a challenge. I couldn't look at it without wanting to pit my fangs against it and find out who ate who, because I was sure I'd win.

"Self-Loathing?" I blurted out the instant I recognized that feeling, "What are you doing out here? There's no need for a nightmare this deep. Nothing could make these dreams worse."

"I'm not a nightmare," she retorted sulkily, "I hope you've figured that out by now. Did that look like I was trying to scare anyone?"

"No, you were eating," I defended, "But that didn't make any sense either. I've never seen anybody eat a dream."

We walked in silence. I hadn't realized we'd started walking, but something in my head had dragged my feet along the trail leading to my Muse. She had that kind of effect on me, even when I was arguing.

"I haven't done it in a long time," Self-Loathing explained eventually. She sounded calmer, more distant, but still emotional. "It shocks me when I do it, makes my memories a bit more vivid. That's what that was, a memory. Not a dream like you're used to. Instead of making something up, the person was reliving something so bad it comes back to them when they sleep."

"That doesn't sound like something I'd want to eat," was all I could think of to say.

"I told you, it's a shock," she answered peevishly, "It wakes me up. I keep slipping, forgetting things, and brooding." There was another silence. She'd been walking a few paces behind me, and I looked back, wondering what her expression would be like. It was hard to tell. Bits of her peeled away as I watched, leaving behind—well, I wasn't sure yet. I saw glimpses of a face that looked human, with dark skin and black bangs.

While I registered that she started talking again. "Anyway, I eat bad things. It's why I was made. When I eat a dream like this it's like I'm biting off a bad memory. The human doesn't forget. They just can't bring it to mind anymore."

"That's why you came out here, to help dreamers?"

I guess my tone had been a little too pointed. Her voice came sharp and angry as she responded, "Stop trying to convince me I'm a good person. You don't know anything about me, Fang. All you see is what I show you, and you don't seem to understand that either. Wasn't it obvious I was waiting for you? I knew you'd find some way to sneak out and see your girlfriend. You're totally predictable. You're exactly what you look like, and I can twist you to do anything I want. It's so easy."

I wanted to argue, but I couldn't because of what was happening to her. It wasn't like she was changing shape. Lots of people can do that, folding in on themselves or growing or becoming something else in a blink. She did that all the time. This was like we were walking into a wind and it was stripping her away. I could see what was underneath now, and it was something I'd seen before. She was becoming a human child with skin a heavy tan and black hair and eyes, but there was something different this time. Her crude smock had a ragged rip in it in the middle of her chest, and all around the tear was an old, dry stain, black with hints of red around the edges.

I could feel it too, although I didn't think I was changing. No, I just couldn't see it. "What's happening to us?" I asked aloud, "I don't want to fight with you."

"Yes, you do," she sniped back, but the edge was gone from her irritability. "Haven't you ever been this deep? We're just becoming what we always were. You're not good at saying it, but you think I'm weird and pathetic and all you really see in me is your own hunger."

She was right about that. That little body she was wearing now was too real, too detailed. It had a scent. She'd gone from something I wanted to punish for trying to be strong to something so weak I just wanted to feel my teeth close around it. I shook my head to clear it and nearly walked into a rock.

I hadn't been expecting landscape. There was no pretense of sky above us, just a dead void, but there was ground under our feet. Kind of. Mostly it was rocks, treacherous gravel and boulders sticking up like, well, fangs. On a shallow rise in the middle of the rocky field loomed a house, looking more dilapidated and empty than ever. What brought my Muse into this place? Did she know she was here?

The feeling of something pushing against me got stronger, but this time it was wind, a biting breeze that circled the house as we climbed up to it. As I padded up the steps onto the porch I had to remember I was talking. "If you think I don't care, why were you waiting for me?"

"I know you care," she answered, but that was all she said. Irritation gnawed at me that she'd ducked the question, but I was watching for that anger now. That was the Dark staining my feelings.

So instead I watched her as we walked through the front door, and as she passed the doorjamb she reached out and pulled a splinter of wood from it. She chewed on that pensively while we walked down the hall, then another hall, and when she swallowed it she trailed her fingertip along a side table, then licked the dust away. When her finger was clean she plucked a dead rose out of a vase and tore it apart and ate it, bite by bite. I felt my hackles rise sharply when she did that. That was my love for my Muse she was chewing on.

Was this the third hall we'd walked down? The house wouldn't cooperate tonight. It didn't want to let us in. Looking around, I saw the eyes. They watched from every wall, and some of them were weird, animal eyes or eyes even stranger. An eye the size of a volleyball stared at me as I walked by it, with an iris that was a mess of purple and red lines and a pupil shaped like an hourglass. The Dark was getting to my Muse, too.

A little bitty hand grabbed my collar, and I nearly bit it as I was yanked to the side. Self-Loathing pulled me through a strangely undersized door in a corner, and while she fit, I didn't. I couldn't seem to make myself smaller either, because I felt like bristling and being as big and menacing as I could. I pushed that feeling away and wriggled, twisting stubbornly until I managed to get through the gap, because on the other side of the chokingly tight door was the parlor.

If the house itself was acting weird, this room was exactly the same as always. A wall full of windows looked out over the sharp rocks surrounding the building and the black, empty sky. Four ivory statues were sunk into the walls watching my Muse, arms lifted as if to ward her off. And she sat in a rickety, oversized wooden chair and held her face in her hands and wept.

There was no sign she knew we were here. Probably she didn't know. She didn't have to. Looking at her, being near her was enough. I was struck by those gaunt hands, and the threadbare lace that covered the backs of them. They trembled. She was breathtaking, every part of her perfect. She was one single, pure thing, this sadness, but she hadn't faded. She wasn't simple, just consumed by her feelings.

A spider drifted down on a thread toward her hair. I'd seen it before. Everything in this house replayed over and over. I felt my gut tighten with anger as a little dark hand reached up, caught the spider, and Self-Loathing popped it into her mouth and swallowed it.

"The blood was right," she announced distantly, smoothing a ruffle down on my Muse's shoulder, "I think she's dead. She's dead, but nailed in place by her own guilt. That's what this place tastes like. No wonder she was able to challenge."

That raised a question, which let me push aside my resentment. It took effort. Couldn't she see I wanted to be alone with my Muse? "Why is Lily Regret, and you're Self-Loathing? Aren't they the same?"

"Am I the same as Lily?" Self-Loathing replied. She kept touching my Muse, straightening her dress, pushing back her bangs, all of it compulsive but gentle. "You've never had to understand the difference, but this girl does. I can taste it. She's wrapped in pain, in the horror of her own actions, but she's not like me. I do the things I do because of the kind of person I am. Whatever she did, she doesn't blame herself. Not really. She did the best she could when every option was a nightmare. She hates what she did, but not herself. She wants it taken away."

Her voice had gotten vague, and so had her expression. She looked almost like a dreamer as she leaned forward, whispering, "If someone else could take responsibility for her crimes, the person who didn't want to do them could rest."

I had just long enough to feel a flash of gratitude that I'd dealt with so many dreamers. Before Self-Loathing finished talking, before her mouth started to open and reach for my Muse's head, I was already galloping around behind the chair. As my head twisted around and I sank my teeth into Self-Loathing's leg, the rest of my emotions hit me. She had tried to eat my Muse. Burning with fear and anger, I flung her as hard as I could into the wall.

I'd done much worse to her in play, but this time I was trying to hurt her and that made the difference. The yell she let out was raw pain and fear, different from when we did this for fun, and her leg was bleeding—or maybe oozing. That wasn't enough to satisfy me, but before I could leap after her the whole room lit up silver.

The light wasn't all that bright, but the house had been dim and the Dark outside stifling. A black and silver fish swam through the air into the parlor, arriving through a door that of course hadn't been there when I looked last. Even the scales and ribbons of fin that were black gleamed, but the silver glowed, lighting up the room like a trail of sparks.

I wasn't angry anymore. Why had I even been angry? I was worried, instead. I couldn't really hurt Self-Loathing. As far as I knew nothing could kill a Demiurge, but I could hurt her feelings and they were fragile enough. She hadn't meant to hurt anyone. She'd been obeying some strange instinct, being whatever she'd started out as before a hundred lifetimes and a thousand victims had made her what she was.

Her black eyes were focused now, looking at me, and she wasn't angry either. The stain had disappeared from her crude dress and she showed no sign of damage as she climbed back to her feet. Coy had chased the Dark away just by entering the room.

"Oops. That looks kind of intimate. Did I come at a bad moment?" she asked. Her scales were stripping away, leaving her a white silhouette of a girl sitting with her legs crossed above the fireplace. Her voice teased, but it was the way Jeffery teases me. There weren't any barbs in it.

"I think you came at the best moment," I told her bluntly. "Now I know why no one comes this deep into the Dark. It's not safe."

"Oh, I know. I can feel it," she agreed pleasantly. She didn't sound like she could feel it. "Most of the Dark likes me once I started acting like a nightmare. Once I passed your Gate it started trying to push me out, or get into me. I'm going to be glad to get out of here. I was hoping you'd come too, but I didn't know you'd have company!"

"I'm not the person you'd be dragging him away from," Self-Loathing assured Coy. Actually, she sounded kind of embarrassed. "He came here to see his Muse, and I latched on without asking."

"He has a Muse?" Coy asked. She sounded nothing short of delighted, and leaping off the mantel her scales closed around her again, letting her swim in a circle around the chair. After a few orbits she stopped, floating in midair, and the fish peeled away to let the upper half of the girl grip the back of the chair and lean in close. "Pretty. I love it, Fang. This is a nightmare's idea of pretty, isn't it? This whole house is like a painting. This is why I wanted to try being a nightmare. She must make you explode with ideas."

"Kind of," I admitted. Nobody talked to me like this. I didn't quite know how to deal with it. "It's more like she makes me feel like I can come up with my own ideas, because I know where they start. I guess."

"Purpose. She shows you your own creativity," Coy agreed, "I understand that. I hope I do. I've been trying to do it for humans since I was dreamed up." Turning back to my Muse, she asked curiously, "Can you hear me, Miss Muse? I'm Coy. What's your name?"

"I don't think she can hear you, or me, or anybody," I told Coy, shaking my head regretfully. "I don't even know her name. No one does. All she does is cry."

"She can't hear you," Self-Loathing put in, "I'm sure of it. Or rather, she can hear you but she's not listening. She's not taking it in. It's just something going on in the background while she thinks about what happened to her."

"Wow," was Coy's response to that. "I feel sorry for her. It just makes her even more pretty, doesn't it? No, she's more than pretty. She's beautiful."

I had to nod. "Yeah." What could I add to that?

Coy swam away from the chair, but her scales were still peeling away, and it was the girl who floated next to me and laid a hand on my shoulder. "I was going to see if you wanted to come with me and play with some dreams," she explained, then corrected herself. "Well, no, I was going to beg and wheedle and do whatever I could to persuade you. I think I can be a nightmare and a fantasy at the same time, and I want you to see it. I want to see what you do, too! I can't take you away from your Muse, though. I mean, I wouldn't be able to live with myself."

"No, he should go," Self-Loathing interjected again, "Hanging around this far into the Dark wouldn't inspire him." She walked up to me, and this little girl body was so much more alive than her other shapes, but so small. She had to reach up to pat my other shoulder. "Go on. Don't worry about me. I'm getting out of here as fast as I can, but messing with dreams isn't my thing. I'll see you after you've had your fun, maybe."

I heard tightness in her voice, but what could I do but take her at her word? She was right that I needed to get out of here. I actually worried, just for an instant, that she might attack my Muse the moment my back was turned. I knew she wouldn't do anything like that.

"All right," I told Coy, "There's nothing much to see when I get into a dream. I mostly just chase people. I can't imagine what you could do to frighten someone!"

That made her giggle, and as her scales and streamers closed around her to become a fish, she told me, "Come and see!"

She swam out through the door, and I loped after her.

So I ran through the Dark, wondering about how much brighter it looked as we passed the Gate and headed back into familiar territory. Through the grey I followed a glittering silver and black shape which wriggled and darted and seemed determined to veer aside to pass through any patch of landscape we passed. Some of them were quite strange, and as I leaped from platform to platform over grinding spikes I wondered if Coy had forgotten I can't fly.

We were headed for the border of course, but my next surprise came when she turned aside while it was still just a dividing line in the distance. She was moving slower now, and as I caught up I suggested, "Aren't we going to cross into the Light? Making a bad dream worse isn't really that exciting. A dreamer on this side is going to spook at almost anything."

"Exactly," she told me in satisfaction, scales dissolving and whirling around her as she sat as a girl in mid-air, craning her neck around. "I got an idea on the way. Having a giant black wolf running behind you really focuses the imagination."

There was something about her tone of voice, there. I was getting the feeling that Coy thought everything was funny. Maybe over in the Light it was. "What are—" I started to ask, but I didn't get to finish.

A dream started forming ahead of us. I barely got a glimpse of a dreamer, still a vague shape that seemed like a man. Before he could focus on himself the murky bubble of his dream crystallized around him. Before I could focus on the bubble Coy slapped me on the haunch and urged me, "Go! That's what I want, a fresh one!"

"But—" I tried again.

"Go go go go go!" she stuttered at me. I didn't understand, but I understood the urgency and the surety in her voice. I let myself trust her and threw myself forward on all four feet as fast as I could. I barely felt the surface as I broke through into the dream. There hadn't been time for it to become solid. The dreamer was still dazed, taking a few vague steps through shadows that hadn't taken shape. The dream was nothing but shapeless anxiety right now.

That is, it was until a nightmare stepped into it. As little and raw as it was, I dominated the dream just by standing there. Shadows became trees, wet grass, and the occasional thorny tangle. It was the kind of scene the dreamer expected to find a wolf in. Coy hadn't given me any instructions, but I knew how to be a wolf. I bared my teeth and stepped forward very slowly, growling low and raw and hateful. That sound let him know that this was personal, and he started to stumble backwards, about to run. It was really pathetically easy until the fox fell like a star from the sky.

That was the only way I could think of it. It had to be Coy, but she'd become something like me, but not at all like me. She was slender and no more a fox than I was a wolf—just something sleek and fluffy and canine, but every hair made of liquid silver that caught every glimmer of light. Compared to me she was tiny, and poised and nimble where I was a bulky, threatening mass.

She looked over her shoulder at the dreamer. It was a woman after all, now that it had taken shape. Then Coy turned her head to look at me. That little body was so gleaming and graceful, her white eyes so enigmatic. She was gorgeous, and I acted without thinking. I abandoned the dreamer and pounced.

She wasn't there when I landed, of course, and my teeth tore nothing. That was what I'd expected, what I wanted. Off to the side I saw her darting with the twisting grace she'd had as a fish. I couldn't lose track of her in that silver body, so I lunged again, bouncing off a tree and knocking the trunk askew. I'd become big without thinking about it, and the dreamer must have thought I was enormous.

After that I chased. There was no mental challenge to it, but physically I was trying to catch the wind. She could leap up onto a tree branch, but wouldn't stay there out of reach. She'd drop down on the other side of a bush, making me duck around at first until I got impatient enough to start leaping over them. The dream got bigger and bigger, and she ducked down little cliffs as I catapulted over them, and we played hopscotch over boulders with me always a step behind her, teeth snapping shut inches behind the tip of her tail.

I forgot about the dream or the dreamer until Coy took a sharp turn and ran right by the dreamer, leaving me facing the person I should have been scaring. It jolted me. For an instant I noticed the feel of the dream, nervous and excited, afraid but exhilarated rather than terrified. I saw the forest around us as an elaborate obstacle course that went on and on, where we'd run amidst trees that were now intricately twisted and decked with leaves that glowed faintly in the night. In every hole, under every bush, eyes watched, but only the woman in front of me knew what they meant.

Coy disappeared in that moment. I barely caught a glimpse of her diving through the edge of the bubble, leaving me alone with the dreamer.

I had only one target left. I showed the dreamer my fangs again and started to lurch forward—and before my eyes the woman melted into a fox. Not quite as glitteringly pretty, but she had become Coy, or the best copy she could make herself. So I barreled forward and bit down on empty air as she leapt out of reach with Coy's same speed and agility, and almost the elegance. Instinct took over again. I charged, and swung around trees, and jumped over rocks and ran over the tops of hollow logs as she darted through them. I could feel the fear tightening around us in the dream, but also the thrill of it, making my heart and the dreamer's pound faster.

Until I chased her up the top of a hill, and she turned and looked at me with a human's eyes and waited in trembling anticipation as I closed the distance and my jaws clenched around her neck.

The dream popped. I'd barely felt the touch of her when it did. I skidded to a halt, panting heavily, twisting my head from side to side as I tried to take stock. We were still well inside the Dark, and a few wisps of emotion lingered from the dream, but they didn't feel like anything I knew.

Everything was normal, but it didn't feel normal. Coy drifted up to me, and her black brushstroke lips pulled into a triumphant smile. I understood the triumph of making a great dream, but my heart was still thumping and I couldn't let go of the feeling of those final moments.

"Was it exciting after all?" she asked, playful but soft. I could hear uncertainty. She wasn't sure if it had been as good as she'd expected?

It had been better. "I don't even know if that was the word for it," I stammered, "Even Jeffery doesn't make nightmares like that. She was afraid, but she wanted to be afraid. How did you do that? Did you see the forest at the end? I'm surprised it broke up with the dream. It was so detailed, I thought we'd have a new landmark. Some place built by a dreamer just for the chase."

That made Coy giggle. She sounded as hyper as I felt! "Wouldn't that have been something? But at the last moment there was nothing there for her but you. I bet she'll even remember you when she wakes up. I hope she does. You made her feel something she'd never imagined, and she had to know how it ended."

Coy's hands were all over my neck and head, rubbing and scratching, and I gave her a few licks. I'd have been embarrassed if the rush weren't still hanging on, but mostly I was just impressed that she even tasted like paint. For someone who could change shape in a dream so easily, she really knew exactly what she was.

"I wonder if we could do it again?" I asked dizzily, "Not the same way. If I put on spikes and made myself monstrous, and you become something really predatory, we could hop into a dream just as it formed.

Then we'd play friendly with the dreamer, but as soon as anything else took shape we'd start chasing it. Could we make the dreamer change into some kind of nightmare? Teach him to chase, make him see himself as a monster for a little while? Make him like it?"

It was electric. My whole body hummed with inspiration, and images and thoughts were flickering past so fast I just had to grab the best ones. I looked up into the face of a rice paper white girl with triangular eyes that matched my hunger and imagination with their own. Hands cupped my muzzle, even whiter and more slender than-

-a girl, a young woman in a dress as threadbare and moth-eaten as it was elaborate, whose hair gleamed just shy of black and whose gauntness was the picture of someone who'd cut away everything about herself except her very core. The girl who was supposed to be my Muse, the one who inspired me.

I staggered back, hard. Was I in love? Could I have abandoned my Muse and fallen for another girl instead? No, I looked at Coy and she was beautiful, but I didn't feel that tightness in my chest. But the sight of her made me want to find another dream, to try and surprise her with my own ideas as she surprised me.

I didn't let Coy ask what was wrong. "I—I —" I couldn't lie. "That was incredible. I mean, that was incredible. I don't have a word for it—" I babbled.

"Beautiful?" she asked teasingly, drifting forward. She was in no hurry.

Still, it was like doom approaching me. I ran around in a circle, babbling, "Yes. Yes, it was beautiful." Oh, Hell, had it been beautiful. "But it's not what I expected, either. I have to go think about it, okay?" I made myself stop and look her in the eyes. She deserved this. I was panicking, but it would be unforgivable to be rude to someone who'd done this for me. "Thank you, Coy. I mean that, thank you. But—"

I lost my nerve. I turned and ran.

Sweet Dreams are Made of Teeth

I felt bad almost immediately, and for most of the run back to the Gate I just tried to sort through it all. Coy wouldn't be hurt. There hadn't been a trace of it in her expression or attitude. I was able to let go of that worry, at least. But this was the second time that being with her had made me feel like I was doing something wrong behind my Muse's back. I was pretty sure I wasn't, but it felt too much like it. I needed to see her, to remind myself why I'd picked her.

The problem was, she was still in the deep reaches of the Dark past the Gate. I was on edge enough that I was having trouble picking her trail up, but when I did it seemed to be in that direction. Going back there would just make things worse. I was probably still a little messed up from visiting the first time.

I had a solution. The taste of her bitter, guilt-curdled blood would drive everything but her out of my mind like it always did. So I headed for the Gate itself and the town around it and particularly for Bar Number Three.

I was already calming down by the time I trotted through the winding streets and saw what looked like a blank, boarded-up building in front of me. Coy probably deserved an apology, but I'd get my feelings straight and then figure it all out.

Sitting hunched up by the door with arms wrapped around its knees was someone who was not just scrawny, but an actual stick figure. It was even made of wood, studded with nails ranging from voodoo doll nails to railroad spike size, many of which pierced its black, splintery limbs and body completely. It was a girl, I thought from the long, limp hair. I already knew she was Self-Loathing before it occurred to me that slumped over in defeat is not a look many nightmares take. I guess I just knew her by now, no matter what she looked like.

I stopped at the door, right next to her. I wanted to go in, wanted to taste my Muse, to lose myself in her again. My shoulders knotted up, tense with frustration and even a little anger, before I let it go.

"Self-Loathing..." I began uncertainly.

"It's okay," she urged me gently, "I just wanted to apologize."

She always surprised me. She sounded so frank and sincere, rather than out of control. My thoughts drifted to the body she was wearing. I'd instinctively thought it was just meant to be pitiful, but it was no worse than what a lot of nightmares and demons looked like. What I noticed instead was that it didn't make me feel much of anything. She had a talent, almost a genius for looking like something desirable. If she didn't look like that now, it couldn't be an accident. She was trying not to distract me.

"For what?" I asked her as I took in this change of mood.

A badly carved face looked up at me, sad but in a stylized way that didn't really wrench the heart. Again, I knew that had to be deliberate. It was strange to realize that someone was actively trying to not manipulate me. "Fang, I've got a hundred things I should apologize to you for, but trying to eat your girlfriend because I was jealous has to be the worst yet."

"You were freaking out," I told her sympathetically. I was sympathetic. How could I blame her for that? "I was freaking out. Neither of us were thinking clearly. If I'd known how badly that place gets to you, I wouldn't have gone."

"I knew," she told me, her head falling forward again, and she couldn't keep the bitterness out of her voice. "I've been there before, lots of times. I knew how it makes people crazy, and I knew that something bad would happen and we'd fight. I knew all of that before I went and waited for you. I don't know what you must think of me."

All right. "If I tell you, will you believe me?" I asked her carefully.

Her face lifted sharply. "What?"

Now it was me who had to sound even and sincere and not try and lead her. "I think that you think you know what I think of you already. If I tell you what I really think, will you believe me, even if it's not what you expected to hear?"

Despite the gobbledygook that had come out as, she seemed to understand. She nodded, staring at me with eyes much shinier than the rest of her painted wooden body.

"I think you're smarter than me," I told her as simply and casually as I could manage.

"What?" she asked again, but with surprise, not disbelief. That tiny difference made me feel tremendously relieved.

Digging my muzzle in behind her, I levered at her lower back, urging her to her feet. "Come on. You're probably better off at home than in a crowd. Let me walk you there."

She staggered upright, tall and gangly in this body. At least I'd broken through her mood. If I needed any more evidence, patches of grey started to creep over her as she told me, "I don't understand. Whether or not I am, why would that be what you think about me?"

"Well, how old are you?" I rejoined as I gave her another little push around her lower back, and we both started walking.

"You're not supposed to ask a girl that," she answered immediately.

"Why not?" I enjoyed her playful tone, but I just didn't get the joke.

That brought her up short the way it had me, but it got her to answer me, so I was fine with that. "All right," she confessed, "But I'm not sure what to tell you. Humans hadn't really learned how to mark time when I was born, and no one else did. From the histories they put together now, I think about ten thousand years. But since you've only ever lived in the Dark, does that number even mean anything to you?"

Well, no. "Then tell me in a way that does mean something. Who in this city is older than you?"

She had to think about it again. "Some of the dream painters, maybe. I think some of them are the same as the ones I knew back then. It's all kind of vague. There are a few very old gods that humans made still lingering around as Demiurges. Demiurges were more important to humans than power back then."

"But you're not really sure?" I asked. Partly I was trying to make my point, and partly I was curious now. "What about Lily? She says she's one of the original fallen angels."

"I don't know," Self-Loathing answered distantly, "I don't know what goes on behind the Gates. It's a one way trip, except for angels and demons, and they're crazy. They all tell a different story."

"But you came to the Dark before her?" I pressed.

"Yes. From the Light, and from the human world. We used to be able to go back and forth. It wasn't easy, but humans could open a way. Now the angels and demons pick a fight if anybody tries."

"All right," I acknowledged, but now I had to make my point. "Think about all that you've seen. You said that I'm easy to predict, and for you I bet I am. You've seen everything. You can turn into anything you want, and that doesn't affect you at all. I don't even know what you are, but it doesn't matter. There aren't any others like you anymore, are there?"

"No," she admitted distantly. There was an edge there, but whatever ugly memories I'd stirred up were getting lost as she tried to follow my thought.

"On top of that you've eaten people, and not like I would eat them. You've let them become part of you. Lots of people. Lots and lots and lots of people, right? So when I talk to you and I can think past the way you make me want to play with you—" I was definitely, definitely glad I couldn't blush. "-I'm talking to this person who knows things I can't imagine and has thought of everything I could say before I say it, usually. Not always, but usually. I wish you were happier, and you can drive every thought out of my head just with the way you look sometimes, but those aren't the first things I think about you. Mostly it's just that I know someone who's really smart, and I'm really simple. It's amazing."

I felt awkward at the end of a speech like that, but it seemed to have worked. She was certainly listening, and she'd changed shape completely. She looked kind of human now. She was still thin, but in a willowy and elegant way. She was trailing a loose white dress, but the nails were still there, sticking through it. Her hair was still long and fell back heavily, but now it was pale blonde.

As I peeked up at her, she peeked down at me and asked, "Would you like to taste my blood, Fang?"

"What?" She'd floored me again. "I've- haven't I tasted it before? Er, several times?" Did she really have to make me talk about that? At least she only looked a little chewable as she said it.

"No, you only think you have," she explained. She sounded vague and sad again, but in more of a thoughtful way. She really was always a mystery. "That was never my blood. Not actually mine. It was just part of whatever shape I put on for you. When I tasted your Muse I wondered if my real blood, from my original body, would be as strong."

She wanted me to feel for her like I did for my Muse. Or did she? Was it something I wasn't willing to give her, or did I just assume it was?

There was no time to figure anything out. A figure dressed all in black dropped onto the street in front of us. From the roof, maybe? He grabbed one of Self-Loathing's hands before she could back away and lifted it to his mouth. His hands and his face were red skinned, sleekly handsome, and he had little horns.

"If the puppy isn't interested, I wouldn't hesitate a moment to accept an offer like that, Lady Masochism," he told her. The drawling tone, arrogant, dismissive of me and purring over the name she'd rather people didn't call her confirmed it. He was a demon. That demon.

"The offer isn't open to you," she told him stiffly, tugging at his grip on her hand. It didn't budge. I knew that as a Demiurge she couldn't really be killed, but it only occurred to me at that moment that there was no guarantee it made her strong, only immortal.

"I'm sure you'll think of something to offer me instead," he continued, a hard edge lending threat to a voice that pretended to be jovial. He took a step back and pulled her two steps forward, reaching his other arm out playfully to receive her. "You haven't been available to your favorite clients in ages, My Lady. Some of us can't wait any longer."

"I told you—" she squealed, an edge of fear and anger in her own voice, but that would only make him more determined.

"She's with me, demon!" I barked at him, "Push off, and she'll see you when she feels like it!"

He'd been deliberately ignoring me, but the insulting tone got his attention. Instead of drawing Self-Loathing into his embrace, he held his other hand up and flexed it twice. He was reminding me of blades I'd seen spring out of it as he told me coldly, "I've been amused by the mystery of why she favors you, mutt, but my patience is—"

He liked to talk too much. I was in the air before he cut himself off, and my teeth closed around his face before he could do anything about it. I jerked my head hard to one side, and his face still hung in my teeth as I landed on all fours behind him and tried to keep terror from collapsing my knees under me.

I could feel the fear running through me like ice, but instead of attacking back he let go of Self-Loathing and stumbled away from both of us. He'd flung both hands up over his face, but kept them enough to the side that he could fix an eye on me. Which meant I could see just enough of what he was hiding.

What I'd ripped away had been a mask, like Lily's. What was underneath was a lot less pretty. It was… meaty and bulging and deformed, and the eye bloodshot, and I was glad I couldn't see it better. This wasn't scary, it was just gross and ugly.

"Well?" I growled around the face I'd stolen. I didn't make the threat directly.

I was right. I hadn't needed to. He'd do anything rather than let us or anyone see what had been hidden under there. With the stiffness of someone fighting panic he pulled himself up straight again, telling me, "You learn entirely too fast, mutt. Keep her, then."

He turned and ran down an alley that seemed to open up just for him to escape through. It looked like he pulled a hat out of somewhere and covered his face with it, but I only got a glimpse. Hands grabbed my collar and dragged me around. Self-Loathing stared down into my face. Her skin was ashy with fear, but she yelled furiously instead. "Why did you do that? He would have killed you!"

"You didn't want to go with him!" I yelped helplessly. I didn't understand this anger! Hadn't I just saved her?

"No, but I've lived through worse. You should have run away!" she insisted.

"I won, didn't I?" That lasted for about half a second. Her glare said everything. "Even if I'd lost, it was worth it. I'd risk myself to protect you."

"You weren't supposed to care about me that much!" she shouted, and I had just enough time to see the tears moving down her cheeks before she slapped me and stomped off.

If that really was as hard as she could hit she wasn't strong at all, but it wasn't the physical pain that shook me. I just sat down in the street and stared at her until I saw her go down the stairs leading into her salon and slam the door behind her.

What had just happened?

I went back to Bar Number Three. I didn't know what else to do. I was starting to get the feeling that whatever I tried, something different was going to happen.

I wasn't disappointed. I could see the dingy door to the bar down the street ahead of me when I heard wings flapping heavily above me, and with a fall of feathers and some drops of blood I thought were theatrical Lily fluttered down for a landing beside me.

"I smell wounded innocence from all the way across town, and it turns out to be you, Fang," she greeted me playfully, "Why am I not surprised?"

I wasn't in the mood. On the other hand...

"Lily, I—" I started, "You—" I didn't know how to say it.

To my relief, almost all of the teasing smirk disappeared, and she just stared at me, then crouched down and laid a hand on my shoulder. Red eyes looked curiously into mine, the same red as her lips and her hair and her fingernails. Lily had a theme too, and it made me feel more comfortable with what I was trying to say.

"You want advice about girls, don't you, puppy?" she asked, sounding mildly surprised.

At this point I was starting to feel like everyone I knew was smarter than me. Again. "Well, you're—" I started, but she cut me off.

"—the only girl you know that you're not in love with?"

I nearly fell on my back, I scrambled backwards so fast. My hind legs fell out from under me, and I was sitting on my tail and still trying to backpedal. My mind just stopped. When it started again, it was only to feel guilty as I blurted out, "I'm only in love with one girl!"

I only knew how afraid I'd been she was going to tease me about this when I felt the relief that she didn't. Instead she stood up, closing the gap between us, and slid her hand between my ears. "All right, puppy," she urged me, "You haven't got the slightest idea why asking me was such a bad idea, so maybe for you it won't be. Come on. There's something I'd like to show you that will help."

A little tug with her fingertips on my collar, and then her hand slipped away as she started walking. I got up again and fell in beside her. "I just thought you'd know a lot more about this kind of thing than I would," I explained helplessly.

"That's why it was dangerous to ask," she answered. Her tone sounded whimsical, but I knew she was teasing herself, not me. "You wear your heart on your sleeve, so I'm betting I know most of this. Can you give me a little hint about what's going on?"

"If I really knew, maybe I could figure it out myself," I told her. I could hear bitterness in my own voice. "I have a girlfriend, and nothing's changed about how I feel for her. It's just that I think Self-Loathing is jealous and wants me to love her. I'm not sure. She doesn't make any sense. I don't mind that she doesn't, but she's more upset every time I see her. I don't know what to do about it."

"And the fantasy girl?" Lily asked. She'd kept her voice casual, but it was the question I'd been trying to avoid.

"I don't think she's in love with me, or I'm in love with her," I answered. I knew I was talking around the point, and it wouldn't do me any good. It didn't.

"But you're not sure," Lily concluded. She reached out again and squeezed the back of my neck. She really did sound like she was trying to comfort me, and gratitude hit me in a rush.

"I don't understand anything that's going on," I admitted, hanging my head almost to the street. "I'm completely out of my depth, aren't I?"

"In here," Lily urged me, and another tug on my collar pulled me in the front door of a plain white building several stories tall. It was almost a tower.

Inside, there were stairs. Lots of stairs, and doorways, scattered everywhere and at every angle with no apparent rules or pattern.

"I've seen dreams like this before," I remarked curiously as we started climbing a staircase. Soon enough we reached a landing and it bent, and as we walked up the new flight of stairs the old staircase was above our heads.

"Some ideas sink into the minds of humans hard," Lily explained distantly, "I find this place interesting not because it's a new idea, but because it doesn't belong to anyone. The building just seems to have happened, and the person I'm taking you to meet moved in afterward. In here."

We passed through an archway like any of the others dotting the walls, and instead of coming back out into the tower this one led into a single airy room with a balcony at the far end. The whole thing was made out of plaster or white adobe or something like that. I didn't know much about building materials, but the rough texture was interesting. There really wasn't any furniture, there was just this one thing filling most of the room.

"I've seen this before. She's Jeffery's Muse, isn't she?" I asked. The room was full of shapes. Big shapes, little shapes. Some of them were flat and crawled across ceilings, others were massive and free floating, or interlocking. Most of them were in motion, changing shape rather than position, but creating little corridors through the geometric jungle. I didn't understand much of it, but when a regular shape like a box but with many sides all folded up into a single, flat series of intricate lines, I knew that it was supposed to mean something.

"His Muse, and the closest thing he's got to a girlfriend," Lily replied. Amusement crept back into her voice as she added, "You and he are so much more alike than you realize."

I blinked. "I thought you and Jeffery—" I began, but as I was pausing to figure out how to put it delicately she started to laugh. In fact, she reached over and rubbed me between the ears again.

"That's exactly why you're having problems now," she told me cryptically, although she still sounded pleased. "You're trying to think like a human. You've learned a few of their rules, but you can't really understand them. You were never a child, you don't have parents, and you don't know anybody who's ever had a real relationship. Your fish girl probably knows more than you do about what human boys and girls want from each other." Lily was smirking now, but again it felt like she was teasing herself. "Probably a lot more. Good dreams tend to be predictable."

Not that I'd seen, but that hadn't been meant for me anyway. "They're the only rules I know," I pointed out, "And they feel right. I don't want to cheat on my Muse, Lily. That wouldn't be right." I was pretty sure about that, even if I didn't know why I was sure.

"But that's not your problem, is it?" she asked me, sharp but not accusing. "Your problem is that you don't know what cheating on her means."

I sat down on my butt again, hard. She'd pretty much nailed it on the first try.

"Is it just the three of them?" Lily asked distantly, reaching up to poke at a silvery sphere above her head, which folded in on itself and became the same, but inside-out. "I haven't had time to watch you closely, puppy."

"I can't handle three!" I told her despairingly. Actually, I felt a lot better already. I had no idea what to do, but at least someone understood the problem.

"How do you feel about them?" she asked me, then changed her mind. "No, that's too big a question, isn't it? What do you like about them? What do you want from them?"

I shook my head, waggling it like a dog as I puzzled that out. "My Muse, I guess... I just want to look at her and love her. That's enough. She doesn't have to do anything. She's perfect like she is. If she loved me too, that would be even better. I'm starting to think she does."

"Mmm-hmmm?" Lily encouraged.

"Self-Loathing," I hazarded, "I don't think I'll ever understand her. I'd like to get to know her, but I could do that the rest of my life and I wouldn't be finished. And I want to, uh... play with her every time I see her."

Lily didn't make a joke, or even smile. She was just watching the twisting geometry around us as she listened.

"And Coy, I guess... I want to make dreams with her. To hang out. To learn from her, and maybe teach. I don't know. It's more like how I feel about Jeffery than anything. I just like her, but I feel like she and I want to be the same thing, and Jeffery is something above me."

"I don't hear much competition between those, puppy," Lily pointed out, giving me a friendly little smile. "Do you?"

I had to admit, I didn't.

"You know what you want from them," Lily told me in the firm tones of someone finally giving advice. "Just take each of them on her own terms. What you feel for one of them doesn't make a difference in what you feel for another. Deal with them how you want to deal with them. The fantasy will always be friendlier than you are, your Muse is never going to talk to you, and expecting the Demiurge of Self-Loathing to do anything but act crazy is a fool's game. Accept them for what they are, and find the way you want to be with that person, and stop worrying about things none of you know how to feel anyway."

"Okay," was all I could say. I was still absorbing it. I looked up at something like a tube snaking through itself over and over and blurted out, "What is she?"

"I'm not sure. I think only Jeffery really thinks it's a 'she'," Lily answered distantly, "She was never human, and she's not from beyond either of the Gates, and she's not a nightmare. There are other worlds than the dream world and the waking world. She may be from one of them."

"And you and Jeffery…?" I asked cautiously.

She laughed, quite loudly and with obvious relish. "Heaven, no. He's not my type, puppy. I don't think he has any interest in the kinds of things I find attractive in a man. If I spend all my time with him, it's because I don't think we're going to know him for very long. The only difference between you and Jeffery I can see, puppy, is that he's never going to be content with anything. He's made the biggest splash any nightmare knows how, and that's not enough. He's trying to find out how to do something bigger. Eventually we're going to lose him."

She'd drifted back into distant thoughtfulness, and I guess I answered the same way. "He has to be himself."

"You nightmares are the ultimate career men," Lily told me, and waved a broken wing at the madness of angles and curves around us. "Not many of you know that girls exist, and when you do—this is what you look for, just something that makes you want to throw yourselves back into dreams."

"That's what we are," I echoed.

"Well, let your girlfriends be who they are, okay?" Lily told me simply, "And don't worry about whether one of them actually is your girlfriend. For you that's just a word. It doesn't mean anything."

"I love words that don't mean- whoah!" That was Coy, bursting into the room from the balcony, and she exploded in black and silver streamers as she pulled herself up short. Floating in place as a girl, and she stared at the geometric riot of Jeffery's Muse. "What is this thing?"

"I'd love to tell you," I assured Coy warmly, "But a friend of mine is really hurting right now. I don't think I can make her any happier, but I'm going to try."

And I ran out down the twisted staircase. I had to try and find Self-Loathing again.

If I could track anyone, I could track Self-Loathing. She and my Muse were burned into my mind, and I just had to keep moving until I caught the trail that was her. That gets a little confusing near the Gate because of everyone else around, but I only needed a general glimpse to tell me she was where I'd seen her last.

She wasn't even inside. As I came running down the newly cobbled street, I saw a nightmare standing at the top of the stairs leading down to her salon. He was something tall and gangly with a spiky silver mane, and the girl whose chin he held had to be Self-Loathing. She looked almost human, although her blue dress puffed out a lot around her hips and made it impossible to figure out how old she was supposed to be. It did show off a lot of leg. What was important was that her body was actually white cloth stuffed taut to convincingly fill out that human shape. With the long, needle-like spikes that came out of this thing's fingers, I could see why he'd find her appealing.

Unfortunately for him, she looked pretty appealing to me too. I didn't bother with a greeting, an introduction, or even a warning. I charged up to her and I wasn't sure if she even heard my padded feet thumping on the bricks until my teeth closed around her calf and she was ripped out of her customer's grip. I thundered forward, shaking her once as she let out a squeal and her springy red curls thrashed. Then I threw her into a wall, hard, and when she landed her ceramic eyes stared up at me in shock.

The giggle fluttering under her voice sent a thrill down my spine as she exclaimed, "Fang!"

"I'm really sorry," I sort of panted and barked back at the thing with the spikes, "Miss Self-Loathing is going to be kind of busy after all." Glancing back at the doll girl in question, I bared my teeth widely and growled, "Very, very busy."

That got her giggling again, which almost made me giggle and break the mood, and she sounded bubbly with excitement as she told her customer, "He really is sorry, but I'm also really going to be busy!" With that she staggered to her undersized feet in their shiny black shoes and tried to run away.

I didn't let her. She'd taken about two steps when I lunged, leaping the last few feet to grab her by the throat. Whatever she was stuffed with was soft, but only gave a little, and I could hear her yelping and feel her arms thrash as I swung my head and my whole upper body back and forth and then flung her way up into the air.

This body, delicious as it was, was too clumsy to escape me. She must have realized that. As she fell she was already changing, and when she hit a rooftop with a grunt of pain she got up as something new. I didn't know what it was. It was the size of a large cat, but skinny and its arms were wings. She was still made out of sewn up white cloth, and eyes made of pink beads peered nervously down at me. There was something delicate and graceful about her, too. Something that was still feminine.

She looked delicious.

This body would be much better at running away, and I didn't want to give her time. I jumped up and grabbing onto an overhang that stretched out in front of a nearby building, impressed myself by jumping from there to the top of a sign, and used that as the stepping stone to launch myself at Self-Loathing, open jaws leading.

I got a blurred glimpse of panicky pink eyes, heard a high pitched whimper that could have been fear or anticipation, and I wasn't sure if she knew the difference. My teeth closed on nothing. She had thrown herself off the top of the building, glided down to the street, and was racing along it on skinny stick legs, sometimes hopping into the air and fluttering and swooping ahead to gain some distance.

She wasn't fast enough. I jumped heavily off the roof and was running when I hit the street, my whole body bending as I raced after her as fast as I could. Or rather, not quite as fast as I could. The chase was my specialty, and when I saw that twisty girlish body sprinting away from me I wanted to catch it as soon as I could. That meant running just a little slower. Then when I got close I put on burst of extra speed, startling her into taking off on those brand new wings—right beside a long, uneven palette of crates. I didn't know why they were there, and I didn't care. I sprinted up them like stairs and as I jumped off she flew right into my teeth.

This body was small and my fangs went all the way through it, a thrill that had most of the street staring at the noises we made as I chewed and shook her, then threw her down onto the bricks so I could pin her down and rip. But when I did she sprung back up again, getting bigger until a liquid silver gazelle gamboled away, the single spiraling horn in its forehead gleaming as she looked back at me.

I think it was about that point when we both started laughing and didn't stop.

I was still laughing, although raggedly and out of breath, when I came barreling out of a side street, twisting around to face the way I knew Self-Loathing would be coming. She was there and had changed shape yet again. I'd lost count of how many girls she'd turned into only to be caught. She was back to the form I had found her in, the doll of a young woman in a frilly dress. Maybe all that had changed was that she moved differently now, rocking forward and back on her tiny feet, bending in a way that hinted much better at the slender, vulnerable curves the dress was hiding.

She wasn't running, or waiting to be caught. She was staring up at a signpost. At least, someone had put up some sort of signpost and the dream painters had come along and covered it with a mural instead. I thought they tended to blur and distort their images to give an impression rather than what had happened, but the black dog poised in mid-air was unmistakable, and the red mask in his mouth was a demon's face. They'd decided to paint my fight.

I was kind of worried Self-Loathing would have another fit, but that pose was only flirty, and when I padded up to look at the picture myself she reached out and pulled my head away from it. Instead she started walking, although there was something more like a skip in her gait. I didn't know how she had the energy. I was all but exhausted. I wasn't sure she had a choice, granted. Walking in those hard shoes and tiny feet must have been its own special challenge.

"Did you know what Nick could have done to you when you defended me, Fang?" she asked, a question that made it clear that we weren't going to forget about the painting after all. She didn't sound mad or hysterical, thankfully.

"I saw him take out Lucy once," I admitted cautiously. I shivered at the memory of blades leaping out of a wall. Yes, it was entirely too easy to imagine that happening to me. "That was probably the tip of the iceberg. But that was why I did it. He couldn't have beaten Lucy in a fair fight, and I couldn't have beaten him. So I made it an unfair fight. Everybody's got their weaknesses."

"He's not going to be happy that everyone knows," she continued pensively, "He'll have to change how he looks now. He's very proud, and he might want revenge. Or he might not. Demons are crazy, angels are crazier, and demons that think they're angels are the craziest."

If he snuck up on me, I was dead. I swallowed that thought and realized that Self-Loathing's hand was on my neck, remarkably human in its shape and delicacy even though I could feel how it was made of padding. She kept sliding it up and down my shoulders, pushing up my collar at the top. We still weren't fighting over this.

"I'm not going to back down from protecting you. You're my friend," I told her, and then added a lot less firmly, "I hope you're right that he might let it drop."

"Maybe," she commented distantly, "He might like that you were able to defeat someone stronger than you, since that's how he views himself. Or he might resent that a mere nightmare was able to show him up. No one in the Dark is a nice person, and the fallen angels really are crazy. I worry sometimes that you seem to think Lily is your friend."

"She is my friend," I insisted immediately, "She wouldn't hurt me. Maybe other people, I don't know. But not me."

"She wouldn't hurt you much," Self-Loathing added mournfully, staring down at me as we walked, "But she'll tease you cruelly when she's in the mood, and play games with you that you can't win, and she'll lie. You should stay away from her, and you should stay away from me. I'll do all those things to you worse than she ever will."

So that's where this was going. I jerked my head around and grabbed her wrist in my teeth, but I only bit down lightly. Instead I licked her captured fabric skin over and over as I met her gaze affectionately.

It seemed to work. Her stitched mouth smiled again. And I noticed something over her shoulder.

"Is every painting about me today?" I demanded, annoyed and embarrassed.

Self-Loathing looked back, rubbing her freed wrist, and giggled again. The Dream Painters had decided that a huge pile of random junk was worth their attention, and after coating it in some grey sludge they'd painted a dark forest scene on it. They weren't done, but all it really took to identify me was my head and my teeth, and I vividly remembered this dream and always would.

"It's not about you, it's about her," Self-Loathing answered. She meant Coy, the vixen in silver scales and tassels just a step out of my reach. While we watched, the painters started on the dreamer, standing in the back and watching us with awe.

"She deserves the recognition," I admitted, "The Dark's never seen anything like her."

"Sometimes I think I can read you better than you know yourself, Fang," she responded, her tone suddenly playful and her smile getting wider. "You want to do that again right now, don't you? Without both of you together, this dream didn't happen."

I was going to learn to blush at this rate, but it was easy to push aside that feeling. I was more worried she'd explode again. Instead she seemed calm and friendlier than ever. "I want to be with you, too. I want a lot of things," I answered her, and I meant it.

She was looking at the painting. I thought the dream painters had exaggerated things. I was sure I hadn't looked that feral and savage in the dream. I hadn't been trying for that at all.

"These paintings are going to be seen by everyone, and there are probably more of them. You're getting a reputation of your own, Fang." The smile she suddenly turned on me was… admiring. My hind legs nearly fell out from under me again. Why would someone like the ancient and beautiful Demiurge of Self-Loathing look at me like that? Then I looked over at the painting. Well, for that maybe I deserved it. And I'd beaten that demon unfairly, but in a way that had been the contest and I'd still won.

Since I didn't know what to say, she continued, "Go on, Fang. You've spent a lot of time with me already tonight. It wouldn't be fair for me to ask any more. If you can go find her and keep this up, there won't be anyone in the Dark who hasn't heard of you. I'd like to see that."

"I still don't—" I started to say, but I could see the look in her eyes. Firm, but not angry. She meant it. At least, that was everything I could read. It was stealing over me again that she was going to keep surprising me for as long as I knew her.

"Go on. It's what you want, I can tell," she urged me. It was almost a command. "We've had our fun, and I feel almost alive again."

"If you're sure," I repeated. There was absolutely no way I was going to let her feel like I was abandoning her, but I could only take her at her word, couldn't I?

"I need to be alone anyway. You've given me a lot to think about," she answered, her tone getting rather distant.

I gave her something else to think about. I grabbed her through that dress, bit down hard on something soft underneath it. Then while she was still squealing I let go again and turned around and trotted away, tail wagging.

But as soon as I knew I was out of sight I started to run, and all I could think about was Coy.

I hardly had to start looking for Coy's trail. I just knew where she was. I'd never been able to track someone so easily who I'd known so briefly, but running a dream with her had been pretty intense. So intense that every muscle felt charged as I ran flat out for the border.

In the distance I saw a dream pop, and instead of leaving behind a haze it left a few mirrors standing on their own where it had been. Seconds later a new mirror sprung up a few feet away, and in a blur mirrors burst out of the ground everywhere, of all sizes and shapes. Most were full length and clumped together to form short walls, so I found myself in a haphazard maze surrounded by reflections of myself on every side. Distorted reflections, not bent like a funhouse, but showing me leaping at the glass or covered in particolor scales, or… well, every one was different. Even before I saw the black and silver fish swimming up into the air from the center I knew who was responsible for this.

Fortunately, it wasn't much of a maze. Even when a particularly long wall got in my way I'd just bend a mirror back and run over it, or knock one down. Toward the center I ran through faint streamers of mist in weird colors that must have been from the dream, but they felt refreshing, like a pleasant mist of ice rather than grippingly cold. When I saw a mirror that was embedded in a large, wardrobe-like cabinet I jumped up on top of it so that I could grin up at the hovering goldfish.

"I guess you don't need my help after all," I told her excitedly, and tucked my tail underneath myself before it could embarrass me.

"This is the first time I've gotten something like this as a nightmare!" she corrected me. Scales streamed off of her so that she could drift over to me as mostly a girl. "I'm really proud of the dreams I'm making here, but I got lucky this time. This dreamer must have had some weird self-image issues. They had practically no shape, but when I started peeking out of mirrors the dream took off. The weird thing was, he—or she, or whatever—was still scared. You can tell we're still in the Dark. I think I've done something for that person, but I haven't a clue what."

She was babbling at me in excitement, and I had to sit on my tail really hard to not pick it up from her. I wanted to hear more. "But you've gotten this to happen in the light?" I pressed.

"Oh, sure," she gushed, "But that's different. Over there I knew what I was doing, and it was still pretty rare. You can't tell me you haven't gotten a dream to hatch yourself, can you? I wouldn't believe that."

"A couple of times," I admitted. "Not much." I was melting under the look in those eyes. It was the same look Self-Loathing had given me. Had I really become someone worth admiring? When did that happen? I just knew she was going to ask me for the details, and I suddenly wanted to change the subject before she found out just how really few times I'd done it. And then I suddenly wanted to change the subject because I had something I really wanted to ask.

"If it's not rude, Coy—why did you come to the Dark anyway? Was it for me? It would be really hard for me to move to the Light, and I'd have to think a whole lot of someone to—" I broke off wending my way haphazardly through that question when Coy started to laugh, light and bubbly and happy.

"You sound so scared!" she told me, and there was that hint of teasing almost buried under her affectionate smile. "Are you worried I'm in love with you?"

A moment later she added offhandedly, "Well, maybe a little." She said it like it just didn't matter. "You're the first nightmare I really met, and I couldn't stop thinking about you. The way you chased me wasn't what I was expecting at all. It wasn't mean, you know?"

I didn't know. "Uh... no. I don't understand," I informed her, feeling a little guilty about it.

That just seemed to make her smile more widely. "No, you don't, right?" she enthused and started to circle around me, still a girl but with her scales and tassels whirling close around her. "It's just natural to you. That's what I saw. It made me wonder if maybe there wasn't much difference between the Light and the Dark after all, and what it would be like to be me and inspire dreamers my way, but do it as a nightmare."

"And you just changed, just like that?" I asked disbelievingly, staring at her. The Light hated me. I could feel it the moment I stepped into it.

"Close," she confirmed, sliding up to grin at me face to face, "It was easier than I expected. It was just attitude. I had to change my colors to make myself even a little scary, but once I went into a dream and didn't try and pull it into the Light but just accepted it—that seemed to do it. Now I'm fine."

"Wow," I answered. I felt a little stupid saying it, but that word summed up everything I felt about her at that moment. And then the itch hit me again. "Do you want to do another dream together?" I asked in a hurry. My tail had slipped out, and started thumping on top of the cabinet.

"Oh, would I!" she burst out just as fast. Neither of us realized we were leaning forward until our noses bumped. It hadn't meant anything, but we still pulled back in an awkward hurry. "Do you have any ideas?" she covered.

"A few," I conceded. A few? I was drowning in them. I wondered if we could get a dreamer to try and rescue Coy from me, and what that would be like?

"Too bad," she shot back gleefully, "We're doing mine first. Come on! Let's find a dream! Fresh ones are best."

So she swam off, scales closing around her, and I leapt from mirror to mirror for the fun of it until we were clear of the little landscape she'd inspired and running through the emptiness beyond. I might have shouted something when we saw a dream sparkle and close up. It was a good distance from the border and getting anything but fear out of this dream would be challenging, but we plunged into it anyway.

Inside, the dream was already taking shape. The dreamer was a well-defined young man in another forest. The trees were sparse, but the forest dim. Too many spider webs, too many little noises, and he was walking fast only to be brought up short by a wide, dark pool. Ripples rolled across its surface.

Coy had disappeared, and I tried to lurk in the background, lying still, just another dark shape and another sense of dread in a dream full of both. The ripples had been the dreamer's imagination, but it was Coy who rose from the water. I knew she was Coy. She looked like a human woman, but much more curvy than her usual shape, with very long hair and pointed ears and an inviting smile. She wore nothing over her body of liquid silver, but I was no expert on human nudity. I knew she was beautiful like the fox she'd been before.

The dreamer liked it. He stepped forward, reaching out a hand to her, but the moment he took hold of her arm she twisted and mewled at him in wordless anger. Yanking her arm out of his grip, she turned and ran, skipping over the surface of the water.

That had to be my cue. I leaped to my feet and rushed over to the dreamer. I paused beside him, staring after Coy and growling softly. Then I launched myself forward, racing around the edge of the pool to chase after her.

We ran, and although it took him a minute, the dream worked. The dream shifted, and the dreamer caught up in an instant, running by my side as we followed Coy through the threatening forest. I lagged behind, letting him lead by a pace. This was his hunger and his chase now, but I ran next to him as the beast he was thinking like, and when Coy swerved aside or ducked behind cover a couple of times it was I who changed course and flushed her out again.

The dream looped and looped, letting us run on and on until we suddenly hit another pool. This one was wider, more rocky, with a little waterfall. Coy ran across it, but her feet sank into the water about an inch and stuck. I thought it was her choice rather than the dreamer's, but she turned back to watch us close in with a very convincing expression of innocent fear.

We reached the bank. The dreamer's arms were out and he pulled Coy off her feet, dragging her into his arms. This wasn't a good dream, and we weren't going to let it drift that way. Coy struggled and whined, but he kissed her—and then her body went even more fluid and limber, she reared back with fangs in her mouth and lunged forward to bite him like a snake.

We were left in the drifting clouds of a broken dream, dark but threaded with colors. I could feel the hunger of it clinging to me, the playfulness, the fear and the cruelty. There was something else, too.

I couldn't help myself. I started laughing and told Coy, "That was something, wasn't it?"

Coy's arms were around me before I knew it, and she kissed my cheek. She'd gone back to being a girl again, or at least a black and white painting in the shape of one. I stood there, then protested weakly, "I thought you weren't in love with me?"

"No, I said I was," she corrected me, "But not much. And I meant that, too." She hovered close to me, sitting on nothing, and laid one arm over my back to toy with my fur. "I can't believe a little crush frightens you. I'm sure you like me back."

"I have a girlfriend," I pointed out, and I couldn't believe how desperate that sounded, like an excuse rather than a reason.

"So?" she replied easily. She wasn't bothered at all, and somehow that made me start to relax. "I don't want to take you away from her. We don't like each other that much. I should have known you don't get a lot of friendly kisses on this side of the border, huh?"

I certainly didn't. I lifted a hand to my cheek where I could still feel the kiss, and there was a faint oiliness of paint there. "You rubbed off on me," I observed, and just didn't know how I felt about that at all.

"In a friendly way," she assured me, almost smugly, "Maybe I just felt I wanted to mark you, leave a piece of me with you so you can remember how we feel right now. How do you feel, anyway?"

She knew the answer to that, and I remembered Lily's advice and embraced that feeling. "Like I want to do another dream!" I barked.

We were both on our feet again, although hers didn't touch the ground. "There's one!" I pointed out and rushed eagerly forward. Scales and streamers, black and silver, swirled together to form a gleaming fish that swam shoulder to fin with me as we raced for the pearly black bubble near the edge.

"This one looks a little weird," she commented, "Let's see what's inside!"

It did look weird. It was too solid and opaque to be this close to the Light, and streaked with all sorts of colors. I wondered what it was going to look like inside and sped up, throwing myself against the surface because it was going to take some force to get inside.

Instead it tore, resisting only an instant before coming apart in tatters around me. I hit the ground and rolled, confused, and then a foot came down on my neck.

I tried to push against it. I might as well have been trying to shift the Gate. The foot was tiny but chokingly heavy and strong, and as I bent my head up and rolled my eyes back I knew what I was going to see. Pinning me down was a human child, a little girl with long coppery pigtails and a hyperactive grin wearing ludicrous pajamas with ducks and rabbits on them.

"Dark, it's Lucy!" I shouted as best I could, "Coy, run! Run, please!"

But Coy just floated a little ways away amidst the ruins of the fake dream. I couldn't help but notice that her fish body glittered and her fins were long and trailing and billowed around her. I just wished she looked afraid. "Why?" she asked in a baffled tone, "It's just a lucid dreamer. I like getting to talk to a human sometimes."

"I'll explain later, just run, please! Do it for me!" I begged. I could feel tears stinging my eyes, and I felt strangely guilty about lying to her. I wasn't going to explain later. I was going to be dead.

Coy hesitated another moment. She was obviously nervous, but she trusted me and she spun around to swim away. Too late. Lucy drew a pin out of her hair and threw, but what slammed into Coy was a barbed metal harpoon. Coy yelled in pain and collapsed to the ground.

There was no blood. That was how I knew it was serious, not drama. And if it hadn't been serious, the chain running from the spear to Lucy's fist meant Coy wasn't getting away.

"You're just the monster I was hoping to catch," Lucy told me gleefully, "I wasn't sure how to track you down, and now I don't have to. You know there are pictures of you all over the Dark these last few nights? When I saw those, you went right to the top of my list."

I stared up at her upside down face, and I could hear my heart pounding. "Let me up and I'll kill you instead," I snapped back at her, trying to sound fierce even though I felt terrified. "You might as well let the fish go. She's from the Light. She's a fantasy, not a nightmare, and she's not on your list."

Lucy's foot ground down harder. I wheezed, but I was watching Coy. Watching her flopping and gasping, only able to make little whimpering noises. And looking at me.

Lucy had noticed. Tears started to fall, one after the other from my eyes as she regarded Coy's struggles. "You say that, but it looks like you've gotten to her," Lucy told me with relish, "And she's gotten to you. That you're able to care about someone else makes this even better."

I struggled, legs scraping underneath me, my body twisting. It was agonizing, but if I could stop needing to breathe—it was still useless. A dreamer was precisely as strong as she believed herself to be. Lucy was a mountain.

And she giggled, watching me fight. "Do you know what it's like having a nightmare, wolf?" Lucy asked me playfully. When I just growled back, she answered herself. "Imagine your life is nothing but pain and fear and you can't wake up and you're sure it will never stop. That's all you can think about, pain and fear. It pushes out everything else and there's no way out."

Her hands moved again. Another spear plunged through Coy, pinning her into the ground. We both tried to yell in pain, but what came out were only strangled gurgles.

"This is great!" Lucy told me lustily, "I'm just going to let you go. Maybe you'll learn your lesson, or maybe I'll catch up with you later. But from now on all you can do is suffer and remember that you deserved this."

I wanted to close my eyes. Instead I watched her yank the first harpoon back into her hand by its chain. As she lifted it, it became a hammer—big, impossibly huge, and it slammed down on top of Coy. When the hammer lifted again there were just scales and bits of streamer. They evaporated as I watched.

Lucy's foot pushed down tighter still, until I couldn't breathe at all. She leaned over me, explaining briskly, "Don't worry. You definitely have to die, so you won't have to live with this forever. Next time I catch you, I'll have found out whether it's even possible to make a nightmare feel guilt."

Straightening up, she stretched out her arms, one holding the hammer which shrank back into a sadistically barbed harpoon. She announced, "I think I can wake up now. It's been a good night."

The weight on my neck disappeared as Lucy popped like a bad dream. I pushed myself to my feet, which was difficult only because my legs felt so weak. Coy was just gone. There was the other spear, driven right into the featureless ground that is most of the Dark, but that was all.

I rushed over to the spot and planted my nose against it. The trail isn't really smell, but it helps, and I latched onto the Coy I knew in my head and started to track her.

I was immediately aware of the smudge of her lip paint on my cheek, and that was it. It wasn't just that I couldn't find her, there was no Coy to track. There was no Coy. There was no Coy anywhere. Coy didn't exist.

I started running. I could hardly feel my body move, but I sped like the wind over the blank groundscape. Up ahead I saw a bad dream, dark and glistening. I kept running until I drove myself right into it, and I had a confused impression of bones and rotting, grasping things. What I saw was the dreamer, a human not quite grown. I didn't give him time to run and be chased. I just leapt up and grabbed his throat in my teeth and tore it out, and the dream convulsed and came apart.

I could just barely see another dream off to the side. I started running.

I ripped another chunk of out a dreamer's chest. This one was particularly stubborn. A bite or two, once a limb came off or they thought they should be dead—that woke most of them up. This one lingered, and I tore and tore and tore, but he wouldn't die. Each piece I pulled off with my teeth made the dream clench with pain, but there was no blood or gore, just unidentifiable chunks as if the dreamer was made of plastic. I'd stopped caring if dreamers or their dreams made sense. Eating his face made the difference. When I bit down on that he finally let go and woke up.

The fog left behind by this dream was an acrid and nearly solid mass, pain without reason or mercy. I didn't care how much of it got on me. What I cared about was that I was standing around and there were more dreams out there. I sprang forward out of the cloud, and Jeffery grabbed me.

He and Lily were just there, waiting for me, and I'd jumped right into his arms by accident. I twisted, but his grip locked down, wrapped around my shoulders, looped around one of my forelegs. I started to thrash, but he was as strong as I'd always suspected he would be. That barely adolescent body with its innocently handsome face and short gold hair hid the power of a nightmare who'd gorged on fear I couldn't imagine, and he knew just how to hold me where I couldn't get leverage. I jerked and wrestled with him anyway, and we lurched and staggered, but I couldn't quite throw him off.

He was yelling something. "Fang! Fang, wake up! Talk to me, Fang. Are you listening?" I yowled back and threw myself from side to side violently, but I just couldn't get free of him.

"He's faded so far, Jeff," Lily told him in a tiny voice, "I don't think he can understand us. Did you see what was inside that dream?"

"He's not faded at all," Jeffery wheezed back, "He just wishes he was."

I screamed as loud as I could, a noise that wasn't animal or human or anything specific, and dug clawed fingers into the blighted, ashy earth that dream had left behind. I couldn't get Jeffery off of me, so I started dragging him forward. He hardly weighed anything, but he could dig in as strongly as I could.

"We know Coy is dead, Fang," I heard Lily say.

Coy was dead. I stopped fighting, stood there on four splayed legs, and I whined as I panted for breath.

"Lucy did it," I husked, then started babbling. "I can't kill her for it. I can't do anything to her. Nobody can do anything to her. The worst you can do is wake her up, and she just comes right back. She can do anything she wants, and she just decided to kill Coy on a whim."

"Fang…" Lily whispered. I thought her hand was on my head, but I was shaking and wasn't sure.

"You're right," Jeffery told me, his voice hard and barren. "Lucy kills all of us in the end. She's going to kill you one day, and she'll kill me if I give her time. We know that, and we've always known that, and you thought it was better to be a good nightmare than a safe one. It's not any different because it was Coy."

"Coy didn't know!" I shouted. Then something inside me gave up, and I fell on my belly and put my hands over my head. Jeffery had already let me go. "But you're right. Lucy is Lucy. Coy didn't know what could happen, and I led her right to Lucy. I made her a target. I killed Coy. Jeffery, I killed Coy, I killed her!"

It was Lily who crouched down beside me. It was her hand on

my shoulder, and her gentle voice asking, "Is this the first time you've lost someone, puppy?"

"I've never had anybody to lose," I answered sharply. I was sniffling and sobbing pathetically, and I didn't care because I didn't need my pride anymore.

"What do you think Jeffery would do if Lucy had killed you too?" Lily went on calmly.

"I would move on," Jeffery answered for me, "I have things I need to accomplish."

I could hear the faint raggedness, the stiffness in his reply. He was lying. That made muscles that were locked up tight in me go limp.

"I don't want to be mean about this, puppy," Lily informed me, her hand stroking my neck while her voice became more firm, "But unlike you two I know what it's like to see a friend die and to lose something you didn't think you could live without. You knew that, right?"

I knew it. I hadn't thought about it. I hadn't wanted to think about it, because when I started to I knew that she might have had to endure what I had just gone through more times than I could count. "How do you go on?" I asked desperately.

"By going on," she told me plainly. Her voice was even, and her cherry red lips and eyebrows were flat. She looked almost emotionless. This was fact, not reassurance. "By not living in what I've lost, and living for what I still have and what I'll have in the future."

No, she was too emotionless. She was lying, too. She was just better at covering for it than Jeffery was.

As wobbly as I was, I pushed myself to my feet. "That doesn't make me feel any better," I told her emptily.

"But you're moving forward again," was her reply.

So I did. I padded off into the Dark. I still had Jeffery and Lily, and I was going to find the other things I hadn't lost.

There was one thing that was supposed to keep me alive, that I was supposed to value more than anything or anyone else. I hadn't thought about her once until now. The house was nearby, and for the first time I caught it when it wasn't stopped somewhere scenic. It drifted, throwing up ripples around it as if the surface of the Dark were a pond.

I crawled up the stairs and padded inside, dragging my feet. I felt as heavy as an elephant, and the hallway around me looked decrepit and lifeless. No eyes watched me pass. The parlor was at the end of the hall at the back of the house where it ought to have been. Where it never was.

My Muse might have been asleep. No, she didn't sleep, but I couldn't hear her sobbing and her breathing was regular and only faintly ragged. Her hands still cupped her face, and between her fingers leaked tears, slowly and one by one but never stopping.

There were tears in my eyes, too. "You're so beautiful," I burst out, "You're so perfect. I don't appreciate you enough. I could have tried—"

I stopped, and I didn't know what to say or what I'd been trying to say, but I wanted to say something. So I screamed as loudly as I could, angry and roaring, and I threw myself against the wall and bashed it with my shoulder. Then I knocked down a credenza, which shattered from how hard I'd battered it, and I charged another wall and let my body strike it sidelong, and then again.

It had hurt, which meant I must have been trying to hurt myself, not the room. No, never that. The room was part of her. Panting, I staggered over to the chair I had been careful not to touch and nearly collapsed against it. My head fell into my Muse's lap, covering it—I'd made myself big again during my rampage. And I cried, not loudly, but I couldn't stop the tears.

"I'm sorry," I told her, and I could hear the whine in my voice. "I love you, and not anyone else. I know that. I never doubt it, not really. So why do I hurt for other people, but never for you?"

Of course, nothing happened. I just lay there, studying the laces tying her dress tight in the front. Some had snapped, but underneath was more white silk. Little ruffles had been embroidered everywhere, most of them in a deep burgundy, and the moth holes were so numerous that some went through several layers to show pale, greenish skin underneath. And she was thin, like someone who didn't eat quite enough. Everything about her said that she was cast off and ignored and left to rot, even by herself. Even by me.

I could feel my heart stirring in my chest, even though it hurt to think about anyone being so perfect. Every detail of her was part of the whole. When a dreamer saw that she had no eyes, what did they think? Did they see their own crimes? And then I finally noticed the smell.

Flowers. I could smell flowers, light and sweet and intoxicating. Not a strong scent, but I had a good sense of smell. I had been smelling this since I walked in the front door and hadn't realized it, but it had been getting stronger the whole time. Now I lay at her feet with my head in her lap, and I breathed deeply the familiar scent of strange blossoms with teeth and eyes I'd torn from a newly born nightmare. My Muse didn't move, but at some level, in some way she knew I was there, and no matter what I had done this was how she felt when I was near.

"What's your name?" I asked her softly. She didn't answer. She never had. But after a while I rose carefully up to my feet and walked out of the house, more slowly but with a lighter step than when I'd entered. That was love, without reason or understanding or blame. When we were together, we had been a little more whole.

We had made each other feel like we deserved to live. Now I needed to visit someone who would let me feel that I was alive already, and remind me that everything could be sharp and vivid.

I was more than a little hesitant setting foot back in the city around the Gate. I expected the buildings and the noise and the presence of other people to be oppressive, but they weren't. That was good, because it took me a while to find Self-Loathing. Her trail was faint, and I kept wandering off it before realizing I was going in the wrong direction and turning around.

I was getting close, and the trail was getting stronger. I galloped down what I was sure was the right street. Ahead I could see the dangling red sign of Self-Loathing's salon, but when I saw what was across from it I ground to a halt and nearly tripped over my front feet.

An empty lot had positioned itself there, which was not terribly uncommon, but the dream painters had been to work. They had covered every square foot of it with one painting and in the center, painted in glistening silver and black strokes, was a goldfish impaled and stuck to the ground with a spear. A mallet was thundering down over her an inch from making contact, and off to the side Lucy wielded it in both hands. My head was just visible at the edge of the painting, pinned by Lucy's foot, and more than anything else I was struck by how Coy's eyes and mine were fixed on each other.

A few locals were standing around and staring at this recording of Lucy's latest murder. Their expressions were grim, but that was all I really noticed about them. Only one caught my eye.

Self-Loathing was kneeling in front of the painted Coy, rocking forward and back and mumbling to herself. She rarely copied an old body, but I'd seen this one before—the little human child with the black hair and dark skin, almost a parody of Lucy herself.

She looked more and more wrong as I crept up on her. There was no shine to her hair, or subtleties to her skin. She looked like plastic, or plaster, anything but flesh. In one hand she held a crude parody of a straight razor, with a blade made out of chipped stone badly tied to a rough wooden handle. She kept cutting her opposite wrist with it. As soon as something dark and colorful would start to ooze out the cut would close, and over and over she whispered, "Why? She was so easy to kill. Why doesn't it work on me?"

I reached out and touched her hair with one hand. When I did some of it fell off, brittle and hard, and shattered into dust when it hit the pavement. This was what fading looked like. She was becoming a parody of herself, until there wasn't enough person left to remain alive. Maybe as a Demiurge she couldn't crumble or evaporate enough to

Sweet Dreams are Made of Teeth

die, or maybe she could. Soon it wouldn't matter. A jabbering statue with no thoughts was dead as far as I was concerned.

I grabbed her shoulder and shook her. More bits came off and she gave under my claws, but getting her attention was all that was important. "Self-Loathing? Self-Loathing, it's Fang. I'm here, I came back. Can you wake up?"

When Jeffery did this to me, I hadn't wanted to listen. There didn't seem to be anyone to hear, now. "Why? Why why why why? Why isn't this easy?" she whispered. It gave me a little hope. They weren't exactly the same words. That suggested there was something left. How long had I been gone, punishing dreamers? How long had she been this way?

I had known that just words wouldn't work. I tried something more direct. I bit her again, and since she was kneeling I locked my teeth around most of her throat and shoulder and bit down fast and hard. It was affection and desperation and I drew blood, and when I did I yanked my head away and retched.

It was foul. No, it wasn't merely bitter or bad tasting. It was rancid and unclean and festering and congealed. My stomach kept heaving, and if I ate anything I would have thrown it up. By the time I got myself back under control, I knew it hadn't worked. She just kept mumbling and cutting herself. The bite hadn't healed, but it was merely a new wound in a body already disintegrating.

I couldn't stand to watch it. I threw my arms around her shoulders, engulfing that little body, and squeezed her to me. My face pressed to hers and I grabbed her wrist in one hand, holding the knife away so she couldn't cut herself any more. It was useless, but there hadn't been any plan to it.

"Are you going to leave me, too? I don't want to lose you," I whimpered.

Her whole body sagged, and in surprise I let her go as she fell sprawling onto her back. The knife just rolled away. "How can you say that?" she whispered up to me in bleary disbelief.

All I felt was relief. I'd shocked her back into thinking. Now I just had to keep her from falling back into whatever spiral of blame and suicide she'd been mired in.

"I don't want to lose you," I repeated stubbornly, dropping back onto all fours and leaning my head down to rub my muzzle against her shoulder. It should have been her chest, but a wet stain blackened the middle of her makeshift smock. Even faint, that diseased smell was so sickening I couldn't make myself touch her blood again. "I don't know what you are to me, but it's something I can't give up."

"How can you say that?" she demanded hoarsely, "I murdered her. I sent you out to her because you were making her a target. I was willing to take the chance you'd die too rather than let her have you."

She pushed my muzzle away with one hand, but while she was stronger than I expected I didn't let her push it far. "I don't believe that," I told her bluntly.

"Fang, look at yourself," she snapped back impatiently, "You're in agony. I did this to you. I did this to her. That wasn't an accident, it was deliberate. You have to hate me for this. You don't have any choice!"

"I don't believe it," I repeated. I had to sound firm, because she could make herself sound absolutely sincere. "The worse something is, the faster you are to think it's your fault. Do you think I don't know how to do that too? You're lying to yourself more than to me, and I don't believe it. There's nothing you could say that would convince me it's true."

She just gaped at me. The smell kept getting stronger, and I was ready to think it was deliberate, some attempt to scare me away. It didn't work, and I had an instant to wonder if that's why she changed tactics and disappeared.

She didn't actually vanish, but that's what it seemed like until I spotted the dull grey-brown sparrow speeding away and over the opposite roof. She'd changed shape in the blink of an eye and run away from me. It was better than fading, but I had no intention of letting her run and hide, maybe to never come back and face that it wasn't her fault.

I planted my nose against the pavement, trying to ignore that horrible mural, and followed Self-Loathing's trail. At least, I tried to follow it. There were hints. I knew she was somewhere, and felt a suspicion that she was moving deeper into the city rather than heading away, but that was all.

There was no point in complaining that I'd never heard of anyone who could disguise their own trail. She could change shape more freely and easily than anyone else I knew of. She'd hidden her trail and might be able to do a dozen other things I wasn't aware of. She wasn't a nightmare, and the same rules didn't apply. I was just lucky I knew her so intimately, or I might not have even had this vague sense of presence and direction.

This wasn't going to lead me to her. But the chase was everything I was. I knew how to hunt.

Which meant that a few minutes later I was padding up to a place I normally avoided. Above me loomed the Gate itself, and I stepped out of the city streets and into the jumble of bones and debris that formed the low hill it sat on. The Gate was enormous, towering over the city itself, made of dull, dark metal and set in a massive frame of stone. Everything was carved with gargoyles and occult looking sigils and broken sections of inscription. Most importantly, the Gate was closed.

It was always closed. I didn't know what it took to open it. Demons got in and out through a smaller door set into the base of the main one. It was little and cramped, and guarded on either side by solid black angels with intricate, fiery pentacle halos and blades that burned with black fire. If the other demons let them look that much like angels, they were probably even tougher than they appeared.

Passage in and out of the little door was slow, and there was a line waiting to get in. The demons standing in it watched me suspiciously, and each other, and the angelic guards who watched us back. I wasn't welcome this close to the Gate, but they hadn't decided to stop me yet.

I looked at the line, but I hardly had to. The crowned and multi-headed serpent, the elegantly muscled goat man, the woman with metal spikes stabbing into and out of her skin—I dismissed all of them at a glance. What I charged up to was the bent remnant of an angel whose wings weren't so much mutilated as gangly and half plucked. One tiny, shriveled arm hung limply, and the other arm was as long as the rest of the body. The face twisted like half-melted wax.

I planted myself right in front of Self-Loathing and told her, "No demon would choose to look that pathetic. They'd wear a disguise."

"Get out of my way, nightmare. I don't know what you're talking about," she answered in a gravelly voice but with a halting, unsure tone that clinched my certainty.

"Is this the only way you can kill yourself quickly?" I asked, "Even a Demiurge doesn't come back if they pass through the Gate."

I didn't get a chance to tell her that I wouldn't let her. I could see it all in her expression of shock. I'd read everything right, and she knew it. Which was probably why she shrank so fast I barely caught it even though I was watching, and something like a long-legged rat scurried away through the refuse.

I chased after it. She was still hiding herself from me, but it wasn't working as well. I had a general idea which direction she was in and I stormed after her as fast as I could safely go. I'd have run faster, but this was about finding her, not outrunning her, especially as my knowledge of where she was got more and more vague. She was hiding herself better again, but she'd stopped moving and I knew she was close.

Now the problem was that I wasn't sure where I was. I'd ended up in a part of town I never went to. There were still shops, but there were more weird brass domes or cubes with no obvious features or entrances, and things like that. I couldn't figure out what any of the buildings were. Passersby were few, and none of them were anything I was sure was a nightmare. One looked so human I thought he was a lucid dreamer, but he was slightly transparent and being carried by a hulking, tiny-headed brute with no face. One of the things I had to step out of the way of looked like a rolling ball of something that fell between flesh and meat and had too many eyes and tentacles. None of them looked like Self-Loathing in disguise, and that was the important thing.

She was close, though. I knew her too well. Everything about her was familiar, and that trail told me she was here. Somewhere. Generally.

There was only one building nearby I clearly recognized a door to, so I pushed it open and ducked inside to make a quick check. A quick check became a long stare. I was in a shop, but there was no merchandise. Instead there were big, round mirrors spaced haphazardly on walls, floor, and ceiling. Each one had trim so complicated it was either geometry or occult. I didn't know anything about either, or care.

There was only one being in the room that I could see, but Self-Loathing could make herself small and I wasn't sure how small. This thing seemed to grow out of the ceiling like a tree, made out of dozens of long greenish-grey tendrils that coiled around each other to make a vague humanoid shape. It hung in the middle of a circular desk, and as I padded up cautiously some of the tentacles reached out to fiddle with the shapes around the edge of a mirror set into that desk.

The mirror lit up. Inside it was a city street out of a dream. Except it wasn't a dream. I'd never seen a dream like this. Everything was detailed, every brick had grain, every piece of paper crumpled in a gutter was different, every letter was readable. No one could dream this way, and the cars that sped past and the occasional human walking by were all just as precise. No one was the focus of this scene.

"What is that?" I asked, everything else forgotten for a moment in my bafflement.

Three tentacles dipped down below the counter and pulled up an old silver plate. A face had been drawn on it crudely, and it spoke. "Reality. Nightmare? Rare, never customers. Don't care. Windows to: Particulate world. Nightmares think of as waking world." Its voice skipped around, always harsh or a little screechy.

"You can see into the waking world?" I asked in shock.

"Yes," it answered emotionlessly, "Important to some. Aetherics. Negative possibilities. Exiled naturals. Never nightmares. Not important to nightmares."

No, I suppose it wasn't. To Jeffery, maybe. He studied humans as if they were holding the secret to the perfect dream. Still, it was enthralling. Every human there dreamed, every night. They were all people with lives as complicated as Lily's or Self-Loathing's. Maybe my Muse had started out as one of those.

"It's amazing, but why would the human world be important to anyone?" I asked breathlessly.

I could hear a faint touch of emotion in the thing's voice now. Pity, maybe. "To nightmares, no. Aetherics, humans very important. Want to touch them, hard to do from dreamlands. Others, particulate reality: Important. Rules not same. To be there, we are different than to be here. Gates very rare now. Not allowed, hard to make. But many always watching."

I looked up at the plate. It was hardly a face, just a few lines that moved, drawn on with black marker, maybe. "Then what are you?" I asked it.

A tentacle waved at the door. "Sign outside: Scryer. Dreamers not writers. Nightmares not readers."

"Except you haven't done anything but show me this one window since I got here," I told her, "There aren't any other customers. The shop is closed and the real owner is gone. You just wanted to talk to me about the world you came from without me knowing. You could have ignored me, but you don't really want to give me up."

"I'm doing it for you, not me!" Self-Loathing yelled back to me in a much more familiar voice, a voice on the edge of bawling. "Why can't you get that through your thick skull?"

"Don't go!" I shouted, and turned and started to bolt for the door, but she outsmarted me. Instead of dropping to the floor, the thing rolled forward and became some sort of flattened animal that scuttled across the ceiling as easily as if it were the floor. It was fast, too. By the time I reached the street I could only see some kind of sleek, long-legged thing, less a lizard than a scaly bird, more like a pair of stilts than either, running like a blur down a side street.

Running in exactly the opposite direction of the Gate. She was remembering to mask her trail again, or recovering the ability, or something. I was almost positive she was leaving the city. After that I didn't know anything at all. She could be anywhere in the Dark, and the Dark was endless.

So I had to know where she would go, and I was there waiting for her when she arrived.

She took her time getting there, but I wasn't surprised. When she finally arrived she was creeping through the packed wheat, and I could watch her erratic, hesitant progress by the way the grass moved.

The wheat helped. I didn't really have to hide. She couldn't see me lying behind the porch railing until she had almost climbed to the top of the stairs. She'd gone back to being the little dusky child with the black hair. The stain on the front of her dress was wet now, and around the edges of the black was a lot of red. Stinking drops fell onto the steps as she climbed them.

"You're not going to do it," I told her gently. It was easy to be gentle. I had nothing but sympathy for her. I couldn't figure out why, but what she was doing was obvious.

"Fang!" she burst out, and stopped. She didn't run away. I hadn't even had to chase her to catch her this time, and it was with weary defeat that she sat down heavily on the top step and sullenly stared at me.

"You came here to eat my Muse," I explained to her as I got up and patiently walked over, "Because if you did you'd become the thing I love most, but it wouldn't matter because I'd never forgive you."

"Then why don't you hate me?" she demanded, her little hands balling up into fists and trembling with helplessness.

"Because I don't believe it," I answered. I had reached her, and she hadn't run away. I pressed my face to the top of her head and rubbed my nose against it, and down over her face. For all that she looked human, she felt cold. "You didn't murder Coy and you would never murder my Muse. If I hadn't come here she'd have been perfectly safe. You might have told yourself that you were going to do it right up until you opened your mouth, but you wouldn't have gone through with it."

She was crying, sort of. She had that expression, that tenseness, and her breathing was ragged, but there were no tears. "How can you be so wrong, Fang?" she asked me hoarsely.

"Can you honestly tell me that if I walked away right now and left you alone, you'd go through with it?" I asked her evenly.

She was silent. I'd won, I knew it. Then her fists clenched again, and she shook all over.

"All right," she told me, trying to keep her voice calm, "If this is the only way. If you promise never to see me again, I'll tell you how to bring Coy back to life."

I stopped thinking. "What?"

"That's the deal," she insisted, "I'll tell you how, but it's over. We're not friends anymore. No matter what happens to me, you'll stay safely away."

"She's dead," I explained blankly, "You can't bring her back. She's not a human who leaves bits of herself behind, and you can't bring those back either."

"I can't," Self-Loathing admitted. Her voice was clearer but still scratchy, and it wobbled. "I can't remember how to dream. And you can't, because you're a nightmare. But so was she. Light, Dark, she was a nightmare. She's not dead, because she wasn't ever alive. You're just something people create when they dream."

Her diminutive hand reached out and touched the smudge on my cheek. Black against black, I'd thought it had been invisible. "You have a piece of her, so she doesn't have to be made from scratch. Find a dreamer and they can dream her up again."

It would work. I couldn't believe it, but it would work. It was just a trace, but the kiss was still Coy. And a dreamer could do anything. Absolutely anything. I knew two dream walkers, and one of them was Lucy, but the other wasn't.

I was already staring out across the waving wheat, trying to catch a hint of Anna's trail. But Coy wasn't the only person I cared about. I turned back and touched my face to Self-Loathing's again and told her, "I'm not going to stop being your friend, and I'm never going to leave you alone. You may never believe in yourself, but I do."

Then I ran, jogging slowly at first because I wasn't sure how strong my legs were as I thought about what was going to happen. When I glanced back, Self-Loathing was still sitting on the top step. The stain on the front of her dress ran all the way down now, and spreading around her was a puddle that wasn't so much blood as an oozing goo that was almost dry. I didn't understand what it meant, but with her I was just going to cling to the things I knew and hope that little by little I'd understand more.

Anna. I didn't know her well enough. She was just a lost soul wandering in the Dark. So I ran, and I held my nose to the ground or lifted my head high, always waiting to catch that scent that would become a direction, a knowledge of where she was. All I had to do was keep running. I'd find her eventually.

That was exactly how it worked. I ran, and eventually I knew which direction she was in. I sped up, bounding in excitement until there wasn't ground beneath me. I fell down a hole, righted myself, and landed in a painfully heavy way in some kind of room.

It was like a carousel inside out. Kind of. The room had many sides with wooden walls, and every wall had either a door or an animal carved in relief onto it. The wood was old and splintery, and in some places it was peeling off, wood-colored wallpaper with wood underneath. In the middle of the room stood a little glass table with a key on it, and standing next to the table was a young girl in a white nightgown.

I walked up to Anna hesitantly. I felt small because I didn't have to be big, and her head was above mine.

"Hi, Fang," she told me with serene enthusiasm, "I'm sorry I haven't seen you lately. Ever since I woke up I've been looking around. This place is wonderful. That's just the right word. It's all full of wonder. Everywhere you go there's something like this room, some little mystery you'll never figure out."

I smiled, although that wasn't a very noticeable expression on my face. "I never thought to pay much attention to them," I admitted.

"Really?" she asked brightly, "You should stop and look at where you live sometime. And meet the people. A little while ago I found an angel, a dragon, and a man who wore bits of fur and still growing plants as if they were clothes, and they were all arguing about who made the world."

"Who made the Dark?" I asked blankly. I lived here, and I hadn't noticed any of this.

"No, who made everywhere. This world, the real world, everywhere. They all thought they knew him. Or her. And before that I went down to the very far end where you can't see where you're going, and I met Anubis there. The real, actual Anubis. I'm sure of it. But he'd dyed his hair blue, and he was making mummies out of statues, and he wouldn't talk to me."

If she could go that deep into the Dark safely... but she was a dreamer, and that was why I'd come. "I'd love to hear more. I didn't know about any of this stuff," I told her, "But before we do, can I ask you a favor? I need you to dream something for me."

Pale blue eyes that seemed at odds with her plain brown hair stopped looking around and turned on me. Her smile was just warm and simple. It was so much like Coy's that I felt tears in my eyes again. Her happiness was just happiness. "Sure," she agreed immediately, "I made those three arguing guys some wine, and they got really drunk off of it and had a party. I think I can make anything here."

"Make this for me," I requested. I sat up and very carefully pulled the kiss off my cheek and held it out for her. "She was a dream, like me. I want you to dream her back to life."

Anna took the kiss from me, holding it like it was sticky in her fingertips, and as she squinted at it she told me, "I can't do it, Fang."

"You can do it," I assured her, more vehemently than I intended. "You're a dreamer. The Dark will do anything you want. Anything at all."

"Only if I can imagine it," she contradicted me, shaking her head sadly. "All I have is this little piece. I can sort of know who she was, but it's not clear. Even if I did it would just be a copy, not really her."

"Please," I insisted, and I didn't bother to hide that I was begging, my whole body stretched forward as I stared up at her.

"…I'm not going to, Fang. I'm really, really, really sorry. Maybe if I thought I could do it right, but I can't."

She turned her eyes away from me guiltily as she said that, and it gave me my chance. She was thinking too much. I lunged, claws raised, teeth wide, and closed them around Anna's throat and tore. She hadn't been expecting it, and in the shock she woke up, disappearing in a spasm.

Except she couldn't wake up. As I landed on the other side of her, she reappeared. At least, someone reappeared. She was much taller and older than Anna, but she had the same hair and the same white gown. She was vague, half-defined and thin as skin and bones. Around us I felt a tension. The walls of the room shimmered. I was in a dream, now. Despite the Dark, it felt gentle. Anna was in control but she wasn't really awake, and that was what I'd wanted.

Already she was bending down and picking up the kiss that had fallen when she'd popped. "Can you bring her back to life for me?" I begged, "Please, Anna? It's something only a dreamer can do."

She opened her mouth and said something in dreamer gibberish. Then she smiled and held up the kiss. It floated up a few inches above her, and I thought I saw a phantom brush stroking through the air—until everything froze for an instant, with a clicking sound and a flash of light, and Coy was floating in front of me.

Except she looked different. She'd been a painting, now she was a photograph without color, every shadow too dark and every highlight bleached white. She still had long, black hair and was more or less a girl, but as a photograph she had a much more human shape. I could tell because she was naked, although the shadows and glares were enough that I thought a human wouldn't get excited about it.

"Coy?" I asked worriedly.

"Coy?" she chirped back. Her voice was the same, but it sounded vague, confused. "Yes, that's my name, isn't it? I wonder why. What's your name? Do you want to see what I can do?"

She didn't know me. And as I watched, light and darkness spiraled around her and she became a fish. She became several fish one after another, flat and triangular or long and skinny or graceful and threatening, until after one final whirling of monochrome she settled on a shape. It wasn't a goldfish. I wasn't sure what it was. It was black and too long, with sinuous agility. It looked as much like a dragon as a fish, especially since its fins all ended in long, streaming tassels. At the front end its blunted head was nearly a muzzle, decorated with pearlescent tendrils that moved nimbly and matched the shine of her eyes. Everything about her shone liquidly.

But it wasn't Coy. This wasn't Coy. Anna had been right, and Self-Loathing had been wrong. All I'd brought back was some kind of warped copy.

I threw back my head and screamed, and I kept screaming, trying to vent the frustration I felt. The dream around me let go, but it had been weak to begin with. Anna was gradually shrinking back to her normal self, but she still looked spaced out. Yet as I howled the world shifted underneath me. I hurt and I didn't stop screaming, but the room was gone. I stood now on a tall pinnacle of rock, surround by more rocks in weird, bent shapes that suggested humans crying.

Above me hung an enormous crescent moon, and I thought I caught a glimpse of things curling around the other rock towers.

I stopped, mostly because I ran out of breath, but before my voice trailed off completely the fish was swimming around me in circles. It came apart in spirals of pearl and ink, leaving the girl sitting in the air next to me laughing and apologizing at the same time. "Sorry! Sorry! You just looked so dramatic. I thought I could make you more beautiful if you had a backdrop. I can do better next time."

I gaped. I didn't know what to say, not even when she reached out one hand and stroked my neck above my collar. Out of the blue she added, "Do you think we could do that in a dream? I bet with you as my model, we could make it so a dreamer didn't know if he was crying because he was scared, or because everything was so beautiful!"

And my heart fluttered a little with a jolt of hope. Maybe Anna had brought back everything important about Coy after all.

Chapter Five

LETTING GO

I felt heavy. The hurt in my heart was a dull ache, and I was worried I was fading because I couldn't figure out what I wanted anymore. I needed someone to remind me how to have fun. I knew someone who was good at that. She hadn't come looking for me, so I was going to see her.

I was just a little surprised to find myself standing underneath the red wooden sign with a black razor stamped on it, but I knew Self-Loathing was inside, and if she was seeing customers that might be exactly what I needed. I'd have to remind myself to be polite and not barge to the front of the line.

Padding down the stairs to her little sunken salon, I found the door just slightly ajar and with a certain amount of relief I pushed it open with my nose. Except it stuck. I pushed harder, but it seemed jammed, just a few inches open but not able to open more. There was a little give. I just had to push.

I was touching my shoulder to the door when I heard light,

clipping footsteps, and Self-Loathing peeked through the gap at me. I knew it was her. No one else in the Dark would wear this shape, soft and fuzzy and feminine, standing upright but more animal than human. She had long, spiraling horns and dark, gleaming eyes and a dainty grace. I could hardly even think about what I wanted to do to that shape, because the smell of her wiped out everything in my head. She smelled like a mix of fur and vanilla, and because it was faint that just made me work harder to sniff it up, let it overwhelm me.

It actually took me a moment to understand what she'd just said. "Go away."

I had trouble letting go of her scent, so sweet and rich. It teased me, made it hard to think. "Is it a bad time?" I asked cautiously, "You probably haven't seen some of—"

She cut me off. "Go away, Fang," she repeated. The sound of her voice, tired and angry and defeated, made it a lot easier to ignore what she looked and smelled like. And there was something horribly final about the way she said, "We had a deal."

"I didn't agree to it," I answered. It was dumb, but what could I say?

"You didn't have to," she told me immediately, as if she'd known exactly what I would say. I felt a little ashamed and a lot confused. The dull, resentful anger in her voice and the deft little movements of her sleek new body kept yanking my attention back and forth. I felt like I had no control.

I made myself concentrate. "I didn't agree to it for a reason," I explained to her as firmly and gently as I could, "You're trying to blame yourself for what happened to Coy. It's just something that happened. I don't believe you did it deliberately."

She looked less tired and more angry now, and I could see her tensing up. "Thank you for saying you know what I think better than I do. That makes this easier. Go away, Fang. You're not welcome here as a friend or a customer."

"You can't mean that. You really don't want to play with me?" I pushed just a little more with my muzzle. My teeth were just inches from one of those thighs, and I could feel the door giving.

"Are you going to take what you want from me anyway, if I say no?" she demanded. There was an extra edge to her defiance. Not excitement. Fear.

I stopped cold. I couldn't even say anything.

"I can't stop you, Fang," she went on. Her voice shook, betraying her attempt to sound fatalistic and unconcerned. "You're stronger than me. A lot stronger. But I don't want to talk to you and I don't want to play with you. So either do what you want to me anyway, or go away."

I couldn't possibly believe she'd think I would do that. She had to be—

I'd been about to do it.

I looked at that leg, with its black stripe that reminded me of some kind of nimble antelope. I could almost touch it. I wanted to argue, to tell her that I wasn't like that, but the only reason she was still talking was that I was strong enough to force her to, wasn't it? I sat back and the door closed in my face. Just like that, without another word.

As I walked back down the street I tried to tell myself that she was always doing crazy stuff and pushing me away. She'd never sounded so resigned about it, though. Could I even say I deserved to be her friend, if I respected her so little that the first thing I did was try and dismiss her decisions as craziness?

I was at the door to Bar Number Three before I realized it, deceptively looking like it was boarded up and nailed shut. I pushed the door open, sliding into the hazy bar, worried about what I'd see.

It was worse than I'd expected. Coy was still sitting on a bar stool exactly where I'd left her, staring up at the ceiling. She wasn't doing anything, just staring. Only when I was halfway to her did she suddenly slide out of her seat to meet me, drifting over to wrap her arms loosely around my neck and chirp, "Fang! Can we go? It's so smoky in here. It makes my gills all scratchy."

Sweet Dreams are Made of Teeth

She didn't seem to have gills as a human, but I wasn't quite sure I wanted to understand that. As I tried to let go of my thoughts of Self-Loathing enough to answer her, long wooden slats twisted along the ceiling and the puppet behind the bar leaned forward across it. "She was like that the whole time you were gone. Not a word," Bar Number Three informed me. Its harsh metal voice didn't convey emotion well, but I thought it sounded worried.

"I know," I admitted guiltily. She wasn't showing any sign she heard us talking.

"We offer hope and warning," the puppet went on, "Our belief is that you have taken her out of the Dark too quickly. She forgets who she is. She needs to dream."

"I know," I repeated hopelessly. "Come on, Coy. Let's see if we can't get you some inspiration." It was an odd way to look at it, that the nightmare dreams as much as the dreamer does, but sometimes Bar Number Three reminded me more of a fantasy than a nightmare. He talked like Coy used to.

I just wished it would work. Coy clung to my neck for a few blocks after we left the bar, then turned into that serpentine, pearl-eyed fish she preferred and swam around me with directionless energy until we left the city behind and wandered into the Dark itself.

"Hey, Coy, would you like to play with a dream?" I asked her when I saw the first bubble hovering in the distance. I tried to sound hopeful and enthusiastic.

"Sure!" she agreed eagerly, "I love dreamers!" She did.

"What do you think you'd like to create?" I nudged her.

"I don't know."

And that was it. That was what she always said. "You don't have any ideas you'd like to try?" I pushed. I was trying so hard to be gentle.

"Not really." I wasn't being gentle enough. She was starting to sound a little guilty. She knew, at least, that there was something wrong with her. I thought about pushing her into a dream and letting her find her own inspiration. Watching her swim around a dreamer randomly again, watching him without doing anything, would probably kill me.

"I'm cold, Fang," she informed me meekly.

"Okay," I agreed. The threads of black and pearl she was made of spun and closed tighter, and a tiny little fish wriggled under my collar and clung to me as I trotted further into the shadows. Whatever she drew from me as she rode next to my skin, it wasn't enough. She was fading slowly, and I thought now that she knew it.

I'd made Anna bring Coy back from the dead, and now she was dying again. No. No, I had to face it. This wasn't Coy. It was some other girl with the same name and the same voice who I was responsible for having half-made. She was a nightmare with no theme or sense of herself, and she wasn't going to last long. Coy had known exactly who she was.

I couldn't take it. I wanted to get rid of her, to run away. But when I looked ahead toward the border and saw a dream beginning to take shape near it, I knew what I really wanted. It wouldn't solve any of my problems. I just had to remind myself of why I was content all alone before I met Jeffery. I had to remember that if I lost everything, it would be enough just to be me.

I picked up speed. I could feel the thrill of it already. I wanted this dream. It was fully formed by the time I reached it, and on the Dark side it would be no challenge, but that was fine. This one was just for the fun of it, and as I leaped through the surface I was already growling and looking around for the dreamer.

The dreamer was a man. I thought he might be young, but I couldn't tell. His clothes were really well defined, odd and formal and stiff, but his face was a blur. The whole dream was one long hallway lined with ebony wood with everything ornate and old-fashioned. A giant black dog landing behind him had about the effect anyone would expect. He began to run, and with a bit of honest joy finally flickering through me I began to chase.

He wasn't a good runner, but I had no desire to catch him. I just stayed close, claws tearing up the carpet, fangs looming and half-spread close enough behind that he most likely could feel my breath. The hall stretched and stretched and stretched. This dream wouldn't be fancy or have any surprises. At least I thought it wouldn't, until I saw Coy's face peek out of a mirror hanging on the wall. Then she was standing in a doorway, back to being a human girl except in a grey and white monochrome of shadows and glare. We started passing windows and she was in every one, smiling hopefully as she watched the dreamer pass. I thought he could see her too, but I knew he could see her when ghost images of her started appearing, hovering in place as we passed, reaching out to touch him with transparent hands and then be left behind. Over and over, a trail of them, staring after us and freezing when we got too far away.

Something had changed in the dreamer, and the dream changed. We were coming up on the end of the hallway. The door dragged squeakily open to welcome us, and standing in the blackness beyond was Coy, smiling shyly and holding out her arms to the dreamer.

I didn't get to find out what would happen when we got there. The dream shook, everything twisted, and it broke around me. It hadn't popped naturally. It had been interrupted somehow? As I tried to grasp that I was shoved down to the still-carpeted ground and a foot pinned itself on my neck.

Lucy.

No! I didn't even yell it, I snarled and started to thrash, and the choking strength of the sandaled foot was barely enough to hold me down.

Which meant it wasn't Lucy.

Growling now despite the strangling pressure, I peered up through the clearing fog at whoever had pinned me down. It was, of all things, an angel. Fit, pretty, and basically human. I couldn't really tell if it was male or female, and it held a gleaming spear pointed at my face. It shone too, a bit of the Light glowing in the Dark, all the stronger because it wasn't alone. There were quite a few of them spread out in a half circle around me and Coy.

"I have the nightmare," the angel standing on me announced, "I'm not sure what the other thing is, but it looks harmless. What are your orders?"

Another angel walked over. It hardly looked different from the first one, but it was brighter. It had a more distant look in its eyes, maybe was more muscular. Definitely male, and I thought he was stronger. As he studied me, this new angel commanded, "We'll give it a chance. Nightmare, for what you were doing to that mortal you certainly deserve to die, but I will not sacrifice a greater justice for a lesser one. I'm willing to release you if you can tell me who opened a portal to the mortal world here recently."

"You've heard about Jeffery in the Light?" I asked, stunned and impressed despite myself. Then I wanted to slap myself for being stupid.

"Confirmation. That's the same name," observed a third angel. This one I was kind of sure was female.

"So it really was a nightmare? Not a demon?" the angel in charge demanded impatiently.

The one holding me was getting impatient too. The pressure on my neck made it hard to answer him. He was smart to do it, but I wasn't sure it was enough. Could I force him off? If I did, how could I get Coy and I away alive? It had to be both or neither. Whether or not I could escape, that one thing I was certain of. "You want me to lead you to him," I concluded, "That's not going to happen."

The angels were silent. They didn't seem to get angry very easily. "It's what we had to expect of the Dark's shades. They resist what is right automatically. There's no point in arguing, and one less nightmare is one mortal who dreams in peace. Kill it," concluded the leader dispassionately.

"No way!" yelled Coy shrilly. I'd forgotten about her, assuming she was just floating there blankly again. Instead, she looked tense and furious. She'd clearly been paying attention.

The Dark shook, and the foot nearly fell off of my neck. Shoving myself up, I pushed the angel off the rest of the way and came face to face with myself. Sort of? A black dog much bigger than me with white fangs reared in front of me. It was some kind of statue, and another sprang up, and another, to the roaring sound of crumbling rock. They didn't do anything, but they were big and they looked much too dangerous. Coy was carving the Dark again and she was angry, but she either couldn't or wouldn't hurt anyone.

I didn't really want her to. I wanted her to do what she'd done, which was give me the chance to bolt past her, yelling, "Come on!" Black and white writhed around the girl, and it was the little sucker fish that lodged itself under my collar as I ran, and ran, and ran, and ran.

It looked like we'd gotten away. There was no sign of the angels anywhere, and the way they shone with the Light should have made them visible from a long way away. Coy must have thought we were safe, because she wriggled out from hiding, growing into the sort of catfish eel she seemed to prefer and swimming alongside me again.

"You saved me! Both of us!" I panted. It gave me more hope than I'd felt for too long.

"I'm glad it worked," she admitted, then giggled. It had a kind of guilty sound. "Fang, what do you think that dreamer felt?"

My heart suddenly ached again. This was a hope I didn't want to feel. "I don't know," I evaded, "You really had an effect on him. Where did you get the idea?"

"I don't know," she repeated vaguely. Then the foggy tone gave way to enthusiasm again, and she went on without being pressed. "I just liked watching you, and I wanted to be like that, but different. And that was my different. Do you think we could do it again? Just me? I think I could make the whole dream like me, into a series of photographs with the dreamer inside them. I'd like to see how that makes a dreamer feel."

That didn't sound like a nightmare, but it didn't sound like she was fading, either. But would she stay like this? I shouldered the question aside.

"I'd love to, but first we have to find my friend Jeffery. I think there's going to be trouble. Lots of it," I told her grimly.

Coy swam at my side the whole way back to the Gate. I hardly even checked where Jeffery was until I got there, and I had to circle around quite a bit when I did. He wasn't in the part of town I expected. He was in the part Self-Loathing had led me to once, where the Scryer shops were.

It was an odd place where everyone ignored each other and only the glowing, waving tendrils around Coy's mouth seemed to fit in. The trail led me to a three-story tower, bent and ramshackle and made out of plate-sized slivers of something shiny like soap. They reminded me of bits of a dream's shell, if you could somehow break those off. I tried not to get distracted and catapulted myself up the uneven stairs until I could feel Jeffery behind a door I was passing. I didn't even try to focus enough to have hands. I pulled the latch with my teeth and burst into the store.

This really was a store. There's not much physical a nightmare wants to buy, but the things in this part of town must have felt differently. I didn't recognize any of it, but I was only interested in Jeffery anyway. He was turning to look at me, holding a flimsy bird cage in one hand.

"Fang!" he greeted me delightedly, "I haven't seen you in ages. Where have you been?"

"Where have YOU been?" I returned, jarred to a halt mentally and physically. I wasn't the one who'd been mysteriously absent!

"Researching, mostly. Planning. I had to find someone who could talk to the Dream Painters, learn things the demons didn't want to tell me. I had to get one of these." He held up the cage in front of my face as he stepped up beside me. Inside was a bird, although it looked more like something made of bits of bone and junk than flesh. The way it kept moving, it was clearly alive. "That was difficult. The guys who tame them expect to be paid. I had to figure out what they want."

"I've been…" I wasn't sure where to start. "A lot of things. Anna made a new Coy, and I've been taking care of her. She doesn't know how to be a nightmare yet. Or how to be anything."

"I think I'm starting to get an idea," Coy chimed in, her fish body dissolving around her and leaving her seated in black and white in mid-air.

To my surprise, that made Jeffery grin, showing off all of his sharp little teeth. He looked at Coy intently now and reached out to touch her chin, and her hair. Trying to get a feel for how she could look flat and have a shape at the same time, I guessed. "But that's the best part of life. All she has is this simple seed of an idea. We could teach her to be terrifying."

I couldn't figure out why I felt uncomfortable about that, and I was downright surprised when Coy pulled away from his touch and floated around behind me, answering, "No, thank you. I trust Fang."

Of course, Jeffery could read both our expressions. So he changed the subject, rubbing his palm roughly between my ears and telling me, "I wouldn't have time, anyway. My plan is just about ready. I might as well start looking for my target."

I needed to tell him about the angels, but I was burning with this, too. This was why Jeffery had disappeared on me. "What is this plan? You're the scariest nightmare in the Dark. After you broke that dreamer in the waking world, nobody even questions it."

"You're right," he agreed, and now he looked… uncharacteristically awkward. With anybody else he'd be bragging, but this was me and Jeffery. "The Dark isn't enough for me, Fang. It's too simple and familiar. I'm going to break out."

"That rift to the waking world…?" I asked cautiously. This was way out of my experience.

"I'm going to make one that's bigger and lasts longer, and go through it. Nightmares have done it before, once or twice. I like what the world looks like over there. I'm sure I can do it, but not alone." He looked at me very seriously, because he knew what he was asking. "Will you help me? You can come with me, if you want. Anyone will be able to go through."

"Maybe," I told him doubtfully. If he succeeded and I didn't come, I'd never see him again. "That doesn't sound like me. But it does sound like you. I'll do whatever it takes to help you… be you."

I'd put that badly, but his grin of pride and delight practically split his face. "Thanks, buddy," he answered quietly, "I'm going to need a lot of help. Making a big enough hole will be hard enough, but staying alive that long is going to be even more of a challenge. Tearing a path from a dream into the human world is going to get a lot of attention."

I had to warn him. Instead, I was interrupted by Lily. "It already has. And you're planning to do it again? You didn't even try and keep it a secret?" She came soaring down onto an open balcony, and had hardly fluttered onto her feet when she ran forward to grab me and Jeffery by the collars.

"I don't think we need to panic, Lily," Jeffery told her dryly as she dragged us backwards onto the balcony.

In fact, she dragged us off the balcony, broken wings flapping madly as she carried us down to the street. I was too heavy for her, but Coy wrapped her arms around me and lifted too, so I only stumbled around a little as I hit the pavement.

"Panic?" Lily asked archly as she dragged Jeffery bodily down the street, "Do you have any idea how petty and stupid and jealous my family is? They'd rather kill each other than let someone else open up a portal besides themselves. I've kept them arguing with each other by telling them I was leading you by the nose."

"But we've stopped arguing, yes," admitted a very, very deep voice. The thing that slid out to block the intersection oozed and dripped shadow, man-shaped but only defined by its burning yellow eyes and ornate fiery halo. I was getting the impression they didn't show those lightly.

"You don't come out of the Gate much, Baal," Lily told him. She'd let go of Jeffery and become cool and calm in the blink of an eye, watching the newcomer speculatively but with a stance that was all casual theater. Even the way her red hair blew in a faint breeze was a show. There was no breeze, and I knew theatrics when I saw them.

"I don't have reason to," he answered, sliding toward her. Unlike Lily, he didn't bother to hide the malignance in his voice. "No one was opening portals. There was no way to get to the mortal world anyway. But now that nightmare is a resource."

"That nightmare needs to be destroyed," announced another raspy voice. It was a woman, sort of, leaning out of a window above me. She had four arms and something weirdly bladed in each hand. Not an inch of skin showed under leather or metal. Another demon, not as smart or original but still dangerous.

"We'll get rid of all of them. There'll be new nightmares again soon. We'll keep it up until they know their place," put in another voice, and something scaly crawled out of an alley, clinging to the wall. At that point I lost track. Demons stepped out of doorways, dropped off rooftops, maybe a score of them. Way too many to fight, and they all looked like bad news.

"As you can see," explained Baal, oozing up face to face with Lily, "There's still some disagreement on fine detail, but only on fine detail. Your little plaything there is going into a box, and we'll decide what to do with him once he's secured and we've gotten rid of any other nightmares who might know how to pull off his little... stunt."

"I don't intend to go along with this plan," Lily informed him coldly. That was how they all looked, grim and detached and businesslike as they started to close around Lily and Jeffery. Jeffery looked the same. This was going to be a battle of wits as much as force.

"That's why I came personally, and brought so many of our

siblings," the lugubrious black shape answered, "Every one of us outranks you, Lily. You can't possibly win this."

It really was a battle of wits, and the first loser was a demon in the crowd. Chains with barbed spikes on the end fired out of its arm. Lily didn't even have a chance to dodge, and they didn't just hit her, they pierced all the way through. Red blood sprayed when the points came out the other side. Something lumbering and hairy lunged forward and took hold of Jeffery, whose needle teeth were already showing. "It'll still be safer if she's already dead," the thing with the chains hissed.

Lily's blood was all over the street. I could see it dripping, almost pouring off the spikes sticking out of her body. Theater. I knew it was theater, just in time to not be surprised as she grabbed a handful of the chains and yanked the demon that had flung them off of his feet and into her arms. She opened her mouth, and row upon row of crescent curved teeth bit into a neck covered in rusty sheet metal and tore it out. Blood sprayed again, this time black, but it disappeared before it hit the ground as the demon's body bubbled and dissolved down to the chains piercing Lily's body.

As she moved like an eel to intercept the next demon leaping for her I heard Baal sigh, "Thank you, Ganby. And now we have to immobilize the Demiurge, since you've reminded us we can't kill her."

I didn't see what happened next, because I was creeping down the nearest alley. The demons had ignored me entirely, and that was exactly how I'd wanted it. I was sure Lily couldn't win this. Maybe with a surprise I could scatter the pack, and she and Jeffery and I could all escape.

I could feel Coy trembling where she'd hidden under my collar. She'd just been starting to wake up, and now she'd had to witness that, and it was going to get worse. I'd worry about her when I had the time.

When my foot refused to lift, it hit me that I'd better worry about myself. I could feel something hard closing around it. Metal writhed up my legs, thrusting out of the ground and locking around me in rings and collars and vices, and some of them had unpleasantly sharp edges. A human boy rose from behind a trash can. He looked a lot like Jeffery, with blonde hair and a vaguely pretty face, wearing ragged grey old-fashioned clothes. His hand trailed along the wall as he approached me, and the gleam of metal thrusting from the one into the other told me who he was before he spoke.

"Isn't this a delightful serendipity?" Nick asked me with excessively casual pleasure. "I've been trying to figure out what to do about you, but picking a nightmare out of the pack is so difficult. And yet first Lily leads us to the one who opens portals, and then he leads me to you. Patience, so they tell me, is a virtue."

"This isn't going to satisfy you," I growled at him, "It won't prove anything at all." Pride. His pride was the only weapon I had. I couldn't budge, and metal was even locked around my throat. I hoped it wasn't crushing Coy.

"You're right," he admitted, his tone suddenly distasteful, "You're far too damnably smart, and I've warned the others not to underestimate the nightmares. Unfortunately, it's practical. Sometimes even I have to just remove an obstacle and not worry about the style involved."

"It won't get you back in Self-Loathing's good graces," I retorted, more angrily than I'd have liked, "She may be mad at me, but she won't forgive whoever kills me, ever. And she will find out."

He smirked at me. This, the sadistic arrogance in that expression, was why he was a demon. "Has trying to earn her love gotten you anywhere, mutt? I know what she responds to."

I tried to open my mouth, but another coil of metal shot out and wrapped around my muzzle, binding it shut. I wriggled a little. I was wrapped up tight. All I could do was watch.

Watch as the glow came close enough that Nick's back began to hiss and smoke, and he tried to twist around and look without taking his hand off the wall. Watch as a sword longer than me swung upwards, slicing him neatly along a diagonal as he barked in pain. Watch as the shining, white-robed figure stepped past my bound body and Nick's mutilated halves to walk out into the street.

What was left of Nick collapsed into ash. The metal jutting out of the street and wall was slower to dissolve, but with clink after clink, stretches of it fell apart. I shook and struggled, throwing my bonds off in ones and twos until I was standing free in a pile of slowly disintegrating metal.

"Are you okay, Coy?" I whispered quickly.

"I'm cold, Fang," she whispered from under my collar. That was not what I wanted to hear at all.

"Just close your eyes and let me handle it, Coy. This isn't who you are," I reassured her.

I wanted to leap out into the street, but instead I peered around the corner. The fight had come to a stop when the angel appeared. Lily was still struggling, but the four-armed demoness held her tightly, with one of those hands over her mouth to muffle her desperate yelling. Jeffery didn't fight, but he eyed the looming creature that held him, the demons, and the approaching angel warily. He was trying to come up with a plan. So was I.

"Oh look, the prig," Baal announced, oozing up in front of his fellows as the angel walked slowly over to meet him, "It hasn't been nearly long enough, Tzadkiel. You're in our territory and heavily outnumbered, and I hope you realize that. Deliver your message and go back to the Four."

"This isn't a message," the angel answered sternly. It was the strong one, the one that had been leading the others, I was sure. "This is an action. You have allowed a nightmare to open a portal and broken the treaty."

"A declaration of rules the Four made up all by themselves isn't a treaty, you stuck-up credulous thug," Baal replied testily, "We're dealing with the portal right now, our own way."

"Insufficient," Tzadkiel informed him, "To deter another offense, it has been decided to raze this termite heap back to the Gate and kill everything we find in the process. The Dark is long since due to be purged."

The street had gotten very, very still. "I'm not grateful to him for much," Baal answered slowly, "But I do thank our Father for the incredible egos he gave all of you. Brothers and sisters, kill him. All together, please. He's one of Heaven's best, and I don't want him to have a ghost of a chance of winning."

The overlong sword had been slung over the angel's back, and he didn't seem to be in any hurry to draw it. The demons attacked first, too many for me to keep track of. One was kicked away, another thrown, but the angel mostly seemed to sidestep the blades and spikes coming at him. Then something leapt down from above me, some kind of insect monster that had been hidden on a rooftop. Hooking hard-shelled legs into the angel's back, it jammed a stinger into him deeply. He stiffened up just long enough for an arm to come hurtling out of Baal's black mass and whip claws across the angel's throat, tearing it open.

Lily's yelling and writhing were the only sound and movement as everyone caught up with what had just happened. Then, as if it hadn't happened, the angel tore the bug demon off his shoulders so hard it left hooked feet behind, then drew his sword with the other hand.

The demoness holding Lily must have been surprised enough to loosen her grip. Lily yanked one arm free, pulled the hand off of her mouth, and yelled shrilly, "He's a Demiurge, you halfwits! If you ever stopped pretending nothing goes on in the Light, you'd have known he held the Demiurge of Revenge!"

"Justice," the angel corrected sharply, giving Lily a severe glare. She'd stung him.

"An eye for an eye?" she asked.

"And a tooth for a tooth," he finished.

"That's Revenge, not Justice," she informed him coldly. The four armed demoness had dropped Lily entirely. All the demons spread out, circling Justice cautiously.

"Not all of us spend every night praying we could lick our Father's boots again," Baal snapped. His calm and control was fraying, and I could hear the edge in his voice as he instructed the other demons, "Pin him, then. We don't have to kill him to make an example. Just don't hold anything back, and I'll see about reinforcements."

"Don't bother," announced a crisp voice. It was the female angel from before, looking down at the street from a rooftop. "We're already here."

At that point it all got very confused, because everyone moved at once. I glanced at Baal first and saw him collapsing into an oily black puddle, maybe in an attempt to escape. I could see three or four angels dropping off roofs, and Justice was already cutting his way through the demons. The big one that had been holding Jeffery grabbed Justice's arm only to have its hairy hands chopped off. Then Lily raced through the crowd, crouched low and speeding along on blood-colored double hinged legs that had broken out of her pretend shell of humanity. She had Jeffery wrapped in one arm. I didn't make her grab me. I ran flat-out at her side as we tried to put as much distance as we could between ourselves and this fight.

We didn't get very far. It was immediately obvious there were other angels in the city. The occasional scream or snarl in the distance was normal, but there were too many. I looked around and could see a toad covering itself in a shell the color of the shadowed brick wall it squatted on, and a snake made out of a chain of rusted, junked appliances curling up behind a roadside stand. Nightmares hunkering down to fight.

The boom drew us up short. It was loud, thundering over the city and making everything shiver. Lily and I stopped in our tracks, our eyes drawn to the source of the sound.

"Oh, dear Father, no, they're opening the Gate," Lily gasped. She dropped Jeffery onto the paving stones and shook her wings. Bent and bony red fingers were starting to jut out of their already ragged feathers as she took off. We got hit with another boom while she was in midair, knocking her back a pace and vibrating my paws across the brickwork. Bits of shell and feather landed around me as her disguise disintegrated a little further.

She landed again on a rooftop, and while I'm not a good climber I was able to jump up onto a burned-out shell of a truck, make a much riskier and more delicate leap onto a second floor window ledge, then throw myself onto the rooftop beside her. In seconds, Jeffery pulled himself over the side of the building next to me, chuckling darkly, "At least we'll get to see something new from this mess."

"Something...?" Lily asked in surprise, looking around at us. There was a third boom, knocking me over and making Jeffery crouch to keep his balance, and I would have sworn I saw the doors of the Gate budge. I could see the very top of the hill of refuse it sat on from here, but the flashes of black and white didn't make any sense to me.

While I was staring at that, Lily laid into both of us. "What are you two doing? Run! Run, you stupid boys! If the Gate opens and you're anywhere in the city, you're dead!"

Jeffery wasn't impressed. In fact, he'd crawled forward again to the edge of the roof, leaning over it to get a better view. "They're really laying into each other down there. I've always wanted to see those black angels fight."

As he spoke, one of the two black stars scurrying around out there went out. "That's why they sent Tzadki. You'd have to be unkillable to take down the Sentinels." She lunged forward, closing a hand around Jeffery's ankle and dragging him back so that she could grab me by the collar too. "Now run, you idiots!" she chided us. "The angels aren't trying to open the Gate. Someone wants to come out. Someone who'll stomp Tzadki, every angel he brought, and probably the whole city in the process. You two will just be colla—"

She was cut off by a fourth boom, but then it was cut off too. The rolling, vibrating knock ended abruptly in the middle. We all looked, but I didn't know what I was looking at. Nothing seemed to be happening.

"They've spiked it," Lily murmured in amazement, "He got both Sentinels. They've jammed the Gate. This will be over before my family can force it open."

"How'd they do it?" Jeffery asked, climbing to his feet and peering curiously off into the distance.

"Jeffy, this city is still a death trap!" Lily snapped at him. Red eyes turned to me, and I couldn't help but notice her halo starting to glow like the rust was being heated. "Puppy, I knew he was like this, but—"

"Yes, he's like this," I agreed. "You can't argue." What I could do was hop behind Jeffery as she started to drag him away from the view. I wedged my head into his back and shoved, and he and Lily jumped off the rooftop and landed lightly on the street. I was a lot less graceful about it, but I had four feet to hit the ground with and it didn't much matter how heavily.

As I left behind what I'd just seen I heard the screams again, in all directions. Fighting. Cold spiked down my back, and I asked Lily, "We head for the edge of town?"

"If we can find it. The city must be in pain. It'll be a labyrinth by now," she warned me anxiously.

I put my nose to the ground. I hunted for the trail, the one I could always find, the sadness and the bitter blood and the dusty, abandoned mansion of my Muse. Even in this chaos I found it, and I barked "Follow me," and took off.

I was used to the city rearranging itself, but Lily had been right. I saw blocks I'd never seen before, but we passed Bar Number Three twice. We still weren't out of the city either, and I kept having to turn aside at long lines of buildings wall-to-wall with each other. Once we were halfway down a street when I discovered the directions had twisted around, and the trail now led behind us.

The streets weren't deserted. Some kind of bloated, apelike demon I could identify by his burning eyes and red horns told three nightmares, "You'll do as I say because you're trapped in here with me and the bird-wings are killing everyone. Now, do you know what to do?"

"I know," answered the nightmare with the scythe arms, and it slashed one across the ape demon's throat.

I sped up. Until I'd seen that I hadn't really believed the whole city was now a killing zone. I started looking for shortcuts, and broke down a little gate leading into a junkyard of old tires, hopping from pile to pile and out the other side.

As I landed in the street I pressed my nose to the dirt path. Directions had shifted again, and as I turned my head to follow the thread of my Muse, Jeffery yanked it the other way.

"They're really doing it. They want to level the place," he announced in shock.

My eyes focused on one of the angels. I couldn't really tell it from any of the others. It had black hair with glowing white highlights that still made it look pale. They'd only used weapons so far, but this one had her hands flat against the side of a building, and cracks were spreading out over the white stonework in complicated patterns with lots of circles and interlocking lines. The building was going to come down in a moment, like the piles of rubble I'd seen and paid no attention to along the way. In fact, it was only at that point I recognized this white, rough, almost featureless little tower. Jeffery's Muse lived there.

Jeffery had figured it out already. I'd never seen this expression on his face as he lurched forward. It was feral, and he moved like he'd been hit already.

"Are your eyes closed?" I whispered back to the little fish-shaped lump clinging to my neck.

"Yes, Fang," Coy whimpered plaintively. She was too fragile for this. Too pretty. My feet were already moving, speeding me past Jeffery as he mastered his fear and anger enough to master his body, too.

It would be impossible not to notice a horse-sized black dog bearing down on you, and the angel let go of the building and pulled out some complicated thing like a stick with blades on both ends. She shoved it forward to block me, but that was fine. It was the weapon I wanted; closing my teeth around the haft and yanking to the side, I threw her off balance.

She had enough time to yell, "By the—" before Jeffery reached her and his own sharp little fangs closed on her neck.

The body was already coming apart into little stars as I stared up at Jeffery in shock. "Did we do that?"

"Damn right, we did," he shot back. His heart wasn't in it. He ran his fingers over the cracked stone, making sure the building wasn't in danger, and looked worriedly up at the seemingly blank windows up above us.

"We can't take her with us. She's too big," I whispered to him anxiously. I levered him away from the wall with my nose. He didn't want to, but he let me separate him.

A metallic scrape rang as Lily kicked the angel's weapon a few feet down the street. "The angels say that if you're good enough, you don't need gimmicks. I guess you weren't good enough, Marael." The words sounded harsh, but there was a distant emptiness in her voice, something bleak and lost in the way she stared at the blade. I gave her a shove too, and we started to run again.

At the corner I saw one street where the buildings only went a couple of blocks and then stopped. We were at the edge—or I thought we were. I actually saw the streets twist around, everything going blurry. Now the intersection was gone. No, it had moved about a hundred yards down, and what was in front of us was another familiar road from the nightmare part of town.

Except an angel was standing in it. Worse, Tzadkiel was standing in it, the one who called himself Justice. It had taken me a second to recognize him.

Lily had known him in an instant and stepped out in front of us. Jeffery and I watched the angel warily. This one would be much tougher than the last, and not as easy to surprise. Taking him down wasn't even an option, but I was looking for a way we could get past him. I was sure he was fast enough that a wide street wouldn't be enough, and I wasn't willing to lose any of the three people with me.

Lily tried something I hadn't expected. She tried to talk to him, hands raised, palms out. "Tzad, please don't do this. Take our brothers and sisters and go home. Even if you win, you'll be the only one to come back from this alive. Am I the only person on either side who cares what happens to my family?"

"Justice is the only name I go by now," he told her flatly, drawing that sword again. It was as tall as he was, but he held it like a twig. "Justice knows no mercy and no fear. I will do what is right regardless of what happens to me, and I expect the same from everyone who fights with me."

"You have a real name, Tzad," Lily told him. There wasn't any hope in her voice, and she wasn't trying to pretend there was anymore.

"So do you, 'Lily'," he shot back snidely, "But you'd rather use a mediocre name like the mediocre sinner you are."

I could see her trembling and the cracks that ran through her skin, deep enough that hooked spikes poked through on one shoulder. "I don't need a fancy name," she informed him stiffly, "I'm a Demiurge, too. You're facing a stalemate. Neither of us can kill the other."

He bristled. They really could get under each other's skin. "Don't mistake righteousness for stupidity," he told her, his words sharp and deliberate. "If anything, I was surprised the other Demiurges were too cowardly to defend this garbage heap. We even decided on a special way to deal with you." He held out one hand, and the wall he was pointing at lurched. A stone cross bulged out of it, taller and wider even than Justice. "You're going to be given exactly what you want," he finished, "Crucifixion."

If I died, Coy would be dead too. Jeffery didn't need me to survive, but I couldn't imagine either of us would make it if we did this. We were creeping up on either side of Lily anyway. I growled, and Jeffery just smiled, casual and disarming, which was a lot scarier than I could ever look. We wouldn't let Lily fight this monster alone.

Justice's sword had just started to lift when a shaky, feminine voice interrupted, "Don't you dare hurt them."

The block that had been added was the one Self-Loathing's salon was on, and she dragged herself up the steps on one good leg, while the other bent in odd places as though broken multiple times. She was a short, sort of elfin thing with a protruding face covered in ugly burns. All the skin I could see around the torn remains of her gown was covered in burns. She was missing an ear and one eye. I'd done worse to her and she'd wanted more, but I still couldn't pick apart all the emotions I felt seeing her.

Justice glanced over at her lazily. He couldn't lose, and he knew it. When his eyes met hers his expression held nothing but disgust. "Pagan gods. This place is filthy. No, you're something worse, some kind of abomination. You were supposed to be grateful for the gods you were given."

"I know what I am," she agreed, her voice full of venom, for herself as well as for him. "Do you know what you are, hypocrite?"

He actually jerked. He stopped paying any attention to us. The sword pointed at Self-Loathing now, and while he didn't sound like he was losing his temper his tone was emphatic as he corrected her, "I am the Demiurge of Justice, and I have held that title for millennia. You cannot sway me. Everyone in this city deserves death. I could list all of their crimes, including yours."

"Justice, really?" she retorted. She sounded so catty and disbelieving. Irritated, like he was just trying her patience. And as she talked she grew, her hair darkening, her body filling out and her face and leg growing whole again. "Justice works both ways. I see you do a lot of punishing the guilty. You're an angel. When was the last time you saved a soul and led it to Heaven?"

"I don't run into many pure souls, abomination," he answered. Too calm. I knew what Self-Loathing could do to you. I could guess what the body she was changing into was making him feel.

It looked like Lily. Kind of. It was just human, not perfect like the one Lily affected, but it had fiery red hair and a touch of makeup that included vivid red lipstick and nails. A young woman in a thin white wrap that clung blatantly and hinted at anything it didn't show.

She took another step toward him, and she still walked like she was in pain. She was completely unthreatening, at least physically. Even her voice shook as she snapped, "Everyone seems guilty to a hypocrite. It's just so easy to find a reason to punish them, right? I don't need to argue with you. I just have to watch you look at me. You don't know me and you can't see my sins, as much as you'd like me to think you can. But if you really represent blind, impartial Justice, what do you want to do to me?"

"Serpent!" he yelled suddenly. His composure gone he threw something at her, a light that stretched into something sharp, driving through Self-Loathing's upper arm and slamming her backwards. She whimpered, gooey blood leaking around the edge of the wound as she staggered to remain upright. There was too much pain in that sound, and I believed it.

Justice was moving toward her, and I started to move too, but I was too late. Jeffery's arms wrapped around my neck and shoulders again, hauling me up off the ground and letting my forelegs claw the air helplessly. He was too strong.

"She's distracting him, buddy!" he hissed into my ear as I tried to shake loose.

"I can't abandon her!" I whined back. It was nothing like the sound she made as Justice kicked her hard enough that the wall cracked when she hit it.

"She's saving our lives!" Jeffery insisted.

"Not us. She's saving your life, Fang," Lily added, her own arms around me, but gentle. "Are you going to stop her from doing this for you?"

I closed my eyes and dropped to the ground as Jeffery let me go. "There's no punishment sufficient for something like you, abomination," I heard the angel snarl, and the choked off scream Self-Loathing answered him with. She couldn't die. She could hurt, but she couldn't die. I had to tell myself that. I had to stop listening to this.

I caught the trail, focused on nothing but the trail, and was running before my eyes opened. I didn't look back at any of the noises. We had to squeeze to get through a gap between two buildings, but on the other side was a short road with a few buildings hovering around without order, and then blankness.

At least there was a stretch of blankness, shades of darkness and patches of thin mist, up to the wall. The garish, glowing wall striped in color after color. It didn't just glow; it was bright and stretched way up and off to either side like it surrounded the whole city.

"The border? They brought the border to the Light here?" Jeffery's voice was baffled.

"You can see over the top of it. It's still the Dark beyond it," I pointed out. I was as confused as he was. "It's still a big slice of the Light at the back end of the Dark. Can they do that?"

"No, they can't," Lily told us. Her voice was haunted, now. Numb. Much more than it had been while we were in the city. "No one has the power to do this deliberately. Only our Father. Exile isn't enough. There's no escape, and he wants me to die."

She dropped to her knees. Her eyes gleamed, a tear creeping out of the side of one, but that was the only obvious sign she was crying.

"No escape?" Jeffery asked doubtfully. "Getting ahead of yourself, aren't you? It's just a strip of the Light. We can cross it. It's not even that thick."

"I can't," Lily mumbled, but her eyes were starting to focus on the wall of repeating color. She was hoping again, looking for an explanation.

"It's supposed to keep us in, I know, but whoever put it up didn't know much about nightmares," Jeffery pointed out. He started to walk toward the barrier curiously.

"Father doesn't make mistakes like that," Lily admitted mournfully, "And he never intervenes."

We didn't have time, and I couldn't shut out the memory of Self-Loathing being tortured as I watched Lily suffering from her own guilt. I ran, galloping forward on all fours, and threw myself against that wall. As I'd expected, it wasn't solid. It wasn't even more than a couple of feet wide. I felt the warmth, the pressure of the Light, yes, that sense of being out of place, but then I was through and on the other side unharmed.

It wasn't even that bad. I just walked back through it, sticking my head out the other side so that they could see I was all right. Then the giggling distracted me.

Coy had gotten free of my collar, and she was a shining white fish, coming apart in bits as she swam around in figure eights inside the strip of color. She plunged out of it as a cluster of sparkling lights, but they re-formed, settling into a new shape. It was sort of, kind of like her old one. Less a fish and more a constellation, a network of stars linked by lines to form an elegant, distended catfish. When she moved the stars would rearrange and there'd be more or less of them in a new pattern. If I looked close, every few seconds a ghostly image would superimpose itself over her, a painted fish marked with curling brushstrokes instead of scales.

She was beautiful, and I stared helplessly as she exclaimed, "I feel so warm again. Who is this, Fang?"

"Who?" asked Lily sharply.

Who? I turned around and stuck my nose into the stretch of the Light. I let the feel of it fill me, focused on it—yes, 'who'. I was inside someone, kind of. Not really. It was more like I was standing on their tail. "She's right," I told Lily and Jeffery excitedly, "It's two people, I think. We'll find out!" I knew which way to go, and the wall made it obvious. I ran.

Coy followed me, spiraling around my head and body, shining with little stars, dipping in and out of the barrier. I wanted her happy. I did. Happy. I wanted to look at her. This was more original, more of a person than I'd seen her since Anna made her. But. "It's still dangerous, Coy. Can you hide under my collar some more until we're safe?"

"Okay," she agreed, yawning abruptly, and her voice sounded cheerful but sluggish as she went on, "I need a nap anyway."

That was worrying, but what dove under my collar wasn't a meek little sucker fish. It was a belt of stars wrapped around darkness that wove around my neck, a second collar under the first.

Up ahead I saw a gap in the wall, and I could hear Jeffery and Lily's feet closing on me from behind. We had to get out of here, and I believed Lily when she said she couldn't get through the barrier alive. But up ahead was the gap, and in the gap was some kind of box. The gap wasn't very big and we'd been looking for it, but still the box had just been left there.

We reached it, I heard a ragged whimpering sound, and it wasn't a box. What I skidded to a halt in front of was a cage. A small, tight cage, not quite big enough for what was inside. Bent to their knees by the low ceiling were a pair of little horses, their bodies absurd candy colors with gemlike eyes and horns that had been bound together with something silvery. Behind them, stretching out from their tails were bands of color that become a solid path of Light reaching out on either side into the distance.

"They're hideous," Jeffery declared, staring at them with a stunned expression. Lily just broke out laughing. It was a bit hysterical, but it was loud and went on and on.

"What are they?" I asked doubtfully, starting to look over the cage for ways to open it.

"They're rainbow unicorn ponies," Lily laughed. She straightened up and tried to get control of herself again. "I knew human children were getting some silly ideas about unicorns, but I didn't expect them to be this ridiculous."

"They're fantasies," I concluded. Strong ones. I lowered my head and tried to poke my nose between the bars, asking, "Are you two all right?"

The pink one whined louder, and they both tried to push themselves as far back against the other wall of the cage as they could. Drawing back, I realized, "They're terrified of me."

"They're not very bright," Lily agreed. "Not all fantasies are. Not all nightmares are, either."

I glanced at Jeffery. He was quite pointedly ignoring the conversation and trying not to look at the... rainbow unicorn ponies.

"We have to let them out," I insisted, stepping around the cage, trying to find some kind of fastening.

"Maybe Coy...?" Lily started to ask, but I shook my head.

"Let her sleep. I can't help it if they're afraid of me," I decided. There was a lock on one end. I grabbed it in my teeth and yanked. Every violent twist made the fantasies in the cage writhe and whinny, but it was more important to rescue them.

"An angel made that," Lily informed me, stepping close. "Let me."

Leaning down, she touched her lips to the lock. For a couple of seconds I thought it wasn't going to work, and then the lock fell off in her hands. I yanked the door open, lunged inside, and grabbed hold of the silvery strip binding the fantasies' horns together. My teeth couldn't quite sever it, but as I dragged the struggling ponies out the strip pulled loose.

They didn't wait an eye blink. The ponies were already scrambling to their feet and galloping off into the Dark as fast as their pudgy legs could carry them. They were heading for the border, and the Light. Behind them their tails left a trail of rainbow light, but it wasn't very long, and the wall had faded into nothing the moment they got loose. In fact we'd been left all alone, standing in the Dark outside the city.

"The barrier's down," Lily concluded, "In a few minutes the city will be empty of everyone who isn't crazy enough to want to fight. Let's get out of here until the angels are all dead or have run away."

That sounded like an excellent plan. I picked up the trail of my Muse again, a random direction I didn't intend to follow closely. We were really headed for nowhere.

We reached nowhere. It might as well have been nowhere. We were running through an empty stretch of the Dark, flat and dull and grey approaching black. I couldn't see any landscape or even dreams in the distance, and the city was far away.

"Well, they'll never find us here," I commented, slowing to a trot and then a halt.

Jeffery's hand was on the back of my head immediately. He wasn't going to say anything, but he'd thought immediately about how I must feel about what we'd left behind. Truthfully, mostly I felt exhausted and drained from fear.

The fear started creeping back when I heard a series of metallic pops. I looked up and saw Lily standing very straight, staring behind us into the distance. The noise had come from her halo. The fake one made of rust had fallen off in pieces, and floating above her hair was the one made of fire, an elaborate symbol made of smaller symbols that probably no one but an angel would understand. She looked afraid.

"They will find us here," Lily contradicted, her eyes unfocused. I knew that look. She was following a trail.

I put two and two together. "They're your family. You can follow each other," I guessed.

"I didn't know! How often do you think I see them anymore?" she snarled at me.

Jeffery had been putting three and three together. His held her elbow and he informed her flatly, "We're not going to let you run off and face them alone. They're coming, aren't they?"

"Tzad is coming, I know," she acknowledged, looking distant again, "He's like a lighthouse. I must be the same way to him. We can't possibly miss each other."

My mind raced. Unfortunately, it was racing in circles. "Lily can't go into the Light. We could go into the deep Dark. It's bad enough for us—it might extinguish an angel." I might be able to let Coy loose for a while. As long as I came back for her, she'd be okay.

Jeffery was going to put in his own idea, but Lily wasn't having any of it. "Just shut up, both of you," she snapped at us. Reaching up, she ran a fingertip along the edge of her halo, although her skin blackened and smoked when it touched the flames. Her voice was a lot sweeter when she spoke next. "Coy? Coy, little fish girl, can you wake up and help us for a minute?"

I didn't want Coy involved in this, but I didn't want a lot of things right now. I felt the belt of stars under my collar stir, and then wiggle, and then the constellation fish slipped free. Stars spun away, and what was left was a young human woman caught in a black and white photograph. All that had changed was that her eyes seemed to glitter now.

Yawning, Coy floated above my back, seated with her legs crossed in mid-air. "Is there something I can do?" she asked hopefully, "I've felt so useless this whole time. It's all so unpleasant, but I'd like to do something for someone else for once."

Lily actually smiled, and her red lips were good at looking pleased and knowing. "Not just for Fang?" she asked.

They were giving each other an odd look. They liked each other, and I didn't have time to figure out why.

"There's something only you can do," Lily explained to Coy, "Fang says you can shape the Dark almost like a dreamer. Make something big for me? Anything at all."

"I have some ideas…" Coy admitted.

Her tone had been cautious and shy, but her words sent a thrill through me. I really shouldn't have felt so excited at a dangerous moment like this, or been so obvious as I cut in, "I'd love to see them."

"All right," she mumbled, giving me a shy, worried smile. "I liked the theme of stars, and I wanted to see what else I could do with it. So, how does this look?"

She didn't seem to do anything, really. Her eyes might have glittered brighter, showing off the countless points of light that now lurked in her dark irises. Around us the Dark started to spin, mists heaving about sluggishly, until everything froze for an instant like a photograph.

When that instant ended I was standing on a disk of brass, way up high. Cold brass that numbed my feet, a flat ring around a huge sphere made out of some murky blue and pink stone. That was about as far as I got before I realized this was just one ringed planet in a machine so big I couldn't see the other side of it, with long brass arms slowly spinning a stone and metal solar system around what looked like a gigantic gas lamp.

Coy had floated around in front of me, looking expectant. I didn't know what to say. What did I think? I was relieved, I was excited, I wanted- "More," I urged her hungrily.

"Yes, more. Don't stop! The bigger, the better!" Lily yelled, seated demurely on top of a moon whirling past.

Coy laughed, stars closing around her as she spun around in spirals. A star lit up above us, and another, and then off to the side, until the machine was enclosed in a globe of them. Faint blue lines connected them into constellations, but as Coy swam past me again the lines began to move, snaking from star to star, circling each other. They looked like they were playing. Big chunks of ice started drifting up into view, comets trailing fog as they circled about, suspended from balloons.

Then she drifted to a halt next to me, her personal constellation uncoiling to reveal the girl underneath, who asked me worriedly, "But something's missing, isn't it?"

I was grinning. I couldn't help it. A murderous unkillable angel would be here any minute, and I couldn't stop grinning. "Make it dark," I urged her.

She grinned back, and now it was inspiration that sparked in her eyes. "Hold tight!" she warned me.

I took her seriously and sank my claws, front and back, into the brass. It was barely enough. The whole machine shook as a star came streaking down from the heavenly globe, then exploded when it hit the ground far below us. Then another fell. The third hit the solar lamp, and metal screamed all around us as one by one the planets began to fall. I thought mine was one of the last, but everything was a blur of vertigo until it landed and I staggered away from broken stone and bent metal rings, staring blearily at the shattered but still-flickering lamp in the middle of a wrecked solar system. Occasionally a new star would come whistling down and scatter the debris, but things seemed to be quieting down.

One of the descending lights was moving too slowly. Three lights, landing on top of the biggest broken planet, the one with red stripes that was hardly chipped. It was Tzadkiel who jumped further down onto the ripped up black earth, but the female angel that announced angrily, "Is this how you spend your last moments, Lily? Mocking our Father's work?"

Coy floated down next to me, but if her expression of stubborn anger at the angels was as alive as I could have asked for, the last thing I wanted was for them to find out she'd done this. I tugged on her wrist and whispered to her, "Under my collar, please. You've done wonderfully. I hope."

As Coy wrapped herself out of sight around my neck, I watched Justice approach Lily. She looked completely composed, even amused, and hadn't moved from her perch on a merely shed-sized moon. "Actually, I wanted Tzadki to meet someone. They're going to get along like a house on fire, I think," she replied blandly.

"I don't have a sense of humor anymore, fallen. I'm not interested in your jokes. Give me the nightmare." He ordered her sourly.

"It wasn't a joke," Lily replied with serene gaiety, "It was hardly even a metaphor. I even think I hear the pitter-patter of little feet now."

"Busted!" a terrifyingly familiar voice declared. I looked up in time to see Lucy slide down one of the still mostly upright arms of the broken machine, only to hop off at the bottom and come skipping up to Lily and Justice. She had on a white nightgown like Anna usually wore, but with mismatched cardboard wings taped to the back and a halo on her head that seemed to be made of a bent clothes hanger and gold glitter. "I'm just glad to be here," she snickered, "I don't get invited to a lot of parties, but you put RSVP on this one and everything! You know you're going to tell me how you did this before you die, right?"

"Some kind of lost soul," the girl angel commented, "Force her to move on and we'll find the nightmare."

"No, she's alive," Tzadkiel corrected her, "A dreamer who doesn't know her place. I wouldn't let her into paradise anyway."

"Wake her up, then," suggested the third angel, who seemed like a male.

I knew why Lily was smiling and looking so relaxed. Lucy didn't like being talked over. As Justice drew his sword and pointed it at her, Lucy tapped it with her own sword made of two bits of wood tied together. I knew which one scared me more.

Justice moved faster than I really could see, lunging forward so that the point of his sword was suddenly sticking far out of Lucy's back. She didn't pop, and I hadn't expected her to. She'd known this was coming, and the malignant, manic grin widening over her face said it all. I couldn't see her sword swing either, but Justice flew back into the red-striped planet, spraying fire as if it were blood.

The wound closed immediately, but he was panting and looked very grim and composed as he pushed himself to his feet. Now he stood poised and graceful, blade held at an odd angle as he hissed, "Devil child."

"Oh, you're one of the kind I have to kill over and over and over?" Lucy laughed, "This could take all night. I hope it does, because I get to sleep in on Saturday!"

They charged. Justice swept forward, but Lucy was faster. She moved like a pinball, zigzagging across the landscape, a line of white robes and red hair, until angel and dreamer met. Their bodies went staggering away from that contact. Their heads went flying. It didn't kill either of them. Justice's body wobbled and Lucy's seemed fine, but hers groped around blindly as she laughed, and his at least seemed to be moving shakily in the right direction.

The other two angels started to move, but Lily slid off her perch on the moon, calling over to them, "Don't. Please, don't. Can you really do anything but get yourselves killed? Just go home."

The female had to tug the male angel away. They glided off the battered stone planet and began approaching, not Lily, but me. "You're right," she conceded grimly, "We can finish the mission without him."

That alarmed her. Red, tattered wings with hardly any feathers clinging to them unfolded, and she leaped over the angels' heads to land in front of me. I backed up a little until I saw Jeffery lurking behind a giant upturned cog, watching the angels. We were going to have to fight.

Lily was still trying to talk them out of it. "Mission?" she demanded exasperatedly, hands outstretched, "You're the only two left. Admit it. I saw Marael die. I know Kalariel and Masakiel were at the fight with Baal, which means they didn't make it. How many others, Isda? It's just you and Maion now. Are you willing to watch him die for a task I know Father didn't give you that has already failed?"

"It hasn't failed," the male angel, Maion, insisted heatedly. "We took out enough fallen and your little creatures to more than justify our casualties. Now we just have to destroy the nightmare who opened the portal. The one you can lead us to."

"They're not going to listen, Lily," I hissed up at her desperately.

"They never do," she admitted, barely audible. I saw her tense up and take a step forward.

The female angel, Isda, was almost as fast as Justice. I didn't even see her knives until they were drawn and Lily was choking off a shriek. Her hand flew off its wrist to land in the dirt. As Lily gripped the stump, slowing down the blood that was dripping from it and hardening already, Isda explained in a monotone, "What I learned from your little trick back there was that I don't have to be able to kill you if I can cut you to helpless pieces. I have no intention of sacrificing either myself or Maion. We're going to live, we're going to eliminate your little shadow playthings, and we're going to take you back to the Four in bits. Exile has obviously taught you nothing."

I started growling. It was suicidal instinct, but I was angry. Then the world seemed to fly apart. I had to replay a couple of seconds in my mind to realize tons of floating ice had dropped out of the sky and the angels were under the steaming rubble in front of me.

"Coy?" I asked, stunned.

"I tried not to hurt them," she defended plaintively from under my collar.

"She didn't. We're getting out of here before they escape," Lily informed us. It wasn't even a command. She was already running, giving me and Jeffery no choice except to follow.

With the immediate threat out of the way, I could hear the loud thumps and occasional wail of metal behind us. Justice and Lucy fighting was like listening to a train wreck, and when I stole a look back I didn't even understand what I was seeing. I could also see the way Lily was still clutching her cut-off wrist. "Are you…?" I started to ask.

"I'll get a new one if I can't come back and find the old one," Lily cut me off, "Worry about me later. Worry about us now. Lucy's going to deal with Tzadkiel." A quick glance at Jeffery showed that we both agreed with that. As strong as he'd been, that just meant Lucy would hurt him worse. What was going on back there was as crazy as the strangest dreams, a charred and smoking child ripping apart wheels made out of eyes with everything in flames. Was that an angel? But Lily shoved my nose down toward the ground. "We need to get somewhere safe. Is the blind girl's house nearby?"

"It is." I knew that instantly. "But won't they follow us?"

"They're already following us," she hissed. Was that pain, anger, or fear? I risked a glance over my shoulder. Yes, there were two white glows behind us.

I sped up, moving ahead of the others, and followed the strongest trail in my head. My Muse was near, and like usual she'd found a stretch of the Dark's mysterious landscape to settle her house in. I wished I was coming here under better circumstances. Willows, elegant and sad dotted a field bathed in night time darkness under an enormous crescent moon that provided no light. We ran along a stone-paved pathway, teased by the wind—no, cut by the wind. It was cold, freezing cold, one of the harshest colds I'd felt in the Dark, but if it fell even for a moment the air was temperate and gentle.

The house was a black shape looming ahead of us, but I could see the angels' glow creeping around our feet. Panting, wordless, we plunged up the stairs and into the hallway.

I thought the house was asleep. I saw no eyes and everything was dark, bathed in deep shadow so that the furniture was lumpy shapes and musty smells. I didn't know what Lily thought we could do here. The light behind us told me that the angels were able to get into the house just fine. Then I plunged through the door that ought to have led to my Muse's parlor. Her, at least, I would defend to the death. There was no one in this house I would hesitate to die for.

I wasn't in the parlor. That really wasn't a surprise, although I'd thought the house wasn't awake enough to mislead me. I was in some utterly dark room, all alone. My eyes adjusted slowly, but there wasn't much to adjust to. I thought the two shapes were little beds, which meant this was the nursery. Not only was the house a maze tonight, it had separated us.

That meant anything could be happening anywhere, a thought sufficient to get me running again. Any door was as good as any other. I stormed through the kitchen, saw a flash of light through a side door, and charged into an equally dark laundry room only to end up ramming into a huge washing basin, knocking it over and sending me tumbling into a hamper full of clothes.

When I tore my way out, the room was lit up. The angel Lily called Maion was there. He didn't waste any time talking. All he had was a sword, barbed and engraved, but really just a sword. As he stabbed it at me my feet tangled in old underwear. Fabric tore, but it was too late. My chest sparked with pain as the point dove into it.

The discontinuity was alarming. I just wasn't where I'd been anymore. Everything felt tense and vague, and I couldn't make out the shapes of furniture in the darkness, but some things I could see clearly. I recognized part of this feeling. I knew the way fear and anger seemed to hover over me, emotions that weren't mine. I was in a dream.

The anger took over from the fear. I was running down a hallway I didn't know. I didn't mean to be, but someone else was in my skin with me and it was her anger that had taken me over. The knowledge that it was a woman fell into place with everything else. My Muse was dreaming, and I wasn't her nightmare. The angels were the nightmare, and I was her way of fighting back. Instead of struggling, I cooperated. Accepting that made it easy. I drove my own feet forward and let her nudge me.

A mirror on the wall. There were mirrors like windows on every wall, showing different rooms, but this one had a glow inside it. I leaped through, and Isda was much smaller than I remembered as I dove out of a wall at her, teeth gaping for her head. She was fast, too fast, but the knife that caught me in the mouth didn't hurt me. I unraveled and found myself back in another room. That was just fine. I was the only person in this house who knew exactly where every door led.

Maion was facing Jeffery across the kitchen counter when I started struggling out of a floor level cabinet, writhing and snapping because I was too big. In the seconds it took me to get free, they'd both fled.

I caught Isda again. I rose up out of an old cistern in a crumbling pump room, dripping slime, and only the hilt of her knife catching on my breastbone kept my jaws from snapping shut on her throat. I thought I could still get her, but the dream wouldn't let me be hurt and before I registered the wound I'd come apart and re-formed in the nursery.

Coy was everywhere. Constellations and painted fish decorated every wall, and her face watched from every grime-clouded portrait. She'd been taken in as part of the dream, but she wasn't suited to hunting or killing. She was taking part in a way that was much more natural for her.

When I sprang out of a chute into the laundry room again Maion was staring at Coy on the wall, her fish face turned away. I didn't know if he could see her sadness at what was about to happen. As I charged forward the angel turned and swung at me, and it went above my head because I was so small. That was the idea. I dug my teeth into the back of his calf as I passed and ripped, kept barreling through the door in front of me, then hurtled out of the door behind him. Now I was a monstrous thing and he was tiny, and my teeth slammed shut not just over his shoulder but his throat and most of his chest. When my fangs crunched deep enough to meet in the middle, I knew he was dead.

I kept running. Back into the hallway, I took an instant to let the house tell me where Isda was. She was in the parlor with Lily and...

Pain lit me up, then disappeared as the dream burst. With my own ears I heard a choking, gurgling whimper from down the hall, and it wasn't Lily's voice. My feet felt heavy as lead, my body solid and much too damageable as I pounded desperately down to the end of the hall. And I could feel the sharp pain in my side where Maion's sword had cut me.

Isda stood in front of my Muse's chair, one knife pointed at Lily and the other thrust through the center of my Muse's chest, the tip of the long blade sticking out the back. Blood stained the knife, black and dripping, but not a lot. I'd heard the noise my Muse made, heard the punctured bubbling of her voice now, but her face was still hidden in her hands and they were still quiet sobs. The wound hadn't changed anything.

"Another lost soul," Isda complained irritably, "Why did Father make humans the only things you can't completely destroy?"

"Disappointment," came Lily's immediate reply. "I mean, look at what a failure we were. He wanted to start over from scratch with a new design."

After all this, they'd descended into catty bickering. I didn't have to hide my growl as I padded forward. Isda had already seen me. The knife was yanked free of my Muse and pointed at me, still coated with black blood. I could taste the bitterness of that blood in my mouth, and always would.

"She's too fast, you idiots," Lily snapped, making me realize Jeffery was lurking behind another door on the far end of the room, watching. "Just run. If you get away, this is over and she's lost."

That was ridiculous. Neither Jeffery nor I were going to leave Lily to whatever this angel's revenge would be. It was the angel who reacted. Her shoulders shifted and she was about to lunge, and everything became tight and frozen again as the dream re-formed around the house.

Everything felt like molasses now, but the angel was still too fast. She kicked up my Muse's feet, and I saw for the second time the chains linking her to the four frozen statues on the wall. Those chains were sliced apart by a single sweep of Isda's knife.

The dream, which had barely closed, let go again. My Muse had stopped moving, stopped crying, stopped doing anything. "There," Isda spat in annoyance, "Now move on already."

I was going to kill Isda. It was as simple as that. She'd kill me too, but I didn't care. I crept forward, body low, fangs showing. She had to keep her knife pointed straight at me, because when her blank, shining eyes looked into mine I was sure she could see I'd take any opportunity if I thought I could get to her. Lily only had one hand, but her claws were out and her body coiled, waiting like mine, and Jeffery prowled toward us. It was going to be over in seconds.

Eyes were opening on the walls now, watching the angel and watching me. The terrified statues were gone. And my Muse reached over to the little stand beside her chair to pick up a vase of dead flowers. She was just starting to swing it at the angel's face when Isda made her decision. The knife aimed at Lily swung back. Instead of the blade, Isda's fist punched my Muse in the chest, shoving her back into her chair. Or rather, into something that had opened in the back of her chair, a round white hole edged in pearl. My Muse's hands caught at the edge, but as her body dipped back into it I saw her expression change from anger and sadness to relief. At that point something else dragged my attention away. Lily had pounced while Isda's knife was out of the way, red claws were fastened into the angel's wrist, and teeth were heading for Isda's face. Isda had no choice. The knife pointed at me arced back to intercept Lily. She was fast. She was way, way too fast. But I was right there, and as the knife plunged back from Lily's sliced-through face my jaws reached Isda's neck first. I bit, I tore, and the knives went flying, and I landed just in time to see my Muse's hands let go.

She fell back into that white void, eyes closed, and while I was still turning my body and getting my feet underneath me it closed up behind her and the hole was gone, taking my Muse with it.

The eyes were gone. The house was still. I looked up at Lily, prying off the split shell of her mask to expose the haggard, blood-colored demon face underneath. I said the first thing in my head. "You planned this."

I only knew why I'd said it after I'd said it. It was why she'd made me take us here, wasn't it? I looked for the anger inside me, but before I could find it Lily answered sadly, "It was what I was hoping would happen. You may not think that's the same thing."

She admitted it. That stumped me again, and left me with only one question. "Why?"

"It was all I could give her," Lily explained. Her voice was low and gentle and pained, and made me itch with the knowledge that she'd lost more people today than I had. "She wasn't happy, and I couldn't give her peace myself. She'd chained herself down to a lie, but if I cut her free…" She trailed off. She didn't want to tell me this, and the pity of it confused me enough to let her trail her claws around the back of one of my ears as she finished, "She didn't think she deserved to go to Heaven, puppy. I forced Isda to take that choice away from her."

"She never spoke to me. That's how unhappy she was." I was talking to myself, really.

"She's at peace now," Lily promised me, "That's all I can tell you, but it's one thing I'm sure of. She's not gone. She's somewhere… peaceful."

I took a couple of deep breaths, but Jeffery's voice asked, "Buddy?"

There was a request in that voice. I looked up, and looked past him at the wall. It had changed. A huge, lush flower in black and purple with a green eye in the center had been badly painted over most of it. Across that image were raggedly carved the words 'Elaine + Fang'.

"Elaine," I repeated. That was her name.

I smelled smoke. It was creeping out of the corners where the floor met the walls. Then there were flickers.

"The house is catching fire?" I asked dumbly.

"Did you think it could live without her?" Jeffery demanded of me, impatiently yanking on my collar. He was right, of course. We ran out into the hall as the flames became hot, and before the worry could finish forming in my thoughts Coy was there, gleaming starlight as she spiraled around me. The house didn't have any tricks to play anymore, but the fire spread at an outrageous pace. By the time we'd sprinted down the hall and all of us had leapt off the front porch onto the grass I felt painfully singed.

I landed on something soft that squealed, to my great surprise, and rolled off it to find it was some kind of lightly charred stuffed toy, unidentifiable from the holes and one missing arm. It was Self-Loathing. Before I could stand up she threw herself over my neck and whimpered, "Fang, your Muse…"

She wanted me to fill in the gaps, but that wasn't the real question. "I'll be all right. You're alive. Coy is alive. Jeffery and Lily are alive. And if I'd known, if I could have—" It made me shake to say this. The need to start running flashed over me, then was gone. Wearily, honestly, I finished, "I'd have done this for Elaine myself."

"I'm sorry I'm not… prettier," Self-Loathing told me haltingly,

"This was the best I could do until I heal, but I couldn't stay away from you. I can't make myself let you go."

"I know," I told her soothingly. I did. All I had to do was feel that lumpy shape on my neck, or look up into the glowing moon eyes of a star-speckled catfish floating in front of me to know I was loved.

"I should have let you go, Fang," she went on, her voice thick and heavy. "It's not going to end well. I mean it."

"I know," I accepted. I knew she meant it.

"Before this gets any more morose," Jeffery cut in, "What happened to the city?" The hand rubbing between my ears let me know that he could have waited, but he was probably right. We were too exhausted to be talking like this.

"It's still there," Self-Loathing sighed, "The nightmares are angry. They're furious. The angels all died or ran away, and if there are any demons left, they're hiding. Everyone else is nervously looking around. No one really knows what the rules are, now."

He looked as tired as the rest of us, but Jeffery grinned, needle teeth fitting together perfectly. "Good. That was the last obstacle. If we move before the demons recover, there'll be nobody to stop me."

I actually laughed. Jeffery never gave an inch or stopped for a second.

Chapter Six

Exeunt Omnes

Anxiety nagged at me. I let Coy go off and play with dreams on her own, but I had to tell myself she was ready and she'd be safe. It wasn't even the first time, but it still felt like the first time. Now that I had time to myself, of course I went looking for company. I wanted to see Self-Loathing, or maybe Jeffery, and as I trotted through the Dark I hunted around for their trails. To my surprise and curiosity, they led in the same direction. That direction was outside the city. Not just outside the city, past it into the blackest depths of the Dark.

I didn't like this place. I loved the Dark, but this was like going into the Light. Worse. I kept thinking that something was trying to get inside me, change me. And there was no scenery, just shadows fading to black. If I was lucky I'd see a dream flicker in the distance, shrunken and hard and opaque. It made me tense, aware of every bristling hair down my neck and haunches.

The trails were getting vivid, and I was relieved that I hadn't needed to go very far when I saw Jeffery and Self-Loathing ahead of me. They weren't exactly side by side. He strolled along swiftly and easily as if he were at home even back here, and behind him Self-Loathing scurried and peered around like a frightened animal.

She almost looked like a frightened animal tonight. I couldn't quite identify what she was. A lot of it was cat, bright blue, with pointy ears and big, fuzzy paws and a tail and whiskers. Part of it was a human girl, although I couldn't tell what age she was, especially in that loose dress. She might even have been a grown woman. Mostly she was small, hardly bigger than if she'd actually been a cat.

Jeffery saw me at the same time I saw him, and was giving me a friendly wave and shouting, "Hey, Fa—" when Self-Loathing shrieked.

Green, slit-pupiled eyes fixed on me, impossibly large and staring. For a moment she crouched, looking more like an animal than ever, and then she bolted, running away from me and back into the deep Dark.

It would have been nice if I'd been concerned that whatever was wrong with her would get worse back there, but I didn't think at all. She'd looked adorable as a little cat thing. Seeing her running away yanked me forward to chase after her. Her back went rigid with fear rather than flirtation, the muscles of her arms and legs tense. Feet in thick sneakers pounded across the nothing that was the ground here, running on two legs that were way too short to escape me. That was fine. I didn't want a chase, I wanted to catch her. It was bad enough that with every step that ludicrous bell around her neck jingled luridly in my ears.

As my teeth closed that final inch I strained to keep myself in check. I let them sink into her collar and the back of her dress, but definitely not her body, then hoisted her up by the scruff and turned to carry her out. She whined and yowled wordlessly, waving her fists and kicking. Each desperate noise and futile swing jolted me with delicious temptation, but I kept my feet moving and caught back up with Jeffery.

He was carrying something peculiar, a little bird cage with a little bird on a perch in it. A zombie bird, with protruding bone and bits replaced with fragments of tile or glass or any sort of junk. He'd called it a pain canary when he bought it and left it behind in the same weird little store. I was guessing he'd recovered the bird rather than bought a new one. It was ugly enough to be distinctive.

He leaned down and examined the struggling Self-Loathing as he walked, explaining, "Sorry, buddy. She'll be okay. The dream I had her eat must have been worse than I thought. That's good for me, but I guess it hit her hard."

"We'll get her back to the Gate," I mumbled as best I could through a mouthful of clothing. Clothing that teased me with deliciously innocent smells of soap and kitten.

"Please," Self-Loathing mewled, or maybe it was a sob? "We should get out of here. I can walk now, if you want."

"Do you want me to put you down?" I asked fondly. I was trying not to sound so fond I growled at her. She didn't reply, so I let her dangle from my teeth as we hurried back into the merely grey mists we'd come from.

The Gate swam into view ahead of us, a massive rectangular arch towering over a random nest of buildings. When we passed the first street Jeffery leaned down and picked up Self-Loathing, although the bird cage made that awkward.

I was looking at the blank expression on her face, but he put her down on my shoulders with her little legs looped around my neck. "All right," he offered, "Rather than tell you what happened, I'll show you and everybody else. Can you find me some dream painters?"

It was hard enough to concentrate with stubby, clawed fingers gripping my fur so tight I could feel the trembling. I also didn't know the dream painters very well. I pressed my nose to the gravel path and started wandering down the street, sweeping from side to side, following traces and waiting for them to get stronger. When they did I followed those, until Jeffery stepped ahead of me. We'd ended up in a park of packed earth and broken, rusty playground toys. A bunch of chittering animals crouched and floated in front of a posting board covered in the incoherent scrawls dreamers make.

Walking right up to them, Jeffery pulled the pain canary out of its cage and held it up to the dream painters. It chittered at them. They chattered at it. Finally we followed Jeffery back to a heap of collapsed wood as the painters began to work.

The image was what I'd have expected from a dream in the deep Dark. There was no background, just pitch black surrounding the centerpiece. The dreamer wasn't even a child, just a toddler, and while I thought it was a girl I wasn't sure. Soon the dream painters were painting dogs, three of them, biting her. One had its teeth deeply into her leg, and red blood smeared everything.

"You ate that dream?" I asked Self-Loathing cautiously.

"It's fading now," she assured me, sliding down to lie over my shoulders. The arms wrapped around my neck didn't feel relaxed.

I peered up at Jeffery. "I'm not going to guess," I told him, "It has something to do with your plan, I'm sure. Why did you have her eat someone's worst memory?" I glanced at the painting. Yes, memories didn't get much worse than that. If she was dreaming she'd lived through it, but those dogs were trying to tear the dreamer apart.

Jeffery climbed up onto the pile of broken wood, then stooped down a little to talk to me. "Do you know how to open a path to the human world, Fang?"

"You opened one when you made that dreamer into something like you," I countered cautiously. It was all I knew.

"I didn't open it. He did," Jeffery explained proudly, "Dreams connect humans to the Dark. His dream wanted to get out, to switch places and become him, and it made a hole. If the hole is big enough, if it lasts long enough, anyone can go in and out."

"So you're going to make another dreamer's dreams take over his waking self?" I guessed. Glancing at the painting, I corrected, "Her waking self, I guess."

"Almost. Not really," Jeffery hedged. He grinned now, showing every tooth, and he had a lot of them. His mouth was wider than a human's and his teeth much thinner and sharper, but they fit together perfectly. "To make a really good portal, I need to make it so the human can't tell the difference between dreaming and being awake. When they're completely lost, when the waking world and the Dark are the same place to them, they really will be the same place. A hole will open. A nice, big one. And then I'm going to go through it."

"Are you sure it will work?" I asked doubtfully. Something about the idea troubled me.

"It will," Self-Loathing assured me. She pushed herself up to sit on my back, and I could feel fingers digging in, and vines and leaves twining around her arms and legs. "That's how we used to do it a long time ago. With training, with rituals and with medicines, a human learned to open the way. If they didn't know how, the dream painters would lead them from this side. That won't work now. Humans don't care about dreams anymore."

"So I'll have to push her," Jeffery concluded. He stood up straight and added in a louder tone, "I'll need some help. It doesn't seem fair to me that I be the only nightmare who gets to escape."

He wasn't talking to me. Looking around, I saw we'd drawn a small crowd. They'd stopped to look at the painting of the dream and ended up listening to Jeffery. There were a few noises, and all of them sounded positive.

I was going to be the note of dissent. "The demons will kill anyone who tries," I pointed out.

"Ain't 'nuff demons left," snickered a nightmare that looked like it was made out of dirt and mold and slime.

He was right. I wanted to point out that there were more behind the Gate, a lot more, but I knew the answer to that, too. They weren't going to find out what was going on and come out in time to stop us.

"I'll need plenty of nightmares eventually," Jeffery told the group, "Right now, every nightmare who goes out there making the scariest dreams they can come up with will help slow down the demons and Lucy figuring out what's happening. I don't care if you're doing it to escape with me, or to stick it to the demons, or to thumb your noses at Lucy herself. I'll try it alone if I have to, but I'll take all the help I can get."

"I've been holding back too long," remarked a tall, weirdly thin nightmare, a human in maddeningly colored clothes with scissors for hands. Rubbing those scissors across his lips, he added, "And so have my friends. The spot of top nightmare's going to be free when this is over."

That did it. There was a lot of laughter, but the nightmares were splitting up, racing out of the park in all directions. Only when they were gone did Jeffery crouch down again and tell me, "You're the one whose help I need most of all, Fang." His tone held an undercurrent, something wrong. To my surprise, I realized it was guilt.

"If it weren't for you, I'd have faded and been forgotten without ever speaking to anybody, Jeff," I reminded him, "Nothing but teeth in the Dark, not really a person at all. Just tell me what you need me to do."

"For starters, eat this," he instructed me, the dry tone making it clear his moment of doubt was over. Reaching into the cage, he pulled out the little bird thing again and tossed it right at me. I caught it by instinct, crunched it in my teeth a couple of times, and swallowed. It went down like bathing myself in the deep Dark itself. Everything went cold, and all I was aware of was my teeth and the victims around me, especially the little vulnerable thing on my back. Then it passed.

"What was that thing, anyway?" I asked, shaking my head and trying to get rid of the taste.

"I'm not sure. Those things from outside? They catch them from the Light and fill them with the Dark, supposedly. However it works, you get a pain canary. They suck up information about bad dreams. It's how I found our dreamer, and now you can track her, right?"

I lifted my nose to the breeze. There she was. "Like a beacon," I assured him.

Jeffery grinned his best grin again, the delighted one he saved just for me. "Then this is going to work, and I'm going to be the first nightmare to escape the Dark in two hundred years."

"When I'm in, what do you need me to do?" I asked, eying the dream that bobbed and wandered on the Light side of the border.

"The days when you needed my advice to turn a dream are long since past. You'll do better without instructions from me," was Jeffery's reply. I was touched by the pride in his tone, but I'd rather have had an answer.

I went ahead without one. I galloped forward, leaped over the little stones marking the border itself, and hit the dream head-first. For a dream in the Light it resisted quite a bit, but after a jarring impact I fell through.

I knew this was the dreamer. I knew it. I'd followed the trail and now she was all around me. Her dream was one of those simple dreams. She was just a human woman with brown hair in the living room of a house that was mostly wood and lightly furnished. Everything felt very pleasant and tranquil, and her focus seemed to be on the dogs. There were four of them, not all the same size, but none of them very big. Mostly they scampered around her feet as she sat in a rocking chair. They tugged on things and chased each other, and there was always one hopping up into her lap and having its head scratched.

I hid behind a wall in the kitchen, out of sight, but I didn't have much time. The dream had its own tension and was barely hanging onto the Light as it was. My being here was going to tip it into the Dark. I wanted to tip it my way.

A pair of the dogs chased each other past the kitchen door. I grabbed the little tiny skinny one with the spots and yanked it out of sight, ripped it open, and dove into it. The body was way too tight, too innocent and harmless, and I was going to bust out of it if I wasn't careful. Wasting no time, I went trotting back into the room on stiff little legs, wagged a pointy little tail, and hopped up on the dreamer's lap. With a vague and pleasant smile she began to scratch the top of my head. I bared my teeth and growled.

The dream lurched. The lighting dimmed, but mostly I could feel it thrown into the Dark as the mood of contentment was replaced by fear. Around me came a chorus of other growls as my nightmare took over the dream and the dogs caught it. I let the seconds tick by, staring up into her eyes, growling murderously between clenched and dripping fangs, and when I decided she'd shrunk back into her chair as far as she could I lunged up and sunk my teeth into her cheek. I could hear the meaty thumps around me as the other dogs bit down.

The dream lurched again, convulsed. It hurt, and as it broke up I went sprawling, landing on my back in my own body and choking on the terror that hung in a burning cloud all around me. I staggered out, then collapsed onto my belly to cough again.

Jeffery wasn't the only person waiting for me. I wasn't really surprised. "I've never seen so much fear in one dream," Coy told me. There was a certain faint, bubbly flutter to her voice lately when she was a fish, but it didn't hide the doubt and worry. She swam over my head and extended one of the tendrils around her mouth, the glittering star on the end dipping into the vitriolic cloud. "Not just fear," she added, "Pain. This dream really hurt the dreamer."

"It was meant to," Jeffery panted, running up to meet us. He was coming from the direction of the border, although I couldn't see it. I could see the Gate in the distance. Wow. Had the dream really gone this deep?

"She can't remember why she's afraid," Self-Loathing explained. I hadn't even seen her. She climbed up my leg as I pushed myself upright, curling like a snake but warm and smooth. I didn't quite know what to make of the sensation, but it was hard to ignore and the feel of her coiled around me teased at my thoughts even after the shock of that shattered dream. I was surprised to realize she'd wound her way up to my shoulders, and with a touch of guilt in her voice she told Coy, "She has no defenses from it now. When something she loved turned on her, it felt real. I did that."

"And that was the idea," Jeffery concluded. The dream's fog of terror still hung next to us, and he slid his finger through it too, licking the slime off the end. "Yes," he judged, "She'll remember this when she wakes up. More than just remember, I bet she gets rid of the dogs. Now she's ready to believe anything she dreams. This is going to work!"

Coy hovered over me again. Expressions were hard to read in a fish made of stars, but those pearlescent moons she had for eyes seemed troubled to me. Again she ran a whisker through the smoke and announced anxiously, "I don't like this. It's not supposed to work this way." It was me she was really talking to.

It was Self-Loathing who spat back angrily, "A nightmare is what Fang is, and he's good at it. I don't want him to change."

"This wasn't a bad dream," Coy retorted, "The dream was an excuse for something else."

I wanted…

It was too late to stop them fighting. They were face to face above me, and venom dripped in their voices because they were fighting over me as much as what I'd just done. I had to stop this from getting out of hand. I knew too well how crazy Self-Loathing could get about me, and it began creeping over me that maybe Coy could be as bad if she were pushed.

Jeffery stepped in. "Fang doesn't have to do anything he doesn't want to do," he told them, quiet and solemn. He and I looked at each other.

So I just had to figure out what I wanted. Oddly, having Coy and Self-Loathing glaring at each other over my head made it easier. Someone was on my side regardless. "This bothers me, Jeff," I admitted slowly, "Hurting the human on the other side of the dream doesn't feel right. It's not part of who I am."

"Who are you? You know the answer to that, right?" Nobody would ask a question that direct but Anna, and like a dream walker she'd appeared without warning, sitting atop a spring on a contraption too ridiculous for me to make sense of. By now I wasn't surprised to see her, and neither was anyone else.

"I'm the teeth in the dark, chasing you in your dreams," I answered mutedly. "Everything else is extra. But one of those extra things is my friends." I was working it out, step by step. Anna had asked the right question, as usual.

"So who are you?" Anna asked Jeffery next, rocking forward and back on her weird toy.

She'd stumped him. He had no ready answer to that, which was the last thing I had expected. "This is how I find out," he told her finally. No, he told *me*.

This was between me and Jeffery, and I supposed it always had been. "So tell me what we do next," I told him. He'd meant it, and I meant it, and it made him smile. He looked so sinister when he did that, better than his grin. I envied it.

"The next part is all mine," he assured me, "I'll need you to lead me to my dreamer a couple of times until I can follow her myself, but that's all."

Now I showed my own teeth. "Easy enough, then." I had reservations, but we'd worked it out. I was grateful it had been so easy.

Except it hadn't. As I lifted my muzzle and searched around for where the next dream would be, I felt the tightness in Self-Loathing, saw the haunted look on Coy's star-speck face, and heard the silence that had been coming from both of them. Neither one of them liked my decision. I was... I was going to do it anyway. I went back to hunting.

Eventually I left Jeffery crafting some of the most boring bad dreams I had ever seen anywhere. I admired his dedication to his eventual goal, but they really were tedious. What was the point of sneaking into someone's dreams and possessing her friends, only to make them break her dishes or say mean things in dream gibberish?

I needed something more exciting, so as I passed a dream floating just on the Light side of the border I jumped into it and looked around. It was one of the weird dreams, the ones where carrots have street signs on them and little bears wear fake moustaches. The dreamer conversed urgently with the bears while wearing a top hat about as tall as he was. I could certainly shake this up. I crept back behind the dreamer, crouched down, and realized I didn't actually know what I was going to do.

It wasn't that I didn't have any ideas. Everywhere I looked there were possibilities. Being attacked by a carrot with teeth might leave a mark he'd even remember when he was awake. I didn't really want to follow up on any of them. I just sat there for a while and watched, while my presence gently pushed the dream across the border into the Dark. It was interesting, in a way. There were clouds in a sky of shifting pastel colors, and they moved like they were flapping wings as they flew. There seemed to be some kind of story going on. Quite what it meant when one of the bears was dragged forward by the others to the dreamer I didn't know, but I admired the imagination in everything around me. Now the bears were beating the actual stuffing out of the prisoner bear, and more bears dragged in some kind of large plastic display case. The doors began to creep open, and inside was the only thing not painted in colors like pink and purple. It was black, featureless black, some kind of doll, but I only got a peek before the dreamer decided he'd had enough and the dream dissolved.

That left me sitting in the Dark amidst the faint haze of a dream. It certainly didn't feel like me, this mix of the surreal and the purposeful and the creepy. I almost let it soak in anyway, but I spurred myself to get up and move on. I had to face it. I knew who I was, but I didn't feel it. I needed my Muse, and Elaine was dead.

Well, she'd always been dead, I supposed. Life, death—I didn't understand humans and wasn't going to try. I hoped she was happy, wanted her to be happy, but she wasn't here anymore and memories of that pallid, emaciated figure weren't enough. I knew already I was remembering her wrong, and sleek arms of pale skin and stitched fabric and white paper outlined in black paint mixed together. I hadn't been letting myself think of my old Coy either, avoiding thoughts of the sunlight colored goldfish and her beautiful imagination. Thoughts of a dusty, silent house and hushed weeping that never stopped. I wanted those back so badly.

Now I was getting maudlin! I needed to turn to the inspiration I still had. I turned my head, sniffing the shadows until my nose turned under its own power to follow what wasn't a smell, just a direction. It kind of was a smell, too. Leather and bone and burlap, things that tore if you bit down hard enough. Self-Loathing was that way, and she could definitely pick me up.

I found her in the leftover dream of a ruined city, a patch of the Dark that was mostly debris of shattered buildings and the wreckage of war machines, some of them odd and some of them obviously alien. She was sitting on the barrel of a tank. Half of it was melted, but there was still room for Lily and Anna to perch on the machine with her.

"I couldn't go back. Humans don't want me anymore. They never liked me, but they came to me when no one else would forgive. I don't think they'd even see me now," Self-Loathing told them. Little feet dangled over the edge of the barrel. All three looked human. A little girl with brown hair, a grown woman with red hair, and Self-Loathing in-between, blonde and carelessly slender with a body as fragile as her voice.

It was nice. She wasn't wearing it for me, but it was nice. I liked the face, not quite as innocently young as Anna's, but close.

"I think I've been here too long to go back," was Anna's explanation, "I miss my friends and my parents, but I couldn't tell you their names anymore." She sounded scared and haunted. Those weren't emotions I associated with her.

"You're talking about going through the portal Jeffery's going to open?" I guessed as I circled around the heap of bricks and pipes to their side.

"Assuming he succeeds. I think he will," Lily agreed. Her tone was much lighter than the other two, but then they were all smiling now that I was here. "None of us are planning to go, but it's nice to have someone to talk to about the mortal world."

"Something's wrong with Fang," Anna pointed out abruptly. That was the Anna I knew. At the same time, it made me feel kind of awkward and on the spot.

I was saved by Self-Loathing's playful trill. "Really? I bet I can make him feel better." Casually, she extended one of her feet and waggled her toes above my head.

I jumped. The tilted up tank had her sitting high above me, and my teeth snapped an inch below that foot. When I landed on all fours again I felt suddenly embarrassed, but I hadn't thought at all. Those little moving toes were just such dainty things that I'd reacted.

It felt kind of good, and it still felt kind of good as the girls giggled, but not so good that I was going to do it again in front of an audience. Anyway, 'giggle' couldn't describe the delighted evil of the way Lily laughed. It was a pretty good description of the noise Self-Loathing was making. She kept wiggling her toes, and they drew my eyes like lures.

"Something is wrong," Self-Loathing announced abruptly, "Should I try harder? I can make you want me. I bet I can make you forget everything."

I was sure she could. I didn't really want to explain that I was too embarrassed to lose control in front of my friends. Then I just blurted out, "I miss Elaine."

That shut them up. It shut me up, too. We all stood there, silent and grave, until Coy's voice bubbled near my ear, "Come on, you taught me this, Fang. It's easy to find yourself because you're right there. Inspiration is just something you stumble over."

Then she was moving. She'd snuck up on me, and now she wound around and around me, her body too sinuous for a catfish. I could feel it, warm and solid even though it didn't look it as she spiraled and slid over me. Little points of heat marked every star. Gliding free, she offered, "Come on, let's try some dreams. Maybe I can inspire you. You always inspire me."

The offer made me smile despite myself. She knew what I wanted and she was pretty, this fish made of stars. "I just don't feel like chasing anyone tonight," I explained reluctantly. My belly twinged to admit it.

"I think you do," Self-Loathing corrected me. She'd laid herself out along the barrel, and suggested with a lazy and teasing drawl, "You just need to chase the right dream. Run away from him, Coy."

This wasn't the old Coy. I didn't feel this way about her. And then her body lashed, and she sailed away from me in a serpentine weave. The stars that made her up kept falling behind, leaving a glittering path while lines redrew themselves to keep up.

I jumped again. Coy let out a squeal and darted behind a rusting refrigerator. Instead of charging around it I jumped up on top, but she rocketed straight up past me and by the time I thought to bite she was threading into the window of a burned out building. She was laughing.

I gave up and followed the laugh. It hurt my stomach when I jumped up to the next floor and caught myself on the window frame, but I'd stopped caring. We raced down stairs and out into the ruins again. This place was perfect. She was faster than me, but she wasn't trying to get away. There were a thousand places to hide, but I could always follow the trail of stars she left behind.

The Dark seemed to get darker as we played our game of tag in this surreal and abandoned battlefield, until we both stopped at the same time and looked around. The stars she'd left behind had settled and they were the only light now, pale and casting sharp shadows everywhere. I turned my head back to look at Coy, and we both smiled as she dissolved into threads of black and starlight, leaving a young woman who glowed without depth or detail.

I leapt again. I'd caught her by surprise and I knew it, and the thrill banished even the lingering ache in my gut as my open jaws reached for her hip and started to close. Then she screamed.

It was fear, pure fear until my teeth caught what really felt like skin, when it spiked higher with pain. It was over in an instant. I didn't bite down. I let myself fly past her, tumbling as I hit the rocks hard and scrambling as fast as I could to my feet, babbling, "I'm sorry! I'm sorry! Are you all right?"

"Why did you do that?" Coy squealed. She floated in a crouch above the heap, and I had to make myself look at her. The fear and hurt in her expression felt like my heart was ripping apart, and I'd left a wound. She wasn't making it prettier or more dramatic. There was no blood, just dragging tooth marks, smears like scars in her photographic image.

"He likes it," Anna answered for me from the tank. Her voice was as calm and convincing as usual. "He thought you did, too. He thought you wanted it."

"Why would I want him to bite me?" Coy demanded, her voice still shrill from panic. It hurt. It hurt me inside. It hurt me so bad I fell off my feet, curling up as best I could when I couldn't make proper arms. The sense of shock, of betrayal, got so bad so fast that I could barely hear Coy's voice as she exclaimed, "Fang? Fang, what's wrong?"

The pain eased a little, and I lifted my head to look into her face, inches now from mine as her arms slid around my neck. She didn't care if I'd attacked her, she just didn't want me to hurt. I should have felt better. I didn't. My insides were a knot, and I couldn't focus on her. It was like I was being pulled away from her toward… the dreamer.

"That thing…" I wheezed, "That thing I swallowed." That was it. The knot in my gut was finally starting to fade. Enough that I could start pushing myself upright again, although Coy still clung to me. The other girls were watching me closely, too.

Something else hit me. "Jeffery fed this to me. This is part of this plan. He set me up? I can't believe it. I can't believe Jeffery would do this to me." That hurt too, but it was a different hurt.

"Jeffery cares about you, puppy," Lily told me as she slid off of the tank, "I don't think he cares about anyone else but you."

Coy's face, so much closer, told a different story. Jeffery's name had made her expression darker. I was stable now, so I... I didn't quite know what to do. I couldn't bite her, and nothing else seemed strong enough. I pressed the side of my muzzle tightly to her cheek and whispered, "I'm so sorry."

Louder, I told them all, "He'll have an explanation. He'd better. I'm going to find out what it is." Then I ran. I could find Jeffery with a bag over my head. I almost felt like that, trying to shut his dreamer out of it.

I found him not in a dream, but arguing about them with other nightmares. He sat on a wrecked car that wasn't part of any other landscape. Half his attention was on the nightmares, and half on the dream that bobbed solemnly nearby, a gleaming house-sized ball amidst the flatter grey of the Dark.

"I think it's going to start paying off any—" I heard him say before his head turned to me. I wasn't all that close, but he didn't have to hear me. Just because I'm a better tracker didn't mean Jeffery couldn't find me in an instant if he wanted to. "Fang!" he called out to me loudly, "Is this the good news?"

With that the dream nearby popped, although only Jeffery seemed to be paying attention to it. I growled, trotted to a halt, and demanded bitterly, "So you knew? You've just been waiting, watching dreams play themselves out, until this happened to me?"

"You—" one of the nightmares started to say, and something inside me came apart. It was Jeffery I was mad at, and I didn't like bullying people. Reputations were supposed to be based on the dreams we create, not who's stronger than who. I was just so mad that thoughts like that tore into bits as I turned to the stranger and growled, staring into his eyes as I put all my fury and bitterness into that sound. I didn't care how big he was, or how raggedly sharp the edges of the obsidian he was scaled with were. I felt contempt for his claws. I just showed him my teeth and took a step forward.

He took a step back, and I wanted to take another step forward, to vent my anger on him and the disdain in his voice. Jeffery's voice dragged me out of that by cutting in, "Anything between me and Fang is between me and Fang, Tet, but finding out why he's mad at me is more important than letting him teach you that lesson."

Just like that I rounded on him, glaring down into that pixie innocent face. "Why am I mad? You fed me this thing and made me a timer for your plan. I thought there was at least something you cared about more than this doomsday dream you're making, or however it works. I didn't think you'd use me this way." I just spat all my feelings out at once.

The growl had worked. Nobody found this funny. Looking into Jeffery's face I felt just a tiny bit of my anger let go, because neither did he. "I didn't think it would be a burden," he answered me solemnly, "And no, that doesn't justify it."

He wasn't used to being wrong, and he didn't know what to do. He just stood there, staring up at me, completely still. He was still because he'd let me do anything I wanted to him as punishment. It was the only apology he knew how to make.

I was still mad. I was seething with it. "Not a burden?" I demanded, "What did you do to me?"

"The pain canary is fixated on the dreamer," he explained in monotone. "Not her dreams, on the dreamer. I've filled her dreams with betrayals. I knew that one of them would come true, and when it did, if she made some connection between the dream and what happened when she was awake the canary would react."

"React?" I asked disbelievingly, "You didn't ask yourself what that would do to—" I couldn't finish the sentence. My gut knotted up again. It was sudden, much faster than the other spasms, and agonizing. It wasn't like being stabbed. It was like being mad at Jeffery. It was that kind of pain, a gouging heartache that wasn't a part of me and I couldn't stop.

"Again?" Jeffery asked in alarm. The others were focused on me now, although they didn't want to get too close to us. "It's happened again already? How many times has it happened?"

"I don't know," I wheezed as the pain started to recede. The only good part was that I felt a lot less angry. There hadn't been room in me for two hurts like that at the same time. Panting, I explained, "They keep getting worse. I don't think I noticed how it started. I'm sure this is at least number four."

Jeffery's cheek twitched. That was all, but it told me everything about how troubled he was. "You can hock it up, Fang. It won't hurt you, and if you'd really absorbed it this wouldn't be happening. Just spit it out while I figure out what to do next. This is moving a lot faster than I thought, but it can wait while I make this right. If I can make this right."

It was moving too fast? I followed that thought. "You need my help again," I told him, "You do. Or you're going to lose this." When he didn't speak immediately I added pointedly, "It's different if you ask."

"We have to move her to the next stage," Jeffery told me, suddenly all business. We were deliberately ignoring the other nightmares trying to listen in. It was, after all, between me and Jeffery. "I need pieces of her. Pieces of her and her dream, and I need to mix them with the pain canary. If you're willing—"

I cut him off, "You don't have time to explain. Got it." I was already moving. Jeffery's dreamer wasn't anywhere yet, wasn't dreaming, but it wouldn't be long. I knew humans spent more time awake than asleep. That time seemed to get lost before it got to the Dark. I ran toward the border. The dream would start near there, and I smelled traces leading me on, suggesting where the dream would begin. I just had a knack for tracking.

I could hear Jeffery yell behind me, "And don't hold back. The bigger the scare, the better." That was fine. Breaking into the waking world was Jeffery's thing, not mine. Dreams were my thing, and I was back in the mood.

There she was. I didn't bother with subtlety, and leaves and branches splintered and flew about as I crashed through the hedge that marked the border tonight. The trail led toward the dream bubble ahead of me. It gleamed more than most, as colorful as gasoline, and it had closed fast. I had a brief impression that it would be hard to get into, so I threw myself against it forcefully. There was a jolt, but I broke through and landed in the dreamer's house again.

This dream was different. It was sluggish. Everything moved slowly and with effort, and sometimes things smeared, and absolutely everything smelled funny, kind of sickly sweet. The dreamer was with a man, and despite the muddy haze he was obviously someone she knew. The way they hung off each other, someone she knew well, romantically.

Well, Jeffery's game with these dreams was betrayal, and I could play it. I waited until she turned her back to fiddle with a fireplace, charged through the gooey atmosphere into the room, ripped at the back of her dream boy with my teeth and dove into him.

Then I waited. I hid, refusing to take control. I let the dreamer and her dream boy gurgle at each other affectionately while the dream melted and ran. Now they were talking in her living room, then they were driving in a car, then they were sitting on her couch without ever having moved. The dream didn't even seem to acknowledge that there was a nightmare hiding in it. We were still firmly in the Light.

Then he leaned in to kiss her, and I took control. I had to fight for it, not against the shell I wore but the viscous drag of the dream itself. That was fine. I reached up with great drama and pulled off the dream boy's face with his own hands, and then I ate it.

That did it. Now I could feel the dream lurching, stuttering as it moved toward the Dark. The dreamer stared at me, whining rather than shrieking. I'd almost forgotten she was afraid of dogs. I ripped another chunk out of her dream boy's arm with my teeth, tearing my claws free. When I'd swallowed that I followed up with a piece of her couch. I wasn't going to have time to get a better sample, so I lunged forward and shut my teeth around her face. She didn't so much scream into my mouth as the scream filled the dream around us, but as the dream popped I swallowed, fast, so I wouldn't lose it. It tasted like the stinking, burning smoke I was left in.

I staggered out of that, my stomach in knots again, churning uncomfortably. Jeffery was racing up to my side. He'd followed the dream through the Dark, but it must have moved faster than it felt. I could feel his hands grip my shoulders as he urged me, "Spit it up, buddy. All of it. The bird, everything."

I was grateful for those instructions. My body heaved, and it felt grotesque, but I sicked up the painful mass in my belly. What splattered onto the ground was the pain canary, more or less. It was bigger, bloated and fleshy and oozing, hideously malformed with none of its limbs in the right place. It didn't look alive anymore. I wasn't sure how alive it had ever been. I didn't suddenly feel good now that it was gone, but I did suddenly feel like myself again.

A rhythmic clattering marked the nightmare shelled in shards of black rock running up on all fours. Jeffery broke off a piece of the canary and lobbed it at him. "Eat that," Jeffery instructed tersely, "We can't push the dreamer anymore. She'll ruin her own dreams now. Now we push the waking world to match her dreams, and since we can't touch the world itself we'll mess with its dreams. That will lead you to whoever's dreaming about our target. Make them think she's a monster, or just make any dream with her in it a scary one. It doesn't matter how they react. They'll do something, and she'll fill in the gaps for us."

He was grinning again, his teeth peeking out slightly from sheer satisfaction. I took no satisfaction from this plan, from the things it was doing to the dreamer or how convoluted it was, but I liked seeing that expression. Jeffery was brilliant and he was making the impossible fall neatly into place, step by step.

The grin lingered, but he really did try to focus on me again, hunching over me and suggesting, "Go rest somewhere, Fang, okay? It's not my place to say this, but thank you. I have to stay here and wait for the others, but you should get out of this for a while."

I nodded. Boy, did I want to get out of this for a while. But, "We're just going to forget what happened. There's nothing we can do about it. So when you need me again, call."

He nodded. He didn't know what to say again. So as I straightened back up and started wobbling toward the Gate, I changed the subject. "I need a drink to get this taste out of my mouth."

I never really had learned to socialize with the other nightmares like Jeffery wanted. Still, there was something comfortable about sitting in front of the counter in Bar Number Three listening to Coy and the Bar talk about making dreams beautiful. Lily kicked her foot idly as she sucked something brown through a straw, which was one of the least glamorous things I'd ever seen her do. And Self-Loathing lay curled up on the bar stool next to me, something blue and sleekly furless and feline that watched me with oversized purple eyes.

The others merely waited, but for me this was a break stolen in the middle of the storm Jeffery was building, and I tried to enjoy it. In fact, I felt like I'd finally relaxed enough to do something I wanted.

"Our frustration stemmed from precisely that source, fishfishfishfishfish," Bar Number Three grated with mechanical excitement, "Our creator believed in interjecting the unexpected and senseless into the mundane. The unexpected and senseless was already in every dream. We were unnecessary."

"And if you try to add the expected and sensible it's boring and doesn't work anyway, right?" Coy agreed, plucking at the strings that moved Bar's puppet body while she sat on his counter. "I'm trying to learn how to string all the senseless stuff together, to try and make it seem like it makes sense and doesn't make sense at the same time. I'm getting some interesting reactions. Sometimes it scares them, sometimes it doesn't, but it makes the dream more intense. You might have fun making dreams like that."

"We feel temptation," Bar admitted, his voice whining metallically, "It would be difficult to uproot ourselves now, and difficult to return. We have come to enjoy using our talent to make drinks."

"Speaking of which," I interrupted in a low voice, afraid there might be no way to ask for this casually, "Could you make me one of my specials?"

It didn't work. After a few moments of fiddling Bar Number Three passed me a clear and diminutive glass half-full of what looked like ink, and he and Lily and Coy didn't seem to notice. But Self-Loathing sat up on her stool, staring.

I would have to let her react however she reacted. My muscles tightened and fear teased over me as I lowered my muzzle to the glass and darted my tongue out to lick some of it up.

It was worse than I'd remembered, but at least I was ready. My whole body locked up, keeping me from jerking away from that shocking bitterness, and I'd wanted it to be worse than I remembered. That was exactly what I wanted. I let the taste drive everything else out of me but the feeling of biting a pale, eyeless ghost, the touch of her, the unwelcoming bleakness of her house, the despair that carved everything she was, and my desperate need to break through that despair and meet the person underneath.

I panted as the shock wore off, wondering if I could handle another taste or the ache of missing Elaine that came with it. I wasn't sure I'd get another chance. Self-Loathing was sliding off her barstool. The feet that touched the floor belonged to a doll. She liked being a toy. This one was more crude than any before, almost featureless and made out of something tougher than fabric, roughly surfaced when it touched me and smelling intriguingly of old leather.

Too stiff to bend, she collapsed on puppet joints at the hips and just leaned up against my haunch.

She wasn't going to complain, or go crazy. It was a wonderful feeling. I gave in to temptation and dropped my face to the glass again for another taste. For a moment I couldn't register anything but Elaine's pain, so sharp that the taste of it took me over. Then as I came to, it was to hear Coy's bubbling voice and be teased by the awareness of Self-Loathing's tiny body and the smell that made me wonder if she would be perfectly, chewably tough.

I knew I only had moments to enjoy this, but I still felt a flash of anger as an unfamiliar voice said, "You're Fang, right?"

I looked behind me, and I had to admit I was impressed. She looked absolutely, unremarkably human, with strawberry blonde hair, youngish but adult and dressed in the dull, sheathing clothes I saw a lot of in dreams. It was the kind of harmless façade a nightmare could use to create any sort of terror, and the eyes were a nice touch, twitching and jerking hyperactively in completely different directions from each other.

So I let my resentment slide and asked, "What does Jeffery need me to do?"

"I don't know," she explained bashfully, her sandals dragging on the floor while her eyes rolled independently, "I wanted your help finding him. I found his dreamer, and something's wrong. Her dreams have gone back to the Light, and when I tried to fix that I couldn't get in. I mean, I couldn't get in at all. It was like it had some kind of shell."

To me that sounded weird, and I wondered if Jeffery expected it. Then I noticed that Lily and Self-Loathing were both sitting up straight, looking at each other. Whatever that meant exactly, it meant that something was going on.

My break was over. It was time to see this through to the end. I wasn't looking forward to telling Jeffery goodbye. In the end, for us, everything but dreams was a brief distraction from the main event.

He was just aiming bigger and striking faster than I would. "I'll go find him. He'll know what this means," I assured her.

"No, he won't," Lily corrected me, drifting up next to me with her fallen angel walk, "I'd bet on it. I'll come with you."

"And I'm definitely coming," Coy chimed in. I felt her lay herself over my back as a fish, body looped and twisted around so that her stars showed against my black. "Maybe getting out on my own was good for me, but I've had enough. I'm not letting you out of my sight until we've made some dreams together again."

I expected Self-Loathing to say something, but she didn't. I glanced back, and that ivory-yellow crude toy body leaned against the base of the bar and watched me with charcoal smudge eyes. I gave up trying to guess what that meant. She wasn't making a fuss or offering to come along, and that color still made me think temptingly of fresh bone.

Just to be sure I made a snapping motion at her, and then swung my head from side to side a couple of times until I caught Jeffery's trail.

He wasn't hard to find. For me he never was, but I tracked him down at the border where I'd expected him to be. I didn't even recognize what it was imitating tonight. On the one side everything was dark, and then there was this thick, hazy greenish wall edged in broken lines, and on the other side it was light. The nightmare with the scissor hands was with him, holding the head of the pain canary up on the tips of its blades.

"Something just happened," Jeffery informed me as I came running up, "The pain canary's dead, and you look like you have more bad news."

There was a quick hailstorm of snowy white feathers as Lily landed next to us heavily, but she rose gracefully again from her crouch. "Your dreamer's fighting back, Jeff," she informed us. She almost sounded accusing about it. "Did you think she wouldn't?"

"If you've made another Lucy—" began the scissor-hands nightmare, but he shut up when Jeffery and I looked at him. We didn't even glare, but it still stopped him cold.

Jeffery and I seemed to be the only people who wanted to solve this as a problem, anyway. "One of the nightmares who're trying to help you says your dreamer's having good dreams now, but she can't get into them," I reported.

We stared at each other blankly. I supposed we were running into the same dead-end thought. If she'd somehow recovered from the shock, any dream so tense a nightmare can't break in at all should be well inside the Dark already. Jeffery managed to think it through to the next step, and looked up at Lily. "She's controlling her dreams without waking up enough to leave them. Do you know how she's doing it?"

"There's a whole world out there they live in when they're awake, Jeffy," she replied, her voice arched and exasperated, "They can reach into the Dark much easier than we can reach them."

Suddenly he was smiling, a little bit of a smirk, a little bit of a small, ingratiating grin. "I know, that's why I'm going to all this trouble. I want to see it for myself."

I couldn't believe he was being this patient. "I think we're running out of time," I pleaded, at least trying to sound gentle and polite, "Please tell him what you know?"

"It won't help, is the problem," Lily explained. She perched a fist on her hip and looked between us with a sort of wistful smile. "Do you even know what doctors are?" Of course we knew that. Humans dreamed about them all the time. When she saw that we did she went on, "They have medicines for dreams, boys. Medicines for how you dream and how you think. It's not subtle and it's not art, but she knows you're hurting her and she's found a doctor to lock you out of her dreams until she recovers."

"As long as she's willing to trust him," Jeffery pointed out. We'd all but killed her ability to trust.

But it would recover fast, so I started running. Jeffery was hardly a second behind me, then sprinting along next to me. We both knew what had to be done, but I had to do it. I was very good at following a trail. I was going to exploit that edge.

As we broke through the slightly sticky barriers on both sides of the border I heard Lily calling, "I can't follow you there, boys. I just can't. Good luck!"

But Coy could cross. I had lost track of her, thought she was still catching up, but she zoomed out ahead of me as we galloped across the bright and colorful blankness of the Light. Her stars gleamed, growing brighter until she burst into flame and a fishlike dragon as bright and yellow-orange as the sun dove back and forth, trailing fire and laughing, "Fang! Can you feel how warm it is here? Why haven't we gone here before?"

Was the answer because I was afraid this would happen? "Later, Coy. I have to focus," I barked up at her, and I did. Jeffery's human's dream had ended, and there were only the slightest traces of her to follow. Humans dream over and over, and I was looking for where the next one would start.

I was too late. I knew it had begun because the trail was suddenly clear, and in a few moments we could see the pearly bubble of it. We raced toward it anyway, and only Anna's voice suggesting, "You'll only hurt yourself if you run into it like that," made us grind to a halt in front of the dream instead of trying to break through.

I smacked my head against the surface anyway. It really was like a shell, harder than rock and completely rigid. The shine was so bright it partly obscured what was inside, but I could see the dreamer drift through a sparsely decorated building, talking to other humans while they all moved very stiffly. Standing on my hind legs, I tried my claws, but it was a complete waste.

Anna touched the surface too, feeling it rather than trying violence. Jeffery hadn't bothered. He hovered over Anna, asking her, "Can you get us in? I don't know if one dreamer can change another's dream."

"I'm not going to try. I'd rather she wins this fight, honestly." Anna's voice was as calm and pleasant as ever, and she looked entirely awake. So awake that there was a hint of bitterness in her expression, although I couldn't hear it in her voice.

"You haven't tried to stop me so far," Jeffery pointed out, confused.

"Tigers are beautiful even when they're eating people, but I don't feed someone to a tiger. I wouldn't really want to shoot the tiger, either. It's the same with nightmares." Her little knuckles rapped on the surface of the dream, and she nodded in satisfaction. Rather like the satisfaction on Coy's face as she hovered behind Anna, glowering at Jeffery.

"I don't even understand what you just said," Jeffery argued helplessly. He really wanted to change her mind, but I hadn't thought for a moment that would happen.

"It only has to make sense to me," came Anna's answer.

The dream vanished, and that was what I'd been waiting for. There'd be another, and if she hadn't woken up it would be soon, and nearby. I cast my head around, looking for the trail, the hint of where she was even though she wasn't really here. It was very soon, and very nearby. I could feel it, I just started knowing which direction she was in, and I jumped and the dream closed around me. I was already inside.

Everything was fragmented, moving in stutters, but the dream seemed to function. It was still taking shape, a street forming for the dreamer to be gliding down rather than walking. There was just the faintest tingle of anxiety in the air. I was here at the start, but the dream didn't want to give in to me. That was fine. I didn't want this one to just fall into the Dark. We were locked in here together, and I had the time to do this right.

Of course, if we were locked in here together and the doctor had made her hard to scare, I'd have no way of escaping if she decided to kill me.

People formed, the usual vague mannequins mixed with a couple with real faces who were people she knew. I waited, sitting behind a car, not really hidden. She wanted to ignore me. What I hoped was that she couldn't ignore me completely, and I got my wish.

She didn't react in any obvious way. It was just that the same face started repeating itself among the passersby. Some woman with a coat watched her wherever she drifted. Her doctor was protecting her from nightmares? Well, here was a nightmare and she wanted to be protected.

From there it was obvious. I slid up behind one of the doctors, sliced open her back and entered the skin as surreptitiously as I could. A little nudging and the doctor I wore walked boldly up to the dreamer and they started talking in pleasant, soothing gibberish. The doctor grew taller too, and began to glow. The dreamer really wanted to be protected. Jeffery had gotten his hooks into her deeply.

Which was why I pressed my face forward through the doctor's, not quite ripping it. It molded around me, the doctor becoming a huge, black dog that staggered toward her, teeth snapping in clumsy but feverish hunger.

The dreamer screamed. The dream jerked, but didn't break. Every doctor on the street now had the face of a growling, snarling dog. The dream jerked again, and this time it broke. The smoke had a truly repulsive smell and feel. I padded out of it dizzily, emerging into the Light in time for a shadow to appear in front of me, a very loud thump and crunch to sound, and a barbed spear point to come to a stop half an inch in front of my face.

"Hey!" yelled Lucy's voice from behind the large and apparently fish-shaped stone shield in front of me, "How'd you do that? Did you do that?"

"I think I should have," came Anna's bland, mournful reply, "You shouldn't do this, Lucy. I guess it's easy to think of nightmares as our enemy, but you can't kill a whole race of people just because a few of them scared you. Doesn't that seem unbalanced?"

"Scared me?" Lucy laughed, "Scared me? They never scared me enough. I'm protecting everyone else. Not that they deserve it, but

I'm keeping monsters like this one from ruining the only escape anyone gets from life."

There was a wheeze, and it was Jeffery's voice. That sound was all too familiar, too much like the sound I'd made with Lucy's foot crushing my neck. I could feel something too, something warm slithering up my back, and then Coy whispered into my ear, "I don't know what's happening, Fang. It's so nice here. How can things like this happen? And she just beat up your friend Jeffery like he was a doll."

Instead of getting to answer her I heard Lucy announce, "Anyway, I'm taking them both. This one, and the one making the dream. Speaking of which," and her voice shook the Light as she yelled, "I see the rest of you out there! You can run this time, but the more nightmares you cause, the sooner you'll see me again!"

I had… seconds. I had Coy, and Lucy hadn't really seen me. Maybe we could get away… and leave Jeffery to die. Or I could try and save Jeffery, and Coy would never leave me, and Lucy would kill all of us. Anna wasn't going to stop us and she wasn't going to save us. I had to save Jeffery. I could feel the heat of Coy's burning fish body against my neck. I couldn't let her die again.

I thought the tightness crushing my heart would kill me first as I whispered to Coy, "I don't think we're going to make it, Coy, but I have to save Jeffery." She didn't like him. "He was my first friend. I need you to do one of two things. Run away, right now, as fast as you can, or try and distract Lucy."

I felt even more of a traitor as Coy wriggled out from around my neck and cooed to me, "I pick distracting her."

Lucy wasn't saying anything on the other side of the shield, so she must be preparing to do something. Whatever it was, Coy interrupted it. She sailed out from behind the rock, a young woman like a cut-out hole to blue sky and lazy clouds. "It was you, huh?" I heard Lucy call, "That's a nice look. I don't get to kill a monster twice very often!"

She knew the new Coy was the old Coy? I only cared for an instant. Then Coy screamed, and light blazed everywhere.

Fish. The air was full of fish of all shapes and sizes, all of them glowing like little suns that darted this way and that. There was a horrible tearing sound and something swept through them, rending most of them into loose sparks, but there were too many to take in one blow. Too many, and now massive stone planets were hitting the ground with echoing thumps.

It was chaos, and I ran. I ran from stone to stone, and when I was between them I trusted the blazing fish. Lucy's laughter never stopped, and I heard crunching and cracking and hissing noises. Then I hit a gap where there'd be nothing between me and Lucy if I ran out. I saw a little copper-headed girl in a ridiculous black coat throw a hatchet into one of the burning fish, which turned into stone and fell loudly to the ground. But it happened on the opposite side, and as Lucy's head followed the statue's crash I lunged. Anna sat there with her head lowered and eyes closed as I passed. I saw Lucy's head begin to twist back, but that was perfect. All she could have seen was a hurtling black shadow before my teeth hit her throat and I yanked as hard as I could.

She popped. She disappeared, woken up by the surprise and pain. I collapsed to the ground next to Jeffery, panting weakly as the jolts of fear came slower and slower, and Jeffery pushed himself awkwardly up onto his elbows next to me.

"You took out Lucy," he told me in a tone as stunned as I felt.

"I got lucky. It was a trick," I replied immediately.

"No one will care it was a trick. I don't care," he husked. Jeffery was actually looking admiringly at me?

There was a flash of blue, and arms as warm as sunshine wrapped around me. Relieved, ecstatic, Coy crowed, "You're alive? You really won? I wanted to save you, but all I could think to do was just make stuff and hope that helped!"

"You saved me, I saved you, and the dream worked. I'm sure of it." I sat up again, and Jeffery climbed to his feet as I assured him, "She'll be terrified of the doctor until the memory fades. I don't think she'll let the doctor protect her."

"But Lucy's after us already, and she'll be back," Jeffery pointed out. "The dreamer's fragile. She can't tell what's real anymore. The moment those medicines fade we have to hit her hard. She'll break, and so will the wall between us and the waking world."

I didn't like that description, but I was distracted by Coy drifting around in front of me. She only floated there for a moment, so that she could peer into my eyes searchingly before moving on. It was enough. Her own eyes were the sun and the moon, side by side in that blue sky. It was beautiful. It also wasn't a nightmare. But I would rather she was beautiful and herself than what I wanted and not herself. That thought was a little dizzy.

"I like the new look. Are you planning on keeping it?" I asked her, hoping she couldn't hear any worry in my voice.

"…No, I don't think so," Coy answered easily, "I like it, but it's not quite me, and the other look doesn't fit here. Does it always have to be daytime here?"

"It's the Light, not the Dark. It's different," Jeffery told her. I felt an edge of irritation at his tone, but at a time like this I understood his impatience.

"So? I'm not asking it to be bad," Coy contradicted him confidently, "How about…"

She drifted off, her eyes closing into slight crescents. She hung in the air silently, then with a shuttering click everything I could see changed.

It was night time, in a swamp. But it wasn't really dark, and the scent hanging sweet on the breeze came from the blossoms weighing down the branches of every tree. Fireflies drifted lazily over the water in imitation of the brighter lights from cozy little cottages I saw here and there on the little hills that poked out of the marsh. While I watched, one of those houses got up on long bird's legs and waded delicately over to set itself down beside a second house. In the distance I heard happy shouts and faint music begin.

A catfish made of stars whirled around me as I stared. It was, very definitely, the Light. There was no questioning it. The Light, at night. Next to me Jeffery admitted with reluctant admiration, "Don't ever ask her to do things our way, buddy."

Coy giggled, one of her whiskers playing with my ear. I glanced at Anna, still sitting next to us. She was smiling again.

It was a shame we didn't have time to stay. For once, I hardly felt unwelcome as a nightmare in the Light. I pushed myself up completely instead and started nosing around for the trail of Jeffery's dreamer.

Jeffery's dreamer wasn't here, of course. Once I'd found her for him, I left Jeffery tracking her dreams. He watched them as the doctor's power let go, and corralled other nightmares to help. I had something to do before I rejoined him.

I hadn't expected this quick little errand to take me to this night-time garden, with its willow trees that waved in melancholy under the pressure of a bitingly cold breeze. It was one of the prettier places in the Dark. If it were less stark it could have been the swamp Coy had created in the Light. There was nothing remotely cheerful about the square of charred wood and ashy dirt at the center of it, where my Muse's house had stood at the end.

This wasn't a place I wanted to sightsee. Not now. I didn't pause my impatient gallop for a moment. In fact, I let my feet thump into the dirt hard, so that the spectral grey figure standing in the middle of the ash could hear me coming. She had just enough time to look over her shoulder and recognize me before I closed my jaws hard over her upper arm and yanked Self-Loathing off her feet, dragging her along as I turned and headed back toward the border.

The giggling shout of, "Fang!" and the solid feel of my teeth biting into her gave lie to the body she was wearing. She looked like a young woman, ghostly and transparent in a long dress and long hair that both blew around in the wind. Everything was a brighter or duller grey, even the halo above her head. It had been a somber look for a somber place, and I was happy to drag her out of that mood.

Her arms quickly wrapped around my neck and shoulders, holding her feather-light body to me as I ran, which let me explain, "Jeffery and I are about to spring the biggest dream in two hundred years. I wanted you there to see it!"

"Six hundred years," she corrected me in a tiny voice whispered intimately into my ear, "Time in their world is very rigid and countable. Drakul broke the soul of a man six hundred years ago and escaped through the hole it left. No one really knows what he became on the other side, but humans still tell stories about him. I remember."

"That's the kind of legacy Jeffery would love," I chuckled. I was following the thread of Jeffery's trail, and getting near. I couldn't see him or the dream ahead, but only because of the clutter. Mostly it was megaliths, great standing stones alone or stacked like doorways. There were a couple of statues of squat, crudely carved human figures, and here and there balls of light would chase each other around some stone icon, or a cluster of pumpkins with glowing faces would decorate the base. I checked the location of Jeffery's dreamer while I ran. She wasn't in the Dark, but I thought the next dream would be here. Or somewhere around here.

"Fang, Anna keeps messing up my decorations!" Coy squealed, a catfish-headed comet rocketing around from behind an obelisk to orbit me petulantly.

I wasn't going to get into a fight between two people who could tell the Dark itself what to do. Instead I slowed down to a trot, Self-Loathing still trailing off of me as light as a ghost. "Why did you two start dreaming up all this in the first place?"

"Because I don't really want to watch," Coy admitted sheepishly.

"I… hope the human recovers," I agreed. That was all I understood about my feelings. Feelings that were seriously distracted as I felt Self-Loathing's teeth close on my ear. It wasn't much of a bite, but it was affection.

Anyway, we weren't alone. Nightmares watched from on top of the stones. Lily had found one lying on its side and was sitting on it next to Anna. Jeffery paced around what must have been the innermost stone circle. I knew what he was doing. He was tracking his dreamer.

Who had just appeared in the Dark. "Off! Off!" I barked at Self-Loathing, leaping forward again. "It's started!" I yelled to Jeffery as I ran past him, "I'll lead you to it!"

"Both of us!" Jeffery instructed, falling in beside me, "You just have to be in the dream. I want your face all over it."

That was all we had time to say. The dream closed in front of us, toward the edge of the rambling field of stones Coy had built. We broke through the surface, and 'broke' was the right word. It had barely formed, but already it was tense and didn't want to let us in.

Inside, I could see the effects of Jeffery's plan. This was a simple dream of the dreamer going about her life, shopping in some kind of huge store. The place was laid out exactly, cans and jars and boxes, rows of vegetables—they were vague, but there were a lot of them. We'd busted in so hard I bounced off one of the other humans pushing a shopping cart. Bounced hard. I didn't budge them at all, and instead blearily watched them stroll past, pause to pick a box off a shelf, study it for a few seconds, and put it back.

I reached out and tried to push the box back off the shelf. It wouldn't move. This wasn't a dream, it was something from the waking world. We couldn't touch it. No... it was a copy of something from the waking world. The annoying, threatening buzz from lights that flickered on and off, the cobwebbed murk that lingered in every corner, I bet those were from the dream. She was dreaming and awake at the same time, copying what she saw.

I did what I'd been told. I lurked behind an aisle divider as Jeffery crept up on the dreamer. The dream had already been tense. Now that we were in it things started getting more detailed. It was weird to be able to look at the boxes next to me and read that they were filled with cake mix. The other people in the dream were becoming more real, too. The human I'd bumped into now wore a ratty suit in dark green, but as his face filled out it wasn't human. It was mine. I glanced around and saw the same transformation come over another shopper, who now had the head of a black dog with very prominent teeth. Then the face faded, but another human walked around a corner wearing it. I noticed the lettering fade from the boxes and cans, but not because the dream was easing. Some of them had labels with dogs on them, and those were getting bigger, more boldly colored, their expressions growing more threatening. I'd infected this dream with her terror of me just by being in it. So what was Jeffery doing? He was at the far end of the aisle, talking to the dreamer as if he was just another customer.

I couldn't hear them and wondered if I could sneak up enough to make it out. Instead, I felt the dream shudder. So soon? Glancing at the walls of the room, I found one where the surface of the dream showed. The bladed end of a harpoon was sticking through it, and through the soapy surface I could see the spear was stuck through a wrist whose hand ended in scissors.

I had done my part for Jeffery. He'd have to handle the rest. I rammed myself against the dream's membrane, shoving until it gave and I forced my way out into the chaos of stone pillars and yelling outside. As I passed, I yanked the spear out of the scissor handed nightmare's wrist and spat it aside. Now it wouldn't break the dream, and maybe the nightmare would recover. He had an ugly look in the glinting eyes under his huge, pointy hat and he crept off behind a statue, probably trying to circle around Lucy.

Lucy stood in the middle of the ring, holding someone's head down onto the altar and twisting an enormous screw that passed through the victim's belly into the stone. The red hair, the feminine body with its tangled white wrap, they were obviously Lily even before Lucy exclaimed delightedly, "Wow, what does it take to kill an angel, anyway? The last one never did die. Don't worry, he sure won't be getting up any time soon. Maybe you'll still be here when I'm done and I can experiment."

"Lucy—" Anna pleaded, reaching out and taking the other girl's shoulder. It was the most aggressive thing I'd ever seen Anna do, and apparently Lucy agreed, because she spun around and backhanded Anna across the face hard enough to send the girl in white flying. Anna hit a stone megalith head-first, slumping down to the ground and flickering on and off as the shock failed to completely wake her up.

If Lucy did that to me, or to any of the nightmares here, we'd have splattered. I stepped into the circle anyway and shouted, "Lucy! Don't you have some unfinished business with me?"

It really didn't matter what I'd said. I had her attention. She stopped abusing Lily, although the metallic sound as she pinned a metal plate over Lily's head wasn't pleasant. I had all of Lucy's attention. She was wearing some kind of ridiculous armor made out of cut-out cardboard boxes, but the sword she pulled into existence from behind her back was metal, bigger than she was and jagged-edged. Of course, she could kill me with a straw.

I'd meant to stall her, distract her with taunts. Nightmares surrounded her, most of them hiding and waiting for a time to strike. Instead I heard Coy squeak, "Fang, what are you doing?" She hovered in front of a nearby stone in girl shape, watching me. And across from her, Self-Loathing was doing the same thing. I glanced at both of them in horror, in full view, but all I could do was try and keep the distraction going.

So I growled and took another couple of steps forward. How big could I get? I dwarfed Lucy, for all that would help. "You're outnumbered, little girl. Badly, badly outnumbered. And all we have to do is wake you up," I snarled at the pigtailed murderess.

"So?" she chirped with glee, "That's all you can do. Look at her!" She waved a little hand at Anna and continued, "Traitor girl is fine. And you know what's great?" She leered now, showing off lots of pearly little milk teeth. "You can't wake me up. Anybody who jumps me from behind tonight is going to be in trouble, 'cause I won't be surprised."

Bravado. Keep her talking. Why weren't Coy and Self-Loathing running away? They just kept watching me! I ran my tongue over my teeth and retorted, "That's fine by me. It means that when we hurt you, you'll stay hurt. You can spend the rest of the night in pieces until you wake up naturally. Maybe that'll teach you a lesson."

Noises behind me. Jeffery's dream started to echo with scratchy sounds. I could hear distant barking. If I accomplished nothing else, I was giving him time to finish.

Lucy wasn't paying attention to that. She was laughing, "Doggy, you are so cool. You talk like me, do you know that? But see, I do learn lessons. I learned a whole new trick from your fish girl the last time we met. Watch this!"

A second Lucy slid out of the first as I watched, stepped forward and waved her sword a couple of times to show me she wasn't just a statue. That left the first Lucy to spin around. The nightmare with the scissor hands, one good pair left, had been creeping up the back of the altar. One swing of her sword and he came apart in halves, with a spray of blood that faded in seconds.

The Lucys stepped up side by side, one fingering the edge of her weapon as the other asked me glibly, "Hey, what about you? Did you ever learn to feel guilt? Will you feel any when I do this?"

She was moving, both of her. One of her was speeding toward Coy, and the other toward Self-Loathing, swords raised. I was moving, too. She was so much faster than me, but I was nearer. My body crashed into Lucy's, knocking her out of her charge and sending her tumbling. The terror of what had almost happened to her hit Coy, and in a spray of stars she ducked around behind the stone and disappeared. She was safe. My eyes dragged themselves over to Self-Loathing and the sword stuck through her gut, pinning her to the rock behind.

I hadn't realized I'd made a choice. I hadn't had time to think at all, to wonder who would survive or what I should do. I'd just chosen. I wasn't sure what it meant, but the glassy, hopeless stare Self-Loathing gave me told me that she was.

I didn't know what to say. I didn't have time, because she made a little croak and fluttered her arm, and I rolled to the side. It had been a dumb choice, but I got lucky—Lucy's blade, swung sideways, passed an inch over me because I was on the ground. As I turned my head I saw Tet behind her, the obsidian covered nightmare. He leaped off the pillar toward her head, and Lucy twisted around to jump up to meet him with a noisy fist to the gut.

Except the Lucy who'd swung at me was swinging again, and I had to scramble backwards as the blade slammed down where I'd been. Then Lucy's voice came from everywhere, skipping from Lucy to Lucy. "Remember—" "—when you said—" "—I was outnumbered—" "—doggy?" They laughed. There were too many of them, chasing nightmares everywhere. Would the girl with the mismatched eyes survive the hook a Lucy had driven into her from behind? The skeleton with the face of a clock was dissolving already after a Lucy had smashed his head in with a hammer.

I didn't see Coy. She'd run away. Please, let her have run away. I did see Self-Loathing and Lucy lifting her chin to examine why she wasn't dead. Self-Loathing ignored Lucy, staring emptily at me. I took my first step, my brain flickering to try and figure out how to save her, when she threw up.

I stumbled, almost fell from surprise. Lucy pulled back in disgust as Self-Loathing retched at her emptily. All the Lucys stopped. Then Self-Loathing retched again, and out of that ghostly mouth tumbled a man.

He was rough, hairy, with a badly cut beard and hair. Instead of clothing he wore a wrap of crude cloth, and the axe in his hand had a blade made of chipped stone. It still looked entirely painful as he backhanded Lucy across the face with it, chortling and gurgling in satisfaction. And Self-Loathing heaved again, and again. A thing like a man-sized rat fell out, emaciated and green-skinned and rotted to the bone in places, and when a Lucy immediately stepped up to chop its head half off with an axe of her own, green hairs crawled up the shaft. That Lucy immediately started coughing up blood, and collapsed on top of the wounded rat. Next was another man, in an elegant black suit stained with red, who fastidiously drew a shaving razor and beckoned invitingly to still another Lucy. Then came something haphazard and malformed like a mottled grey baby, and after that I lost track.

It wasn't like many of these things could fight well, but the Lucys seemed confused. They moved jerkily, unable to keep up or fight with the kind of speed she could summon when there was only one of her. The remaining nightmares saw this, and I saw the wandering-eyed girl pull herself off the hook, leaving a trail of her own blood, and drive the spike into the head of the unmoving Lucy that had impaled her.

I looked back at the dream. Something was happening in there. The dream shrank as the dreamer stumbled, yelling or babbling things I couldn't hear, away from dog-faced people gathering around her. Shaking and crying, she rushed into a little bathroom and looked into the mirror.

Her reflection looked back at her with my face and lunged out of the mirror. Except it got sucked back in as it did because the mirror was a hole, dragging the entire dream into it. Jeffery tumbled out as it shrank. In the blink of an eye there was just him, standing next to a rectangular tear like a doorway opening into the bathroom I'd just seen. A bathroom where I could make out the faint smudges on some of the tiles, where every word of a sign about washing hands could be read, where if I looked closely I could see every strand of the hair of the woman sobbing on the floor.

"I did it... I did it. It's time to go, Fang!" Jeffery husked between a few weak, stuttering chuckles.

"I'm not going, you know that!" I snapped at him, already looking back at the melee I'd left behind. Uncoordinated, confused, no one

Lucy could keep up. Each one that was killed popped like a waking dreamer—and then a new Lucy split off from one of the others. Somewhere, one of them was still laughing.

Jeffery's hand grabbed my collar. He was going to beg. "I don't want to go, Jeff, and you do. Goodbye. Thank you," I repeated.

The weak laughs stopped, and his hand pushed me away. It wasn't hard. It was deliberate, and I took the hint and ducked behind the nearest column as he announced loudly, "Aren't you a little late, Lucy? Weren't you trying to stop me from making one of these?"

I wasn't sure how many nightmares he saved with that, but the Lucys were reduced to fumbling as one of them leaped over the crowd, landing with a thump on this side of the ring, laughing hyperactively as she rose up to charge him. Except I ran around from behind the megalith and sunk my teeth into her shoulder, yanking her off her feet. I was betting everyone's life that this was the real Lucy, that any of them was the real Lucy if she looked out of its eyes.

As my teeth bit in her laughter choked off, then came back. She twisted around, grabbing at my collar, grabbing at my face and taunting, "Sorry, doggy. I told you I was expecting it. I mean, it hurts, but I bet it doesn't hurt as much as if I do this!" Her groping hand closed on one of my back teeth and snapped it out of my jaw. The pain exploded through me, but following it came something worse. I was the teeth in the dark, and I'd lost one of them. I felt… cold. My feet moved like lead, but she'd let go of me to hold up her prize, and I made the last couple of steps and threw her into the hole Jeffery had made.

She was just gone. The other Lucys were gone. Their weapons were gone, but not the damage they'd done, and my tooth was gone, too. The coldness sucked at me, but I was more than teeth. I was the chase, the black dog, more than just one thing, and a gap in my fangs might make me scarier. It still ached, but I was stable as I turned my head and told Jeffery, "You did it, Jeff. Get through before it closes."

"Goodbye, buddy," he answered haltingly, quietly. Nightmares stared, but his last words were going to be for me. "Maybe I'll even see you in my own dreams."

He stepped past me into the gap, and as he did I turned and blocked it with my body, so I couldn't see what happened to him and neither could anybody else. "I know what Jeffery promised you," I growled at the remaining nightmares, "But he's gone, and to honor his memory he's the only nightmare going through this portal tonight. None of you could do what he did. None of you even thought to try. He's the only nightmare who earned it."

I glared down at them as I swept the ring with my eyes. Down? I hadn't realized just how big I'd made myself. Size wasn't everything, but it held them, let me call out, "Anna? Are you okay? Can you come over here? Maybe you can close it."

"I have her, Fang," Coy's voice answered me. It was subdued, haunted, but clear. It was the first time I'd seen her walk, escorting a shaky Anna up to me.

Even as I watched, Anna blinked, her blue eyes clearing and focusing on me, soft voice promising, "I'm fine. Even something like that can't wake me up."

I nodded. Nothing that happened in the Dark could wake her. So I lay my muzzle behind her head, and with a swift jerk I threw her through the portal too. She was gone, and I didn't get to wonder if it had woken her up at last. Beside me, Coy squeaked something too weak and choked off to be a scream and she collapsed.

It was jarring, and the other nightmares were watching me for weakness. So I stood there, glaring, and added coldly, "And in case any of you are thinking of twisting a dreamer to make a portal of your own, I want you to remember that Lucy's gone. I'm not, and unlike Lucy I can find you." I didn't know if they were swallowing it. I could hardly hear my own voice. I listened to Coy's wheezing, and told my feet to stay where they were. This was something she could only do for herself, that she'd have to do for herself, needed to do for herself.

"I'm cold, Fang," she whimpered, a curled up shape of stars and whiskers on the ground beside me.

I... I could give her a hint. "Who are you?" I husked back. That was all I could do. Any more would kill her tomorrow, rather than letting her die today.

"I'm the dragon of the divided waters, star of the heavens, fish of the oceans," she mumbled. Her body stirred, flopped once, then lay still again. "No... no, that's just a shape." She took a few breaths, but each one came weaker than before. "I'm a dream. The dream that stays with you in the morning because you didn't know something so strange could be so beautiful, or that you could be responsible for it." The stars dissolved, and she pushed herself up on pale arms from an overexposed photograph until she stopped, her head hanging. "That's not... enough. That's not a person," she whimpered, and then gasped, "But I am a person. I'm Coy. My name is Coy, and that's who I am."

She was shaking, but she sat up and I felt a tiny hand close on my haunch, squeezing a fistful of fur. I couldn't look straight at her. I had to watch the nightmares. They had to remember me like this, an implacable force rather than just Fang. They'd seen me get rid of Lucy, maybe forever. I needed them to think that wasn't an accident. I needed them to fear me.

Finally they all looked away, and some started getting up and walking off. A light flickered out on the ground in front of me. I looked back. The portal was closed. Strength drained out of me, but I still had enough to support Coy as we walked out into the ring. It wasn't empty, but the nightmares were leaving and I had to get Lily free from where Lucy had fastened her to the altar. The things that were left were ignored me, anyway. They were things Self-Loathing had vomited up, the ones that hadn't been killed. Most of them looked more or less human, and as I watched they drifted, not walking but dragged inexplicably away. Most of them seemed to be headed in the same direction. Toward the far-off Gate.

There was no one pinned to the monolith by a sword anymore. I didn't know what to make of it. So I looked around among the surviving cast-offs for something I recognized, but I didn't see anyone until I lifted myself up on two legs in front of the altar and closed my hands on the screw holding Lily in place. Another pair of hands, small and brown, were tugging on it already. From the other side of the stone a little girl with deeply tanned skin and black eyes and hair told me solemnly, "Thank you. I'm not strong enough anymore."

I gave the bolt a twist, forcing it to turn. Self-Loathing lost her grip and began to slide away from me. My arm lashed out instinctively, grabbing her by the wrist. Tethered by my hand, pulled on by a force I could feel testing my grip, she floated there and stared up at me with those bright eyes. All she wore was that crude dress with the black stain of dried blood on the front. "Thank you, Fang," she told me. She smiled weakly. She was still staring. I'd never earned the affection in her face, or in her voice. "You're still trying to save me, but it's too late. I don't know where the title went. Maybe to one of the others. I finally get to move on."

She wasn't being pulled toward the Gate. She was being pulled toward the border. "You're going to Heaven?"

She giggled, and it was that playful, bubbly sound I'd always loved to hear. "Heaven? You think Heaven and Hell are my only choices?" she asked me teasingly, her smile widening, "Someday you'll figure out for yourself that angels are crazy. I won't get to be there. Wherever I'm going, you can't keep me for very long."

She was right. The pull had gotten stronger. It was going to start dragging me pretty soon. When I didn't say anything, she went on, "Let me go, Fang. It's time. I don't want to hurt anymore."

I couldn't say what I felt. I couldn't look into those eyes, hear those words, and bite her like I wanted to. I glanced at Coy and asked desperately, "How do humans—"

"They kiss," she told me solemnly.

Right. So I pulled a little harder, dragged Self-Loathing up to me and my face to hers, and I touched my lips to her forehead. I hardly had the mouth for it, but it was all I could do. "Let go, Fang, and don't look," Self-Loathing whispered, "Don't drag this out for either of us."

So I let go, and I turned my back, and I pried the plate off of Lily's mouth, and by the time I glanced back by accident the little black-haired girl was long since gone. Lucy had done something to Lily's hand, but she worked it back into shape enough to lay it on my shoulder as she sat up awkwardly. "I saw them, puppy. They were terrified. They all know you're the top nightmare now."

"Good," I grunted, "Maybe they'll be scared enough to think I'm actually going to keep them in line. By the time they know I won't, I hope they'll have forgotten trying to copy Jeffery. Let them make their own dreams their own way, not his." I leaned over then and nudged my muzzle against her cheek, adding, "Goodbye, Lily. You, at least, I'm sure I'll see again."

Coy had recovered a lot more than I'd thought, because the hands gripping my collar were unexpectedly strong. "If you try to leave me, I'll follow," she warned me immediately, "I don't want to live without you, even if I can."

Lily merely stared at me thoughtfully. "You're taking her back to the Light?" she guessed, her voice light but sharp and cagey. I couldn't help but grin, despite it all.

"She's not a nightmare, not really. She won't find out what she really is in the Dark," I explained.

"But you're a nightmare, Fang," Coy insisted. She dragged my face away from Lily, made me talk to her instead. "You are. It's who you are, and I know you can't stop."

I grinned wider, up into that frozen, monochrome photograph of a girl's face with its deep shadows and bleached highlights that made her more of a portrait than anything human. "You're right," I conceded immediately, "I'm not going to stop being a nightmare.

But maybe I can learn to be a better nightmare over there. I met someone who crossed the border once to learn more about herself, and I've always wanted to try it. Why not now? Do you want to come with me?"

Pale arms flew around my neck, looking weirdly flat even though I could feel the shape of them as Coy squeezed. "I really, really do. I want to go there, but not without you."

"I'll see you, Lily. I'll see you soon," I told Lily as I started to pad away, heading toward the border and the brighter horizon I could see in the distance. Coy swam excitedly around me, darting and circling, moving so fast her stars seemed to juggle.

"I don't want you to change your colors," she told me, "We'll have to change somehow to fit in over there. It's too warm. I think you could get away with silver highlights. Humans would love you in silver and black, don't you think?"

I laughed. It was weak and tired, but I laughed, and as we passed the last of the standing stones I assured her, "I'll give it a try. I've always loved silver and black, and you're right. I want to stay me, just become a little more."

Epilogue

The wonderful thing about Scryers was that they didn't use mortal rules or the rules of the Dark. They used their own rules, and they could show you things easily that should have been impossibly obscure. That you wanted something might be enough for them to find it. So Lily peeled a sheet of paper off of the mirror. She knew she'd found the newspaper she wanted. The photograph on the front page said it all.

She was several years older, and the black and white disguised the copper color of the pigtails, but that was Lucy. Bruised, starved, with a broken nose, but the face was the same and the expression that stared challengingly at the camera was so very her. Around her neck hung a tooth that could have come off a dinosaur, tied to a loop of string. Lily couldn't help but smile as she read over the article. The mysterious slaying of a 'local' couple had taken an even stranger turn. The bodies had been partially eaten by the murderer, and when their daughter was taken into custody she showed signs of having been badly abused over a period of years. All of this was still unconfirmed, naturally, but an inside source reported that instead of the quiet, withdrawn girl reported by neighbors, the daughter had blossomed after her parents' death, and the only concern was that she might be too aggressive to mix with other teenagers yet. It was, Lily thought, all so very, very perfect.

But that was the past. The future was opportunity. Running her thumb over the imitation newsprint, she thought wistfully of the mortal world and the humans in it. Her family was huddling behind both Gates, watching each other suspiciously and not wanting to make the first move. It looked like Lucy had no need to punish dreams anymore. It was time for Lily to look into opening a real, proper portal at last. Her way, of course.

About the Author

Richard Roberts has fit into only one category in his entire life: 'writer.' But as a writer he'd throw himself out of his own books for being a cliche. He's had the classic wandering employment history—degree in entomology, worked in health care, been an administrator and labored for years in the front lines of fast food. He's had the appropriate really weird jobs, like breeding tarantulas and  translating English to English for Japanese television. He wears all black, all the time, is manic-depressive, and has a creepy laugh.

As for what he writes, Richard loves children and the gothic aesthetic. Most everything he writes will involve one or the other, and occasionally both. His fantasy is heavily influenced by folk tales, fairy tales, and mythology, and he likes to make the old new again. In particular, he loves to pull his readers into strange characters with strange lives, and his heroes are rarely heroic.

A Taste of

Richard Roberts

Chapter One

On the last day before I got my super power, I was sulking because I didn't have a super power.

"That's not going to work," Claire warned me.

"It will! I've been studying my Dad's notes," I snapped back.

She tilted her head down and looked at me over her glasses. "You can't give yourself super powers with a double-A battery, Penny."

"It's not the power," I explained. "It's the frequency. Get it just right and it resonates with your whole nervous system and gives it a jolt. I've seen Dad do it. If you have powers, they go off!"

I snapped that at her, too. I was frustrated! I clipped the wire another millimeter and looked at the wavelength reading on the meter. It went down a notch, like it was supposed to. I was dreading the next question. She was going to ask that question.

"So what's the frequency?" Claire asked right on time.

I collapsed on top of the workbench and confessed, "I have no idea."

Claire giggled, but at least she tried to restrain it.

"I was reaching. I knew I couldn't just guess. I don't know. I guess I hoped I'd get lucky," I grumped.

Claire put her hand on my shoulder. "We're supposed to be working on our science fair projects. Mr. Zwelf is being really nice about it."

I pushed myself back up and insisted, "This *is* my science fair project. It will work! I just have to steal my Dad's notes and do the math. And measure my body weight and stuff. There's a lot of math." A lot of math. A really stupifyingly tremendous amount of math. Pages upon pages of math. Even with a calculator, I'd be up all night handling the algebra.

"You know inventing and science are two different things, right?" Claire had the world's most teasing grin. Like, you looked at those teeth and you couldn't be mad at her for making fun of you, because it really was all in good fun. That's how it worked on me, anyway.

"So what are you doing for your science fair project?" I demanded. I actually hadn't wanted to know. Any excuse to be lab partners with your best friend, right?

"I'm already done! I blind tested photos of Mom when she's using her powers and when she's not using her powers on a bunch of boys. They couldn't tell the difference, which shows her power must be psychic, right?" she answered, so very casual.

"You want your super power as bad as I do!" Hard to sound accusing with a grin like the one stretching my face all of a sudden. This stuff was no secret, but, criminy, obvious much, Claire?

"It's still good scientific method," Ray pointed out, sliding down the workbench with his textbook. If Mr. Zwelf hadn't come down on me and Claire arguing, he wasn't going to pitch a fit if Ray made three.

I turned to him. "What are you doing for your project?"

He shrugged. "I don't know. I'm atrocious at science fair projects. I can never get an idea until the last minute. Right now, I'm looking through the book and hoping inspiration leaps out at me."

"You have trouble with science fair projects? You?" I asked, honestly blown away. Ray was the smartest kid I knew. My folks were celebrated super geniuses who had a framed letter on the wall from the UN thanking them for saving the world, and Ray was smarter than me. He could probably do the stupid math in Dad's notes. I wasn't looking forward to it.

"It's so meaningless and arbitrary. I might as well be measuring plastic cups to find out which ones are more dense," he griped, propping his elbow on the workbench and leaning his head on his fist. His blonde hair was so fluffy, it hung right down over his hand.

Ow! I still had the current on. I'd zapped myself on the antenna. Wasn't much of a charge, but still. I shook my finger and pried out the battery, but I didn't have time to dismantle the antenna. The bell rang.

"Lunch time!" Claire squealed with delight, stretching her arms above her head as Ray stared.

Love triangles suck.

"Why are you so dramatic today?" Ray asked as I sat down with my tray across from him. Just me and him at our table. I could listen to that inexplicable English accent the whole hour. He didn't know where it came from, and I didn't care.

"I'm not being dramatic today," I argued, trying not to be dramatic about it.

"Yes, you are."

I lifted my head in a show of innocence. "I'm not being dramatic. My parents are dramatic. Mom can reduce a mugger to tears with a speech about the statistical chance of ruining his life going up with every crime. You were there. He was bawling like a baby."

"Does she really prepare those speeches ahead of time?" he asked, grinning. Ray spends half his life grinning, and a third of his life sleeping, and the remaining sixth happens when I'm not around.

"She has a flow chart depending on circumstances. I got to draw the lines the last time she updated it. I was seven." I added that last part because, you know, it's beneath my dignity now.

"You're being dramatic for you," Ray pointed out, zeroing back in on the argument.

He was totally right, but I was saved from admitting it, because Claire had arrived. She brought her lunch, so she should get to the cafeteria early, but she'd never been big on hurrying. I bet her Mom trained her to be fashionably late.

She was heading straight here, so it looked like she'd be sitting with us today. Okay, I needed to watch that snippiness. Claire sits with me most days, it's just that Claire is welcome anywhere. Like most lunch rooms, the cafeteria of Northeast West Hollywood Middle is laid out in an intricate map of feudal kingdoms. The performing art kids have three tables, the computer science kids have a table, me and Claire and Ray have a table. Claudia has a table all to herself, poor girl. I'd invited her over to sit with us once, but she refused. Since Marcia had pulled the "sit with her, then make her the butt of all the jokes" trick on her once, it was hard to blame her. You can't help some people, much as you might want to.

Speaking of Marcia—thinking about Marcia, technically—maybe Claire wouldn't be sitting with us today after all. Marcia made her friends scoot over and pointed at the bench. "Space for you, Claire!"

No, Claire was sitting with us. She gave Marcia a smile and a shake of the head, trying to be polite, but walked right past. Marcia looked like someone'd stuck a rat up her nose. She should have let one of the other girls give the invite. Marcia is a Mean Girl, and she sits at the Popular Table, and, yeah, both exist and everybody knows it. I swear they were only popular with each other, but somehow they were the Popular Girls, even though it's Claire that everyone really likes.

I think our table is the "extroverted geeks" table. Or maybe it really is the "children of superheroes" table. Of course, both leave Ray out. He's quiet with other people. Eh, who am I kidding? The three of us were filed firmly under "other."

"Is Penny still desperate to get her powers?" Claire asked as she slid into place next to me.

"I had managed to distract her until now," Ray answered.

I threw my hands up in the air. "What's wrong with wanting to get my powers as soon as possible?"

"Didn't your parents' powers only surface in college?" Ray pointed out. I think I'd strangle myself if it took that long.

"Mom's power emerged at about my age." Claire was so breezy about it, but everybody knew she'd inherit The Minx's abilities. She'd be less like her Mom if she were a clone. Blonde, wavy hair, a curvy figure *already*, delicate, blonde doll face, all lips and eyes – pretty much the opposite of my shapeless stick topped with brown, braided pigtails. On her, glasses looked like fashion accessories.

"I can't even be positive I'll get powers. My Dad's thing with science is a brain mutation. He identified it. Mom's a regular human," I grumped.

Claire unbuckled her lunch box with a beatific smile. "My father probably had super powers. I should be a shoo-in."

Ray blushed visibly. Okay, maybe I blushed a bit, too. Claire really didn't know who her father was. Apparently there had been a lot of candidates, thanks to her mother's power of Clouding Men's Minds. If 'minds' was the right word.

And Claire was looking forward to inheriting those powers.

Thank goodness, Ray also wanted to move on. "There's no way your mother is human. Regular humans can't do that," he insisted.

"Chess grandmasters are regular humans. She says it's just focus and study, like Sherlock Holmes." Contrary to what I'd just said, I agreed with him. We'd been passed on the road by a police chase once, and she'd gotten on the radio and told them where to set up a road block, and they caught the criminals. She'd been able to explain it, but when she got to calculating how fast the criminals had intended to drive rather than how fast they were driving, I gave up. I knew she wasn't perfect, but, when villains heard The Audit was coming, they used to give up right there, and I couldn't blame them.

Claire passed me a cup of real gravy, which I poured on the school's bland Salisbury steak. Cutting a slice, I took a bite. The rich gravy made a world of difference. Claire's lunchbox is a collectible antique with Krazy Kat on the cover. Her Mom feeds her like a princess. My Mom makes me buy a cafeteria lunch. I would never have asked, but Claire shares the wealth automatically. She has those looks, and she's generous and kind. Is it any wonder her Mom got a full pardon when she retired? Of course, she'd saved the world a couple of times. What kind of crazy supervillain tries to destroy the world?

Half of them.

I stopped jonesing for super powers before I started and dug into my lunch. A little gravy made the mashed potatoes stop being pulped cardboard, too.

Claire gave Ray a chocolate cupcake, which must have made his sandwiches a thousand times more bearable. Ray eats like he's on the edge of starvation. As skinny as he is, his metabolism must burn like a blow torch. He got done in mere minutes and asked, "How did the big German test go?"

"Nicht so gross. Got a B," Claire admitted.

Ray looked at me.

I couldn't think of any way to brush it off.

I let out a sigh. "I got a C."

"Ow. Really?" asked the boy who never got less than an A on any test in his life.

Not that he was trying to be mean. He was trying to be sympathetic, which made it worse. "I'm pretty sure I'm going to get a C in the class," I admitted. I winced, my whole body tightening up, but it hadn't been… that bad to say. Just pretty bad.

Ray tried to comfort me. "Everybody has subjects they just don't get. Languages are yours, I guess."

Claire nodded.

"I'm not supposed to have bad subjects! My parents are the two smartest people in the world!" God, it dug at me. It dug right at my heart. How could I even explain this to them? "Can you imagine the look my Dad gave me when I brought home a B in Algebra II? He was trying to not let me know how disappointed he was. That's the look he had!"

"You weren't even supposed to *be* in Algebra II. You and Ray are the only kids going across to Upper High for Geometry, and you're getting an A in that," Claire pointed out. She was trying to cheer me up, not blow me off. She didn't get that it just didn't matter.

I couldn't help but feel bitter. Or cheated, maybe. Some kind of ugly emotion, anyhow. "I just want my super powers to activate now. I won't even have to worry about this stuff. I'm smart enough to get this frequency stimulator thing Dad designed working, at least," I grumped.

The bell rang. I wasn't done eating. Oh, well, I'd had the good stuff.

You want to know how good friends Claire and Ray are? When we got up, I noticed a plastic case in her bag. She'd gotten a new superhero collectable figure. She and Ray can geek out about them for hours. They'd kept their mouths shut about it not to rub it in. Then I'd spent the whole lunch period talking about super powers anyway.

We all had PE together. Half the class was spent changing into and out of our gym clothes, which I bet is why we only had the class on Wednesdays. Sometimes we could get together and talk, like when we were standing in line for the horse. Today was basketball, so no luck there.

The game went about like expected. Two random kids were picked as captains. The boy picked Ray second to last, and the girl picked me last. I wasn't the last person picked, though. The boy still had one more person to pick. Claudia, of course. Ray and I ran around the edge of the crowd until someone threw the ball over everyone's heads, and I jumped up and grabbed it.

Ha! I wasn't the greatest dribbler in the world, but I was in the clear because I hadn't been in the pack in the first place. I dribbled right past Claudia, who didn't even try to stop me, and found myself face to face with Ray. He wasn't a good runner, and he was already so winded I was able to duck right by him. Unfortunately for me, Claire had been lingering on the edges too. She snatched the ball in the middle of one of my clumsy dribbles and passed it to Li, who was a way better shot than either of us.

Still, face to face to face on the basketball court had been cool. I was considering chalking up this gym class as a rare success when the boy captaining his team started to yell. Not "yell," exactly, but he had a nasty tone as he told Claudia, "What is wrong with you? You just stood there! You really are slow in the head, aren't you? At least try to play the game!"

I wondered if I should get Miss Theotan's attention, but it wouldn't do any good. If she'd witnessed it personally, she'd come down on bullying like this like a ton of bricks, but she was on the other side of the court, and if a teacher doesn't see it, it didn't happen. Instead, Claudia turned away from the boy without a word. The crowd of kids taking the ball away from each other again and again turned and lurched in our direction with Claudia in the middle of it. She grabbed the ball as it went past, tossed it over everyone's heads, ran through the crowd, and caught it herself, then launched it from the three point line and sank the basket.

You'd think that would get everyone gabbing and circling around Claudia and she'd finally be popular, right? No, that's not how it works. All of a sudden a girl was complaining to Miss Theotan that it wasn't fair that one team had one more player than the other team, and, as Ray and Claire and I stood around feeling helpless and guilty about it, Claudia ended up sitting on a bench for the rest of the game.

That put my mood right back in the dumps. I dodged Claire and Ray both when class ended, and with it the school day. I didn't step out the school doors until it was exactly time to meet my Mom, driving up to take me home. She didn't ask me about my obvious bad mood, so I didn't have to tell her about the test.

Nothing eases the sting of social injustice like knowing you'll soon have super powers to help you combat it. Nothing eases the sting of lousy test scores like knowing you'll soon have the ability to absorb and then apply abstract data far beyond mere human limits. If they ever really integrate psychological theory, my Dad will be impossible to live with. Until then, us normal humans have a shot at outwitting him.

Not a good shot. He's still a genius. Still, I had the advantage of experience. I wandered into his office. To my delight, I found him at his computer with an e-reader laid on either side of his keyboard, scrolling slowly down a web page with lots of text and a few teeny, tiny diagrams. The curiosity bug had caught him. He was researching. He'd have no attention left for anything else until it all came together in his head.

Or not. As I picked my way through the stacked up books and lifted the first pile of printed paper to peek at the title "Subliminal Paralyzation Cascades" he spun around in his seat and greeted me. "Hey, Pumpkin! How was school?"

I pointed at the "Pumpkin" jar. He put a dollar in it blithely. It hadn't made him stop, but the penalty really supplemented my pathetic allowance. "Princess" is five bucks, but I'm saving that jar for emergencies.

I needed a plan.

"Where's that paper on the antenna thing that resonates with the human nervous system?" I asked. My plan? Pretend it was something totally normal to ask for.

Dad took off his work glasses, which folded up as he scratched his head. "If you want me to build you one, the answer is 'no.' The shock is too dangerous to be used casually, and not dangerous enough to be a weapon. It didn't even bring Marvelous' powers back. Really a failed project."

That was not good news. Not for my plans, and not for one of the nicer superheroines. "Is she okay?"

"Beebee took a look at the release records and worldwide superhuman crime reports. She says the odds of any criminal being near enough to LA and crazy enough to try a hit on a depowered hero are insignificant," he answered. Beatrice Benevolent Akk, would be my Mom. Officially retired, as was my Dad, but still neck deep in the community.

"Not what I meant, Dad. Will she get her powers back?" I pressed.

"She says her powers will return when the curse is broken."

Oh, the weight on those words. We had this argument again. "Dad, I can't believe you still don't believe in magic."

He argued back as if this were the first time. "Pumpkin, I've done the analyses. She's inherited a tone of voice and sensitivity to electrical currents that allow her to initiate some very complex energy chain reactions with precisely formulated sound wave patterns."

I pointed at the jar. Money in the bank.

"So she can cast spells," I translated back to him.

"They just happen to sound like incantations," he insisted.

We glared at each other. Then I realized he'd taken off his glasses, so I took mine off to make it fair. We glared at each other a few seconds more, then both broke down laughing at the fuzzy-edged blob arguing against us.

"So, where is that paper on the nervous resonating antenna thing?" I asked.

He looked around the room, then his eyes drifted down the rows of piled up books, drives, notebooks, clipboards, and sheaves of paper. Got him! He'd started analyzing his own pattern of clutter. He knew it well enough to figure out the system when he needed to. "Under the Audubon Field Guide. I'm still not going to build you one."

I scooped it out. No title, but the first paragraph talked about matching neural electromagnetic resonance. He loved printing out his work. Good for me!

"I need to do it myself anyway," I evaded. "It's for the science fair."

"How is school? Report cards will be coming in soon. Were you ready for that German test you were worried about?"

EEK.

Okay, shake it off. Not literally. He didn't notice me freeze up. I flipped through the pages laying out the engineering of the antenna. "I don't think I have time to talk, Dad. I have to do a lot of math. Really a lot of math. Really, really a lot of math." A different sort of horror crept over me at the thought. Urgh.

"Yeah, I bet. Good luck, Pumpkin," he urged me. I pointed at the jar silently. I would have liked to gloat that I was cleaning up today, but I was trying to keep from fainting.

I could do this. I got the trig and calculus textbooks off of the kitchen shelf, praying I wouldn't need to use them. I got my custom smart phone (like Dad would let me use a brand name when he could spend three weeks making one that works across all platforms) to use the calculator functions.

So many equations. Okay, I had to know the percentage by mass of each element in the antenna. I ran into Dad's electronics workshop and copied down the label on his cheap spares. It didn't matter what they were as long as I had the numbers, right? That gave me three variables he had down with Greek letters, and I plugged them into the next equation, which… took differentials of sines and cosines. He had to be kidding me. I dug out both books I'd been hoping not to use. I'd seen this stuff before. I just had to find the cheap rules and apply them… Okay, no. No, this was too complicated. I had to understand what I was doing. How did you get the first differential of a sine function?

I didn't know. It just… it just didn't make any sense. There was something there. I had to know because the waves from the antenna when they traveled through my skin had to become waves that would merge with waves in my axons, causing a chain of…

I could almost see it, but those words didn't make sense. What was I doing? It was like trying to call The Mona Lisa a painting. Just work out the math the cheap way. I'd need my body mass index; that was in the next equation. Of course, I needed my real, exact body mass index, not just some rough approximation by comparing weight and height, or whatever the rule-of-thumb trick was.

I didn't even know the rule-of-thumb trick. I'd need a machine just to get my body mass index.

Whining in frustration, I threw Dad's papers across the room, then threw my notebook with my fumbling math after it. I'd probably gotten the math wrong anyway. And I was good at math!

I lay down in bed and put the cover over my head. It wasn't nearly bedtime. I would spend the rest of the day sulking and trying to avoid the issue and maybe tomorrow I could come up with a new idea. I had to hurry. I could hide a C on a test from my Dad, but not my report card.

And what was I going to do about the science fair anyway?

The alarm on my phone woke me up the next morning. I didn't want to get out of bed. I stared at the ceiling for a while, but I'd already outsmarted myself. The phone was out of reach of the bed, and I had to get up to turn off the alarm, and after that I might as well go take a shower.

The sky was black outside, and I was all alone in the house. Technically, I wasn't alone. Mom and Dad were there, they were just fast asleep. I tied my pigtails into braids myself. Dad made me a machine for when I don't feel like putting forth the effort, but he'd tinkered with it yesterday. The little hands had extra fingers, and the access plate looked new. No matter how lazy I felt, I wasn't going to risk it. I could tell just by looking that he'd messed something up. Dad's inventions always do what they're supposed to do, but sometimes don't do what you think they're supposed to do. Something about the extra grabbers looked wrong to me, and, if I couldn't put a finger on it, I wouldn't let them put a finger on my hair.

The scrambled egg maker, on the other hand, was a godsend, since it's a miracle if Mom ever makes breakfast. She's right; I'd hate it if she pulled her Audit routine at home, and she needed a break. Not that she could stop herself completely. Halfway through my cereal bowl I heard her door alarm squeak, and, as I reached for my backpack, she stuck her keys in the side door and opened it for me.

As she pulled the car out of the driveway, Mom asked me, "Still brooding, Penny?"

I'd just sat through breakfast grumbling about my parents' super powers. "Yeah, I guess. I don't know what to do for the science fair."

Just saying that gripped me. That's all I needed, an F for not presenting anything at all. I had no ideas for what to do to replace the antenna. None. I still wanted to make the antenna.

"Want any advice?" she asked.

"No." If I talked over the science fair thing with my parents, sooner or later my grades in German would come up. Most likely sooner. I was hemmed in on all sides.

At least my Mom has a light touch. She let it go, although she gave me a concerned glance. I wouldn't be at all surprised if she'd timed it precisely to give the maximum amount of sympathy without making the recipient feel pressured.

The brooding didn't stop when I got to school. What was I going to do for the science fair? I wanted to invent something, really bad. I wanted to make that antenna. It wasn't even about zapping myself with it for super powers now. It clawed at me that I'd stared at a few pages full of math and they'd beaten me utterly. I'd had reference books, but they didn't help, because none of it had made sense. The device and the calculations were two different worlds that I couldn't connect.

Making that connection was Dad's super power. I didn't have it. I didn't even have a hint of it, like I was going to grow into it.

The bell rang. I was sitting in my chair in History class, and I hadn't heard a word. I'd read the whole chapter ahead of time because World War I was such a bizarre war, but that wasn't the point. I'd been wrapped up, brooding the whole time. This was tearing me apart.

I slipped out into the hall and laid my back against the cement block wall of the hallway. I had to do something. I had Geometry next, across the street in Upper High. I'd always kind of known it would be easy to skip out on that class, because nobody was tracking that I'd been to the other school that day. It hadn't been important until now.

I walked around the school to the science lab. I'd left the parts in there. It would work. I couldn't do the math, but it ought to just work. It was the most obvious thing in the world. If the antenna was the right length and you touched it, it would zap you.

I stopped in front of the classroom. I could see kids at their benches through the door's window. Of course, a class was taking place now. There'd be a science class every period.

"You are entirely unable to leave this invention thing alone, aren't you?" Ray asked from behind me.

I flinched. Of course, there was one person who would track whether I'd been to Geometry, because he took the course with me. He'd even guessed where I would come.

I turned around to see Claire standing right next to Ray. They were both missing class to talk me out of being an idiot.

"It's driving me crazy, okay? I just need to try. I need to fiddle with it until I've proven to myself I can't do it and I don't have any choice but to let go." I hunched my head down between my shoulders. Guilt clawed at me, but I'd be in more trouble going to class late than skipping it anyway. I wasn't walking away from this.

"Were you able to get hold of your Dad's notes?" Claire held her hands clasped behind her, the picture of innocent concern. Even her dark blonde hair just made her look more sincere and charming than if she'd been a pale blonde. Claire was so much better looking than me; her power would come out any minute.

That was crazy thinking, getting mad at Claire for being such a good friend. I was just so frustrated. "It was like Dante's Calculus Inferno. There was no way," I whined.

"You're not Brian Akk, and you don't have to be. You're Penelope Akk," Claire reminded me. I wanted to pop her for that gentle, talking-me-off-the-roof voice—so imagine if she hadn't used it.

"It doesn't matter. I can't get to the parts now. I just can't let it go!" I growled.

"If you get an hour to show yourself that it doesn't work, will that help you?" Ray asked.

He knew something. "Yeah, it will."

He started grinning again. I must be seriously flipping out if he'd been frowning this long. He did know something. "Come on," he told us, and we followed him down to the other end of the hall, past the computer science lab to the… other computer science lab.

I'd never actually been in this one. He pulled the door open, revealing a lab empty of kids or teachers. Half the computers were in bits. This wasn't a schoolroom.

"Miss Petard lets me help her with hardware repairs when I'm ahead of the class," Ray explained grandly. That "when" would be "all the time," but he didn't say it.

"I can't steal the school's computer parts!" I squeaked in horror.

"You don't have to," he promised, as smug as if he'd been waiting for that objection. He stepped over to a set of shelves, scooped up a pile of cards and drives and cords, carried them over to the nearest table, and dumped them on it. "All broken. She never throws anything away. You just need the parts, don't you?"

Claire, bless her as the best friend a girl could have, heaved a toolbox onto the table.

I grabbed a screwdriver and opened up the casings. A length of copper wire, any battery, it wasn't a complicated device. It had to… what was the word? Modulate? It wouldn't be exactly the same signal constantly. It had to work in a pattern. I needed… I didn't know the name of the part I needed. I tried to pry some electronics off of a circuit board with a screwdriver, and it snapped in half.

"FRACK!" I didn't quite swear.

"What are you looking for? Maybe we can find it," Claire asked.

I shook my head. "I've got what I need here. I just need to rearrange things."

"You can't rearrange a circuit board. They're made that way in a factory. You'd have to recycle the whole board and start from scratch. We don't carry blanks." Ray was trying to be gentle, but it was useless because he was wrong. Or he was right, kind of.

Recycle. I'd have to recycle the whole board.

"I need… metal cutting tools," I begged. Was I begging? My voice sounded so quiet. Yes, I needed those tools. I couldn't let this go.

"I don't think there are any in a computer lab, Penny," Claire warned.

Ray's eyelids lowered, and his grin widened. He'd thought of something. "There aren't, but nobody's using the shop classroom in the morning."

"There's a shop class?" Claire and I asked simultaneously.

"It's downstairs," Ray told me, grabbing our hands and pulling us out the door.

"There's a downstairs?" Claire and I asked simultaneously.

He dragged us down to the corner stairway. There were the stairs going up, like I'd expected, and there were stairs going down. I'd been to Northeast West Hollywood Middle for three years, and I'd never had any idea these were here.

It was like a sign. The tools I needed were down there. I skipped down the stairs ahead of Ray and ran down the short, blankly white hallway. One of the doors said "Shop," and I flung it open. I walked inside and was surrounded by ugly, crude versions of all the mad machines in Dad's workshop that I'd have to find the names of.

I knew what I needed. Gears, lots of gears. I found them. Magnets, electricity. I flipped on a saw and sliced pipe into thin slices, then squeezed them in a vice. It was obvious, wasn't it? You could recycle anything. Even energy, sort of.

Stop trying to find words. I didn't know what I meant, but I could see it.

I twisted the top segment into place. It looked like a centipede. I sighed, put the soldering iron into its brace and turned around to lean against the table until my muscles stopped shaking.

Ray and Claire stared at me like I'd made a second head instead of—

"What is this thing?" I asked, looking at the contraption in my hands. Large portions of it had no cover plates. There was just no way I'd made gears that tiny, much less fit them together.

"Shouldn't you know?" Claire asked me. She and Ray really looked scared. No wonder. Was that a psychotic break? I felt so tired now, but relaxed. Well, if I'd stressed out so badly I'd made this ridiculously intricate piece of modern art, my parents would be sympathetic. Therapy wouldn't be so bad.

"I think it's just—" I started, absently twisted it in my hands. It resisted, but turned, like a crank. And just like a crank, it kept turning. Then it flipped, grabbed my hand with its many legs, and crawled up my arm.

Claire squealed, but I wasn't afraid. I'd made it. I knew it wasn't going to hurt me. That was about all I knew.

Ray got there before either of us. "Penny, you made that. You have super powers!" he announced.

My eyes stung. He was right. He was so right! I lunged forward and grabbed both of them and squeezed them in a hug. I felt a little electric feeling as Ray's not-as-skinny-as-I'd-have-thought chest pressed against me, and he must have felt the same about Claire, but... forget that!

"I have super powers!" I crowed, my voice squeaking like a mouse. "Just like Dad's ... ! Almost like Dad's." I saw Dad work all the time. He had to do research, lots and lots of research, and he knew exactly what he was building ahead of time and what it did when he finished.

"I made this," I said, pulling back and holding up my hand as the little automaton crawled up that arm and fastened itself around my wrist like a bracelet. "I have no idea what it does."

"It's an inscrutable little machine, isn't it?" Ray admitted, leaning down to peer at the snowflake gears.

Who cared about the details? I was a superhero!

THE ADVENTURE CONTINUES IN...

AVAILABLE WHEREVER BOOKS ARE SOLD

Thank You for Reading

© 2011 **Richard Roberts**
http://frankensteinbeck.blogspot.com

Please visit http://curiosityquills.com/reader-survey to share your reading experience with the author of this book!

Catch Me When I Fall, by Vicki Leigh

Seventeen-year-old Daniel Graham has spent two-hundred years guarding humans from the Nightmares that feed off people's fears. Then he's given an assignment to watch over sixteen-year-old Kayla Bartlett, a patient in a psychiatric ward. When the Nightmares take an unprecedented interest in her, a vicious attack forces Daniel to whisk her away to Rome where others like him can keep her safe. But when the Protectors are betrayed and Kayla is kidnapped, Daniel will risk everything to save her—even his immortality.

Exacting Essence, by James Wymore

Megan's nightmares aren't normal; normal nightmares don't leave cuts and bruises on waking. Desperate, Megan's mother accepts a referral to a new therapist; a doctor dealing with the business of dreams—real dreams. The carnival of terrors that torments Megan nightly is all just a part of the Dreamworld, a separate reality experienced only by those aware enough to realize it.

On her quest to destroy the Nightmares feeding from her fear, Megan encounters Intershroud, the governing entity of the Dreamworld, and must work with her new friends to stop the agency from continuing its evil agenda, and to destroy her own Nightmares for good.

Caller 107, by Matthew Cox

When thirteen-year-old Natalie Rausch said she would die to meet DJ Crazy Todd, she did not mean to be literal.

Whenever WROK 107 ran contests, she would dive for the phone, getting only busy signals. At least, with her best friend, even losing was fun—before her parents ruined that too.

Her last desperate attempt to get their attention goes as wrong as possible. With no one to blame for her mess of a life but herself, karma comes full circle and gives her just a few hours to make up for two years' worth of mistakes–or be forever lost.

Fifteen, by Jen Estes

Ashling Campbell is her generation's dreamwalker, which means instead of getting beauty sleep, her nights are spent astral-projecting fifteen years into the future. She meets her fiancé, hangs out with her grown-up friends, and witnesses her own execution at the hands of a throng of bloodthirsty demons.

It's "13 Going on 30" meets "Buffy".

CPSIA information can be obtained at www.ICGtesting.com
Printed in the USA
LVOW11s0108311215

468558LV00003B/146/P